Greig Beck grew up across the road ... Australia. His early days were sp... reading science fiction on the sand. ... computer science, immerse himself ... industry, and later received an MBA. Today, Greig spends his days writing, but still finds time to surf at his beloved Bondi Beach. He lives in Sydney, with his wife, son, and an enormous black German shepherd.

Llyfrgelloedd Libraries

Please return/renew this item by the last date below

Dychwelwch/adnewyddwch erbyn y dyddiad olaf y nodir yma

Maesteg
01656 754835

awen-libraries.com

ALSO BY GREIG BECK

The Alex Hunter Series
Arcadian Genesis: Alex Hunter 0.5
Beneath the Dark Ice: Alex Hunter 1
Dark Rising: Alex Hunter 2
This Green Hell: Alex Hunter 3
Black Mountain: Alex Hunter 4
Gorgon: Alex Hunter 5
Hammer of God: Alex Hunter 5.5

The Matt Kearns Series
Book of the Dead
The First Bird

The Valkeryn Chronicles
Return of the Ancients

KRAKEN RISING
GREIG BECK

momentum

First published by Momentum in 2015
This edition published in 2015 by Momentum
Pan Macmillan Australia Pty Ltd
1 Market Street, Sydney 2000

Copyright © Greig Beck 2015
The moral right of the author has been asserted.

All rights reserved. This publication (or any part of it) may not be reproduced or transmitted, copied, stored, distributed or otherwise made available by any person or entity (including Google, Amazon or similar organisations), in any form (electronic, digital, optical, mechanical) or by any means (photocopying, recording, scanning or otherwise) without prior written permission from the publisher.

A CIP record for this book is available at the National Library of Australia

Kraken Rising: Alex Hunter 6

EPUB format: 9781760301293
Mobi format: 9781760301309
Print on Demand format: 9781760301316
Print format: 9781760301361

Cover design by Pat Naoum
Edited by Tara Goedjen
Proofread by Laura Cook

Cover images used and altered under the Creative Commons Licence 2.0:
Raymond Zoller: flickr.com/photos/klamurke/2999223504
Joseph: flickr.com/photos/umnak/13002208153

Macmillan Digital Australia: www.macmillandigital.com.au

To report a typographical error, please visit momentumbooks.com.au/contact/

Visit www.momentumbooks.com.au to read more about all our books and to buy books online. You will also find features, author interviews and news of any author events.

When I look down into the abyss,
Down into the merciless blackness,
Colder and deeper than Hades itself,
There I see the Kraken rising.

Kraken Rising, Greig Beck, 2015

To my big, beautiful Jess, my silent shadow, who was always there. Gone now, but I'll never forget you.

PROLOGUE

Southern Ocean – Edge of the South Sandwich Trench – October 12, 2008

Five hundred feet down, the silent leviathan glided through the water. At that depth there was just the faintest trace of sunlight penetrating down to create wave-like ripples on its surface, but below it, there was nothing but utter darkness.

The USS *Sea Shadow* was an experimental design submarine. Based on a miniaturized Ohio Class design, the 188-foot craft had an electric drive and high-energy reactor plant that allowed it to navigate the seas in total stealth. In addition, nano-paint on echo-free tiles reduced the chance of detection from active sonar – it was effectively an ocean ghost.

For now, *Shadow*, as the crew affectionately knew it, carried only conventional impact torpedoes, simply to add test displacement weight. The rest of its armament stores were empty, but when the craft was fully operational, it would be crammed with enough weaponry to obliterate anything on or below the water. The new design submarine was fast and invisible, and as far as the navy was concerned, was a high seas game changer.

The test run was watched from naval command with a mix of pride and trepidation. *Shadow* was in international waters, which would have made it diplomatically awkward should it have been detected. Even though the closest high-tech power, Australia, should not have possessed the technical capabilities to see or hear it, training runs in this part of the Southern Ocean were necessary and extremely useful as the environmental conditions were as hostile as they could get. And if the Aussies *could* find them, then the project would be determined a fail.

Today's exercises were to be carried out on the edge of the deepest trench in the region – the Southern Sandwich Trench, just off the Antarctic's coast. Muddy plains, abyssal mountain ranges and crevices that fell away to 26,000 feet into the Earth's crust, dominated the ocean floor here.

Captain Clint O'Kane stood on the command deck, shorter than the rest of his crew, but his authoritative presence made him seem like he towered over every one of them. His dark eyes were unreadable, as they reflected the green glow of the instrument panels.

O'Kane was relatively young, but had been a mariner for two decades. Still, he felt his heart rate lift as he passed over any of these deeper zones. It was the trenches that worried all submariners. These cold black voids were worlds of crushing depths, permanent blackness, and were most often shielded from them as the deep water made the liquid compress enough to repel most of their sonar pulses. And every now and then, when something did bounce back, more often than not it could never be identified. In that mysterious darkness, there were temperature fluctuations and flow variations that defied explanation, and every mariner felt there were things down there that saw them, without ever being seen themselves.

This trench had an additional reputation – it was the Southern Sea's Devil's Triangle. Dozens of ships had disappeared down in these stretches of water. And aircraft had also vanished, like the 1920 disappearance of *Amelia J* – a low flying spotter plane that gave a single fear-filled message: "*It's coming up*", before disappearing from radar, never to be seen again.

O'Kane would sail into the teeth of any battle that he was commanded to, against any odds, and never even blink. But he always slept better when they were well away from this particular deep-water stretch.

"Contact."

The single word was like a small electric jolt to his gut. He casually approached his sonar officer, standing just behind him, and outwardly radiated his usual calm.

"Distance?"

The officer calibrated his sonar, and concentrated. "Five miles, coming up out of the abyssal zone."

"That deep?" O'Kane grunted. "Biological?" He knew that sperm whales could get down to nearly 7,000 feet to hunt in the total darkness for the giant squid.

He waited. The officer's face was creased in concentration. Beside him, O'Kane could see his screen, the winding sonar line passing over the long darker stain on the sensor. The man leaned even closer to his console and also pressed fingertips over one of his microphone's ear cups. He shook his head and shrugged.

"Nonmagnetic signature, but *unknown*."

O'Kane groaned. They had an online identification library of blips, pulses, and pings for every deep-water biological creature and geological movement. Their library also stored the propeller sounds of the world's entire naval fleets – they should have been able to isolate, and then identify, anything and everything below the water.

He remembered Fuller's Law – *nature provides exceptions to every rule*. O'Kane ground his teeth. Meaning, he was back to relying on experience and his gut.

"Give me bearing and speed."

"Sir, relative bearing is sixty degrees, three miles out over the trench and speed is at twenty knots, variable. Rising, and moving into a parallel course."

O'Kane grunted his approval. *Parallel was good*, he thought. At least it wasn't moving any closer. "Too fast for a whale," he said.

The sonar officer half turned and pulled one of the cups away. "I don't think it's a whale, sir. It's not making a sound ... and it's big, very big." He frowned and swung back. "Doesn't make sense." The officer rotated dials and leaned forward for a moment, his face a sickly green from the monitors. "Whoa."

O'Kane didn't want to hear that word from his sonar man. He began to feel a sudden slickness as beads of perspiration popped out over his face and body.

The officer spun. "It just turned towards us, and speed increased to fifty knots."

"Fifty knots? Not possible." O'Kane's jaw set. "Sound red-alert. Come to twenty degrees port bearing, increase speed to maximum."

He exhaled through clenched teeth. Anywhere else he would have immediately surfaced, but doing so here would mean exposure to the unfriendly satellites he knew were always watching. He could not risk breaking cover over a damn sonar shadow.

"Object now at 1.1 miles and closing. Collision course confirmed. Not responding to hailing, sir."

O'Kane had only one option left – *to fight*.

"Ready all torpedo tubes. Come about eighty degrees starboard, and then all stop." The huge steel fish yawed in the water as it moved to face its pursuer. O'Kane grabbed the back of the operator's chair, as incredible centrifugal forces acted on the huge armor-plated body.

"On my order." O'Kane planted his legs and stood straight, waiting.

"Five hundred feet, collision imminent. Closing to 480 feet, 430, 400 ..."

It was too fast, and O'Kane knew it was probably already too close. "Fire tubes one and two. *Brace*." He gritted his teeth.

"Firing one and two – *brace, brace, brace* ..." The echo sounded as his order was relayed to the torpedo room.

The order was drowned out by klaxon horns. O'Kane felt the slight pulse that went through the superstructure as the torpedoes were expelled from the nose of the submarine. He held his breath, his eyes half closed as he waited for the sensation of the impact detonations, and the destructive shock wave that would follow.

Seconds stretched ... nothing came.

O'Kane opened his eyes. "Status update."

"Negative on impact, sir. Bogey seems to have, *uh*, vanished." The sonar operator spun dials, and hit keys, his face dripping sweat now. "It just ... " He shook his head. "Something's wrong."

"Impossible. It must have dived." O'Kane felt his heart racing. "Let's give it some space. Full speed astern." He felt the thrum of the engines kick in and looked to the inside wall of the submarine, as if seeing through the inches of steel plating. His gut told him it was still there.

"Come about, ahead full." The USS *Sea Shadow* jumped forward as the high-energy reactor gave the drives immediate power.

Go, go, go, O'Kane silently prayed.

The operator suddenly jammed one hand over his ear cup again. "It's back – a hundred feet, fifty ..." He balled his fists and spun, his face contorted.

"*Where ...*" O'Kane almost yelled the words. "*... where the hell is it?*"

"It's ... on us."

The crew and Captain Clint O'Kane were thrown forward as the submarine stopped dead in the water. He held on to an instrument panel and then started to slide, as unbelievably, the huge craft was tilted. The sound of metal under pressure immediately silenced the yells of the crew. There was nothing more terrifying to submariners than the sound of the ocean threatening to force its way in to the men living in the small steel-encased bubble of air below the surface.

O'Kane looked at the faces of his men, now all turned to him. There was confusion and fear, but no panic. They were the best men he had ever served with. For the first time in his long career he decided to break protocol.

"Blow all tanks, immediate surface."

The order was given, and the sound of air rushing from a compressed state to normal atmosphere, as it filled the ballast tanks, was like a long sigh of relief throughout the underwater craft. O'Kane's fingers dug into one of the seat backs as he waited for the sensation of lift. It never came.

"Negative on rise. We're still going down." The operator's voice now sounded higher than usual.

The command deck tilted again – nose down, now leaning at an angle of 45 degrees.

"Full reverse thrust!" O'Kane yelled the command, and he immediately felt the engines kick up as the screws turned at maximum rotations. He leaned over the operator again and looked at his screen. He knew the result without having to see the numbers.

"Descending." The officer now calmly read them out. "800 feet, 825, 850, 880 ..."

The USS *Sea Shadow* had been tested to a thousand feet, and could probably withstand another few hundred. But beyond that ...

O'Kane exhaled as the sound of hardened steel compressing rose above the thrum of the engines.

"Something has us," he said softly. It was every mariner's nightmare – the unknown thing from the depths, reaching out and taking hold. He knew how deep the water was here, but it didn't concern him. They would all be dead and pulverized long before they ever reached the bottom.

Anger suddenly burned in his gut. *But not yet*, he thought. O'Kane spun. "Get a Cyclops out there, *now*."

Hands worked furiously to load and shoot the miniature wireless submersible that was a torpedo with a single large eye for a nose-cone. Inside the fast moving craft was a high resolution streaming video camera with remote operational capabilities.

"Cyc-1 away, sir; bringing her back around." The seaman worked a small joystick, turning the six-foot camera craft back towards them.

O'Kane leaned closer to the small screen, waiting.

"*Sea Shadow* coming up on screen, should be … *oh god*." The seaman's mouth hung open.

O'Kane stared, feeling his stomach lurch. Nothing could ever prepare any man or woman of the sea for what confronted him on that tiny screen. O'Kane pushed himself upright, and slowly looked down at his right hand, spreading his fingers, then closing them into a fist. *In the hand of a god*, he thought.

Into his head jumped a few lines of a 200-year-old poem by Tennyson, and much as he wanted to cast it out, it sang loud in his mind: *Below the thunders of the upper deep; Far, far beneath in the abysmal sea; His ancient, dreamless, uninvaded sleep; The Kraken sleepeth.*

No, not sleeping, thought O'Kane, *now awake.*

He raised his eyes back to the screen and continued to stare at the thing that engulfed his entire submarine. Rivets popped in the skin of the vessel, and then the super-hardened hull started to compress. The 33-foot diameter submarine began to buckle, and he saw that the automated distress beacon had been activated.

"We're gonna breach."

The shout came from behind him, and he spun, roaring his commands. "Sound general quarters, increase internal pressure, close all watertight doors, shut down everything nonessential, and watch *for goddamn fires*."

The hull groaned again as they continued to descend into the darkness.

"What do we do?" The seaman at the screen looked up at him with a face the color of wax.

O'Kane could feel the crew's eyes on him; he could feel the fear coming off them in waves. His hand went to the key around his neck. The high tech, prototype submarine had self-destruct capability. He alone could trigger it.

"What do we do, sir?" The man gulped dryly, his face twisted.

If there was one thing O'Kane was sure of; while there was life, there was hope. His hand fell away from the key.

"We pray."

CHAPTER 1

The Kremlin, Moscow – Basement Level 9

The interrogation rooms deep beneath the Kremlin were reserved for the most important and high value type of guests. The rooms were a brilliant, surgical white, and insulated to contain the screams that frequently emanated from within. The shiny tiles also it made the individual rooms easy to hose out.

The man strapped to the gurney in Ward-5, Level-9, had a metal spike extending from one of his nostrils, with wires leading from it to a box that sent a mild electrical current into the area of his brain between the hippocampus and amygdala. Captain Robert Graham, former head of the US Military's Alpha Soldier Research Unit of Fort Detrick's Medical Command twitched and babbled nonstop. His lips were flaking, split, and parchment-dry.

Doctor Dimitry Liminov rolled back one of Graham's eyelids to examine the bloodshot orb. Captain Graham showed no physical response to the touch. The prone man babbled on, a zombie husk, more dead than alive, disgorging secrets like a recording machine set on eternal playback as his life drained away.

Liminov wrote some more on a chart, threw it onto the nearby steel table, and then pushed out of the reinforced double doors. As they hissed closed, the single glass porthole in one of them showed two huge guards stationed outside. The final click sounded, leaving nothing but the soft fevered whispers of the man on the table.

Set into the concrete floor, behind the few items of furniture, there was a six-inch grate over a drain, and if anyone had looked closely they would have seen the tiny red electronic eye that extended on the end of a questing worm that rose up and then turned slowly to further investigate the room. After another second, it snapped back down and disappeared.

Just below the sound of the babbling man, there came another noise – a low grinding accompanied by a gentle vibration. It continued for another twenty minutes, before a circle appeared around the outside of the drain, this one nearly two feet wide. A wisp of smoke lifted from it as searing heat was exposed to the air for a moment and the noise was shut off. Once again the questing worm poked its head up to examine the white-tiled room, and judging all was in order, snapped back.

There next came the sound of concrete moving, and then the grunt of human strain. The circle lifted, and like a giant stone birthday cake, the many layers of reinforced concrete, steel, and tile rose into the air – a massive two solid feet of it – and then impossibly, it was laid gently beside the hole as if it was feather light.

A figure appeared next. A wetsuit still damp with the waters of the nearby Moskva River clung to its muscular frame. Alex Hunter pulled himself out of the hole, moved quickly to the door, and carefully stole a glance through the single portal. Both guards were still at either side of the frame, the noise inside of the room contained by the soundproofed barrier.

Satisfied, Hunter crossed back to Captain Graham, strapped down on the steel table. Hunter took the wetsuit-hood from his head, and stared down, his gray-green eyes expressionless as he examined Graham's drawn and tortured features. Moving quickly now, he drew a small box from a pouch at his belt, and unwound a wire and clip from it. This he then attached to the metal probe extending from Graham's nostril. He waited a second or two for the readout on the small screen to calibrate the brain function of the man.

Hunter grunted, and then spoke softly, his voice carrying via the tiny device at his temporal bone behind his ear, to be relayed back to his home base.

"Brain dead. Orders?"

The response was calm and deep. *"Termination."*

Alex unclipped the wires and replaced the box back into his belt pouch. Next came a syringe, which he held at Graham's neck. He paused, looking down.

"You deserve a lot worse." Alex stared at the man who had tried to capture and either kill or experiment on him. Captain Robert Graham's work had saved his life, had roused him from a lifelong brain death to becoming the extraordinary being he now was. But then, when the military scientist tried to repeat the experiment, he had failed time and again. His response had been to recover Alex – by any means – and then turn him inside out to see why he was a success when hundreds of others had failed.

Alex's eyes began to burn with fury as the memories rushed back. Graham had unleashed killers upon him – their orders to bring him in dead or alive. The final insult came when Graham had threatened his family. And now, what had Graham told the Russians? Who else now knew about him, about Aimee, and Joshua?

Alex's teeth were bared. "You deserve this hell." He knew the empty shell couldn't possibly hear him, but also knew that if circumstances were different, he would have killed the man anyway. And that death might not have been so … easy.

"Your lucky day. My orders are to release you."

He inserted the needle, injected the amber fluid, and then placed a finger on Graham's neck, feeling his pulse quicken, flutter, and then abruptly stop as expected. The alarm that followed wasn't.

The banshee shriek that tore through the room meant either he'd been seen, or the life-sign monitor had a fail-safe attached – it seemed they wanted Graham to keep on living in his own private hell for a long time to come.

"*Shit.*" Alex moved quickly to finish his job – he withdrew a small vial of greenish fluid from another pouch, carefully unscrewed the lid, and then poured the contents over Graham's face. The flesh sizzled and started to cave-in on itself – there would be no pictures of the man left to parade on the Internet as some grisly warning to the West.

He had seconds now. Alex lifted a metal stool, stabbing it into the overhead lights, plunging the small tiled room into an eerie darkness lit only by some dotted red lights on the myriad of machines monitoring Graham's body.

Alex looked towards the door. "Party time." It burst open.

Doctor Dimitry Liminov pushed into the room, and immediately froze. He would have been expecting to see the prone figure of Captain Robert Graham, but instead was met by the sight of a tall figure all in black, whose eyes shone silver in the darkened room. Liminov's mouth opened and closed for a second or two.

"*Gv ... gvar ...*" The call to the guards was barely above a whisper. Liminov sucked in a huge breath, turned, and then shouted: "*GVARDIYA, GVARDIYA!*'

The doors exploded open again, and Alex pushed past Liminov on his way to meet the new arrivals. As the first man entered the room, Alex grabbed him and dragged him in hard, flinging his six-foot frame up against the white tiled wall. The guard's impact left a red streak as he slid to the ground and lay still.

The next guard had enough time to bring around his rifle stock and swipe it across Alex's cheek; the crushing impact was brutal in the enclosed room. Before the guard could recover from sweeping his gun across the intruder's face, Alex had delivered a flat strike across his throat to silence him. The man grabbed at his neck before he was punched once in the temple. He fell like a tree, unconscious before hitting the ground.

Liminov's screams contained notes of rage and fear, but Alex continued to ignore him, and lifted a metal stool, breaking off one of its legs as he moved to the door. He used the length of steel to jam it through the handles, effectively locking Liminov in.

He then turned to the Russian scientist. Alex's face showed an ugly crush-mark on his cheekbone. The flesh rippled for a moment before the wound stopped bleeding, and the bones popped back into place. The skin started to crawl closed over the trauma mark – weeks of healing in seconds.

Liminov's face twisted in recognition. "I know who you are. You are Captain Graham's prize lab rat, the one they call *the Arcadian*. You're too late ..." Liminov backed up, keeping the silver table containing the moldering pile of flesh that used to be Captain

Robert Graham between himself and Alex. "He has already told us everything."

Alex smiled without humor. "Not everything." He moved around the table and grabbed the shrieking scientist. "You have no idea who I am." He dragged Liminov towards the table. "And you have no idea what else is in here with me."

Alex pulled Liminov around to force him to look at the dead American captain, pushing his head down hard.

"Now tell me how you were just following orders." Alex's voice was without pity. He pulled Liminov upright. "You and your president need to learn not to touch our stuff."

"I'll be sure to give President Volkov your message." Liminov spat the words into Alex's face. "And then let him know who sent it – you'll never be able to stop looking over your shoulder. You, your family, your friends, not even your son, *Joshua*."

Alex's cold smile dropped at hearing the name. "Yes, we should all keep looking over our shoulders." Alex suddenly twisted the man's head until it sat backwards on his neck. "And I think he'll get our message now."

The door shuddered as men started to heave against it, trying to get inside the room. Alex dragged Liminov's body up over Graham's, and then reached into his belt pouch. There was a gas disk that he stuck to the wall, and then punched hard – a thick, green gas started to jet from its sides. The chlorine gas was a heavy, stinking gas that destroyed the respiratory system. Without at least a charcoal filter gasmask, no one would be entering the room. It also created an impenetrable fog, concealing him from the door's glass portal.

Alex held his breath and shut his eyes, moving by memory to the hole in the floor. He eased into it, and then gently dragged the huge circular block of stone and tile back over the top and lowered it down over him, sealing the hole like a massive cork.

In another few minutes he was swimming beneath the dark water of the Moskva River. *I love it when things go to plan*, he thought.

The first underwater mine detonated fifty feet from his right. The instantaneous change in water pressure created a shock wave that pummeled his body and made his ears bleed. Alex hung, momentarily stunned, before jolting into action.

The Moskva River mines were probably strung in a cordon around the Kremlin's underwater side – too deep to affect shipping, and probably residing near the bottom – and were remotely detonated or activated by movement. Either way, they created a deadly explosive net around the building.

Alex sensed the second mine looming before it detonated. This one was coming up fast, and was only ten feet from him. Though he spun and kicked away furiously, the proximity of the explosion was like a giant hammer compressing his body and brain.

He kicked hard, using legs and arms furiously to swim deep. He grabbed onto some debris sticking from the silted bottom, and held on. His eyes widened as he saw the circular shape slowly rising from the silt before him. The mine immediately detonated, its compression blast battering every cell in his body. His eyes closed and his breathing slowed, as his mind took him somewhere else.

*

Alex Hunter floated, drifting and dreaming. He was freezing, and things lunged at him from the darkness – things with gaping mouths, or horned beaks, slick tentacles, or scaled talons. Claws ripped at him, determined to tear him to shreds and devour the morsels. They scratched, bit, and stabbed at his body. He was pushed and bumped, and the horrors shredded the fabric of his garments, the same as they tore at his sanity.

He wanted it to end, wanted his peace. A tiny voice whispered to him: *it only hurts for a while, and then all you're left with is a small scar and a smile.* Who said that? He remembered: his *father*, from so long ago that it was just a faint echo in his memory.

He then saw the boy, his son Joshua, saw his face as he waved to him while he was being carried away. Then a beautiful woman, with night-dark hair and ice-blue eyes. She smiled and leaned forward to kiss him. *Aimee*, his mind whispered. *I'm so sorry.*

They're all gone. Another voice now, the sly one that tormented him. *You left them.*

Never, he shouted in his mental chaos.

Yes, you left them. Alone, unprotected. You were weak, selfish. They could already be dead, and you let it happen.

Never! Anger boiled up within him, making him feel hot, red hot, the air around him crackling with furious energy. There was a sharp pain in his shoulder, but when he went to bat it away, he found his arms were held tight. He floated up, not to the surface of freezing water, but to consciousness. Then he heard the voices, heard and felt the rumbling of the truck, and felt the chill against his skin.

Alex stayed motionless, just letting his senses catch up. There were Russian voices. He was stripped to the waist, his wetsuit removed, and he was tied to a wooden pallet. He opened his eyes a slit. It was near dark in the back of the truck, a single lantern swung overhead, but it was more than enough light for him to see clearly.

He heard the men around him talking about being near the Lytkarino District – he knew it – fifteen miles from the Kremlin, and now they were heading back there. He must have floated in the river for miles. He saw that the men wore police uniforms. They must have dragged him from the river.

"You feel ... he's very hot ... too hot for a normal man."

There was a hand on his chest, and then another.

"He has a fever?"

"Maybe, but now you watch," the voice said in Russian.

Alex saw the man lift a small blade, and touch it to his shoulder. The truck hit a pothole and the blade penetrated deep. He felt the sting of the knife, and then the familiar burning sensation.

"*Ach* ... no matter. Now, you watch," the man said quickly to his comrade, dragging him forward.

Alex knew what they were seeing; the wound would bubble and hiss like acid, as the flesh knitted back together, his metabolism healing the cut almost immediately. A wonder to them, and probably why they were transporting him to the Kremlin, rather than simply leaving him locked in a prison cell at the local police station. He knew when he got there, he was as good as dead, or nearly dead – they'd do to him what they had done to Graham. They'd strap him down, interrogate, and torture him. But his unique metabolism would continue to regenerate him, keeping him alive, so they could question and torture him, over and over, forever.

He waited, counting the seconds. There was a third man, dozing, and another in the front cabin, driving. He needed to be silent, and needed the vehicle. He waited, counting the seconds. The pothole jerked the truck to the side and rattled its frame. The lantern arced, its light swinging away from Alex on the pallet. In the split second it took for the light to swing back, the men's faces when suddenly illuminated again immediately twisted in shock as they found a half naked figure looming up, shredded rope dangling from each wrist.

Alex grabbed the two who had been delighting in their surgical examination of his flesh and cracked their heads together – a little too hard, as blood spurted and the skull of one depressed. He let the bodies drop, and grabbed the dozing man, and flung him from the back of the truck, his body tumbling into an overgrown ditch. If the policeman ever woke, it'd be hours before anyone found him or he could stagger back to his base.

Alex peered through the rear window panel at the driver – the older man oblivious and driving with half lidded eyes. Alex quickly moved to the rear of the truck and scaled the outside of the bouncing vehicle, clambering along the top. In the distance he could see the glow of the city coming up fast. He hurried, swinging along down with the slimmest of handholds, and then in a single motion, he ripped open the driver's door and shoved the startled man aside. Before the driver could even speak, Alex had gripped the wheel, and took control of the gears and pedals without the machine slowing. He turned.

"*убирайся!*" Alex roared.

The Russian word for *get out*, struck the policeman like a hammer, freezing him momentarily. Alex leaned closer and bared his teeth, and that caused the driver to burst into action. Even though the truck was doing sixty miles per hour, he spun, opened the door and leapt.

In the side view mirror, Alex saw the man land, bounce, and then lay still.

"Bet that hurt." He grinned and then swung the wheel at a widening in the road. The truck groaned as it turned hard, and then he jammed his foot down, and accelerated back along the dark road.

Alex reached for the police radio and began moving the dial up the frequencies, searching. In another moment, he found the correct numbers. There was nothing but white noise, but he knew this was simply camouflage – there were people listening, his people.

"Arcadian, coming in." He ground his foot down on the accelerator.

CHAPTER 2

Project Ellsworth – English Antarctic Research Project

Professor Cate Canning's hands shook. "Okay people." It felt like a thousand butterflies swirled in her stomach as her finger hovered over the button. "Are – we – re-*aaady?*"

It didn't matter what the half dozen scientists and engineers crowded into the makeshift laboratory behind her said because *she* was ready, the equipment was ready, conditions were perfect, and she alone would make the final call. She was the leading evolutionary biologist in the United Kingdom, and it had taken a lifetime of research, planning, fundraising, politicking, and then bloody arm-twisting, to even get to prototype phase of the exploration of the subsurface lakes below the Antarctic ice.

It had been tough – there was international pressure to ban all human activity on the southern ice sheets ever since the huge, unexplained algal blooms had been seen off the coast in March. So far, the total scientific ban had been kept in check with the counter argument that the blooms were strange but a common occurrence – one theory was that there was warm water welling up from a deep fracture somewhere – and that *warm water* conjecture made Cate even more curious, and determined.

And then, just when the road seemed to be getting ever steeper, a bluebird of good fortune had landed on her shoulder. Just months ago, NASA reported that the Hubble Space Telescope had picked up water vapor plumes emanating from Europa, one of the tiny moons of Saturn. Up until that point, the astral body, first discovered in 1610, was of little interest to anyone other than Galileo and a few dozen astronomers. The tiny ball was comprised of silicate rock with an iron core, and an outer covering of solid ice – interesting, but unimportant. But with the water plumes there came proof of liquid below that frozen coating. And where there was water, *there was life.*

Mankind would send eyes to Europa in a mission due to launch in 2022. Suddenly, the race was on to see what was under the astral body's ice. The eyes they would send would not be human, but needed to be able to see below the ice, *from* below the ice ... exactly what Cate was working on. Suddenly people wanted in, and Cate had sewn up a funding deal with an American research company, called GBR. They'd fully funded Cate's project for the next decade, with her having full autonomy – it was almost too good to be true.

Cate stared at the stratigraphic mapping screen before her. Of the 400 lakes below the Antarctic ice, the newly discovered Lake Ellsworth was one of the largest and deepest. It would prove the perfect test bed. Cate had seized their chance, and now they were here, at the point of launch.

"Are we ready?" she repeated.

This time, shouted assent from the assembled team.

Cate exhaled slowly, absorbing the moment. The Ellsworth project was a test run for navigating the hidden oceans of Europa. But it was more than that – the subsurface lake had not been disturbed for many millions of years; it would be a window into the Earth's prehistoric past. Cate bet there was life down there, and more than anything, she wanted proof of life.

Cate smiled, and then pressed the launch button, wishing she could go with it.

"Good luck, Flip. Go fetch," she whispered and sat back to wait, and watch.

*

The miniature probe, nicknamed *Flipper*, and with a picture of the famous aquatic mammal painted on its side, was only six feet in length. It was packed with instrumentation, had a heat source at one end, and also ended in a rotating diamond-tipped drill. It would melt its way through the dark ice, cut its way through the granite crust, and then drop into the liquid it found below. There, its tanks would fill, giving it neutral buoyancy and allowing it to hover midwater, slowly rotating, and capturing streaming and still images until its batteries were exhausted.

Flipper would not be coming home. Above it, the hole it had created would immediately refreeze after it had passed by, sealing it in. This was a requirement of the approval process – *Flipper* was fully sealed and sterile, as no contaminants must be allowed to enter the pristine environment they expected to find below the rock and ice. The gigantic body of water had lain undisturbed and unseen by mankind for countless millions of years – humans were now as alien to it, as it was to us.

Flipper's high-speed drill went from a grinding to a furious whir as it broke through the crust of granite and then fell through space. It took several seconds before it hit water that was blacker than hell itself.

It sank twenty feet before slowing, to then hang listlessly. The water was warm and deep, and at the point where *Flipper* entered, it went nearly 2,000 feet. The enormous body of water was 160 miles long and 50 miles wide – it was more an underground sea than a lake.

The sterile drill tip was automatically jettisoned, exposing a bulb end that was a single curved sheet of toughened Plexiglas. This bulb was lit by a ring of halogen lights surrounding a lens that was motion sensitive. *Flipper* was a six-foot Cyclopean fish that watched, tasted, and listened as hundreds of instruments came to life immediately recording, organizing and assessing the details of its environment. It also began a series of pings designed to echo-map the exact size and shape of the world that had become *Flipper*'s new home.

The sonar pings emanating from the probe were captured and read when they were bounced back from a solid object – in some directions it took many minutes for the reflected waves to return. They were invisible, and inaudible, to most creatures ... but not to all.

"Reading *Flipper* loud and clear; good signals, hale and hearty." Doctor Arkson Bentley's face creased in confusion, also making his long, thin nose wrinkle. "Hey." He suddenly leaned forward, placing his fingertips over one cup of his earphones as he glanced at Cate. "You're not going to believe this, but I've got another signal – electronic pulse."

"Sonar echo?" Cate asked, not looking up from her own screen. "Gotta be."

Bentley's frown deepened. "No, I don't think so. It's weird, like a beacon, keeps repeating over and over."

"Cancel it out – must just be echo distortion," Cate said distractedly to her senior scientist.

"You got it, boss." Bentley removed the signal from their scanners. The scientist then ran the data through his computer, organizing the information and deriving a geological profile of the huge sea deep below them. He watched as the contours started to be painted onto his screen; cliffs, valleys, mountain peaks, and then, the geology moved. Bentley froze, and then jerked upright in his seat.

"*Whoa, whoa, whoa*, I got something else – big, distant, but it's there."

"What now, Ark?" Cate skidded over to the scientist's sonar screen. "What do you mean, contact? Is *Flipper* going to run aground?"

"No," Bentley said. "We're not going to run into something, but it looks like something might bloody well run into us."

"A jelly-sheet maybe?" She frowned and peered over his shoulder at the screen. A jelly sheet was a huge clump of free-floating algae that hung like a curtain in deep subterranean water. Some of them could be a dozen feet across and solid as pudding.

"Only if the clump has learned to swim at thirty knots," Bentley said quietly.

"Thirty knots? Oh my god, is it proof?" Cate slowly rose to her feet as some of the other staff around them turned to look at Bentley's computer. "No, must be a sheet of ice that's calved; still sliding through the water." She was playing her own devil's advocate, but in her gut she hoped against hope.

"Not a chance," Bentley said, his eyes glued to the screen and one hand up to the headphone cup over his ear. "The water temperature is subtropical to say the least." He concentrated on the pulses bouncing back from *Flipper*'s sonar. "Closing, closing ... there." He pointed. A blip finally showed on his screen. "Still a thousand feet out, but coming in at fifty knots now."

"Fifty knots? That's impossible; nothing can travel that fast underwater." Cate looked back at the camera feed. There was nothing but the halogen's glow on a crystal clear empty blackness – the lights not even showing the snowy particle debris usually seen in warm waters.

Bentley leaned forward. "Holy shit, closing in, coming right at us." He shook his head. "Whatever it is, it just accelerated to eighty knots."

The other scientists jostled behind Cate, pushing and shoving like teenagers at a rock concert.

Carl Timms, lead engineer, and the only game fisherman in the group, had wide eyes behind thick glasses. "That's an attack run." He nodded at the screen. "And we're sitting ducks."

"500 feet, 400, 300, 200 ..." Bentley's voice was becoming shrill. "In range of the cameras ... now." He pointed.

The crowd surged back to the screen showing the black void miles beneath their feet just as *Flipper* swirled as something shot past it, creating a liquid tornado around the probe. The motion sensors ignited secondary flashes as the still camera captured image after image.

"Can we stabilize?" Cate felt the knot in her stomach start to tighten again.

"No, we just have to ride it out and hope to god we don't rupture a buoyancy tank and sink. All we can do is pray *Flipper* slows enough for us to ... *oh* ..." Bentley's mouth hung open.

A huge eye momentarily filled the screen. It was lidless, round, and white-rimmed, and its pupil was a goat-like slit. Cate sat back, not being able to help feeling that there was a cold intelligence behind the momentary gaze.

The image changed to a furious, boiling movement, and then there came a sound like an electronic scream, as if the probe was shrieking in fear of its life. The screen went dark, then there was nothing.

"It's gone," Bentley said into the silent room. "Everything's gone. It's all over."

Cate sat down slowly, feeling dispirited, but also elated. *All over?* she wondered. *Hardly,* she knew, feeling a swelling in her chest.

Bentley rewound and then froze the last of the images. He whistled. "Oh my god." He sat back.

"Alpha predator," Cate said softly. Framed and frozen on the small screen was the eye. There was no real way to judge scale, but she knew she was seeing something of titanic proportions.

"Now *that*, is an eye." Bentley clapped his hands and rubbed them together. "That's a big blimmin', beautiful eye."

"Oh, it's much more than that, Ark. It's proof." Cate stared off into the distance, as she slumped back into her chair, a dreamy smile on her lips. "My proof of life."

CHAPTER 3

Chinese Antarctic Research Outpost – Xuě Lóng Base – Yesterday

Chief mining engineer, Zhang Li, knelt among the debris. The vibrations from the huge rock cutter ran through him, even making the old fillings in his back teeth ache. But he felt or heard none of it as he broke apart and examined the heavy rock he held in his hands.

Gold, he grunted and broke away the shard of stone with the gleaming metal streak. A good rich vein, he thought, letting the gold nugget piece drop to the tunnel floor, keeping the other. Gold wasn't the type of riches he sought, but instead, substances worth a thousand times more – REEs, or rare earth elements, the small but vital components used in computers, lasers, and also sophisticated military hardware. It was this scarce treasure they sought from the ancient Antarctic mineral beds.

He grinned and rubbed at the rock piece he still held, knowing what he had was a speck of dust compared to the magnitude of what he had found. He looked around at the tunnel walls, ceiling, and floor – the deposits were old, rich, and very high quality – probably the largest undiscovered deposits left on Earth.

"*Hiyaa*." The yell and its echo was lost among the monstrous drilling. Zhang Li's heart swelled – he'd done it – potentially, billions upon billions of Yuan worth of raw material for the People's Republic of China. He would be famous, and feted, maybe even by the president himself.

He pushed the rock into his pocket, already planning his country's and his own future. China was rising to adulthood, and growing with it was a hunger for raw materials, prestige and power, and also, for risk taking. Five years ago, in breach of the global Madrid Protocol's Antarctic Treaty, he and a team of engineers, geologists, and miners, along with a military support contingent, had been dispatched to the Antarctic.

Week by week, over the years, they had built their machines, and then commenced their digging below the snow and ice. It had been difficult, and lives were lost – but below the ice, that's where the value lay – in the ancient bedrock. Much of Antarctica was composed of rocks almost four billion years old. It contained nearly all of the Earth's history locked away, and hidden below a thick blanket of white snow and dark ice.

Secret mining here would be an engineering feat beyond comparison. Zhang Li's grin widened. But engineering was what Zhang Li lived and breathed. He had graduated with honors from Massachusetts Institute of Technology, and then he, and another student, had been hand-picked straight off campus, to work for a small research company called GBR. That company specialized in fossil fuel research, and he still wondered what happened to the tall girl with the ice blue eyes and night-black hair – *Aimee*, he remembered, *Aimee Weir* – brilliant, and better at her job than he could ever be. Everyone expected it would be her to become famous. But now he was here, and it would be him that would be remembered.

Mile after mile below the Antarctic ice Zhang Li and his team had tunneled, first following the signatures from the satellite spectrometry and ground penetrating satellites, and then once locating the mineral traces, following them down to their lodes. Along the way there had been accidents, and there had been mysteries.

He remembered one particular core sample: the drill-pipe had been withdrawn from two miles below the snow, ice, and rock, and its contents laid out on the plastic sheeting for examination. There had been silence for several minutes, as the scientists, geologists, and engineers had stared in confusion, their steaming breath rising around them.

The previous core samples were laid out on tables like long rods of sparkling diamond – some green, some blue, some brilliant white, all displaying the varied and magnificent mineral colors that had accumulated miles below the Antarctic's surface. But the new sample was different – the stone gave way to something else at the tip ... something that bled.

The flesh, if that's what it was, was mottled green, and the liquid, the blood, that leaked from it, had a bluish tinge. But it was the eye-watering smell – ammonia, and near overpowering, that had chilled the men far more than the freezing temperature.

"We hit something," Zhang Li had said, wishing he could wipe at his streaming eyes, but the huge gloves made it impossible.

Sho Zhen, their head geologist, and his only friend on the mission, frowned down at the congealed mass. He ran two fingers over the sticky sample. "Something alive."

Zhang Li saw the sudden alarm in his friend's face. "*Pah.*" He stared at Sho. "More likely some sort of fossilized animal preserved in the ice."

"But, we were *below* the ice." Sho Zhen looked up into his face.

Zhang Li shook his head. "The Russians have been bringing up lumps of mammoth flesh from their frozen tundra for centuries." He glared for several moments, until the man nodded. "We need to move the drill location, and then recommence." He headed for the door. "See to it."

Zhang Li snorted as he remembered. They'd closed that drill location, stored the strange flesh, and then within a day, had forgotten about mysterious sample. It was of no consequence or interest to the mission.

Zhang Li ground his teeth again as the mind-tearing sound of the huge circular rock cutter dragged him back to the moment. He pushed his hard hat back, wiped his brow and then squatted next to some dinner plate sized shards of stone, one in particular catching his eye. He turned it around, and frowned down at it. He then grabbed at the others, turning some over, sliding them closer and then rearranging them like a jigsaw.

His eyebrows knitted. Millions of years ago, the area he was in was probably an ocean floor, and the soft mud had taken an impression. In the matrix he could make out a fossil imprint – a circle, nearly two feet wide, serrated at its edges, and in the center a hole. He placed one of his fingers into it, and it sunk in to the second knuckle.

The thing reminded him of something he had glimpsed at the Beijing Maritime Museum – fighting scars on an ancient sperm whale hide. He couldn't quite place it in his memory, and gave up. Zhang Li got to his feet. Like a window on a world long past, the ancient continent gave up its secrets to those it determined were worthy, but today, he was not to be one of them.

The rock cutter made a high, screaming noise that made him wince. He had been part of the deep dig for years, and knew every pitch, clank, grind, or whisper that came from the huge boring tool, and this was the sound of the giant circular blades spinning in space.

Voices yelled for a halt, and Zhang Li jogged down the tunnel. The air was still thick with floating dust that stuck to the skin, and combined with perspiration to run like oil from the men's faces. His dig foreman, Li Peng, waved him over.

Zhang Li nodded to him. "What is it?"

Peng shook his head. "Not sure. We've opened a cavity – a big one." He looked briefly over his shoulder before turning back to Zhang Li. "There's also a signal emanating from inside. It was trapped behind the rock face."

"A signal – man made?" Zhang Li stepped past him. "Looks like the earth has done our tunneling for us. And now, we better make sure we really *are* alone."

*

Zhang Li ran for his life. His breathing was ragged and hot, and he blinked at stinging perspiration that ran greasily into his eyes.

They were all gone now – the engineers, the workers, and even the military guards. He cast his mind back; the first few had vanished in the night – simply wandered off in the darkness they had thought – cold madness or got themselves lost somewhere in the newly discovered labyrinths. But then more disappeared during the daytime dig, sitting down for a break, or moving into a side tunnel to take a piss, always by themselves. One minute they were there, and the next they had vanished as if they had been nothing more than smoke.

As their numbers dwindled, some of the men had said they saw their missing comrades and had rushed headlong into the dark after them. Their screams and scuffmarks on the cave floor were all that remained.

Zhang Li had followed once, and then seen them – the *guilao* – ghost people. One of his missing security men had stood there in the darkness, unmoving, unnatural. The guard seemed glisteningly wet, and though his mouth was open, no words came. Sho Zhen, the geologist, had approached – he took only two steps before the guard had attacked ... or rather sprang at his colleague so fast that he seemed to fly. From there, reality had become a confused nightmare.

He changed; it wasn't a guard at all, but something stinking and fleshy that stuck to his friend, sucking on to him, and agonizingly impaling him to then drag him away screaming into the darkness. Zhang Li had remained standing rod-straight for several minutes, mouth gaping, feeling nothing but a warm wetness spread at his groin. He slowly wiped a hand over his face, feeling the slick perspiration.

His remaining team had gathered behind him, demanding he return them to the surface. But instead, his jaws clenched with determination – he was the leader of the team, and a respected scientist, not some superstitious villager. His guards had guns; he needed to take control. He decided then; *he would do it, bring them all back safely.*

Against their wishes, Zhang Li had taken their remaining crew and ventured down into those dreadful, stygian depths. Drag marks against the stone marked their path, and deeper and deeper they had descended, until they eventually found their answers ... the horrifying answers to his missing team members.

... and now those answers pursued him, the last man left, all the way to the surface.

CHAPTER 4

Buchanan Road, Boston, Massachusetts – Midnight

The floorboards felt cool and smooth under Aimee Weir's bare feet. She knew just where to place her toes so the boards wouldn't creak.

This was a habit now, waking at midnight, usually jolted alert by fleeing nightmares about her past, or chasing the specter of a love long gone. Perhaps it was her young son, Joshua, who kept the ghost of Alex Hunter alive. Joshua's features and his unique abilities reminded her every minute of every day of the Special Forces soldier who changed her world. His presence lingered in the dark corners of her mind, refusing to dissipate. *I'm right here*, Alex seemed to say, every time Joshua smiled up at her.

She stopped in front of her bedroom, deciding. Her partner, Peter, slept soundly, and only a small part of her wanted to return to share the bed with him. She had wanted a father for Joshua, and Peter had played that role. But as much as he loved her, and maybe she even loved him, there would always be a ghost between them that refused to be exorcised.

She passed by the room, and placed her hand on Joshua's door handle. She smiled and shook her head; she checked on him too much – every night when she woke – worried that if people knew about Joshua, knew he was Alex Hunter's son, they may try and take him from her. Or perhaps even worse, she would wake up one time and find that he had been nothing but a mirage. He was the only good thing she had from those strange times.

Last look, she thought and quietly opened the door. It was cold – strangely so – the curtain billowed from a slight breeze. The window was open, and it shouldn't have been. She frowned and her head snapped around to look to the bed. It was empty.

Movement drew her attention back to the other corner of the room, and her breath caught as a large shape loomed. There was a single red dot where two eyes should have been. Aimee screamed.

*

Offutt Air Force Base, Nebraska – US Military Space Command, Classified Division

"Sir, extreme intrusion – Buchanan Road."

"What the fuck?" First Lieutenant Sam Reid leapt to his feet, the huge HAWC towering over the soldier leaning in at the doorway.

At thirty-nine, Sam was the oldest HAWC in the ranks, but he was the strongest, and the best military tactician on the team. He was also crippled from the waist down, as he had suffered the brutal shattering of his L1 and L2 spinal plates, and worse, had had his cord severed.

But advancements in experimental bionics and battlefield armor had meant test pilots were needed – Sam had enthusiastically volunteered to try out the new MECH suit, or part of it. The Military Exoskeleton Combat Harness was the next generation heavy combat armor. On Sam, the half body synaptic electronics were a molded framework that was built on, and into, his body – light, flexible, and a hundred times tougher than steel. Sam was as good as new, except now the big man could run faster than a horse, and kick a hole in a steel door.

"Buchanan Road …" There was a near imperceptible whine of electronics as the mountainous HAWC spun back. "*Goddamnit*, that's Aimee Weir's place. *Shit*."

He punched a button on his desk's comm., breaking through to his superior officer.

"Boss, Aimee Weir's house, *trouble*. I'm patching it, and coming through." He turned back to the soldier at the door, as he placed a small plug into his ear. "Switch it through, Shorty … and link in the team."

"You got it."

The young soldier sprinted away, and Sam jogged down the hallway to the Hammer's office. He pushed at the door and went straight in. Even as he got there, the wall was opening, revealing a huge screen.

Colonel Jack "Hammer" Hammerson, commander of the secretive HAWCs division within the US Special Forces, was already in front of the screen. He half turned, the granite-hard expression telling Sam the man was already pissed off.

"Talk to me, Reid."

Sam listened to the comm. plug for a second or two and then pointed. "Data link coming through now. We've got two intruders in the house, got past our surveillance. They're good."

Hammerson's screen split to show multiple darkened rooms. There was a single adult male, flat on his back in a doorway, a spreading bloom of red on his chest. Two large men, in blackout clothing and cyclopian night vision gear, were in the child's bedroom. One of the men held Aimee by the hair and shook her as he shouted into her face.

Hammerson's jaws clenched, and Sam heard something deep in the man's chest. He could have sworn it was a growl. Sam stepped closer to the screen, enlarging the child's bedroom view. "They're looking for Joshua; they can't find him."

Hammerson didn't blink. "Take 'em down."

"Do we want to find out who sent them?" Sam asked.

"They can talk to me via an autopsy." Hammerson turned, his eyes merciless. "Proceed with the order."

Sam nodded, and touched the button in his ear. "Alpha team, go on insertion. No warm bodies."

The man on the screen punched Aimee in the face, and then lifted her again by the hair. He continued to shout at her.

Sam's teeth ground in his cheeks. Personally, he wanted them alive. Not from compassion, mercy, or because he really wanted to talk to them. Instead he wanted five minutes alone with them. Sam's huge hands crushed into fists.

*

Joshua Weir curled up small. He barely breathed on the top shelf of his closet as he peeked from behind the wall of soft toys, Star Wars Lego, and boxes of broken Transformers. The room was near pitch dark, but he saw the men as clearly as he saw in daylight.

Mommy was in trouble and he watched as the men shouted questions at her, and shook her by the hair. While one man shouted, another man was flipping over the bed, and pulling out drawers – they would find him soon. Joshua eased back, but clutched a swimming trophy in his hand. The small silver figure on top, standing with raised hands, was now a sharp spike. The man hit Mommy, and Joshua's hand tightened on the trophy.

Uncle Peter came into the room, fast, and seemed at first confused, and then frightened. One of the men in black struck him across the throat and he went to his knees clutching his neck. Then another pointed a gun at his chest that barely made a noise, and Uncle Peter fell backwards.

"*Peter!*" Mommy screamed as her potential protector first went down and then went to sleep.

Joshua turned his head to the dark doorway. He heard the other people coming, silent as ghosts, too silent for the men in the room to hear. He listened as they came up the stairs, and also crept on the roof. He knew they came to help. He didn't know how … he just … knew. He also knew something else, and he urgently leapt from his hiding place.

Joshua landed on Aimee, causing the man holding her to leap back momentarily. The small boy immediately wrapped his arms around her eyes and ears, shielding her. He squeezed his own eyes shut, just as the window frame exploded inwards, and a small stun grenade detonated on his bed.

"It's okay, Mommy," he whispered, but knowing she couldn't hear as he lay across her, shielding her. Like magic, and before the flash had even dissipated, there were several more huge black-clad bodies in the room. There was a soft sound like someone spitting, and the two men who were hurting Mommy just fell down.

A blanket was thrown over Joshua and Aimee, and Uncle Peter was also lifted from the room.

Mommy started screaming then, and calling his name over and over. But Joshua reached out to her, talking softly, telling her they were safe now. She pulled him to her, hugging him tight.

Joshua looked back, just as they were being bundled from the room. He knew the bad men had no breath left in them and were dead.

Good, a tiny voice whispered to him. He smiled at that.

CHAPTER 5

Aimee sat in the back of the black van as it sped away. There were three men and one woman in the back with her. She didn't know them, but knew who they were – HAWCs.

Peter lay flat on the floor, his head propped and his chest bandaged. He groaned and coughed wetly. Aimee reached down to wipe the hair from his forehead.

"He'll be fine. Collapsed lung, but otherwise, it's through and through. He's lucky." One of the men wiped blood from Peter's chin, and then read some figures from a small electronic pad they had stuck to his chest to monitor his vital signs.

"Lucky," Aimee repeated, looking at Peter's drained face. She felt sorry for him, but also something else – she suddenly knew that even though he was a good man, a good provider, and a good role model for Joshua, he could never be their real protector.

She turned to Joshua and he smiled up at her. In his face she saw him again, Alex Hunter, that specter from the past. She smiled back, amazed that her son seemed unfazed by the night's brutal events. Instead, the boy turned to one of the HAWCs, and reached across to touch one of his gloved hands. Across the back of the knuckles and fingers was armor plating. Joshua made a fist and rapped on it.

"I bet that would hurt."

The big man looked down, and grinned. "It's supposed to."

Joshua nodded, as though this was the answer he expected.

"Ma'am." One of the HAWCs handed her a small pellet, and he pointed to her ear. "He can hear you as well."

She nodded and inserted it.

"Aimee, are you okay?"

She closed her eyes, immediately recognizing the voice. She couldn't decide whether to be angry or happy. "You know I am, Jack. You've been watching me, haven't you?"

"Yes," Jack Hammerson said softly.

"For how long?" she asked.

"We never stopped."

She exhaled. "Thank you." She had thought Joshua was a secret, now she knew differently. Strangely, rather than inflame her, it calmed her. If Jack Hammerson had known for five years, and done nothing, then they never intended to take him away at all, she rationalized. In fact, while she had been abominable to the HAWC leader in the past, he had secretly been guarding them all along.

"I'm sorry," she whispered.

"The sins of our past ... or perhaps the sins of others, now carried by you, whether you like it or not. I'm the one who is sorry, Aimee."

She leaned back. "So, what now?"

"That depends on you. Say the word, and you can go back to your home, or a home somewhere else. We'll patch up Peter, and generate a cover story." He paused, waiting.

"For how long? Until someone finds us again?" Aimee lowered her voice and turned away. "That was no random break in, they wanted him, didn't they, Jack?"

"We think so. The secret's out – the Israelis know about Alex Hunter now, so do the Russians. They captured one of our people, interrogated him. Probably learned everything there was to know about him, and the people around him," he said. "More worrying is the Chinese joining the party. We know they have their own Advanced Soldier Program. Getting a little crowded now." He sighed. "A lot of choppy water, Aimee."

She shut her eyes. "Is anywhere safe?"

"Nowhere is ever really safe. But there are places that are safer than others." Again he waited.

"What about Joshua? I know, you know, he's ... *different*," she said.

"He might be. But my only interest in him is that he stays happy and healthy. Aimee, we can protect you."

"If ... there's always an *if*." She waited.

"No Aimee, no *if*, no catch ... a request maybe, but no catch. My priority is protecting my country, and its people. That includes you and Joshua. You both can live a happy and safe life under our care and protection. No one will ever touch you or him again. No one will ever even get close to either of you again. A normal life; I promise you that."

"Normal?" She leaned back, knowing that the devil always wanted its pound of flesh. "And the request?"

"Come in and we can talk about it. There's a lot to catch up on." Hammerson ended the call.

*

Captain Wu Yang lowered the night-vision glasses, revealing eyes that were coal dark in a face that looked like it was carved from solid stone. The Chinese captain was tall, even by Western standards. He and his team had benefited from early detection and then cultivation of the XYY chromosome phenotype breeding programs – the extra Y chromosome in males delivering height, strength, and aggression well above average, and ideal for roles in the Special Forces arm of the People's Liberation Army, or PLA.

Breath hissed from between Yang's clenched teeth, as he turned away from the breached house in Boston, heading for his car. There was no need to wait for any result – his men were already dead, and if not, and they were captured, they were ordered to take their own lives.

Inside the dark car, he sat for a moment, feeling the throb of pain in his head. He gripped the steering wheel, the hard polymer beginning to bend in his hands as his rage built. This was supposed to be a simple mission, to enter the country, take the child, and be gone, all in twenty-four hours. He had erred by not expecting there might be surveillance. *But why would there be*? he wondered.

The wheel began to crack as it bent towards him. Who was this Joshua Weir that he had some sort of Special Forces operatives as his personal protection? Why wasn't he told, so he could successfully execute his plan?

The top of the steering wheel snapped off in his hands, and he exhaled, releasing the building pressure. It was over, and he had failed. All that remained was to leave the country and report the result to his Controller, Chung Wanlin – and this was not going to be well received.

Yang sped away from the sidewalk, his large calloused knuckles beginning to bend the remaining portion of the steering wheel once again.

CHAPTER 6

Beijing – Central Military Commission

General Banguuo Tian read the report on the Xuě Lóng Base in Antarctica for the second time, this time slowly and with growing interest.

The secret Chinese project, one of hundreds being undertaken globally, had been an REE mining program undertaken by the Ministry of Land, Resources, and Mineral Exploration. The military's limited involvement had been the supply of a few basic support personnel.

Now, all communication had ceased; it seemed they had all vanished. Banguuo knew they had satellite links, radio, and in emergencies could tap into Australia's phone system to reach one of the dozens of safe houses situated down there. It was simply not feasible for all of those contact pathways to go dark all at once.

He placed the report carefully on his desk and steepled his blunt fingers. The report suggested possible causes, such as cave-in, gas leak, or electro-magnetic disturbance, and he could guess at a hundred other benign reasons for their non-communication. *But*, his own parallel intelligence report mentioned intercepted chatter from Australia – the Australians were radar-scanning the base. They had also performed a high level fly-over, and if the Australians had ground penetrating radar, they might have picked up the below-ground activities. This ally of the United States would not hesitate to pass on the information, and it would then find its way to the American Antarctic base at McMurdo.

The tunneling work beneath the Xuě Lóng Base was close to a pocket of the frozen continent designated as restricted by the Americans. Military map code Area 24. It was termed a *forbidden zone* by his US military counterparts. He snorted his derision – the American designation was worthless – China's rising power meant nothing was restricted or forbidden to them anymore.

Normally, this eventuality would only have mildly interested him, and he would have left it to the mining ministry to sort out. But there was something in the report that grabbed his attention. Banguuo's jaw worked, as his eyes traveled over the paragraph again. There was an unknown signal emanating from this Area 24. The code ciphers had already identified it as being a unique automated distress signal from an American naval vessel, registration unknown.

Area 24 was over two miles below the rock and ice. The signal was no communication aberration, but instead was coming in over the secret frequency used by American submarines when they were in distress.

There was no formal naval notification of a missing vessel – ship *or* submersible. But not everything that occurred was broadcast. Banguuo knew of America's secret *Sea Shadow* project that was shut down after the experimental craft had vanished. He remembered at the time having one of China's submarines search for it.

"Nothing ever stays hidden forever," he said quietly, as his blunt fingers now drummed on the desk.

Maybe we now know where it was really lost, he thought. The signal was so deep beneath rock and ice it was only through chance that they had picked it up when the mining team had broken through a rock wall into a subterranean void.

What if somehow the submarine got trapped under a shelf or in some sort of cave? The signal was so deep that it could not be detected above the ground. *Perhaps we are the only ones to have received it. What if the Americans don't even know it's there? Maybe we have the only tunnel down to their experimental submarine.* Banguuo sat back, his mind working. An opportunity to leap decades in submarine research and development, offered to him on a plate. Who could refuse? His grin widened.

He needed speed, and he needed a crack team. He had just the thing in mind.

CHAPTER 7

US Naval Pacific Command Headquarters – Honolulu, Hawaii, Island of Oahu

"This can't be possible." Five-star General Marcus "Chilli" Chilton's eyes moved over the information brief. "The *Sea Shadow*? Our *missing Sea Shadow*?"

Jim Harker, his staff sergeant, nodded. "We believe so. It's the correct frequency and automated coded message. And it gets weirder – it's coming from designated Area 24."

"*Area 24*?" Chilton groaned. "And it just started up all by itself?"

"Maybe, but we don't think so. It's a fluke that we even got wind of it. The signal was in an old parcel of data sent by some Brit exploration team that's drilling into the Antarctic ice. They've got funding for another round of digging, and wanted some previous data verified, so they forwarded the packet to one of our scientific teams, who detected the buried signal. This data they sent is years old, but …" Harker shrugged. "The *Sea Shadow* was, *is*, nuclear powered, so the energy source would have continued to fuel the signal beacon for as long as it remains operational."

Chilton sat back. "How could it *be* operational, when it vanished years ago in abyssal water? We spent months looking for it, but in water that is some of the deepest in the ocean." He frowned. "And then it ends up in Area 24? That's damn well miles away … and miles inland."

"And two miles down, under the ice and rock." Harker tilted his head. "But we know there's more under the Antarctic ice sheets than just snow, ice, and rock, don't we?"

"That's why we quarantined the area," Chilton said.

Harker raised his eyebrows, further wrinkling an already heavily creased forehead. "So here's my wild theory: what if the *Sea Shadow* found a way in, or was sucked in ... all the way to Area 24?"

Chilton sat staring at the data sheet in his hands. His large head lifted. "Who else knows about this?"

Harker exhaled. "I think more people than we'd like. This is where it gets choppy. Two hours ago, several Chinese high-speed choppers were dispatched to their Xuě Lóng Base in the Antarctic. This has been followed by the *Kunming*, one of their new guided missile destroyers. We've plotted its course – it looks like it's on its way there. You might have expected a supply ship, or even an engineering vessel. But instead they're sending an attack and defense craft packed with enough armaments to start a war. Bit extreme for a quick run down to resupply some hungry scientists."

"What have they said?" Chilton asked.

"Nothing plausible," Harker replied.

"So ..." Chilton's eyes narrowed. "The *Kunming* is making its way down to the Southern Hemisphere, by itself. There are no joint war games planned, and there has been no official explanation." Chilton looked up from under heavy brows. "Somehow they got access to that data. Hacked ours, or the Brits'. And you think they're making a run for the sub."

"It's a possibility." Harker shrugged. "It's what we'd do if we were them. But maybe they didn't have to hack anything. Their Antarctic base, the Xuě Lóng Base, is supposed to be a weather research station, but really it's just cover for a rare earth minerals mining. We know they've been deep excavating for years. Maybe they went deep enough to pick up the signal themselves – just decided not to tell anyone."

Chilton laughed softly. "Again, probably what we'd do."

"So far, the Australians' request for notification of intent has been met with silence from the Chinese," Harker said. "But we've been picking up a lot of chatter between Beijing and their Antarctic base – or at least we did – it went offline a few days ago. Been nothing but silence since. That also could be the problem."

"I don't like it." Chilton's voice was basement deep. "And I don't like where this could end. If that *is* our sub, I want it back ... and I don't mean handed back after the Chinese have pulled it to pieces." Chilton leaned forward. "What do we have in proximity?"

"Not much. Most of the fleet is conducting exercises in the Arabian Sea or in port. We do have a fully armed Seawolf in the Southern Pacific, the USS *Texas*, that was coming in for some down time, and guess who's onboard?" Harker raised an eyebrow. "Commander Eric Carmack."

Chilton started to smile. "Good, and just what we need: a wise head and a steady hand. Divert them – priority order. I want the *Texas* down in the Southern Ocean, ASAP." He seemed to think for a moment. "Also, alert McMurdo. Who's down there now? Is it still Benson?"

Harker shook his head. "No, his tour finished last July. On deck now is Sergeant Bill Monroe. He's currently got a squad of twenty soldiers, just regulars; engineers, comms. specialists and some medics."

Chilton nodded. "I know 'Wild' Bill Monroe – good man. But if the Chinese have sent fast choppers, I'm betting they'll be dropping some hard asses onto their base." He sat, rubbing his chin for a moment.

"Get a secure line through to McMurdo. I think we better let Monroe know what's going on." Chilton leaned back. "Also get him to take a run over to the Chinese base and have a little look-see at what they're up to. I think we, and Bill Monroe, need to be ready for anything."

*

Xuě Lóng Base – Antarctic ice surface

The two sixty-foot Chinese transport helicopters landed heavily on the hard packed snow, sending any loose flakes into a furious cloud that swirled around the large craft.

They had +-+-ed the absolute end of the fuel distance having last tanked up in South Africa. From one craft, a crew of men and women disembarked – a dozen of them, and set to unloading equipment, and supplies. From the other, a very different set of human beings – twenty of them, all over six foot, broad, but moving smoothly and efficiently, in whiteout fatigues, and carrying packs. Over most shoulders were slung skeletal automatic rifles.

The group made their way to the entrance of the camp. It was a submarine portal-like door, with spinning lock wheel and combination pad. The entrance tunnel led to a connected set of reinforced boxes, amounting to about one hundred square feet above ground. They waited, the twelve-person science team, engineers, and machinists, all lining up at the entrance but all keeping clear … for one man.

Captain Wu Yang pushed his goggles up on his forehead and strode forward. He let his gaze travel over the assembled men and women, barely concealed contempt in his dark eyes. The PLA captain was tall, like all of his team, but even he was dwarfed by one of them – the massive soldier standing at Yang's shoulder was another half a head taller. At around seven feet, the man's oversized, broad features and diastemic space between his front teeth told of acromegaly, the trait that produced gigantism in humans. But the man, Li Mungoi, was not just a freak of nature, instead he was the first of the *Hǔ Zhànshì* – the tiger warriors – the enhanced combat soldiers produced by the secretive new warrior program run by the Ministry of Military Biological Research, and headed by Minister Chung Wanlin.

Mungoi's intellect was little better than that of a child. But he was as strong as three men, utterly merciless, and loyal to Wu Yang without question.

Yang smirked at the look of fear on the civilians' faces. The PLA captain could make grown men pale, but Mungoi made them sick from fear. He was the monster at Yang's back.

Following Yang's failed mission in America, this assignment would be different. He would determine the nature of the signal emanating from under the rock and ice. If it was the missing American submarine, he would take legitimate ownership on behalf of the People's Republic of China under the Maritime Law rules of fair salvage.

Yang looked up at the giant. He had everything he needed, every advantage, and he had Mungoi. This time, there would be no distractions, no failure. *Nothing else mattered* – he turned to briefly face the science team – *nothing*.

Yang grunted his approval at the lit code pad. "Good. Power and heating intact." He held up one finger to the scientists and then turned to his men, nodding to several. He keyed in the code and spun the door lock handle and tugged. It swung open with a hiss of escaping air. He drew his handgun, letting it hang casually at his side for a moment, and then he and half a dozen of his soldiers pushed in quickly.

CHAPTER 8

US Naval Pacific Command Headquarters – Honolulu, Hawaii, Island of Oahu

Five-star General Marcus Chilton entered the room with James Carter, the Secretary of Defense. They spoke softly for several seconds, and then Chilton shook the man's hand before they broke apart and Carter took his seat. Chilton nodded to the other members already around the long table – General Walt O'Gorman's bulldog expression didn't flicker. He sat with other armed forces generals, chiefs of staff, and a smattering of other senior politicians.

His staff sergeant, Jim Harker, mouthed the word, *ready*, to him. Chilton nodded and placed a hand on the back of his chair and remained standing. "Ladies and gentlemen, a collision of events is occurring."

The table quietened, all eyes on him. "Many of you remember the experimental submarine, code named *Sea Shadow*, that disappeared in the Southern Ocean, along the edge of the South Sandwich Trench in 2008. The miniaturized submarine had an innovative electric drive and high-energy reactor plant and was as close to invisible and soundless as a sub can get. Inexplicably, it was lost with all hands, and never found."

He looked at the faces around the table, everyone was hanging onto his words. "Never found, perhaps until now. As long as the submarine is intact and has power, it will continue to call to us." He looked at each person in the room again. Secretary of Defense James Carter nodded imperceptibly, and Chilton continued,

"Well, we have recently detected what we believe to be our missing submarine calling to us."

There were murmurs and then a round of applause. Chilton held up one large hand.

"That was the good news." He smiled without mirth. "So, here's where it gets messy. The signal was found buried among other old data, and it was detected coming from approximately 2.25 miles below the Antarctic ice and rock – from Area 24."

Frowns, and then rushed voices. Chilton held up a hand again. "It sounds impossible, I know. All our submarines have a coded emergency beacon running on an undisclosed frequency. Its unique call signature is as identifiable as a fingerprint – and it's ours all right." He exhaled. "And how is it possible? Damned if I know. We have theories, none of them verifiable … from here."

"Is a salvage mission being organized?" General Steve Warneke asked evenly.

"Yes, and it seems not just by us. At 0800 hours EST, the Chinese Luyang III class destroyer, the *Kunming*, entered the Southern Ocean. It is fully armed, and has refused to state what its purpose is, or to even respond to international hailing."

He picked up a remote and clicked it once. It brought up the Chinese base on the edge of the Antarctic. "This is the Xuĕ Lóng Base. We expect it is the anticipated destination, and is situated only three miles from Area 24."

"Oh shit, you think they're making a run for the sub?" a senator asked, leaning forward in his chair. "They heard the signal as well?"

"I believe so," Chilton said evenly and moved to the next image. The screen now showed a sea of white, with a few flat roofs poking up from the snow. The camp was in a basin valley, and there were a few small mountain shoulders crowded in behind it.

"Bill Monroe took a little trip over there a few hours back for a look-see. He reported a couple of helicopter loads of personnel arriving. He said the size and the way some of them moved made him think they were serious military. Interestingly, no people were rotated out."

"How many does that base hold?"

"About two dozen ... mostly engineers, science staff, and a few standard soldiers. Now there is easily that many packed in there. Way too many people to inhabit the base. Above ground, that is," Chilton said, lifting the remote again.

He clicked and the next image shown was taken from a high altitude satellite. "We knew they were mining, but kinda makes you wonder what else they've been up to. Our Aussie friends had picked up quite a bit of chatter that abruptly shut down about a week ago – the radio and comm. sets were still functioning, and open, but nothing was being transmitted – they simply stopped talking. Beijing is understandably frustrated." He shrugged. "If it was our base, and they went dark, I'd want to know what happened as well."

"They all disappeared?" General Warneke's brows raised.

Chilton tilted his large head. "From above ground anyway. So ..."

He clicked again. This time the images were stratigraphic sonar images that peeled back the surface layers, one after the other – the snow, the ice, then the rock. "Now we can see what they were up to: serious mining." The next image was a computer model of an interpretation of all the sonar readings represented as a 3D graphic. It showed tunnels leading out, and down, for many miles. "They're digging – mining, or building deep fortifications. Whatever it is, their actions are expressly disallowed under the International Antarctic Treaty of '59." He shrugged. "Doesn't matter, but what does is, we believe they've detected the sub's signal, determined what it is, and have decided to investigate."

He tapped some more keys, increased the range and depth of the sonar mapping. Hundreds of miles of tunnels and cave systems were shown like dark threads, leading to the massive dark mass of an underground lake.

"Reaches all the way to the Area 24 quarantine zone. I think they broke into one of the natural caves. Had to, they were already close." Chilton waved the image away and turned. "I don't care if they have a birthday party down there, or a funeral." He rolled massive shoulders and sat down. "But they've dropped soldiers onto the ice, and now they're going to plant a warship down there." He clasped his big fingers together. He turned to James Carter, waiting.

"Talk to them," Carter said. "Get someone on the line right now. Before we bump chests, let's see what they have to say." The secretary of defense tapped his knuckles on the table. "Then we can decide on what comes next."

"I've tried," Chilton said.

"Then try again; I want to hear," Carter responded quickly.

Chilton nodded and swung around to Jim Harker. "Jim, get me General Banguuo in at the Central Military Commission. Patch it through right here, right now. He's a straight shooter, and someone who won't hide behind protocol."

Harker stood and called through on a small secure line. Chilton waited, looking up at the screen. It still showed the tunnel systems under the Chinese base that extended towards Area 24. In the center of the large table, a black disk with a speaker in the top crackled for a moment. There were some clicks, and then an educated, relaxed voice came through.

"General Chilton, this is a pleasure to talk to you again. How long has it been?" General Banguuo seemed to be barely holding the smile embedded in his words.

"Long time, General." Chilton leaned forward. "The last summit was nearly three years ago now."

Banguuo grunted. "Only three? *Hmm*, and now, here you are again."

Chilton noticed that there was no surprise in the man's tone. "General Banguuo, you're a very busy man, so am I, so let's get right to it." Chilton stared straight ahead. "Why is the *Kunming* in the Southern Ocean?"

"Simply supporting our citizens." The answer was too quick.

"You don't need a Luyang III class destroyer for that, General. Or twenty Special Forces soldiers dropped onto the ice. We would be happy to extend our own resources from our base at McMurdo, if you feel you need more support. Just ask."

"There is no Chinese Special Forces on the ice. And I think your base at McMurdo has done enough." There was no warmth in the response.

Chilton frowned. "I caution you about placing your navy in that area. Maybe we should come and join you – lend support – make it an international effort. Make sure other people down in that region don't see a warship as being ... provocative."

"Provocative?" Banguuo sounded like he growled. "What is in Area 24? What is so valuable that it is worth making our people disappear over? *These* are the things that are seen as provocative, General Chilton. These are the things that lead to ... a dark place. We should all think very clearly."

Chilton's frown deepened. "Area 24 is a contamination zone, to be avoided. That warning is for everyone – us included."

"But *you* enter it. And we now know that you have been intruding on our Antarctic bases territory. We also have sophisticated satellites, General. Following your intrusion, our people are missing, but you warn *us* to stay away from our own base."

Chilton held up a hand to the secretary of defense, stopping him from interrupting. He knew Banguuo, and could sense the tension in his voice.

"General, believe me, I don't know what you're talking about. We don't know anything about your people. As for Area 24, it is off limits to everyone – because of contamination. Please stay out of that area, for your own good."

"Now you threaten us? You overestimate your global authority." Banguuo's voice rose in pitch.

Chilton waited, feeling the tension in the air, like it was adding weight to the atmosphere. He wondered who else was in the room with the Chinese general.

"General Banguuo, we don't – "

"I suggest, General Chilton ..." The strange new voice that had come onto the line was nasally and cutting. "If anyone should stay out of the Southern Ocean, *for their own good*, it is you."

The line went dead. It felt like all the oxygen had been sucked from the room.

"Who the hell was that?" Chilton finally asked.

"That ..." James Carter exhaled, "... was a damned nightmare, and why your man acted like he had a rod up his ass. It was Mr. Chung Wanlin, both the Minister of National Defense and Biological Research, and also a fervent nationalist."

Chilton sat back slowly as General O'Gorman leaned forward, one fist clasped in the other. "Did he just threaten us?" He snorted. "Stay out of international waters?" He smiled to Chilton. "When it comes to those type of messages, I don't hear too good. You, Marcus?"

Chilton smiled. "Well, kinda just makes me all the more interested. I've dispatched a Seawolf down for a little look-see. It'll be there in a few days."

"I'll need to brief the president. He's not going to like it," Carter said.

"He's going to like it less if we get pushed out of the Southern Pacific." O'Gorman's expression was flat. "Or if they get their hands on our leading edge submarine technology."

"And what do we do if they fire on us?" Carter turned to him.

"Sink 'em – we've got the firepower to take 'em to school." O'Gorman's smile had little warmth.

"Or they sink us." Chilton stood and paced for a moment. "As a kid I remember watching this great boxer called Jersey Joe Walcott – best boxer alive. He took on this flash new kid who was small, with a short reach, and had this funny way of moving around the ring. His name was Rocky Marciano. Walcott had the height, the reach, and the experience. Then Marciano stopped his funny way of moving, planted his legs, and caught Jersey Joe off guard with a big surprise uppercut – sank him – game over." Chilton came around the table. "Either way, we sink them, or they sink us, it could mean all out war." He paced again. The room was now silent, watching him. "We need to get in front of them. If they've got a path to our sub, then I want to use it – with or without an invitation." He stopped moving. "I need more time and more options." He turned, searching for one man, and finding him.

"That means you're up, Jack."

Colonel Jack Hammerson, who was seated at the back of the room, stood, saluted, and left without a word.

*

Jack "Hammer" Hammerson skimmed through the reports and images, stopping at the signal analysis of the buried pulse. Naval Comm-Sec had identified the unique frequency signature as that belonging to an experimental sub that vanished in 2008, and Naval Command wanted it back, or obliterated – either was fine with Hammerson. But first they wanted line-of-sight confirmation ... and that's where he came in.

Hammerson knew the location well – Area 24 – a labyrinth of caves leading down to a primordial world. It was his office that had recommended designating it an international forbidden zone. He knew there was absolutely nothing else down there that could send a signal of any shape or form. Hammerson had sent a team there five years ago. Of the twenty men and women that went in, only three walked out. The reports from the survivors told of a place that was alien to a human being, as if they had set foot on Mars ... except perhaps a thousand times more hostile. Humans didn't belong down in those cave systems.

Hammerson had no idea how an American submarine had found its way in there. But he was damned sure that the question about the crew's likelihood of survival should be answered with a conclusive *deceased*. Whether command realized it or not, he knew his job was not rescue, but location, confirmation, and probably destruction of the American asset – nothing more, nothing less.

Chilton needed to thread a team in there. Enter the Chinese Antarctic base, locate their tunnel system, and then use it to find the submarine. If at all possible, they were to minimize lethal action against the Chinese nationals. Hammerson snorted – *like the PLA were going to let them just walk in there*. He knew they'd be fighting the Chinese all the way to hell, and given their recent attack on Aimee Weir's house, that might be just how he'd like it to be.

Hammerson sighed, dropping the folder. The other complication was that by the time they got there, managed to work their way in, and down the shaft, the Chinese would be days in front – way too much ground given. He needed another option. Something a lot faster and more direct.

Hammerson opened another folder, covering other nations' work on the frozen continent. He stopped at the British section –

Project Ellsworth. It was one of theirs. The funding company, GBR, was a US military research arm.

Jack Hammerson refamiliarized himself with the project and personnel, and then sat back. *Looks like we've got an elevator*, he thought, and smiled as he lifted his phone.

CHAPTER 9

Southern Ocean, northern coast of the Antarctic

"What've we got, seaman?" Alan Hensen was Chief of Boat, known as the COB, and second in command of the USS *Texas*. He stood behind the communications officer with his hands resting on his hips.

"They're hailing us, sir. COB to COB." The comms officer, Schwab, turned briefly to Hensen first, and then swung to Commander Eric Carmack. "Commander Chen Leong."

Erik Carmack folded his arms and planted his legs, looking at the banks of screens, focusing in at one in particular. It showed a satellite image of the *Kunming*, and approximately 1.3 miles to its south was a computer representation of the outline of the USS *Texas* below the water. The destroyer was dwarfed by the huge deep-sea fish, both in physical size and firepower.

"They're turning front on, sir." Schwab's voice carried a hint of strain.

Carmack nodded. It didn't matter if they tried to present a smaller target, the *Texas* had eight 660-mm torpedo tubes, and an armament of Tomahawk cruise and Harpoon anti-ship missiles, Mark 48 ADCAP torpedoes, as well as a full kit of mines. The *Kunming* was a powerful destroyer, and on the water it would be a formidable adversary. But down in the deep, it was the *Texas* that was the real killer fish ... and the *Kunming* knew it.

"Take the helm, Chief." Carmack let his COB take over, knowing the man would be a commander himself soon, so experience in real confrontations was invaluable. His job was to be a mentor, and that was why he was here.

"Aye, sir." Hensen turned to his comms officer. "Open a frequency. Invite them to tell us what they're doing down here, Officer Schwab."

Schwab opened a hailing frequency and sent the message in dual languages – English and Mandarin. "Responding now." The Chinese verbal response was captured, recorded, translated, and then fed onto a screen before the comms officer. Schwab read it and raised his eyebrows.

"They ... demand we surface."

"Do they now?" Hensen asked, with a flat smile. He turned to Carmack. The commander nodded, knowing what the COB had in mind.

"Light 'em up."

Lighting them up meant that the weapons system would be brought online and electronic targeting would commence. The *Kunming*'s counter measures would immediately see the scan net being thrown over them.

Hensen straightened. "Go to BS1." They'd war gamed against the Chinese, and every time they did, the quantitative gaming programs found them unpredictable, either overconfident of their own abilities, or prepared to use bluff belligerence, that nearly always went bad. BS1, or "Battle Stations One", was the Seawolf submarine's lowest level of combat readiness, but still meant closing off waterproof bulkhead doors, weapons checks, and being in a state of dive readiness.

"The *Kunming* is demanding we cease our aggression," Schwab said.

Hensen grunted. "Ask them again what they are doing in international waters. Their presence here is itself an act of aggression."

"They've lit us up, sir." Schwab's voice had an edge this time.

The *Kunming* had plenty of rocket-propelled depth charges, which were dumb weapons and only useful in a straight-line pursuit. But they also had smart missiles that calculated a submarine's position, then simply dropped into the water, to propel down at speed. They were fast, *bullet-fast*, accurate, and deadly.

Hensen radiated calm. "We expected that. Keep an eye on their batteries. Get the flying fish ready, just in case." The *Texas* had the latest anti-missile defenses, such as A3SM Mica Sams – a torpedo-like capsule containing a medium-range Mica missile that was tube-launchable at any depth. If the *Kunming* launched, the Micas would burst from the water, hunt 'em down in the sky, and take 'em out.

"They couldn't be that stupid," Hensen said evenly.

"There's obviously something they *really* want." Carmack raised heavy brows.

"Let's tighten up." Hensen eased back. "Got to BS2." Horns blared and the lights went red in the command room. The faces of the men were radiating the green glow from their screens and all radar, sonar, and targeting equipment was focused on the Chinese destroyer.

"New message, sir." Schwab watched the screen for a moment. "They say they are awaiting instructions, and ask us to be patient with them. It may take some time."

"That's not what they really want. They want us to pause and think about it, put us in a holding pattern." Commander Carmack's eyes narrowed. "Check with HQ on vessel activity around Hainan."

Hensen spun back to Schwab. "Get NAVCOM on the line. Find out what fleet movements are occurring in the South China Sea."

Schwab opened a coded frequency and sent the information packet. In a few seconds, he turned and lifted one ear cup from his ear.

"They've got two signatures at the Yulin Base – big fish – both possible 096, Tang class, plus a whole lot of other traffic from the surrounding areas."

Alan Hensen straightened. "So, now we know why they want us to burn up time while they stretch us. In forty-eight hours the odds will have moved against us." Hensen turned to Commander Carmack.

The commander's brows were knitted. "Speak to Chilton, Alan; we need instructions, and the clock is ticking. I think we'll need a few extra friends down here."

*

Colonel Jack Hammerson stood behind his desk, waiting.

Alex Hunter entered the room, saluted, and then sank into the chair.

"Sir."

"Good work in Russia." Hammerson allowed a small smile. "Our Intel obviously missed the motion sensitive mines in the Moskva, huh?"

"Yeah." Alex snorted. "That detail might have helped." He grinned at Hammerson. "Head's still ringing."

Hammerson laughed and then shrugged. "Anyway, glad you're back in one piece." He sighed and sat back. "The world is turning, son, and there's much to do."

Alex angled his head, frowning as though distracted. Hammerson watched carefully as Alex got slowly to his feet, his brow creased. He waited, observing his soldier. Alex Hunter, the Arcadian, was the first man, the *only* man, to ever survive the experimental Arcadian treatment. He was an elite Special Forces soldier brought down by a catastrophic battlefield wound that was described as terminal. Hammerson himself had approved the treatment, as Alex's chances of survival were minimal at best, and the odds of a recovery were zero.

But Alex did survive – *more than survive*. When he woke from his coma, he was something vastly different. The treatment was designed to give severely wounded soldiers their physical and cognitive abilities back and improve wound healing – get them back in the field. But something unidentifiable in Alex's system caused an unexpected amplification of the side effects – he didn't just get better, he became something far more ... formidable.

There was always a price, and Alex continued to pay it – his mind had been ripped in two. Alex Hunter, the original Alex Hunter, was still there. But deep inside there lurked another. The Jekyll to the Hyde. This "other", was a personality far more ruthless, brutal, and unpredictable. Alex kept him chained up, but any bond can be broken. This was the beast Hammerson always watched for.

Alex continued to stare off into the distance as Hammerson examined him. The young soldier was like a son to him, but one who he had burdened with great gifts or a great handicap. Now Hammerson was going to ask him to head back down below the ice, where five years ago the man had lost an entire team. It was also a place that still haunted Alex's nightmares, with the things that lived down in those starless depths always with him.

"Alex ... *Captain Hunter* ..." Hammerson said, and Alex's eyes flickered. "What do you know about the *Sea Shadow*?"

Trance-like, Alex continued to stare. "I've heard of it." The frown was still creasing his brow. "Experimental sub that went missing in the Southern Ocean, years ago."

"That's right. Missing since 2008, up until a day ago." Hammerson watched Alex closely. After a moment, Alex turned his cold, gray-green lasers back on him, the gaze penetrating to his core, assessing him.

"You've spoken to Aimee."

Hammerson knew it wasn't a question. And also knew it would be a waste of time trying to poker face the guy. Hammerson nodded. "Yeah, it's all okay."

"Something happened to her." Alex suddenly leaned forward. "Joshua ...?"

Hammerson held up a hand. "There was a minor altercation at their home. They're all fine. We took care of it."

"I need to see them." Alex stood.

"Not yet." Hammerson lowered his brow. "I said they're fine."

Alex started to pace. "Need to see them." He was like a caged beast. "Need to see them now ..."

"*Sit down!*" Hammerson's voice boomed in the small room, and he got to his feet. "This is not a fucking democracy, son. You want to do your own thing, then go back to wandering the streets at night, dismantling muggers, and living off the land." He stepped closer. "But if you want to help, want to help Aimee, Joshua, all of us? Then shut up and listen."

Alex gripped the seat armrests, but didn't sit. His face contorted and his fists clenched. The air in the room felt like it crackled with tension, and Hammerson tried to remain as still and calm as he could manage. He could see there was a battle taking place inside the man; it raged and tore at itself, warring between logic and insane fury.

Hammerson didn't blink. "I said Aimee and Joshua are fine. Do you trust me?" He waited for several seconds, and then banged a fist on the desk, making everything jump. *"Do – you – trust me!"*

Alex crushed his eyes shut, and the muscles in his neck strained like cords on wood. His hands on the armrests gripped until the wood started to make a splintering sound. Finally, he nodded and eased back into the seat. His eyes stayed shut, but the tension in his jaw began to relax and after another moment he exhaled long and slow, opening his eyes to focus on Hammerson.

"Yes."

"Good." Hammerson sat down slowly, feeling the perspiration run down under his arms. "Aimee is fine. And you know you can't see her … yet."

Alex nodded again. "She still thinks I'm dead." He looked up. "When?"

"Soon." Hammerson smiled, keeping his face expressionless. "Listen up; we don't have much time, and this is critical."

Alex exhaled and nodded again. Hammerson continued, "The *Sea Shadow*'s automated distress beacon just triggered, or was finally detected. The kicker is, it's coming from under the Antarctic ice."

Alex looked up slowly. "Beneath the ice?"

Hammerson nodded. "We found the signal, and so did the Chinese. They sent a destroyer, the *Kunming*, down there, and we think they're going to make a run at it." He shook his head. "Can't let them do that." He clasped his hands in front of himself. "We have the USS *Texas* onsite, keeping an eye on the *Kunming*. But in a day or two, there'll be a lot more military assets down there. One false move, and we'll be at war with China." He shrugged. "We'd win, but …" He got up, and went around his desk, picking up a computer tablet and sitting down. He flicked through some screens, stopping on one.

"What we'd end up winning might be a field of ashes." He handed the device to Alex. "We have a range of imperfect options. Any one of them could work, and any one could blow up in our faces with catastrophic consequences. One thing is for sure, we'll end up with a bloody nose."

Alex watched the war game analysis on the small tablet's screen. It showed the two major continents: the USA and China. Lines emanated from each – red lines from China and blue from America. More lines also emanated from the ocean at differing strategic positions. Most of the red lines stopped halfway.

"If diplomacy fails, and there is a launch, we estimate over a thousand nukes would be in the air within the first hundred seconds," Hammerson said. "We'd take down eighty percent of their missiles, but the ones that got through would target major infrastructure, military facilities, and significant civilian populations."

Alex turned to him, and Hammerson went on.

"It'd kill or maim fifty million Americans. On the Chinese side, the losses would be in the hundreds of millions, and push 'em back to the stone age." He exhaled slowly. "Like I said, we'd win, but we'd be hurt bad. Country would be in turmoil for decades." He leaned forward onto the desk. "And once the lion goes down onto its knees, then the hyena close in. What then would Russia do, or Iran or even North Korea? Maybe use the chaos to launch their own attack?" Hammerson said.

"One after the other, or all at once." Alex exhaled slowly. "And that does not have a happy ending,"

Hammerson stood behind his desk. "So, we need to deescalate the situation – fast. We need to remove the original rationale for them being down in the Antarctic. We need to find the *Sea Shadow* before they do. Recovery or destruction, nothing else." He looked into Alex's unblinking eyes. "We also need to defang the dragon that's already down there."

"You want me to go?" Alex asked.

Hammerson nodded.

Alex sat stone-still for a few moments. "You said they were already on their way. By the time I get there, they'll be days ahead."

Hammerson smiled grimly. "We might have a shortcut. You can call it an express elevator."

"One-way trip, huh?" Alex's eyes looked ancient, weary.

"No, we'll *absolutely* get you home," Hammerson replied. "It'll all be in the full briefing."

Alex nodded. "You want me to secure the site, and if the *Sea Shadow* can't be retrieved, obliterate it." He looked up. "What happens if the Chinese refuse to leave?"

Hammerson grunted. "The Chinese have disavowed all knowledge of the team – they don't exist. Send them home, and if they won't go ..." His eyes were lidded.

Alex nodded wearily. "Kill them all."

Hammerson lifted another report from his desk. "Before you get there, I have one more job ..."

He knew this last task was far more delicate – high impact, low mortality. He also knew he made the right call not telling Alex about the Chinese intrusion into Aimee's house to target Joshua. The last thing he needed was the Arcadian extracting bloody payback where he was about to send him. He handed the report to Alex. "Like I said, first we need to defang that dragon."

CHAPTER 10

Xuĕ Lóng Base – Antarctic ice surface

Curious, Shenjung Xing thought. Even from where he stood just outside the door, he smelled the odd odor escape. In the Antarctic, like most frozen climates, the sense of smell was near useless as the cold locked up odors. But the base's escaping air was warm, and carried with it scents redolent of saltwater, copper, and something like ammonia.

Shenjung Xing, the head scientist, and leader on the team, was the chief mineralogist, and an engineer by trade. His second in command was a small, wiry woman, nearly overwhelmed by all her padded gear. Dr. Soong Chin Ling was a rare earth minerals specialist, and had worked with Shenjung for over a decade. Many times they had shared a bed, and many times he had thought of marriage, to have the idea whipped away by the next project. He turned to her now and raised his eyebrows. She shrugged in return.

In a few minutes, one of the soldiers came to the door, and waved them in. But as Shenjung went to step forward, the other soldiers pushed past. Shenjung bristled, but knew that he was in charge on paper only. Until they determined what happened to Zhang Li, and the other workers and security force, he was to follow Captain Wu Yang's instructions like everyone else. The man's face alone didn't invite disagreement. And he tried hard to ignore that ogre, Mungoi, he had with him.

When the scientists and engineers finally got to enter the base, they moved along the corridor, and then into the main briefing rooms. Off to one side was the communication center, next were the dining facilities, and then some of the sleeping quarters and lavatories. The rooms were Spartan, and were as much used for storage as human habitation. It was below ground where most of the action took place.

The facilities constructed on the surface were little more than a cap over many levels of industrious activity below. Access was via an elevator that descended hundreds of feet to the mining platforms and miles of tunnel work.

Sublevels contained laboratories that used sophisticated processes of oxidization, acid baths, and crystallization to remove the valuable minerals, so the few tons of finished produce could be easily, and secretly, transported. Gadolinium, the soft and strange metal, was used in lasers, computer memory, and fluorescent tubes. Already global demand had outstripped supply, and China's appetite for that metal, and other RREs such as terbium, dysprosium, holmium, erbium, thulium, ytterbium, lutetium, and dozens more, needed to be constantly fed.

"Comrade." Wu Yang reappeared, pointed at Shenjung Xing's chest, and then clicked his fingers.

Shenjung hated that, but swallowed it down for the good of the party. He turned to Soong, who had unzipped her coat. "Come with me."

Together they hurried after the PLA leader. Shenjung's feet skidded in something jelly-like. He ignored it, trying to keep up with the longer legs of Wu Yang. At the shaft room he stopped. Several of Yang's men were standing around the elevator shaft – the only thing in the center of the room.

Beside him Soong crinkled her nose. It was here that the source of the smell was emanating from. The cage elevator that sat on top of the shaft was flattened open, its walls now like the petals of a flower. It was as if something had exploded within it and blown all four sides out each way. The heavy, metal roof of the elevator box was lying against the wall, with a huge dent in its center.

"Gas explosion?" Yang asked.

Shenjung approached the twisted metal of one of the cage sides, and crouched to look at the thick bars, twisted like softened rubber. They were coated in something that he dabbed at with his finger and brought to his nose. He recoiled as Soong crouched beside him. He offered his fingers to her. She sniffed at the residue.

"*Phew*, ammonia?" she asked softly.

"Maybe firedamp," Shenjung said. He motioned to the peeled cage. *Firedamp* was a term used by miners as a catchall name for the myriad pockets of flammable gas found, especially in ancient strata. It was usually highly pressurized, easily ignited, and exploded with lethal force.

Shenjung rested his hands on his knees. "Maybe a vent that was ignited by the drilling …" He looked at the ceiling; there was a glistening hue as if the mucus was up there as well. "There are no scorch marks anywhere."

He leaned forward and peered down into the shaft. The mechanisms and railings were all still in place, just the capping cage at the top had been obliterated. It was as if something had boiled up from below, refused to be contained, and like a massive fist, had punched upwards, and then reached on into the base. He shook his head, staring down into the darkness that stretched away, well beyond his vision. He knew the first shaft landing was a good five hundred feet down, and that there were lower horizontal shafts beyond that. Even more, before they reached the floor tunnels where the last work was being carried out.

"So, explosion, yes?" Yang asked. "And what is that smell?"

"It is highly likely it was a pocket of dirty methane that ignited. And then air blowback after the initial explosive expansion caused the damage." Shenjung got to his feet.

"I concur," Soong said, also rising. "As for the smell; it is strange, but the gases can be trapped for many millennia, and other compounds leach in, such as carbon dioxide, hydrogen sulphide, carbon monoxide, and maybe even ammonia sulphides. Caves can smell like old shoes, rose gardens, or even graveyards."

"So, you two both think the explosion killed them all? Then, where are the bodies?" Yang's eyes slid from Soong to Shenjung.

"No, no," Shenjung said quickly. "There are no signs of incineration on the internal superstructure."

Yang looked back to the elevator shaft. "So, Zhang Li took them all down into the tunnel for mining duties – the soldiers, the communications specialists, even the cook?"

Shenjung tried to put himself in Zhang Li's place, trying to determine if there was any reason for him to commandeer the entire outpost's staff. "Cave-in. Maybe there was a cave-in that trapped his mining and engineering team, and he needed the others to form a rescue party. To help him dig."

Yang stared for a moment. "And then the explosion occurred, trapping them all." His eyes narrowed. "*Hmm*."

Shenjung gazed back at the shaft. "I knew Zhang Li. He was an excellent engineer and mining specialist. I cannot imagine any other reason for him to take non-mining personnel into the deep tunnel systems."

"Yes, perhaps this makes sense." Yang's mouth turned down. "If there was a cave-in, and he needed extra hands, he would have used all resources available. It is what I would do." He turned, his expression flat. "But I also would have sent a message to my superiors."

Shenjung stayed silent, and after a moment Yang shrugged.

"If they are trapped, then until we fix that elevator car, no one is going down." He barked instructions, and then turned back to Shenjung. "Get your engineers to repair the cage. My men will assist."

He spun and left, followed by the enormous Mungoi. Several of the soldiers stayed behind, awaiting their instructions.

Soong stared into the dark elevator shaft. She held up a hand, palm outward. "It's warm. The air rising feels warm." She smiled weakly. "Like breathing."

Shenjung grunted. "It's not unusual for the earth to be a few degrees warmer within the deeper geology."

She looked back at him, not convinced. "Would you have taken novice men and women into the tunnels?"

He shrugged. "I don't know. If I was confronted by a cave-in emergency, then I would like to think I would do anything and everything to rescue those trapped."

She nodded and then sniffed deeply. "That smell."

"Stay focused. It's nothing unusual." He exhaled, knowing that didn't feel true.

"*Yi!*" Soong jumped as shouts and a commotion came from one of the outer rooms. Yang's soldiers ordered them to stay put before vanishing toward the din.

A few seconds later, one soldier stuck his head back in the room. "Captain needs you – there's a survivor."

*

The figure was a tiny ball of fear in the ring of soldiers. The huge steel refrigerator door hung open, and inside Shenjung could see that shelves had been shoved aside to accommodate a single occupant.

Shenjung looked back at the miserable being. The man had his hands thrown up over his head and he rocked back and forth, mumbling a single word, like a chant, over and over.

Yang stood over him, his arms folded and his brow creased. When he saw Shenjung, he pointed down at the man.

"This fool's mind is gone. See what you can find out." He went to turn away, but then spun back and delivered a kick to the side of the man's rump. "And make him stop that constant wailing."

The man screamed and rolled onto his side, curling up into an even tighter ball. Shenjung hissed his annoyance at the PLA captain and knelt beside the man. Up close, he could smell his body odor, excrement, and the sharp tang of fear. He had obviously been locked in the freezer for days and not bothered to exit, or even undress, for anything.

"He's in shock," Shenjung said.

Yang's jaw jutted. "And I have two dozen people missing. He knows what happened. You make him tell us, or I will. Quickly now."

Soong was scrolling through the camp's personnel records on a computer pad, and turned the screen to Shenjung. "The man's name is Lim Daiyu. He's the base cook." She leaned forward and gently placed a hand on Lim's shoulder.

"Mister Lim, Lim Daiyu ..."

"*Zhàyǔ!*"

The shouted word made Soong fall back.

"*Zhàyǔ – Zhàyǔ – Zhàyǔ!*" Lim lunged at her, his face streaked with tears and eyes showing whites all round.

Yang kicked him back. "Be careful."

Lim covered up his head again, sobbing. Shenjung clicked his fingers at one of his team. "The medical bag; get me two mls of Librium, quickly."

Yang leaned over the chanting man. "What is that imbecile saying?"

"*Zhàyǔ.*" Shenjung snorted. "Do you not know your Chinese mythology, Captain? *Zhàyǔ* is an ancient evil. It is supposed to be made up of pure yin, and devours men whole." He looked up at the tall soldier. "And it lives in the underworld."

Yang snorted. "Like most demons, I'm sure."

A syringe of golden fluid was handed to Shenjung, and he stuck it immediately into the man's arm. Shenjung handed the empty syringe over his shoulder and nodded to Soong.

She talked softly, her hand on Lim's shoulder. "You're safe now. You're safe, Mister Lim. Do you know where you are?" she asked.

Lim moaned, but breathed deeply, his taut frame visibly relaxing. In a few seconds he nodded.

"Good." She continued to pat Lim's arm.

Shenjung leaned forward. "This is important, Mister Lim. What happened here? Where is everyone?"

Lim shook his head, crushing his eyes shut. "I don't know."

Shenjung put a hand on his shoulder. "Yes, you do. You hid in the refrigerator for a reason. Tell us why, Mister Lim. You're safe to speak now."

Lim Daiyu made a small sound in his throat. "I want to go home, please." He looked up, his face running new tears. "We are all dead."

Yang growled his impatience, and Shenjung ignored him.

"Why do you want to go home? What scared you?"

Lim looked towards the elevator shaft room. "They all went down to the lower levels to find the missing workers. A few of us had to remain here." He rocked back and forth. "It came, came up, took them all. No escape for us …" He howled. "*Zhàyǔ-ǔǔǔǔ!*"

Yang's lips curled. "Superstitious idiot." He kicked the man over, his howl shutting off. "Our answers are not up here. Ready your people. As soon as that cage is repaired, I want the first team to descend."

Shenjung nodded, and then looked back to the elevator room. He felt a warm breeze on his cheek. *Like breathing*, Soong had said.

*

It didn't take long for the engineers and soldiers to agree that the elevator cage could not be rebuilt – time and materials were both nonexistent. Instead, the engineers had straightened the guide-rails and created an open wood and steel platform. The metal sheet that had been the roof of the cage was too buckled to be of use and remained against the wall, a mute but stark representation of the power that had burst forth from the depths.

The first Chinese team descended slowly. Shenjung Xing stood to one side, with Soong crowding in close to him. He felt her small fingers intertwine with his. At the other side of the ten-by-ten platform stood Yang, immobile, a small reflection of the control panel's lights in his coal-black eyes. Other than that small spark, the man might have been made from the same stone just beyond the cage.

Shenjung watched as the rough hewn walls shot upwards as they descended. The crowd on the platform meant those closest to the rushing stone were little more than inches from the jagged, uneven rock. A stumble would mean snagging on the stone and having clothing, and perhaps skin, shredded away in an instant.

Shenjung tilted his head back. There was a dot of light far above them now. The base camp – light and life, now dwindling away to nothing.

The last communication from the former engineer, Zhang Li, was that he was heading down to the lowest level tunnel – half a mile still to go. They would assemble at the bottom, and while Yang would send out scouts, the rest of them would wait for the entire team of engineers, miners, and soldiers to arrive, leaving just a skeleton crew topside.

A mile down now, and Shenjung already felt unsettled. At first they had passed through a layer of bone chilling cold emanating from the dark stone. But now in the depths, there was a warmth and humidity rising around them, and a smell that hinted at something vaguely reminiscent of humid shorelines or rotting vegetation. *Methane pockets*, Shenjung thought. *We need to be careful of sparks.*

They passed by multiple cross tunnels on their way to the deepest level, and finally the elevator whined to a halt with a final jerk and bounce at the bottom. Shenjung cursed softly; it was too much to hope the lights would still be working, and the huge man-made cave was a solid wall of darkness.

Yang ordered everyone off the platform, and immediately sent it back to the surface for the next group. He then turned to click his fingers and point, sending two of his men scurrying off, guns up and the barrel beams of their automatic rifles leading them away into the darkness.

Shenjung noticed all the PLA soldiers carried huge packs, probably additional ammunition, climbing equipment, and supplies. More than he would have expected, and more than any of his own team brought with them. *So much for this being a rapid search and recovery mission*, he thought glumly.

The PLA leader turned to his men. "We need to gather any evidence of the American assault on the base, and we need to locate that source of the signal. This is the priority."

Shenjung cleared his throat. "And we need to find our missing people."

Yang grunted, not turning. "They are either here or not, alive or not."

Shenjung was determined not to let the man ignore the possibility of survivors. "You do care about our people, yes, Captain?"

Yang turned, his dead eyes never flickered. "Comrade Shenjung Xing, I care about our people, and their safety and security. I also care about our people of the future, and their children and children's children, and their ability to live in freedom and prosperity. I do not like an aggressor to have superiority over the oceans where they can seal us off when they choose to. We will locate the missing American submarine, and I expect we will find out what happened to our people on the way." He took a step closer, towering over Shenjung. "Yes?"

Shenjung saw then the zealotry in the man's eyes. The facade had cracked open and the unbending soldier stood ramrod straight within. To this man, Shenjung knew he was necessary baggage at best, and an expendable irritant at worst. He needed to take care. He nodded.

Yang spun away. "Get those lights working. Hurry." His voice boomed in the dark tunnel.

One of Yang's soldiers jogged back from the darkness. "Sir, there are no lights."

Yang made a gravelly sound deep in his throat, and the man quickly pointed his rifle beam upwards as explanation. There was nothing above them – the cords, light fittings, support rails, all were gone – also the land lines for communication. They'd be out of contact until they surfaced. The soldier moved his light and they could see there were fresh gouges in the stone as if some sort of heavy machine had been dragged along, scraping everything away as it passed.

Yang turned to Shenjung. "Rock cutter?"

Shenjung ignored him, moving his own flashlight along the ceiling, and then the walls. He took a few more steps, bringing his light down to the tunnel floor. Something caught his eye, and he went to it, crouching.

"What do you have?" Yang kept his position, obviously not wanting to be seen to scurry after the engineer.

Soong came and crouched beside him. "Is that a boot?"

"Maybe once." Shenjung prodded the shoe. It was peeled open, the toughened leather sides torn apart. He used a knife to carefully lift it. It glistened in his light, and he brought it to his nose, sniffing.

"*Phew*." He dragged it away, wincing. "Ammonia again." He held it towards Soong.

She sniffed, frowning. "Maybe medicine for a foot ailment?"

Shenjung bobbed his head, knowing that traditional Chinese medicines could contain all sorts of strange and exotic compounds. He dropped the boot.

"Yes, perhaps." He stood. "Captain, the machinery should be three hundred feet further along this tunnel branch. It was there that Zheng reported he had broken through into the new chamber."

Behind them, the elevator arrived with the second group of soldiers and engineers. Yang organized them into three groups. A team of five of his PLA would lead out with Shenjung, Soong, and Yang behind them. The central group would be primarily the engineers and miners, and the third would be the remaining PLA, who were tasked with carrying equipment.

They trudged in silence. Shenjung had to unzip his heavy parka, as the perspiration ran freely down his sides.

"Why is it so hot? There is no geothermic activity in this area," Soong said, almost needing to jog to keep up.

"Can you feel it?" Shenjung asked. He held up a hand, the fingers spread.

Soong did the same. "Yes, the air movement again. How can there be a breeze a mile and a half below the Antarctic?"

CHAPTER 11

Sam Reid came down the hallway and saw Alex Hunter waiting at the solid metal doors of the secure elevator that would take him down to the weapons research and development area below the USSTRATCOM base. Like on most of their missions, the special ordnance Alex would need was not in any armory, arms store, or weapon dealer's manual anywhere in the world. Most of it was experiential, or reserved just for him and the HAWCs.

He smiled, easing up behind him, sniper silent, but he already knew Alex could hear what others could not. Sure enough, Alex spun.

"Boss." Sam grinned, holding out a fist for Alex to bump. "Down to the toy store?"

"Oh yeah. Little party down south I've been invited to, need some extra kit," Alex responded.

"I heard," Sam said. "Wish I could tag along, but this damn MECH suit doesn't exactly fit in tight places." He grinned. "I need plenty of space to work my magic."

"Magic?" Alex scoffed. "Is that what you're calling lumbering around, breaking all the office furniture these days?" He laughed easily with his big friend.

"Well, I get to stay right here where it's nice and warm." Sam slapped Alex on the shoulder. "You can freeze your butt off all on your own."

"Hey, maybe I'll tell Hammerson I need a bulldozer – a Samdozer. We'll see who freezes first." Alex raised his eyebrows.

"Samdozer, huh? Yeah, I like that." Sam looked at his HAWC team leader. Hunter never seemed to age; probably another side effect of his treatment. But it was his eyes that carried the scars; they were haunted. "You okay?"

Alex nodded, looking away. But after a moment he stepped in closer. "Aimee's place … there was an incident. You know about it." It wasn't a question.

"You heard about that?"

"Hammerson told me." Alex's gaze was steady.

Sam waved it away. "Was nothing, we took care of it. Don't worry about it."

"Can't do that, Sam, *ever*. What happened?" Alex's eyes bored into his.

Sam remained tight-lipped for a moment longer. "Okay." He guessed if Hammerson had already told him, then what the hell. "We had a minor intrusion at the family home. What we ascertained from the bodies, it was a couple of Chinese Special Forces. They were good, we were better, so they're dead." Sam held up a hand. "And don't sweat it; they never laid a hand on Joshua."

"He was there?" Alex's eyes widened. "He was fucking at home when those torpedoes came in. It was a hit?" Suddenly Alex was in Sam's face. At around six-two, Alex was about four inches shorter than Sam, but the big HAWC knew Alex could tear him in half in the blink of an eye. Sam went to back up a step, but Alex's hand came up fast, catching hold of his wrist.

"What happened, Sam?"

Sam remained calm. "They came in hot, and went out horizontal. We took 'em down hard. But there's no ID, no traces, no leads – like I said, they were good."

"Where are they?" Alex's words now came from between his teeth.

"The bodies?" Sam frowned.

"No, fuck the bodies. Joshua, Aimee?" Alex's fingers started to compress on Sam's wrist.

"Safe – nothing can get to them. Rein it in, boss."

"*Where the fuck are they?*" Alex's words were more a roar. The pain in Sam's arm was now intense, his own huge hand was beginning to go numb as the blood flow was cut off and the bones ground together. Sam gritted his teeth, watching and waiting, knowing escalation was only seconds away. Veins began to show in Alex's temples, and his other hand had curled into a fist.

"I'm not fighting you," Sam said evenly. "But know this, while I'm alive, nothing, nobody, no time, will ever touch them." Sam laid his other hand over Alex's.

Alex's entire body seemed to vibrate, and Sam knew the war with *the Other* inside him was raging. He hoped to god he was able to contain it.

"Rein it in, boss. We're in this together. While you're on-mission, I'll look after them."

Like a pressure cooker having the lid removed, Alex let go of Sam's forearm and stepped back. The veins in Alex's temples vanished and the fire in his eyes subsided.

"Yes." Alex exhaled, blinking. "Yes, I need you to do that, Sam. Be their guardian." Alex looked up, his eyes now dark and haunted. "Where I'm going, things will get a little … crazy. If anything were to happen to me, I need someone here to look after them."

Sam put his hand on Alex's shoulder. "I can do that." Sam didn't bother with the bullshit *you'll be fine* speech. Every mission the HAWCs were assigned to was one where good people died.

Sam gripped Alex's hand. "We are ghosts; in and out without a trace." Alex smiled, repeating the words in unison with the big HAWC. "We are the sword and the shield. If any get in our way, they will fall."

Alex's expression hardened. "Yes, and they *will* fall."

Sam nodded, and turned away, trying hard to resist the temptation to reach down and rub his bruised wrist. One thing he knew for sure: he'd hate to be the guys who tried to stop the Arcadian on this mission.

CHAPTER 12

Hours later, Hammerson sat in his office, flicking through his HAWC profiles. Alex was on his way, and now he needed a backup team. He wanted HAWCs who could secure the Chinese base, and their mining tunnel system, so when Alex came back up, he'd find an open door.

He had no doubt the Chinese would make the job red-hot. So his team needed to be lasers – burn their way in, and then keep the door open at all cost. Hammerson hoped the Chinese saw reason. But there was too much at stake and too little time now. Bottom line was, his team wasn't there to make friends.

Chilton had asked him personally, *The Hammer*, to get the job done, and he'd get it done the only way he knew how, *by hammering*. He sat back and smiled. The toughest jobs were the ones Joe Public never knew even existed … just the way they liked it.

Once again Hammerson checked Alex's vital signs on his monitor – strong and calm – the man could be taking a stroll in the park, instead of where he now was.

*

20,000 feet above the Southern Ocean

The B1R Lancer cut through the atmosphere at 20,000 feet doing just under Mach 2. The high speed, high altitude bomber had departed from the southern tip of Australia several hours back, and was already approaching its destination – the edge of the ice shelf of Antarctica.

The single pilot began to ease back on the throttle, the plane immediately slowing among the freezing clouds, and dropping down below Mach 1 with an associated boom. He turned to look back into the small hold. There was one delivery package – a single passenger, designate unknown. He was simply referred to as *Mr. Hawk*, and that was it.

The huge figure hadn't moved a muscle the entire trip. He sat like he was carved from stone, with hands clasped together and resting on his knees, his head tilted down at the now closed bomb-bay doors. He looked more machine-like than human. The pilot eased back around; he wasn't paid to ask questions.

"Crazy bastard," the pilot whispered. No one was going to survive the descent, even if he was wrapped in all the freaking tech in the world. The bulky outer suit the guy wore had rigid folds between the legs and under the arms. Normally a Spec Op high altitude drop would mean a torpedo frame made of high tensile steel, but as no metals could be worn that would cast a radar signature, it had to be a ceramic and polymer framework. He doubted it would be effective when fighting the cold, and speed, and then there was the final impact with no chute. *At least he'll be an invisible dead man*, the pilot thought gloomily.

The radar pinged and the pilot turned back to the controls momentarily before switching the cabin lights to a deep red. He swung around and held up two fingers. Eerily, the figure was now facing him, and he nodded once. His head and face were encased in a bullet-shaped helmet, his eyes impossible to make out. He could have been a robot for all the pilot knew – a robotic human-shaped wing.

The pilot exhaled, opened the bomb-bay doors, and then hunched over. Even from where he sat he felt the murderous waves of ice-pick cold air screaming up into the interior. He gritted his teeth, and then after another moment, turned again. The cabin was already empty.

"Good luck … *Hawk*."

He switched on the mic. "Package away." He banked and kicked the dart-shaped bomber back up to Mach 2. He'd be long gone before the guy's body even hit the water.

CHAPTER 13

Alex stayed rolled in a ball for the first few thousand feet, falling fast. He needed to minimize surface area exposure to the biting cold. Even though he wore multiple layers, and had a metabolism that could deal with extremes, he would be powerless to stop his extremities freezing solid, making fingers useless when suddenly called to do rapid or complex work.

He had a simple job to do – take out the *Kunming*'s offensive strike capability. The Chinese destroyer could not be allowed to rain hell down on the McMurdo base. *Defang the dragon*, Hammerson had said to him. *Defang the dragon, and then all you're left with is a big ugly lizard*, he thought and smiled.

Alex reached a number count in his head, knowing it was time to slow his descent. He unrolled, opening his arms and legs wide. The effect was instantaneous, as the folds of synthetic material acted like a combination wing and air brake on his body, slowing him from 220 miles per hour, down to just over a hundred.

Alex bit down hard on the air tube pumping warm oxygen into his lungs. The rising atmosphere was punishing as it pummeled his body, and the cold was a thousand razor blades slashing and stabbing at him, furiously seeking any exposed flesh. He grinned around the breathing tube inside the contoured helmet. He was looking forward to hitting the water.

As he finally dropped through the cloud cover, he saw he was slightly off-target. The *Kunming* was a mile out to his left, and he angled his shoulder and one arm to tilt toward it, and then swept his arms back, and legs in tight together. Alex became an accelerating arrow shape. He was an insignificant dot, invisible to radar, and traveling again at 200 miles per hour. Even if someone happened to be looking in his direction, the color of his suit against the leaden sky was the perfect camouflage.

Directly below him, Alex could make out the huge torpedo shape of the USS *Texas*, lying about fifty feet under the surface ... and then, he was in position. Once again, he opened his arms and legs, engaging the folds and struts of his suit to slow his speed – he counted down: nine, eight, seven, six, five, four, three, two, one ... *impact*.

The water surface collision was enormous, battering his entire frame. Multiple smaller bones in his body immediately fractured, and muscle, cartilage and tendon compressed and bruised. He had held his arms folded up and over his skull, but for several seconds he was stunned senseless. It was only the icy water that shocked him back to consciousness.

He sank down several dozen feet, peeling himself from the wing-suit. He'd been lucky, since he'd missed all of the tiny bergs that dotted the water. They were impossible to see on the descent, and even though they might have been little bigger than a coffee table on the surface, below, they could easily be the size of a Buick. If he had struck one of those, he would have been paste and it was game over. As it was, he could feel the massive trauma to his body, but knew that his system rushed to repair the damage, while his mind screamed its urgency – the Southern Ocean, freezing water, the *Kunming*, USS *Texas*. His mind reset, and he let the drop-suit fall away into the dark water, leaving him just in the specially thickened wetsuit, with a slim pack attached to his stomach.

Alex kept the full helmet in place, as it provided both airflow and goggles. The keel of the *Kunming* soon came into view, and in another few moments he was clinging to its stern, praying they wouldn't need to start the huge propellers as the churn would have drawn him in and shredded him in an instant.

His first task was the easiest – he needed to make the vessel go dark. To do that, he'd shut off all incoming and outgoing communications.

Alex opened a pouch in the pack on his front and brought out a flat disk which he attached to the hull, switching it on, so it first adhered, and then started to generate its white-noise net around the vessel. By the time they figured out it wasn't a problem with their own technology, and began a search for the source, the *Kunming* would need to deploy divers before they found it – and that should give him more than enough time to finish his work below the ice.

Alex looked up at the shimmering gray surface, steeling himself and then rising slowly. He breached the surface and paused, taking off the helmet, its air supply exhausted. He let it fall. He then attached caps to his palms. *Time to join the party*, he thought, and began to climb the two dozen feet to the rear deck.

Agony; the cold air on his bare skin was a thousand daggers, but he ignored it and slowly looked along the boat's guard rail – his plan's success was predicated on the crew and officers' focus being on the area where they knew the US submarine would be submerged. Then, one hand after the other, spider-like, he came up the side of the destroyer. He paused again and then slowly lifted his eyes above the railing. He slid over, tossing the suction pads back over the side.

Alex had memorized the Chinese boat's schematics, every room, armament, and crew capability. He had several immediate targets to destroy – the *Kunming* had anti-air, anti-surface, and anti-submarine missiles, deck-top mounted guns, as well as two 30mm close-in weapon systems (CIWS) that would be ferocious against an exposed submarine hull. The upside for him was that the missile launchers were single system, which meant the firing mechanism could shoot multiple missile varieties, but it was the same battery – knock it out, and you take them all out. The other guns would need individual attention.

Alex stayed low and moved fast. He was a dark blur speeding along the deck to his first target. The rear half of the destroyer was primarily multi-function phased array radar – numerous sensors and sonar. Basically, it was the eyes and ears of the ship, which was now blinded and deafened by the white-noise net that he'd attached to the *Kunming*'s hull. Their problem would not become apparent until the comm. team sent or expected to receive a communication.

Alex darted forward again. It was the front third of the ship where most of the dragon's fangs were embedded, and that section was directly under the raised bridge; it would be impossible to avoid being seen. He needed to rely on speed and accuracy, and then be gone within seconds.

Alex flattened himself on the external shielding, and paused to suck in a deep breath. He blinked hard to dislodge ice crystals that had formed on his lashes. His short dark hair was frozen solid against his scalp. His body's regeneration capabilities had to continually work to repair a body under attack from the freezing cold and its determination to turn his limbs, and face, to solid ice. He laid his head back against the cold steel and counted down.

Three, two, one, zero ... Alex exploded forward, his hands going to the pack on his front, and drawing forth several discs that looked like hockey pucks. His first destination was the two 30mm CIWS cannons. To each, he fixed a plasma disc, and pressed down on their timers. He then sped away to the smaller deck-mounted weapons. Once again, he attached several of the pucks, flicking on their pulses, and darting away.

By now, shouts had come from the upper deck, and the sound of running boots on steel. They would find him with their gun sights soon, and he had just one last job – the huge single system multiple missile launcher. No matter what came, this weapon needed to be taken out. Alex ran hard, a puck in each hand, his focus on the central launching barrel, when the bullet caught him in the shoulder, spinning him to the deck.

The bullet was a small caliber high velocity slug – probably fired from a QBZ-95 assault rifle. Alex was glad that whoever had fired it didn't have it on full automatic, as the Chinese gas powered weapon had an 80-round drum, and could spit them all in under a minute.

Alex rolled and came up fast. More bullets pinged off steel around him, and he rolled and ran hard now, swerving and running to complete his mission, and also running for his life. Within ten feet of the missile launcher he leapt, and threw the discs hard – one went in, the other stuck to the outside, near the base – *had to be good enough*, he thought, as there would be no second attempt.

Time to go. He turned, accelerating. More bullets whizzed past – angry lead bees looking to inflict their fatal sting. When Alex was six feet from the railing, he dived, spearing down the forty feet of the raised hull towards the dark water of the Antarctic.

It was like a cold fist on his face and head, but he swam down deep, feeling the grind of the bullet in his shoulder, and aware of the air bubble tunnels the bullets made as they chased him down.

He had about a thousand feet to cover to make it to the USS *Texas* for an underwater entry. The Chinese would have high velocity sniper rifles deployed on the deck now, so surfacing was out of the question. The wound in his shoulder was a dull throb, but the puncture in his suit allowed more of the sub-zero seawater to enter, thankfully numbing the wound, but also freezing his limbs, and making his movements slower and more cumbersome.

The gunfire had ceased, or perhaps his hearing had shut down as he swam. He concentrated on counting his strokes, knowing each one took him six feet closer to his goal, but burned just a little more energy from his limbs, and a little more oxygen from his lungs.

How many strokes have I made? A hundred? More? CO_2 was building up now, entering his blood stream and his brain, and making him drowsy. Flashes of light began to go off in his head, as the oxygen in his lungs was depleted. He was so tired, and all that remained was a calm voice in his head, Aimee's maybe, he wondered, that told him to relax, to sleep. To simply stop and take that first big, deep breath of pure, warm oxygen. He hadn't even realized he had stopped swimming. Then came the soft voice, sniggering at him. *You lose,* it whispered.

As his vision clouded, something loomed huge in the dark water before him. There came a sudden tightness as something circled his wrist, and then wrapped around his waist. He stopped caring, and his body simply hung limply in the thing's grip as it came at his face, pushing something into his mouth.

For Alex, everything went black.

*

Onboard the *Kunming*, confusion, chaos, and shouted orders rolled across the deck and out over the freezing water. Diver detection systems were brought online, and these used sonar and acoustic location to track small movements in the water. Snipers waited, rock steady, for the intruder to surface or for the system to pinpoint his position. Below deck, engineers were running system checks, trying to ascertain if the intruder had disabled any of their infrastructure.

The loud and blaring klaxon horn was finally shut down, but the entire crew was deployed to searching the ship. Seaman Qui Long was the first to find one of the discs, stuck limpet-like, to the top of the 30mm cannon. He tried to dislodge it. It wouldn't budge. He called over his shoulder for assistance, and then drew forth a knife from his belt and tried to wedge it under the object, without success. It was like it had become welded to the steel of the ship.

He called again for help and more sailors rushed to him, as he continued to struggle with the hockey puck sized pellet. He grunted in his efforts. "Stuck tight. Maybe an explosive." His lips turned down in scorn. "Small. Unlikely to damage the armor plating." He gripped it harder and tugged again.

As if in response to his derision, a small red light started to glow on its surface. Unbeknown to the sailors, the plasma-mine had initiated a tiny nuclear fusion. Inside its tiny casing, the miniature reactor collided particles and gamma rays with molten salts to generate trapped energy as pure heat – in two seconds it went from the sub-zero surface temperature of the steel plating to two thousand degrees Kelvin. Qui Long's hands were vaporized to the elbow and he fell back screaming with the skin on his entire body red and peeling, as the now glowing disc sank into the gun, turning the surrounding steel to gray liquid as it went.

The same thing was occurring to all the guns, each of them having their barrels or firing mechanisms melted beyond use. The *Kunming* had just been taken out of the game.

*

Water bubbled around Alex as it rapidly drained away. The tightness around his waist was still there as he moved into full consciousness, and he jerked back, immediately banging hard into the side of the submarine's seal tube.

"Easy there, big guy."

Alex's vision cleared, as the Special Forces underwater portal was flushed and filled with air. Two men in bulky ice-environment wetsuits stood close by, breathers now dangling at their necks. One had been holding him up, and now stepped away.

"Okay, now?" The man's breath steamed in the freezing tube.

Alex nodded and shook more clarity into his mind. The heavy door-wheel was spun from outside, and there came a sudden sibilant hiss, as the watertight seals were pulled apart and the oval door swung open.

He then stepped into the artificial light in the metal corridor of the USS *Texas*, and sucked in a deep draft of the warm air. His exposed skin prickled from the sudden change in temperature.

"Jesus Christ." A sailor stood waiting, mouth open. He stepped back as Alex moved further into the corridor. "*Ah,* Petty Officer Third Class, Anderson." He saluted.

Alex nodded, peeling off his gloves. He went to return the salute, but caught sight of his own hand – it was blue, and the fingers still wouldn't bend properly. He'd only ever seen skin like that on fresh corpses pulled from icy water.

"Commander Eric Carmack sends his regards, sir," Anderson said in a rush.

Alex began to peel himself out of the wetsuit. He felt the pain in his shoulder, and looked down at the ragged bullet hole there. He tugged harder on the neoprene suit and a partially flattened metal slug fell to the deck.

Petty Officer Anderson looked down briefly at the remains of the high caliber bullet. When he looked back up, his eyes went to Alex's wound, and became transfixed.

Alex could feel the familiar tingling over the trauma site, as the bullet wound began to heal, the skin around the meaty hole bubbling, and then pulling closed before the seaman's eyes.

"That ... musta hurt," Anderson said, swallowing, with an attempted smile that was more of a grimace.

"Every time," Alex said, and rolled his shoulder. He turned away; there was no time for conversation. "You have a package for me." It wasn't a question.

Anderson nodded. "Your kit and the skidder is juiced and ready. We also have a medic waiting to see you, if ..."

"Don't need him. Commander Carmack on the bridge?"

"Sir." Anderson pointed. "Follow me."

"I know my way." Alex headed for the bridge and Carmack, feeling impatience rising in his gut. Time was moving against him, the race was on, and he was already playing catch-up. He moved fast down the steel corridor, Anderson jogging in pursuit.

CHAPTER 14

Chinese rescue team – Two miles down and west of the Xuě Lóng Base

Captain Wu Yang held the shard of super-hard steel in his hand, his mind working. The metal had been flattened, impossibly compressed. He felt his frustration welling up. "Just like the elevator cage." He turned, holding it out, and looked along the faces of the assembled engineers and scientists. They stood, shuffling their feet, refusing to return his gaze.

"What happened? *Well?*" His booming voice made many of them flinch back.

"The cutter has been dragged away ... maybe taken into another tunnel," Soong Chin Ling said softly.

"Dragged away; *that's* what you think?" He glared. Soong dropped her eyes, and only one of the group met his gaze now – Shenjung Xing.

Yang flung the piece of steel down the tunnel and the fragment bounced away, clanging off into the darkness.

"This machine" – Yang waved his arm over the debris littering the tunnel – "weighed over a thousand tons and its drill head is solid tungsten." He tilted his head, looking up at the ceiling and then down and around the edges of the huge tunnel. "It is so large that the device should have fully plugged the end of the pipe." He scoffed. "But it's not gone, and it hasn't been dragged away into another tunnel."

Yang walked to one of the walls, lifting his flashlight, illuminating a similar shards of steel embedded deep into the rock.

"It's still here. Except now, what remains of it is crushed into the walls, floor, and ceiling."

No one said anything, avoiding his gaze.

"Just like the elevator cage," he repeated. "What could do that?" Yang placed his hands on his hips and turned slowly, finding Shenjung. "Firedamp again, *hmm*?"

The lead scientist remained mute.

Yang walked towards them. "And if so, then where are they?" He leaned closer to the scientist, becoming infuriated with his calm. "Where is the team, their burned up bodies, blood traces, bones, anything?" He turned again to one of the shards sticking out from the wall, frowned, and leaned in closer. He sniffed.

Yang straightened, and beckoned to Shenjung and Soong, clicking his fingers and waving them closer.

"Smell it."

Soong bent to wipe one of her gloved hands along a shard of twisted steel. She sniffed at it, and then held her hand up to Shenjung.

"The same as in the base, and on the boot."

Shenjung nodded and placed a hand against the rock wall, looking around at the obliterated interior. "If whatever came through here could do that to the cutter, there would be nothing left of flesh and bone, Captain. But, maybe they are not dead, but instead further inside, trapped maybe."

Yang grunted, just as the scouts came running back in from down the tunnel. He turned to them. "Report."

"Sir, we found something, two hundred feet further in. Another tunnel. But it's not one cut by the machines. It seems far older."

"*Ahh*." Yang waggled a finger in the air. "Perhaps our missing base members *did* descend lower. One of Comrade Zhang Li's last communications talked of opening *a void*, yes?"

"A void," Shenjung repeated softly. "Then yes, perhaps they *were* able to descend lower, and avoid whatever catastrophe occurred here."

"There is something else, Captain Yang."

Yang slowly turned. The soldier stood so rod-straight, it was if he were on a parade ground and not deep below the earth.

"Writing. There seems to be some sort of writing on the walls." The soldier stared straight ahead.

"Good, they also left us a message." Yang clicked his fingers. The soldiers fell in around him, and the scientists and engineers were pushed to the rear, their smaller frames eclipsed by the larger men at the front.

Yang looked down along the line. "Comrade Shenjung." He motioned impatiently, and saw the man lean in closer to the small woman beside him.

"You come too," Shenjung tried to whisper. "I think I get a front row seat."

"I'm sure it is whether you like it or not," she returned softly.

Yang walked briskly, Shenjung and Soong jogging to keep up, and not be trampled by the larger men behind them. They stopped at a collapsed wall, where the drilling ended when it had broken through into exactly what the missing Zhang Li had described – a dark void. Yang and several of his men lifted flashlights and panned them around slowly. Though the interior of the new cave was huge, it looked like it primarily sloped downwards, and its structure was vastly different from the tunnels they had been traveling along so far. The drilled tunnel had smelled primarily of cut stone and diesel fuel. But inside the new cavern, it smelled old, ancient, the rocks timeworn. There was a greenish tinge on several, indicating there was still moisture in the air.

Yang stepped lightly up onto the tumbled boulders, some the size of bread loaves, others the size of small cars. He let his eyes move over the broken debris. Shenjung went to climb up beside him, but the rocks shifted, and started to slide underneath him.

"*Watch it.*" Yang grabbed at him, but missed. The table-sized boulder that Shenjung stood atop began to skate down the pile and Soong screamed. Yang knew the rock would flip soon, and the scientist would be crushed.

People scattered ... all but one. Mungoi planted trunk-like legs as the huge boulder came towards him. It caught on the edge of another stone and lifted. Shenjung was thrown to the ground, as the eight-foot slab rose up like the lid of a trap about to close on top of him.

Shenjung rolled and ended up at Mungoi's feet, and the huge man lifted his arms, and leaned forward. The immense rock came down, and was stopped by the giant's hands. Mungoi's feet sunk into the debris to the ankles, and he grunted from the strain. The scientist stared up at him with his mouth open.

Yang smiled and nodded. "Good work, Mungoi." He looked down at Shenjung. "I suggest you watch where you walk, comrade. We cannot be holding your hand every second."

He watched as the scientist got to his feet and dusted himself off. The scientist turned to thank Mungoi, who looked down at him with disinterest, and then simply flipped the huge rock to the side.

Shenjung carefully clambered back up the debris pile, sucking in huge breaths.

"Okay?" Yang raised an eyebrow.

Shenjung nodded, calming himself. "Your man is strong."

Yang turned away. "You have no idea."

Shenjung then pointed. "It is clear that the drill broke through here."

"Maybe." Yang sniffed deeply. "I smell salt." He lifted his flashlight a little higher. "Maybe the ocean. But we are miles from the shoreline." He turned. "What is your opinion?"

Shenjung inhaled deeply. "Maybe mineral salts?"

"No, I know seawater when I smell it." Yang panned his flashlight around at the debris and then behind them. He noticed that the rubble was inside their tunnel, and not the old cave.

"Strange, the wall was pushed inwards. If I was to make an educated guess as to what occurred here, I would say that the miners didn't break through into this cave, but instead, something broke through in on *them*."

Shenjung pointed down at the debris. "Maybe when they retracted the cutter head, they drew the entire wall down on top of themselves."

"Once again, where are the bodies?" Yang climbed inside, and lifted his flashlight. "*Zha-aaaang!*"

Zhang – zhang – zhang – zhan – zha ... The echo receded to a whisper and then vanished.

Shenjung grimaced. "It's big." He turned his face towards the darkness. "And deep, but there is a breeze – I can feel it." He carefully stepped in and down along the debris, and then walked a few paces into the new cave. He stopped suddenly, lurching. "Careful, a drop off."

Yang quickly joined him, grabbing Shenjung's shoulder and pulling him back. He too peered over the edge. They were standing on a shelf of stone, and his light refused to penetrate the dark more than fifty feet into the pit. He picked up a fist-sized rock and let it drop. There was nothing for a few seconds before it struck a wall – once, twice, three times, and again, this time far away.

Shenjung exhaled. "We do not have enough rope."

"Neither did they," Yang responded and turned to several of his men. "Go, scout around. Find how Comrade Zhang Li descended."

Shenjung saw that the soldiers and now his own team of engineers and scientists had crowded into the ancient cave. Yang took him by the arm and walked him several paces away.

"Well, Comrade Shenjung, with the cutter destroyed, it looks like one of our tasks is already at an end. There can be no repair, only replacement – and this will not happen easily." He lifted his chin towards his engineering team crowding into the new cavern. "And so, their usefulness has expired. We don't need to bring them any further on our mission." He paused. "But you must stay."

"Our mission?" Shenjung Xing paled, and then shook his head. "I don't think …"

Yang held up a hand, and the smaller man wilted under his gaze. "We only need one geological specialist … and that will be you. That is an order."

"You can't order me."

Yang snorted. "Comrade, the engineering part of the mission is finished – the part *you* were in charge of. The priority remaining now, is finding the source of the signal from below the ground – the military mission – *my mission*. This is where I take the lead, and you follow. And *that* is an order you will obey."

*

"The part you were in charge of" – Shenjung Xing could have laughed; he never felt *in charge*. He held up a hand. "I am an engineer, geologist, and mining specialist, not a cave expert."

Wu Yang's eyes closed, and Shenjung waited, but after a few seconds he exhaled, knowing further protest would be wasted on the man.

"I will tell them."

He carefully picked his way around the fallen boulders, and gathered his small team. He felt their eyes on him, and spoke slowly.

"There is no machine to repair, recover, or restart. Our work here has completed early." Their faces were blank, waiting. Shenjung cleared his throat. "Until we receive further instructions, we will head back to the surface." He smiled. "Drink tea, relax, and stay warm."

There were murmurs about work, pay, departure, but he ignored them. There was only one person's face he sought out. "There is one more thing; I will accompany Captain Yang a little further into the caves … alone."

Soong came closer. Her lips held a fragile smile. "Calling for volunteers?"

He shook his head. "Not this time, my Soong. You take them back up."

"I'm not a good babysitter." Her smile fell away. "I would prefer to be down here with you."

"I'm sorry, this is not a request. These are Captain Yang's orders, and this time I agree with them. The less people we have down here the less chance more will get injured, or disappear. If we find anything significant, then we can return and decide what we need to do."

"And if you find Zhang Li or his team? What if they are hurt, and need to be carried out?" Soong asked. "We can be extra hands."

Shenjung shook his head. "And what if there is another rockfall, and more are hurt? All we do is create more people needing to be carried out, or more people vanished. We have twenty strong soldiers." He gave her a weary smile, and leaned in a little closer. "I would also like you with me, but maybe in other circumstances." He reached out to take her hand. "Get a message home, and tell them that the rock cutter cannot be repaired. Take our team back to the surface; wait for us there."

"No," she said softly. "I will wait for just *you* there." She turned away and seemed to shiver. "My grandfather used to say: Heaven has a road, yet no one travels it; Hell has no gate but men will dig to get there." She looked up at him. "And Yang is digging you deep now."

His weary smile lifted into something stronger. "We must *learn* what happened to our lost colleagues." He held up a finger. "And my grandfather also had a saying: *learning* is a treasure that will follow its owner everywhere." He grinned. "You see, two wise old men gave good advice to their grandchildren." He squeezed her hand. "I'll be fine. But only if I know that you are safe."

Soong looked at her feet momentarily, before the words rushed out. "Shenjung, I did not come here because of the project." She squeezed his hand hard in return. "I will be waiting for you." She paused, looking like she wanted to say more, or lean in close to him. In the end, she clicked on her flashlight, stepped back, and then turned to the dark tunnel, following the others.

He watched her go, her small light getting smaller and smaller until it vanished completely. *And one joy scatters a hundred griefs*, he whispered. Despite the gloom of the dark passages, and the knot he felt in his belly at the thought of scaling down any further in the dark caves, the idea that this young woman would be waiting for him suddenly filled him with lightness and hope.

CHAPTER 15

McMurdo Base, the surface

Sergeant Bill Monroe stood in his snowmobile and looked out over the bluff. Below was a plain of blinding white, with a few swirling flurries, looking like small ghosts racing each other across the freezing landscape. The wind was only around twenty miles per hour with gusts of thirty – mild. Down here katabatic blasts got up to 250, easy. Still, the chill factor made the wind feel like needle sharp teeth trying to get at his flesh.

Monroe wore standard extreme weather kit, with goggles fitted into a full-face covering. The face plate was padded with insulation on the inside and externally was of a tough polymer that had shielded him from far worse temperatures than these. And he knew well what the cold could do – freeze burn gave black blisters on the skin, the same as if you touched a red-hot stovetop. Extremities exposed for longer periods were lost. Fingers, toes, ears, noses – once the meat was frozen, the cells got ice crystals in them, and the flesh died. Removal was the only option – *lose a bit to save the rest* – it was as simple as that.

His comm. link pinged. "*Captain, come in.*"

It was Jennifer Hartigan, his onsite medical officer. She was smart, wholesomely attractive, and could hold her own in field exercises, stitching a wound, or on the dance floor. He smiled, and guessed this message was going to be about the fancy dress party they were organizing this Saturday night to farewell the day-trippers. He squeezed the comm. link at his neck to connect.

"Monroe. Go ahead, Hartigan."

"Bill, got a message coming in from HQ, high priority. You need to take it."

"Can you patch it?" He frowned at her tone.

"No can do, sir, coded squirt. Not to be delivered over this frequency, or any frequency. You're going to have to be in the chair for this one."

What the hell? he wondered. "Okay, coming back in. See you in twenty."

He took one last look over the snow plain. The shadows were long, the sun just a weak orb sitting on the horizon. *Winter coming, party's over*, he thought. He threw a leg back over the snowmobile and turned it around, quickly lifting the machine to eighty miles per hour, and shooting a rooster tail of white into the air behind him.

Within thirty minutes, Monroe had taken the urgent call from a Colonel Jack Hammerson, acting on executive orders. He was told to expect a Special Forces soldier – no name, no rank – but he was to do everything the guy said without question. Bottom line, he was to link up the soldier with the British scientific team over at the Ellsworth project base.

Cate Canning and her team of Brits were under Monroe's support umbrella, but to date they had pretty much kept to themselves – fine with him – no noise, no trouble. Until now.

As if I don't have enough to damn well do, he thought, as he waited out in the cold for the soldier, getting more pissed off by the minute. He was told to wait, but he forgot to ask, *how long?*

"Who is this guy?" Ben Jackson stamped huge boots beside him, trying to get circulation into his long legs.

Monroe was a fair sized man, but the big soldier trying to stay warm beside him looked down on everyone. He liked Jackson, and if some hardass was going to show up, who better to have standing with him than the local giant? Monroe grinned confidently.

"No idea who he is. But we've been ordered to meet him, get him sorted out, and then push him towards the Brits." He turned. "And now you know as much as I do." He looked up at the leaden sky. "He's too late anyway. With the storm coming in, we won't be going anywhere till it passes on."

Jackson grunted, and lifted huge arms to hold a pair of fieldglasses to his eyes. "Bill, incoming; one o'clock."

Monroe lifted his own glasses, seeing the snow plume kicking in the air. *Where could he have come from?* he wondered.

Then it hit him – *shit*, he thought, as the soldier powered up to them on a high-speed military snowmobile that was more like a torpedo. He wore some sort of armored wetsuit, with full-face shielding ... and he was frozen, really frozen, with an ice crust over his shoulders and arms. The lunatic must have come from the water – how was that even possible? It was an unbelievable 120 miles of exposed granite, loose snow, and ice crevasses.

"Holy shit." Ben Jackson scoffed. "The ice man cometh."

The soldier stepped off the sled and rolled his shoulders, cracking ice that fell from him in large flakes. He flipped his faceplate up. Any thoughts Bill Monroe had about chewing the soldier out vanished immediately. Though the guy had sort-of handsome features, there was something about him that set alarm bells ringing. Perhaps it was the iron-hard physique, or the sense of menace behind those gray-green eyes, that hint of explosive violence barely held in check. Every time that stare alighted on Monroe, it seemed to cut right through him. Frankly, Monroe thought, he'd be happy when this guy, and his secret mission, was just a memory.

The soldier held out a hand, and Monroe grabbed it, shook it, and quickly introduced himself and then Ben.

"Thank you for meeting me, Sergeant." The soldier turned and nodded briefly to Ben, but then immediately turned back to Monroe. "I'll need a chopper and a pilot."

Monroe nodded. "I can fly you," he said, while watching him carefully. "Is there anything else you need? Hot coffee, a few minutes to gather your shit together? If you've ..."

"No. Just to get going."

"Not sure that's a good idea. There's a storm coming in, and I strongly ..."

"Now." The man's eyes never seemed to blink.

Ben Jackson held up a hand. "Sir, Sergeant Monroe is right, down here the storms can ..."

Kraken Rising

The soldier turned to Ben, and the big man's mouth snapped shut.

So much for my big scary backup, Monroe thought. *Fine, you want to go to hell, well then, be my guest.*

Monroe thumbed over his shoulder. "This way."

*

The helicopter descended towards the five figures standing on the snow. All were wearing thick clothing with hoods up and goggles over their faces, making them look like chubby clones of one another. Alex saw that the Ellsworth base wasn't large – one fair sized silo-shaped building and then mostly a temporary set of shelters designed to accommodate the scientific staff while they went about their technical work. Just off to one side stood a structure that looked like a round elevator shaft, rising several dozen feet into the air.

"You know about the *Kunming*?" Alex asked.

Monroe nodded.

"I knocked out their communications. Sooner or later they'll figure out how to get it back online. Once they do, they may decide to pay you or the British team a visit." Alex turned to Monroe. "An unpleasant one."

Monroe nodded. "We don't have the manpower or ordnance to repel a coordinated attack." He smiled grimly. "But we don't intend to surrender the base, or anyone under our protection."

"I know you won't. But you've got the USS *Texas* in your front yard, and they've got a squad of SEALs onboard. Just try not to start a war until I get back." Alex grinned, and then looked to the figures on the snow. "Good luck, Sergeant Monroe."

Alex grabbed his kit bag and leapt free before the chopper had settled on the ground. He jogged to the figures sheltering from the swirling snow. One of them, slightly shorter than the rest, stuck out a hand.

"Mr. Hawk?" The voice was authoritative and female.

Alex grabbed the hand and shook it. "That's right. And you must be Professor Cate Canning."

She nodded and waved him towards one of the small shacks. Inside it was warm, but the floor was wet. Cate and the men started to peel off clothing and boots. One by one they stopped and stared at Alex.

He wore his armored caving suit that would also be his diving gear. It was compression fitted over his frame, from fingertips to feet, the Kevlar thread worked through a polychloroprene material. There were also thin molded sheets of a mottled biological looking material over the biceps, thighs, and chest plate. It made him look like a cross between an assembled robot, and some type of superhero. It also had shielding over the hands and knuckles, and tight against his back was a flattened air tank that contained compressed oxygen.

"That's some suit you got there. You planning on diving or bloody cage fighting?" said one of the youngest bearded men, brows raised.

"That's enough, Sulley." Cate Canning smiled tightly, and then pointed at each of the assembled men in turn. "Doctors Bentley, Timms, Schmidt, and the one with the sense of humor is Sulley." Each nodded, their bearded faces far from humorous. Alex guessed none were happy to see him.

That was fine, he didn't expect a welcoming committee, and in fact was already expecting some sort of passive resistance. He didn't blame them; no one likes to have a huge boot stuck right into the middle of their project, especially one that the scientists had been working on for five years, that he could potentially sabotage. Hammerson would have had to pull a helluva lot of strings, and fast.

Cate walked down a small hallway in the shack and into a larger room, where one entire wall was covered in banks of equipment. "Sulley, get the kettle on. You're on tea duty." She turned. "Or is it coffee for our American friend?"

"Neither." Alex could feel the tension in the room. "Just a briefing, and then I'm ready to go. Time is extremely short."

Cate stared for a moment, her jaws clenching.

"This is crazy," Bentley said, pulling at his long thin nose and then folding his arms. "Even though this position has the thinnest ice coverage for fifty miles, it's still a mile-and-a-half thick layer of super compressed ice, over a skin of solid granite." He turned to Cate, his palms up. "We know, *we know*, there's a gap between the ceiling and the water below, but what we don't know is just how big a gap. The drill *will* end up falling into space, and the impact on soft tissue alone could ..."

"*Flipper* made it. *Orca* will too," Cate said, clicking her fingers and pointing Sulley to the kettle.

"Damnit, Cate, that's just it. *Flipper* was in a titanium and steel armored sleeve. We designed the shielding to protect the submersible and its electronics – not flesh and blood." He thumbed at Alex. "He wants to hitch a ride? Fine, but he'll be dead even before *Orca* is launched." Bentley's face was growing red. "This is crazy. *Crazy!*"

"Might be possible for someone to survive. *Orca*'s gyros will stabilize it, and it's padded to kingdom come," Timms said, looking to Bentley who now glared at him and shook his head. He grinned. "I mean not someone like you, Bent. You're basically ninety percent tea and crumpet, but look at this guy." He thumbed towards Alex. "He looks like he's made of iron."

Sulley snorted. "Nah, the cold, the heat, the pressure; it'll be suicide." He handed Cate a small mug of steaming tea. "But Yanks love that sort of stuff, right?" He shrugged. "His body will give *Orca* some more padding."

"Happy to assist," Alex said without humor.

Cate looked from her team to Alex. He noticed her features were attractive but severe, and her eyes were like shards of diamond. Alex could tell she was weighing something up in her mind.

Bentley exhaled through clenched teeth. "If he damages the probe, we'll end up with nothing. This is a one-off, one-way deal. We can't even recover the probe to repair it, and it's supposed to explore the lake for the full ten months of its powerpack life. If he buggers it up, it's over, and we'll never get more funding for another try."

"Arkson." Cate smiled at Bentley. "I've devoted my life to this glimpse of another world, I think ..."

"Yes, you *do* need to think. If he damages *Orca*, it'll be a forty million dollar piece of junk sitting on the bottom of a sunken sea." The nostrils of his long nose flared, looking like tiny wings. "Cate, *you know* what's at stake here."

Cate bared her gritted teeth. 'Don't get all self-righteous with me, Arkson. The project's funders basically ordered us to assist. They could shut us down a lot quicker than this guy." She jerked a thumb over her shoulder at Alex.

Bentley straightened. "Unlikely. Cate, I know there's more at stake than ..."

Alex had heard enough. "*You* know what's at stake? *I* know what's at stake; *it's you people who don't.*"

The room quietened as if a switch had been thrown. Alex looked at each of their faces. "You don't know a lot." He tried to keep the menace out of his voice, but knew his stare was already making some of the men ease back. "I'm not here to ask or to apologize. But you need to know a few things, *fast.*"

The group waited, and Cate nodded at him to continue. Alex placed his hands on his hips. "Did you know the Chinese have lost contact with their Xuě Lóng Base? Did you know we have a Chinese warship off the coast because they probably think we had something to do with it? Right now, there's an American sub keeping it at bay. But soon there'll be more ships, and then one false move, and there could be a nuclear war. I can potentially stop it, but I need to be down below the ice, *fast.*"

"Did you?" Bentley asked, lifting his gaze to Alex's face. "Did you have something to do with them losing contact?"

"No," Alex said.

"Would you tell us if you had?" Sulley asked from behind Bentley.

"What's down there that's so interesting to you?" Cate asked, tilting her head.

"That's classified," Alex responded.

"Of course it is." Bentley snorted his disdain.

"Something else I don't understand," Cate said. "Since when did your relationship with the Chinese government get so bad? When did you stop talking and start deploying warships?" She frowned. "Something's not right here."

Alex felt his frustration start to coil inside him. "Look, there are ... *other* factors in play. I'm not authorized to tell you, and you're not authorized to know."

"Not helpful." Sulley's voice rose again from behind Bentley.

Alex exhaled, looking from Cate to the scientists. "I know, to you, your project is important. But we are nearing a conflict tipping point, and I'm sure you don't want World War Three starting on your doorstep." He stared hard at Arkson Bentley, and the man held his gaze. "I'm sorry, but in relation to that, your work is to be temporarily commandeered."

"Like bullshit it is." Bentley's eyes narrowed. "No American spook is going to march in here and say, *how are you? By the way, I'm taking over your project because we pissed off the Chinese.*" He crossed his arms over his chest. "You're not going near our probe."

Alex looked along the faces, speaking now through clenched teeth. "Do you really think I care about your fucking probe?" He took a step towards Arkson Bentley, feeling a knot of fury start in his belly. The man went pale behind his beard. Alex's eyes blazed, and without even realizing it, the hand he held up had curled into a fist. "I need to get down there, fast. Your probe is the only chance I have to do that."

Alex waited, but most of the men had stopped looking at him, not wanting to meet his eyes. Only Cate was still staring, and her gaze was quizzical. Alex shrugged at her. "All I can promise is, I'll do my best to protect your probe." He scoffed. "And stay alive."

Silence hung in the small room for a few more moments before Schmidt held up a hand.

"*Ah*, Mr. Hawk, protecting the probe is not the issue. It is certainly possible you can fit yourself into the capsule, we have left the rear mostly vacated for cushioning and to act as a buoyancy tank for when the drill canister is in the water. It must be suspended nose down for smooth release of the probe. But ..."

"But ..." Bentley spoke without looking away from the floor. "On the way down, there will be enormous changes in temperature. To begin with, it will be well below freezing, as it drills into the top layers of snow and ice. But once it strikes the hard ice, *the dark ice*, the heating units are designed to kick in to soften it. The exterior of the probe will rise to four hundred degrees, and the interior, we estimate, will be near two hundred. You will not survive. All we will succeed in doing is depositing a broiled body, in a dark sea, several miles down."

"Your concern is touching." Alex never blinked. "You just concentrate on getting the probe down there, I'll worry about my comfort level."

Cate snapped her fingers. "Hey Sulley, we have thermal sheets that are temperature controlled. They could help."

Alex shook his head. "Like I said, you let me worry about my own safety." Alex lifted his kit and dropped it on a table. He unzipped the bag, revealing several sets of goggles, fins, and a single slim backpack, which he looped over his shoulders.

Cate peered into the bag and reached for one of the other sets of goggles, turning it over in her hands.

"How long will it take … until I make the water surface?" Alex asked.

"The entire penetration?" Schmidt shrugged. "Test sinkings have taken up to seven hours. But we have increased both the power of the drill and the thermal displacement unit. Our estimates are a drop of sixty-seven minutes of high speed ice coring, and then a slower descent through the granite mantle. There's about a hundred feet of dense, orbicular granite. Going to be one bloody rough ride."

"And getting there isn't the only danger." Cate's brows were drawn together. "You have no idea what you're getting yourself into." She crossed to one of the computer screens and flicked it on. She opened a file, and started the video footage, and then turned the screen towards him.

"There's life down there, you know, and not just blind shrimp, or bacterial clumps. There are predators – huge, we think." She stopped the film at an immense eye filling the screen. It was lidless, round and white-rimmed, and its pupil was a goat-like slit.

The eye seemed to stare into Alex's soul. He was momentarily transfixed, and felt his mouth go dry. "Yes." He found it hard to look away, as monstrous memories came rushing back. "I know what to expect." He tried to smile at her, but felt his mouth fail to fully comply. "Unfortunately, I've been there before."

Bentley scoffed. "Yeah, right."

Cate stared at him for several more moments, but there was something in her expression that was more assessing than disbelieving.

Bentley's grin split his face, rising on both sides of his long nose. "Like I said, if the heat doesn't kill you, the vibrations will certainly loosen your teeth ... and then you wait until you meet whatever it was that took *Flipper* out." He finished with a snigger.

"Let's get started," Alex said.

Cate folded her arms. "Listen, Mr. Hawk, or whatever your real name is, I don't care who you think you are, or how many politicians' arms you twisted to get here. Without my approval, you're not going anywhere." She paused, her gaze direct. "Unless."

Alex waited, seeing something building behind her eyes.

"One condition." She held up a finger. "You take me with you."

Bentley spluttered. "Are you crazy?"

Her team crowded around, and even though she was a tall woman, the men seemed to stand over her, their faces twisted in either disbelief or anger.

She folded her arms. "I'm going. I've waited my whole life to get a glimpse of what's down there. I thought that we wouldn't send anything biological until we knew what the contamination risk profile looked like ... well, seems that assessment protocol has been overridden by our clever benefactors." She turned, looking at each of them. "I'm not sitting around up here, when I could be down there." She nodded towards Alex. "Besides, I'll have John Carter of Mars with me." She turned back to Alex. "Deal?"

"No." Alex continued to get ready.

Cate's folded arms seemed to tighten across her chest. "You weren't listening. One word from me, and *no one* is going ... and you can't launch by yourself, tough guy." She smiled. "Besides you're going to need me – as well as being an evolutionary biologist, and the closest thing to a primordial environment expert you got, I've also had medical training. If you get injured, I can help."

Alex continued to work on his pack, and she stepped towards him, wrenching his arm. "I've spent my whole life studying this potential landscape. You'll need me. I'm an asset."

Alex looked up slowly. "Dr. Canning, you've spent your life studying fossilized landscapes or things compressed in shale that have been dead for millions of years; they're nothing like they are in real life." He stared hard at her. "Down there is not our world. Down there, human beings don't belong."

Cate's teeth were gritting, as she wrenched his arm. "But you've got a free pass, huh?"

"Not because I want to go." Alex went back to his pack. "And I don't take sightseers."

"Then all I can lend you is a fucking shovel, mister. You can dig your way down." She turned away. "Have your president call our prime minster. I'm sure they can sort something out in a week or two."

Alex stared at the back of her head with such ferocity, his vision almost blurred. After a moment he exhaled. Why should he care if this woman was determined to kill herself?

"You don't know me, and I don't know you," Alex said evenly. "If you get injured, or in any way become incapacitated, I'll leave you without blinking. That's the way it is." Alex stared at the woman. "Understood?"

Cate didn't flinch. "*HUA!*"

They remained locked together, staring at each other for several more moments, before she finally turned away, shouting over her shoulder, "Get me the thermal sheeting, a dive suit, flashlight, flares, and survival pack. Launching *Orca* in ten minutes, people."

CHAPTER 16

The wind screamed and the Ellsworth team braced themselves against the furious cold, as they gathered around the silo shaped structure. A door, or rather, a panel, had been lifted free, revealing a dark space inside. Alex stuck his head in – it was like a cross between a cylindrical steel telephone booth and giant vitamin capsule. There was not a lot of space even though Bentley and the other scientists had removed some of the compression packing.

The wind was rising, and Alex could feel it trying to work its way to his skin. He ignored it, knowing it would be nothing compared to what was to come. Beside him, Cate shivered with several silver thermal sheets wrapped around her body, and another hanging over her shoulders. Underneath, she wore a black wetsuit, with goggles around her neck as well as small breathing tanks slung over her back.

"Gonna be snug," she said and grinned through clamped teeth.

Alex bet it was either nerves or to stop them chattering. *The woman has guts, I'll give her that*, he thought.

Schmidt pushed his head into *Orca*'s rear cavity, and yelled, "I removed some of the cladding to create a space for you. The bubble here was so the capsule would create neutral buoyancy and float midwater, this end up. That way the submersible would be able to launch in open water, and not end up buried in the silt on the bottom. There is a rim inside," – he said, pointing – "you can use it to crouch on, but for the love of god, try and keep your big Yank feet off the end of the submersible. Though it's toughened steel, if you bend any of the struts, we won't be able to maneuver it."

Alex ignored him, so Schmidt looked to Cate, his expression gloomy. "You know what to do, Cate." He clasped her shoulder, the silver sheets crinkling. "Those thermal covers can take temperature extremes. Stay away from the walls, and you'll be fine." His eyes slid away before she could meet them.

Alex climbed in, and moved to the side so Cate could enter and then crouch in front of him. Both hung onto the side struts, and balanced on a metal rim above the probe's fins. There were bracing bars on each side that they could use as handholds.

Bentley leaned inside. "It's only little more than an hour, Cate, but it'll be the longest hour of your life." He smiled sadly. "It'll be tough, but you can make it." He turned to Alex, his expression hardening. "Keep her safe."

Alex didn't respond – he couldn't – he knew what to expect down there. He would make no empty promises.

Bentley went to turn away but stopped, and instead grabbed Cate's arm. "Cate, *please,* this is mad."

"I'll be fine." She shrugged him off. "Whatever happens, learn from it."

Bentley seemed to want to lean in further, but Alex held up a hand. "You heard the lady. Go back and do your job."

Bentley's jaws clenched momentarily. "Listen, the body of water you'll find yourself in is about the size Lake Ontario – about two hundred miles long, by fifty wide. Also, a mile deep in places. It's a bloody ocean, and it'll be blacker than hell."

Alex checked the tracker he had – the sub's signal was faint, miles away, but it was there. He knew when he got down inside the ice and rock mantle, it would be a lot stronger. He looked up at the scientist. "There's an air pocket above the water, and there's dry land. So, as long as I can get to a shoreline, then I'll be fine."

"You'll be fine? I don't give a damn about you, mister." Bentley grimaced. "You know we have proof of life down there. And you know we're not talking about some tiny shrimp or blind eel. The thing that knocked out our previous probe was big, real big, and you'll be in the water with it."

"I'm counting on it," Cate said. "Just keep *Orca*'s onboard cameras rolling, and we'll make history."

Alex looked down at her and smiled. He admired her. The thought of dropping into the black water, miles below ice and rock, and knowing what was down there, must have filled her with dread – but she was going anyway.

"Let's get on with it," he said.

"Never met anyone in such a hurry to be sent to hell." Bentley pulled his head out of the capsule. "Insane, the pair of you," he shouted.

One after the other Schmidt, Timms, and Sulley either gave the thumbs-up, or knocked on the skin of the capsule. Sulley came back quickly and stuck his head in. "Wish I was going ... " he grinned, "... not." He then sealed them in. Immediately there was total darkness. Alex heard Cate take a huge shuddering breath.

"Hey Hawk, I must be mad, you know."

"You can only die once," Alex said softly. "But it won't be today. And by the way, it's Alex."

"Okay, thanks, Alex ... and call me Cate." She hunkered down.

Alex's eyes were able to pick up the minutest particles of light, and his wristwatch numerals became little beacons, making everything an alien green. He saw her look up at him, her eyes blind in the dark.

There came a double knock against the outer skin of the probe.

"Here we go, ready or not," she said with a tremor in her voice.

Alex reached down, pulling the thermal blanket up over her head. "Cover yourself. Try and leave no gaps at all, and do not touch the exterior of the capsule. Oh yeah, and breathe through your nose. That will at least cool the air down a little, so it doesn't scorch your lungs."

"What about you?" Her voice was muffled under the insulation sheets now wrapped tightly around her.

"Me? Do this every day." He smiled and gripped the steel bracing tighter. Already, he could feel the bone-chilling cold through his gloves – against bare skin his flesh would have freeze-bonded to the steel.

Starting like the buzzing of an insect, and then growing in intensity, there came a small hum from below them. It reminded

Alex of an electric drill starting up. He smiled again. In effect that's what they were jammed into, a giant electric drill about to screw its way down through snow, ice, and rock to a hidden world miles below.

Alex remembered that the first stage of the process was to just employ the drill mechanism to move easily through the surface snow and ice. But when they entered the compacted ice zone, the dark ancient ice that was dark blue and as hard as stone, then the thermal-heating units would kick in.

It would be over in little more than an hour. He just hoped he could withstand it – a lot of lives depended on it. There came a jerk, a thump, and then a sensation of sliding.

"Going down," Alex said, tilting his head back. "Next stop, the lair of the leviathan."

"What?" A muffled voice, from down in front of him.

The cold became more intense, like a physical weight settling around them. Alex shut his mouth as his teeth began to ache. He screwed his eyes shut to ensure that the delicate membranes didn't freeze solid in his head.

His skin began to prickle and sting, and he felt his arms and legs growing heavy. His body was pulling the blood away from his extremities as it automatically rushed to save the brain and internal organs.

His own body's temperature burned hotter than a normal person's, but he knew Cate would suffer if the intense cold continued for much longer, no matter how many thermal blankets she was wrapped in. He reached down to circle her body with an arm, the outer blanket crinkling as it became brittle.

The vibrations that were just a tickle beneath his soles now became a thump, then a grinding, as they struck the first of the dense ice sheets. Pleasant warmth wafted up towards Alex's face as the huge silver bullet's thermal engines kicked in.

He flexed his hands to get the blood flowing once more, and then adjusted his grip on the probe's infrastructure struts. His feet were braced on a three-inch rim running around the interior. Cate was in a similar position, but was facing him, head down, and her smaller body was now folded into his. She was just a lump of silver sheeting. He looked at his wristwatch – already they had been traveling for twenty minutes. *So far so good*, he thought.

He felt the air tickle the hair in his nose. It was getting warmer. He looked up towards the dark rear of the capsule, and heard the sound of turbulent liquid – the boiling water that was created by the ice-melt would first cool behind them, and then freeze, effectively creating a solid plug. This was designed to ensure that no more contaminants could enter the pristine environment below. But it also meant there would be no return journey via this way.

The capsule thumped, slowed, and then shuddered as it impacted with the dark ice. There came a grinding that had Alex clamping his teeth as the vibrations shook every atom in his body – *shake your teeth loose,* Bentley had said – now he knew what the guy meant. The drill sensors must have engaged more of the heat unit's source, as the temperature jumped and an oven-like blast rushed up past Alex's face, searing his skin.

He leaned forward, yelling, "Keep your eyes and mouth shut."

He let go of one of the struts to pull goggles down over his face. His eyes were the only soft organ exposed to air, and would suffer first from the heat. Alex concentrated on his breathing – *in and out, in and out.* Through his gloves, he felt the heat start to make the Kevlar-woven material begin to soften. It could withstand significant heat, many hundreds of degrees, so he felt confident it wouldn't burn or melt. But it was the mask that worried him. If it melted and then degraded, he would enter the water near blind.

Alex concentrated on a soothing image – Aimee Weir, her face, her voice, and her shape. He counted the seconds and ignored the pain, the pressure and the heat. He felt Cate against him. The bulky thermal material seemed flimsy on her now, but as long as she stayed cocooned inside her thermal sheeting shell, she might just be okay ... for a while.

Cate had brought a sheet for him, but he had refused it, making sure she kept them all. He knew that what he could take, she could not. Instead, he crushed his eyes shut and took himself somewhere else. Part of the HAWC training in regard to physical pain was twofold – on one level they were taught how to tolerate extreme discomfort, and to be able to simply ignore insults to their body that would have normal people screaming. The second level was the prolonged agony of significant physical trauma – *torture*. In the event of this happening, they were taught how to place themselves in a state of near hibernation, and mentally remove themselves, leaving their bodies behind, and viewing the insult to their flesh and bone as something that was happening to someone else. Death then became not something to be feared, but a doorway to a blessed release.

Seconds passed, minutes, and then more minutes – each new moment attacking his body and mind. Inside, deep in his cerebral cortex, something stirred, something rebelled at the torment.

Get out! The voice was furious, and created more pain, this time from deep within his skull.

Alex breathed rhythmically, and clenched his eyes even tighter. He tried to focus, but the pain ripped him back, and allowed "the Other" to stir. If it gained control now, he, *it*, was liable to simply try and exit the capsule, destroy it while it was burning its way through ice that was harder than rock.

Aimee, he whispered. His hand on the internal metal strut vibrated, and then his fist tightened, increasing pressure. The steel-titanium blended structure began to bend inwards under his force – it wasn't him doing it, but the other being deep inside him. "Not now, please not now," he whispered over and over, through clenched jaws.

The blistering heat, the ever-present grinding vibration of the drill, and the sensation of pressure on his ears became Alex's world. There was nothing else, until ...

They hit stone, and Alex only just reached out in time to grip Cate and hold on tight to stop them being thrown onto the probe's maneuvering struts. The thermal drill tip retracted, and the circular cutting blades were brought to bear on the rock. The noise was near deafening, and Alex gritted his teeth, and then screamed his anger and pain, fighting back against the thing that wanted to let loose its fury inside the confined space.

You'll die. It'll all be for nothing ...

... unless you use the woman, a sly voice whispered, deep inside his head. *Use her as a flesh cloak – shield yourself – and live!*

Alex moaned. The *flesh cloak* was an extreme Special Forces survival tactic – you used the body of an animal, gutted, and worn as a cloak to stay warm, or cool.

It will work, the voice again, sneering.

Alex shook his head, trying to fling it away. He knew it wanted to take him into its world of anger and madness. The cynical laugh started, taunting him, jeering and mocking, wanting him to let go, surrender to it, and then … it was gone, *everything* was gone, and he felt like he was floating.

Alex opened his eyes in confusion, and it took him a few seconds to determine what was happening, and then it came in an instant: *they were free-falling*. They had broken through the crust that acted as a ceiling over the underground sea.

"*Hang on!*" he yelled, and was relieved to feel Cate cling to him a little tighter. In turn, he jammed his breather in his mouth and then wrapped a large arm around her head – he knew what was coming – if they struck rock, they were dead. But even if they hit water, the surface tension would make the landing traumatic on soft tissue.

He braced himself, gripping on with every ounce of strength he possessed. The longer the capsule fell, the greater the velocity, and then the greater the impact. How long had it been – *five heartbeats, ten?* – eventually they would reach thirty-two feet per second, and they had been falling now ten, fifteen, twenty …

They hit the water at a slight angle. Alex, one arm down and around Cate, was thrown to the side. His head connected with the armor plating of the outer shell. There was nothing after that.

CHAPTER 17

Shenjung Xing heard shouts from within the cave opening, and he clambered back up over the rubble, stepping carefully back into the cavern. A hundred feet farther along, a group of the soldiers were standing before a huge wall of stone, combining their beams of light up onto its flat surface.

Captain Wu Yang looked briefly in his direction, and then back to the huge edifice. As he approached, Shenjung could see the carvings and raised lettering etched deep into the stone.

"*Hoowah*. This is old," he said softly. The work was crude chiseling, but the images were intricate and clear.

Yang stepped closer and placed his fingers into one of the carved lines. "Certainly not done by any of Zhang Li's team. The rock and the markings have an unbroken cover of moss." He rubbed his fingers together, and then wiped them on his pants. As he stepped back, debris crunched beneath his feet. He turned.

"Comrade Shenjung, you are a man who works with rocks and stones, and must have come across cave art before. What is your opinion?"

Shenjung panned his light across the tableau. "I am not a specialist in the ancient works of man, but yes, I have encountered many things before in my excavations." He leaned in closer, bringing his light up and reaching out a hand, first touching the moss, rather than the stone images.

"*Acarospora sinopica*, a lichen; it grows on iron rich stone. But it is remarkable for being very slow growing, and in the right conditions, can live for thousands of years." He half turned. "Current research has found that some lichens may even be immortal." He stepped back, looking up at the wall. "For this depth and covering, it could be at least five thousand years old, and perhaps even tens of thousands."

Shenjung focused on the carvings beneath the growth. There were whorls, strokes, and lines, some carved in, and some raised in relief. Further along, there were depictions of birds, snakes, something that could have been a big cat, and a bison type animal. And then there were the faces: tongues lolling, some gnashing teeth, and many with wide eyes, staring, holding looks of anger combined with fear.

"Look here, this one." Yang pointed, and Shenjung followed his arm.

At the center of the relief was a huge glyph of a small mountain that had what looked like coiling snakes emanating from it, and a giant eye nesting in its middle.

"Their god?" Shenjung grunted, staring for several moments more. "Perhaps our demented survivor was right – perhaps it is *Zhàyǔ*, the devourer of men." He turned. "Remember, it lives in the underworld."

Yang scoffed. "I think I will ignore any intelligence briefings derived from a frightened dumpling cook." He shook his head, his eyes flint-hard. "To me it looks like a representation of the sun ... sunlight. It is telling us that this is probably a way out." He turned away, to more brittle crunching beneath his feet, and stepped away from the wall.

Shenjung sighed, about to follow the PLA captain, when instead he crouched as something caught his eye. The crunching beneath their feet, it wasn't stone chips as he expected, but instead bone fragments – different shaped shards and splinters, the fragments brown and aged and mostly pulverized. He picked up a tooth, a human molar.

"Captain Yang." He held it up.

Yang leaned closer but didn't take it. He shrugged. "Maybe some cavemen got trapped in here."

Shenjung got to his feet. "Cavemen do not create this type of carven symbolism. They paint, using natural dyes, charcoal, and some rubbing." He scoffed at the bone fragments. "And then what happened to them? They're ground to pieces."

Yang shrugged. "The cutter crushed the bones when it broke through."

Shenjung shook his head. "No, even the edges are ..."

"*Captain?*"

Yang turned towards the voice. A soldier, standing further along the stone shelf.

"Steps, Captain Yang. Cut into the cliff wall." The tall soldier stood at attention. "There is evidence that they were used recently."

"Steps?" Yang clapped his hands once, the sound like a gunshot in the cave. "So, now we are getting somewhere. *Hoi!*" He circled a finger in the air, and followed the young man. The rest of the soldiers fell in behind them.

A few hundred feet farther along, the ledge narrowed to about six feet, and then simply ended. Cut into the wall were steps, descending, and also disappearing upwards into the darkness. They were narrow, small, and barely wide enough for a normal foot. Shenjung could see that they changed angles as they descended, before they disappeared in the blackness of the void below.

Yang pointed his flashlight upwards. "To the surface?"

Shenjung also craned his neck, following the steps. "These look thousands of years old. The stone is age-darkened by moisture, and cave gasses." Shenjung shrugged. "Maybe there was a surface when the steps were cut, but that was around 12,000 years ago. Our position now is far out under the ice sheets, so too much ice and snow above us." He stepped back, lifting his light. "However, I would be interested to see where they lead."

Yang turned away. "Lieutenant, beacon signal source and direction."

The PLA soldier held up a small-screened device, panning it around. He then spun back to his captain. "Four point eighteen miles due west, point ninety-two miles on vertical descent ... down." He pointed.

"Good." Yang turned back to Shenjung. "Upwards, is likely to be miles of more labyrinth, or a dead end." Yang brought his light down to the descending steps. "If there is scuffing on the lower steps, then most likely it was made by Zhang Li and his team. If they went down, and our objective, the submarine is down, then we will follow."

Shenjung could tell that Yang probably didn't give a damn about the missing engineers. His priority was the signal, and only the signal. He waved his light over the stone ledge at its brink. "Doesn't look like footprints, more like drag marks."

"Come." Yang ignored him.

Shenjung stared down into the darkness. He had a feeling that the massive hole in the earth was more like a gigantic mouth that was about to swallow them all. He could feel a slight updraft against his face – it felt warm, humid, and there were hints of salt, methane, and an odd sourness among other odors ... odors of living things, or perhaps things long dead. It did nothing to dispel the image of the mouth open and waiting. He followed the PLA captain, but couldn't shake the feeling that sunlight was a luxury he may never see again.

CHAPTER 18

Cate was smashed into Alex's body. Her face became immediately wet, and she knew her nose was gushing blood. The upside was, her goggles were still around her neck and hadn't cracked. She shifted position and groaned. Every part of her ached – muscles, bones, and even though she had covered up as much as she could, she could feel blisters under her wetsuit. But what she felt, and endured, must have been nothing compared to the man above her who hadn't been covered in thermal sheeting and had literally acted as a shock absorber for her body. She had felt him go limp, and knew he was either unconscious or dead.

Inside the capsule it was blacker than anything she had ever experienced in her life, and a moment of disorientation washed over her. Then there came the sensation of the capsule turning slowly as it settled correctly in the water. *That's something*, she thought. She had seconds now before the launch, and blindly reached up to find and then feel the soldier's neck – *thank god, a pulse*. She lifted his mouthpiece and pushed it between his lips, automatically starting the oxygen. She covered her face with her own goggles and jammed in her mouthpiece.

Below them, there commenced a minute electronic vibration running up through the skin of the hull, and then came a more ominous sound – rushing water, welling up. She had a moment of panic, but swallowed it down, remembering what that meant: the outer doors of the capsule had opened, and *Orca* was about to launch.

Here we go, she thought, and reached down to wrap an arm around one of the propulsion struts, and then hung onto the limp form of Alex with her other arm.

Like a ten-foot torpedo being launched from its shaft, *Orca*, the deep-water submersible, began to slide free, taking Cate and Alex with it.

She felt an unbearable sense of alarm, as they were pulled out of the capsule and into the inky black water, miles below the Antarctic's icy surface. Cate screwed her eyes shut and instinctively held her breath.

Darkness, warmth, and saltiness. She opened her eyes. Cate Canning's laboratory readings had told her to expect it, to assume a near tropical environment of a constant seventy-eight degrees in the underground sea. But now, only when she was immersed, could she really believe it. What she hadn't expected was the blue glow radiating down from above – *bioluminescence*, she thought. If she was at the surface, the radiance would still only be like twilight, but at least it wouldn't be anything like the impenetrable nothing that was below her.

Orca pulled them along a few dozen feet below the surface, and Cate's scientific mind took over, and blanked out any thoughts about what could be down underneath. The inky blackness fell away to crushing depths of over a thousand feet, and she knew there were organisms down there, big organisms, and she just hoped she could get herself and Alex to the nearest shoreline before they were detected.

Cate had one hand looped through a strap on Alex's shoulder, and the other she gripped tight to one of the submersible's rear struts. Her shoulders screamed from the strain, but *Orca*'s gentle speed made it easier. Still, she knew if she lost her grip on *Orca*, they would be stranded, and if she let Alex go, his heavy kit would take him down, and he would be lost.

She turned her head to look back towards the surface of the underground sea. She could just make out their bubbles as they merged and then raced upwards. They were a silvery thread that ascended to a watery blue ceiling. She could imagine them popping on the calm sea, and she longed to be up there with them.

She turned back to the depths, and impatience started to take hold. *One, two, three, four* – she kept her mind occupied, and began to count seconds as *Orca* traveled onwards. The submersible's propulsion units whirred softly, almost a purr beneath the water as the hydro-jets pushed liquid back towards them and over a bank of fins that guided it through the depths. Cate had programmed the machine herself, and knew one of its first searches was to be towards the east, before it was to head back out, and then dive deep. They needed to be well gone by then.

She looked back again at Alex's limp body, his large arms and legs deathly still and trailing as they glided along. She wished she could check on him, but for now, hanging on was all that mattered.

Suddenly *Orca* slowed, and Cate's head snapped back in alarm. The cigar shaped machine gave a little reverse thrust, to then hang motionless in the water. The submersible's neutral buoyancy allowed it to be suspended without sinking or rising. She gritted her teeth, as she remembered her own program protocols – it would take audio readings now, and even though the propulsion units were near-silent water jets, it would also shut these off as it listened for the most minute of sounds.

Cate breathed in and out evenly, waiting, impatient, the only sounds she heard were her own exhalations, loud in her ears. She momentarily held her breath, and then there it was, all the clicks, squeaks, tapping, and pops of a living ocean. Around her, stars floated – tiny specks of light, either gliding or flashing before being quickly shut off. It was the silver biological glow of creatures in a dark sea, used for attracting mates, prey, or as a warning. To Cate, it seemed like she was floating in a night sky, not underwater, but high overhead, looking down on the stars in an endless universe.

Orca coming to a complete stop made her feel it was safe enough for her to let go of its strut. She lowered her arm and flexed her fingers, feeling immediately relieved. They were stiff and sore, but they'd be fine. She then dragged Alex up towards herself, looked into his face mask – his eyes were closed tight, but there was still the rhythmic pumping of his breather as he sucked in and expelled air. She decided she'd take the time to better secure him, and she dragged him closer, and unclipped his belt, then threaded it through her own belt at her back, so he was now lashed to her. It would cause more drag, but at least it gave her two free hands, that she could now alternate to share the load.

Orca hung in its aquatic inner-space a moment more before its nose-cone lit up as a bright ring of lights surrounding the camera eye came to life. To Cate in the dark water, it was as if the cigar-shaped probe was like some sort of deep-sea fish that had stopped to search for prey midwater.

The probe's glowing eye created a pipe of light to try and illuminate the void. But it was a hopeless task as the darkness swallowed the glow without ever revealing the hidden world Cate knew was all around them.

But then from the corner of her eye, *movement*. Something the size of a hubcap glided past. It was circular, ribbed, and trailing ribbon-like tendrils. Cate concentrated, straining out from the probe to see it before it moved past the range of the light. Instead of disappearing, it stopped, and turned, drifting back towards them. Cate grinned around her mouthpiece.

You beautiful thing, she thought. *Neuteloid – Cyrtoceras, I believe*. It was banded blue, white, and black, something that never would have been known from the fossil record. The thing was a survivor of the ancient Ordovician Period. Their ancestors were around today, but much, much smaller.

The engines started up again, and the Crytoceras turned and sailed away. She then felt the fan of water on her face as the machine eased forward. She grabbed it and leaned out and to the side again, a passenger watching the strange world go by. From time to time, something would dart away from the beam like a laser had scalded it. The eyes of the sea creatures were probably more adapted to the dark, only ever having to deal with a soft, twilight glow whenever they rose to shallower waters.

Cate thought of her team, huddled together in a cold laboratory room over a mile above her, watching, recording, and marveling at everything they saw via their screens, while she saw it live. She hung on for her life, wishing *Orca* would stop again just for a few seconds so she could claw her way to the nose-cone. There, she could somehow communicate with them, tell them she was fine, and ask if they could *shut down the light.* Though the powerful globes pushed out a lot of energy and lit a pathway some forty feet in front of them, the wall of dark was only ever *just* pierced. But from out beyond the curtain of blackness, she knew its powerful beam would be seen for miles – the speck of white light would attract anything that hunted by sight.

Five hundred and one, five hundred and two ... She counted more seconds as *Orca* sailed on. Her body began to ache again, and she changed her hands on the rail. She briefly wondered what would happen if she slipped – the probe would quickly leave them behind. Her team above may suddenly detect an improvement in maneuverability, but it was unlikely they would know to turn around for her. She could reprogram *Orca.* After all, she was its designer. But she was down here.

More than likely she and Alex would be cast adrift, a couple of slow moving non-aquatic mammals left to float in a fathomless dark sea. She shuddered at the thought and started to count again, trying to remember the probe's search grid, and how long it was before they could expect to near any type of land. Alex had said it would be there, and close. She prayed he was right.

Orca suddenly dropped about twenty feet, and Cate felt a bone-chilling cold as the water temperature plummeted. She had heard there were temperature anomalies down here – silos and columns of hot and cold water. Her group had hypothesized that the warm water columns were caused by hydrothermal means, but the cold columns, they were the conundrum. One theory they had was that there could be a vortex in the underground sea. It literally breathed in and out, sometimes taking in cold water, and sometimes expelling warm. There was evidence for an open vortex, as the expellation had a physical manifestation – just recently a behemoth Antarctic algae bloom was seen off the Antarctic's coast that was so large it showed up on satellite imaging from space.

She'd make a mental note, and hopefully one day they'd get to ... she grinned around her mouthpiece. *One day they'd get to what?* She was stuck here, and the only thing she'd be doing from now on was simply trying to survive.

Cate felt the warm water return as they passed out of the freezing current, and *Orca* rose to its proper investigation depth. She resumed her somnambulant count once again. *Thirteen hundred and twenty-five, thirteen hundred and twenty-six ...*

Cate felt the slight touch of a pressure wave push at her side, and momentarily create more drag on Alex's body as he lurched on her back. A tingle raced up her spine – other than the vortices, there were no currents down here – something in the darkness had just moved past them. From far out behind them there came the sound of thump and then a grinding, metallic crunch that made her flinch. At first she struggled to understand what it was she could be hearing, but then knew it could be only one thing – the shell of the probe. The capsule would have been still floating on the surface, due to the pocket of air trapped inside its rear. It was a bigger physical signature than they were, and it was being destroyed, *no*, she thought, *attacked.*

Shit, how much farther? she wondered, just as the sound of the attacks grew louder, and then ceased. That meant whatever was occupying itself with the probe's shell had either sunk it or had lost interest, and might be now on the lookout for something else – something more palatable. She began to kick her legs, hoping the minuscule amount of extra thrust would help in getting them further away from what was going on, maybe only a half mile to their rear.

She looked back over her shoulder – nothing but darkness and the limp form of Alex. She cursed him, the big tough soldier, now little more than dead weight. *You bastard.* She jerked one arm back, striking him in the back of the head. *Big fucking help you turned out to be.*

Would she cut him free if they were attacked? She'd like to think she wouldn't, but it might not be in her control. And besides, if it came down to both of them dying or just Alex, then she'd vote for life every time. *Sorry buddy, but for all I know you could be a braindead beanbag anyway.*

She turned back to *Orca*, kicking hard now, and biting down on her breathing tube. Her neck and scalp tingled; the darkness surrounding her was impenetrable, but that was only to her.

She knew something was out there now, and could feel the huge presence in the water close by.

She kicked harder, adrenalin giving her a burst of energy. Her breathing was becoming ragged, and she knew she was burning up her oxygen, but wasn't able to help it.

Fourteen hundred and sixty, one hundred and sixteen, two hundred ... she couldn't focus, and whimpered around her breathing tube. Once again, she felt the gentle push of water against her, first from one side, and then seconds later from the other – they were being circled by something very large and very fast. For all she knew, it was close enough now for her to reach out and touch.

What are you? her mind screamed. She couldn't help thinking back to the image of the huge eye she had seen on her screen all those years ago. It had baffled her and most of her marine specialist colleagues. Now, she would find out.

Orca powered on, and Cate and Alex were dragged along with it. She knew that in the control room miles above them, the instruments would be screaming at Bentley, Schmidt, Timms, and Sulley, and they might be whooping with excitement as the sensors told them of the approaching behemoth. Maybe by now they had swapped visuals and moved to either thermal or light enhanced to try and pick up the thing's silhouette.

Cate concentrated, trying to pierce the darkness. Would the thing see them as intruder or prey? Would it matter to the outcome? *No,* she thought. To whatever was out there, there was only one question: *would they be edible?*

Orca's light was a beacon to it – she needed a distraction. Cate eased a hand down to a pouch at her waist and drew forth a flare that she then jammed against her thigh and pushed out to the side to let go. It sank slowly, and she turned to watch it fall away into the void as *Orca* gently pulled her and Alex slowly away from it.

The ball of glowing red light continued to sink, illuminating and scattering tiny creatures as it dropped lower and lower into the darkness. Twenty feet, thirty, fifty. Once again, Cate couldn't help feeling like she was floating in space, but this time, her tiny ship was under attack from some giant alien beast. The human side of her didn't want to know what was out there, but Cate Canning, PhD in evolutionary biology, and the nosy scientist, desperately wanted to catch a glimpse of the creature. It was why she had bullied Alex into bringing her along.

The tiny red halo of flaring light sunk lower, and lower, two hundred feet down and behind them now. Cate had to crane her neck to see it. And then, a feeling like an electric shock passed through her body – there it was. The leviathan moved past the light, its hide painted a hellish red by the flare. It came again, and this time a hubcap-sized eye swiveled to stare briefly at the light, before the creature glided on.

There was an unmistakable, primordial sensation that all humans experienced when they were suddenly in the proximity of a large predator. Cate felt it now, her bladder swelling, making her wanting to urinate, her heartbeat racing, and a swoony, light-headedness overcoming her. It was like when the body was going into shock, it automatically pulled the blood away from the extremities and brain into the torso. It did this in preparation for severe trauma and loss of limb.

Deep down, the massive creature passed underneath the flare. *Four massive paddle-like flippers, and striped, like a tiger*, she thought, as a surge of adrenalin ran through her. Probably the coloring was to make the predator even less visible to anything on the surface by creating a ripple effect. It was hard to judge its exact size from the distance, and in the dark water, but measuring it against the dot of red light that had just been in her hand, she guessed it was close to sixty feet in length.

A pliosaur, she guessed, but a goddamn big one. The massive marine creature swam in the ancient Jurassic-era oceans of 150 million years ago. But to be this size, the thing must have been a species that had simply been labeled Predator X, until it was finally classed as a member of the Pliosaur family only a few years back.

Cate felt her heart rate kick up. The creature had a head twice the size of a T-rex. She stopped moving. *If that's what it is*, she thought, then they'd be lucky to make it much further even if they were in a speedboat.

The creature vanished again, and Cate held her breath, waiting and watching, and then there came a gentle push of water against her body and *Orca* was eased offcenter, its fins angling to put it back on course.

How long had they been traveling under the water – fifteen minutes, twenty, more? Surely they were coming close to their next objective. She tried to remember the configuration of the course she had plotted. The launch, then midway they would stop and scan, and then they would approach a shoreline and breach to capture some surface readings and images. They *must* be close. Wherever they were by now, Cate knew time was up.

If they were to survive, she needed a change of plan, and at present they were vulnerable from every direction – she could at least reduce that by one. She tried to release her grip on the rear strut, but her fingers were locked tight. Fear had caused the muscles to seize up.

Frustration and fear surged within her as, stretched out like she was, her belly and groin tingled as she felt how exposed the soft parts of her body were to the giant leviathan below. Cate bit down hard on the rubber mouthpiece and screamed into the breather, commanding, cursing, and then pleading with her hand to let go.

One at a time, her fingers finally opened and she immediately reached in to the rear vents of *Orca*'s steering system and grabbed one of the struts, using all her strength to bend it slightly and cause the torpedo-shaped vessel into a change of direction – upwards.

In just a few seconds, the nose of *Orca* breached, dragging Cate and Alex up behind it. Cate spat out her mouthpiece and dragged in a deep and humid breath. After the artificial air of the tanks, everything tasted thick, moist, and ... alive. The atmosphere was a deep, shadowy blue, as if a lamp had a colored scarf wrapped tightly around its bulb. She looked up at the twinkling stars of millions of bioluminescent organisms living on the cave roof overhead – they were like tiny blue fairy lights on a black cloth hundreds of feet above them. *Save me*, she wanted to scream at the little stars.

Her vision popped with light, and she felt the lightheadedness return. *I'm going to black out*, she thought. She whimpered, as momentary panic threatened to overwhelm her. *Not now, not now*, she pleaded. Tears blurred her eyes within the mask, and blinking them away, she felt a thrill of hope surge through her. About two hundred feet away was a dark shoreline, with what looked like trees, a forest perhaps? But it was still so far away, and maybe too far at their current speed.

She refused to look back down into the deep, dark water in case the monster was there, coming up fast, its cavernous mouth swung open. More time, just five minutes more, might make a difference. She began to kick her legs again, her thighs burning. She looked over her shoulder and screamed.

"For god's sake, wake up, damn you. Help me."

She let one hand go, and wrenched her arm back, elbowing Alex in the back of the head – once, twice. "*Wake ... the fuck ... up!*"

Just then, several hundred feet out to the right side of her, there was a breach of the surface as a striped hump rose. It glided closer, and closer, passing a dozen feet in front of them, and then out to left where it slid vertically back down, finishing with the tip of a stubby reptilian tail that left a swirl of dark liquid.

"Oh god, no." Cate knew enough about deep sea predators to know that the angle of its descent meant it had dived deep. If it followed a similar attack pattern, surging up from the depths, using speed, power, and surprise to overwhelm whatever creature it hunted, it would come up out of the dark like a colossal missile. They wouldn't be able to outrun it, and they wouldn't be able to get out of its way. They could only wait to be eaten alive.

She finally put her face down, and peered down into the hidden depths. There was one option left. She jammed her hands back into the steering struts and bent the fins with every ounce of strength she had, this time angling the nose downwards. *Orca* began to dive, taking them both with it. She sucked in a deep breath.

Sorry baby, but you have one more job to do, she thought. Cate began to feel pressure on her eardrums, and pulled her arms in, and then pushed out hard, sending the submersible on its way – straight down.

The sleek, cigar-shaped probe powered on into the depths, and Cate began to frantically swim upwards, kicking hard and fast. She kept watching as the strong white beam of light created a pathway into the deep, its white beam a ball of light against miles of blackness. She pumped her legs hard, trying to put distance between herself, the probe, and what she knew must surely be coming up fast from below.

She broke the surface, sucked in a huge gasping breath, and then began to breaststroke hard. She sank under Alex's weight, and once again jerked her arm back at him.

"Please, please, wake up."

She sank again, but just before she went down, she heard a cough. She kicked upwards, and broke the surface.

"That's it, Alex, wake up." She began to swim. "Just kick, that's all I need from you. Kick, *kick hard*."

Cate felt the surge at her back – weak, but it was enough to cancel out the drag his body was making. She dipped her head, trying not to look or even think about what was down there. From deep below them there was the sound of an impact, and then a crushing-crumpling noise that went on for several seconds. She knew immediately it was *Orca*'s toughened steel casing coming into contact with something that probably had a bite pressure in the tens of thousands of pounds.

The shoreline beckoned – sixty feet now at most. She dragged in a huge breath, and started to throw her arms up and over, dragging the water past herself. Forty feet, thirty, twenty, they were only a dozen feet from shore but there was still nothing but darkness below them. There were no shallows, as the shoreline must have been the edge of an underwater cliff, rather than the gradual shallowing encountered on a coastal beach. Her scalp and neck tingled, and once more she felt the sensation of something large approaching.

"*Kick, kick, kick!*" she screamed. In answer, she felt herself speed forward. Alex's legs now starting to churn, even though his head still lolled groggily on her shoulders.

"That's it, harder ..." Eight feet, five feet, she looked down and saw a small rock shelf. She clambered on, not trying to stand with Alex on her back, but instead scrabbling forward on all fours. She dived and scrambled the last few feet onto a gritty shoreline, rolling over on top of Alex and looking back, just as something that was like a striped mountain breached and half rolled, so its huge eye could stare dispassionately for a second or two before it veered sharply away.

The only thing that went through her head was that the huge eye of the beast was different to the one she had seen on the monitor all those years ago. She slumped back against the rock.

CHAPTER 19

Bentley pushed his chair back and got to his feet. "She's dead." He turned to kick the chair across the small room.

"Don't say that," Sulley yelled back.

"The bloody idiot." Bentley pulled at his nose, eyes screwed shut.

"You're an arsehole, you know that?" Timms growled through his straggly beard.

"Game over," Bentley responded.

"Maybe not," Sulley said, furiously hitting keys, and slowly moving a dial like a safecracker. "*Orca* might have just been knocked offline by the impact."

"Knocked offline? *Orca* got hit by a flamin' express train. Whatever hit us had a sonar signature that tapped out around sixty-five feet with a displacement of a sperm whale. If it kicked the shit out of a titanium hull, what would it do to flesh and blood?" Bentley came and leaned into Sulley's face. "You do remember the teeth, don't you?"

"Not all of us are ready to give up just yet," Schmidt said, not turning away from his screen.

Bentley snorted. "Best case is, she's hurt – better send a rescue team. Oh, wait, that's right, there is no such thing." He straightened, sneering. "Better for her if she *is* dead – it'd be more humane."

"You truly are an arse," Sulley said turning in his seat.

"I'm a realist." Bentley sighed. "Better tell HQ." He started for the door.

"The speed – that thing was moving at forty-two knots." Schmidt turned to stare. "Holy shit, it was flying ... literally flying under the water."

"Unbelievable," Timms said. "And how horrifying for Cate, and that other guy."

"The other guy." Bentley paused at the door. "He's dead, she's dead, *Orca*'s dead, game over." He shouldered his way out of the room.

"*Arsehole!*" Sulley yelled, and turned back to his screen. He narrowed his eyes. "What would Cate do?"

"Never give up," Schmidt said softly. "We can give it a while and then try a reboot."

"Good idea. Okay, we wait then." Sulley turned in his seat. "Who's making the tea?"

*

Colonel Jack Hammerson read the data squirt intercepted from the Ellsworth team's update to the UK Ministry of Science. There was no information on Alex Hunter, and he didn't expect there to be. But the two words he dreaded were there: *Probe destroyed.*

Even though Alex Hunter's vital sign monitor was now flat-lining, did he think the man was dead? *Probably not.* Just well out of range, he bet. Hammerson sat back, jaws clenched. Could he risk it all on a wait-and-see approach? *Absolutely not.*

He had no choice, he needed to initiate his backup plan. If the front door was shut, then he'd need to kick open the back one, and forge right in.

The backup team's mission was no longer a *stand and hold* assignment that he originally planned for. Their role had suddenly changed from defensive to offensive and they now needed to go in, *and go all the way down to hell.* He just needed one more member – a guide.

Hammerson picked up the phone, hating himself already.

"Margie, get me Aimee Weir."

*

Cate couldn't breathe. She knew that the Pliosaur could have easily grabbed prey from shallows and even from the shoreline. She and Alex were a tempting morsel of meat, just a few feet from the deep water. She waited, and then surprisingly, a hundred feet further out, the striped hump rose, whale-like, and then slid away, fast.

"Not that hungry, huh?" She snorted softly, but then sobered and quickly looked over her shoulder. "Or did something scare you off?"

A metallic clank from the rocks farther down the shore drew Cate's attention back to the waterline. She grinned.

"Well, hello, you tough little bastard."

It was *Orca*, the probe had beached. The ten-foot toughened metal body looked like it had been run over by a truck. It was crushed in places and had some rips in its super hardened steel skin, showing wires and circuitry.

She nodded to the mangled machine. "Thank you." Then she lay down, aching, still on top of Alex.

Cate felt him stir beneath her, and she unclipped her belt and rolled off him. He groaned and she reached across to grab his hair and lift his head. He was breathing and there was an actual dent in his forehead that was so dark it looked black.

Ouch, she whispered, and pushed him over onto his back. She knelt beside him, and used a thumb to open one of his eyes – the pupil dilated. *Good*, she thought, *no brain damage. But don't know how with that damned ding in his noggin though.*

Alex moaned again and his head raised a few inches. "Wha …?" his lips continued to move.

"Take it easy. I think you've suffered a concussion." She wiped debris from his cheek. "Just breathe, we're okay now."

She shrugged out of her own oxygen tanks, and eased Alex's off his shoulders. He lay back, and Cate turned to the forest, looking along the line of huge trunks. *Alien*, was her first thought. It was hard to think of them as trees, as most were up on multiple stilts, twisting and slimy looking, like in some sort of haunted forest. *Maybe they weren't trees at all, but something vastly different,* she wondered. Many rose at least fifty feet in the air, and ended in stubby palms, but their tips looked more akin to polyps rather than fronds. There were more at ground level, all of them looking soft and damp.

It was strangely quiet, with vapor hanging in the air. It reminded her of a haunted forest, and all that was missing was the hooting of an owl or a headless horseman lurking in the shadows. She continued to search the dark spaces as her gut told her that there was life in there. She inhaled deeply. There was the ever-present smell of warm saltwater, but permeating it was another odor – *mushrooms,* she thought. That's what it reminded her of – composting mushrooms.

Above her the ceiling was black velvet, but speckled with blue dots that lit the environment in a soft twilight. Looking back at the subterranean sea, it was almost an endless flat surface of inky black liquid that swirled and popped as things broke the surface or swirled just out of sight beneath the warm, dark blanket. To one side of them, a huge cliff rose up hundreds of feet, to then curve up and over them as a ceiling. In among the blue lights there were hanging fronds that looked like upside-down corals of all differing hues.

Alex groaned again, and she turned back to him. She frowned. Did the huge dent look different? She placed her fingers gently onto it, and then immediately snatched them back – his skin was hot, damned hot. She leaned forward, and as she watched, the sunken contusion rose and flattened, and after another few moments the deep blue-black bruise lightened to purple, red, and then vanished.

"What the hell?"

Alex sat up, staring straight ahead for a few moments. He got to his feet without a trace of unsteadiness.

"Take it easy." Cate followed him up.

He continued to stare out over the flat water. "It's gone now." He turned slowly, his eyes catching sight of the mangled probe. He half smiled. "Close encounter of the worst kind, huh?" He looked at her, his brows raised.

She shook her head. "Yeah, and you slept right through it, Mr. Big Hero."

Alex inhaled, filling his chest with air. "You got us in safely. Good work, Cate." He smiled. "I owe you a drink."

"You owe me more than that, pal," she said, scowling.

Alex reached for a pouch at his waist, and pulled out a small box. He fiddled with its dials, looking at the screen, and then turned to the forest. "We're not far." He started up the rocky shore.

"Hey, wait, you were just …" She scoffed. "I don't believe this." Then: "Ah, goddamnit," she said, and started to follow.

CHAPTER 20

There came a knock on the door, and Hammerson's PA, Margie, stuck her head in.

"Jack, Aimee Weir to see you ... and she's brought Joshua."

Hammerson nodded. "Thanks Margie, but just Aimee for now. You can take our little friend for a walk around the base. Show him the planes, and the canteen. I think it's mac and cheese day."

Truth was, he wasn't ready to look the kid in the face again. How could he see that countenance – Alex Hunter all over, after he'd just sent his father below the Antarctic ice, and was about to do the same to his mother?

After a few more minutes Aimee knocked and came in. Hammerson got to his feet, and took her by the hand, noticing she looked tired, haunted.

"Good to see you Aimee. How's life been treating the pair of you?"

"Life is okay, and we're good, Jack," she said. "The safe house has small rooms, but at least I don't wake up feeling like I need to be checking Josh every ten minutes. It's safe, I guess."

"Just every ten minutes, huh?" Hammerson smiled, but noticed the sharp look in her eye, and held up a hand. "No, no, I'm not watching you. Just a joke, Aimee."

"It's okay." She relaxed, but still looked strung tight.

"How's Peter?" Hammerson asked, already knowing how her partner, or ex-partner now, it seemed, was faring.

"He's getting better. The doctors say he'll make a full recovery. He thinks it was just a break-in that went wrong." She smiled weakly.

"Good, good. We can bring him in as well, if you like."

"No, it's best if Peter goes back home. It's not right that he got dragged into this in the first place. Don't want him becoming submerged ... like me."

"You're not submerged, or a prisoner, Aimee." Hammerson watched her closely.

"We are and we aren't, Jack. You know that." She looked up. "Will it ever end?"

"If it did, I'd be out of a job." He smiled with little humor. "But for you, yeah, sure. Don't know when, but time passes, things change, people forget. The world and everything in it moves on." Hammerson stood and walked to his desk, and poured a glass of water for her.

She shook her head. "I'm sorry. You've done so much for us. I'm grateful."

"Here, drink this." He left the glass on the desk, and walked to the window. He faced the pane, but watched her reflection. Aimee went to the desk, and took the glass to her lips. As she went to set it back down, she craned her neck to look at the report, reading quickly. She frowned and leaned closer, putting her glass on the desk.

"Zhang Li?" She looked up, her brows knitted. "What's going on, Jack?"

"Chaos," he said without turning. "Subterfuge, war, aggression, and a fight for order." He shrugged. "The usual stuff." He turned and motioned to a chair. "Please, sit down, Aimee. We need to chat about a few things."

"I used to know a Zhang Li, from my university days." Aimee sunk into the chair. "This is no friendly catch up, is it?"

He stared directly into her eyes. "No." He went and sat on the edge of his desk. "The world is tilting under our feet, and we need to act, before we all slide off." He smiled apologetically. "I'm afraid we need your help."

She still frowned. "Me? How?"

He watched her for a few more moments, then exhaled slowly.

"What is it, Jack? No bullshit. You know me." She put down her glass and sat forward.

He nodded. "Here are the facts, all boiled down nice and neat. In 2008, we lost an experimental sub in the Southern Ocean. A few days ago, its emergency beacon fired up ... coming from deep beneath the Antarctic ice."

"What?" She recoiled, confused.

Hammerson half smiled. "Strange, I know. We don't understand it either. But we weren't the only ones to pick up the signal. The Chinese army look hell-bent on getting to it." He looked into her eyes. "They're going into the restricted zone – Area 24."

"Area 24." Aimee sunk into her chair, her eyes haunted. "You have to tell them."

"We've tried, they won't listen to us, and even if they did, they'd never believe us." He watched her. "There's a storm coming, Aimee ... a big, hot, nasty one."

She frowned. "For godsake, Jack, what does that mean?"

He sighed, rubbing one hand up through an iron-gray crew cut. "This doesn't leave this room." Hammerson stared for a few moments until she nodded. "At 0800 Pacific time, a team of Chinese PLA soldiers and a relief team of engineers and miners arrived on the ice, and immediately entered a tunnel system below their base."

He paused, letting the information sink in. "I say, *relief* team of engineers and miners, because their previous team vanished – all of them. Including your old friend, Zhang Li."

"He's not my friend. I mean, I knew him. He was a brilliant geologist and engineer, and got a top job back in China. He was working in the Antarctic?"

"Yes, and now he's gone. Maybe they headed down into the caves and got lost, or there was a cave-in. Something happened down there." He waved it away. "Doesn't matter now. But the new team is headed up by a scientist called Shenjung Xing. He's a moderate, like Zhang Li, also educated in the US, and we believe he, and Zhang Li, will both be open to hearing the truth."

She shook her head. "Wait, I still don't understand. You said, a submarine under the ice ... you mean the ice shelf?"

"No, the ice *and* rock. Somehow, all those years ago, our submarine managed to find a way in. We just detected its distress signal buried in some other data." Hammerson shook his head at her horrified look. "It's automated, we don't expect it'll be a rescue mission. But, what we can't do is let the Chinese military get to that sub first. We're going in to try and talk to them, but ..." He shrugged.

She snorted. "You're going in? And what happens if they won't listen? You're not a negotiator, Jack. You don't bring in HAWCs when you want to talk, you bring them in when you want something obliterated."

"We won't draw first blood, Aimee, if that's what you're worried about." Hammerson remained calm. "But the facts are, a Chinese destroyer is now parked down there. So is one of our Seawolf submarines, keeping an eye on it. Both are nuclear capable." His face became grim. "If they won't listen, we will do what needs to be done to protect our people and property."

"Including starting a war?"

He didn't flinch. "We won't draw first blood."

"You know as well as I do, that if the HAWCs go in, there'll damn well be blood – nothing but blood. That's what you made them for. You *must* fear a war, Jack?"

"Yes, Aimee, we fear war." He sat staring at her for another moment. "But it's our job to make the other guys fear it more."

She scoffed. "And how will that destroyer react when you come back to the surface, and their own team doesn't?"

"Aimee, *you* know what's down there, they don't. Without our help, you really think they'll make it back to the surface anyway?" He tilted his head. "But like I said, we'll try and talk to them. The rest is up to the Chinese."

She sat back, her head tilted to the ceiling. "This is a nightmare."

Hammerson shrugged. "We're out of time and options, Aimee. They'll send reinforcements, so will we. There is no real overt deescalation point available at this time. Someone has to back down, and as it's our technology, and our people, it won't be us. Sorry, Aimee, but we're in the pipe – lock and load."

"Oh for chrissake, Jack, who wins a nuclear war?" Her brow was creased in disbelief.

He shrugged. "They start something, we finish it. If they walk away, we all go home. But if we don't establish our superiority, well, they're already mining illegally, so they obviously have little regard for international law. Our game theorists suggest they'll establish a permanent military presence on the Antarctic. That's right on the doorstep of one of our allies. Added to that, they get their hands on our secret technology, and probably establish sea primacy over the Southern Ocean. Nothing in that scenario is good for our – or the world's – future or interests. Like I said, they pull back, or we push them back."

"No, no, no, that's not an option. You must talk to them – send diplomats, not damned HAWCs, I beg you. You know there's a reason for that saying about *the pen being mightier than the sword*."

Hammerson's smile was lackluster. "You want to know what General MacArthur said about that?" He didn't wait for her response. "Whoever said the pen is mightier than the sword, obviously never encountered automatic weapons." He held up a hand to stop her protest. "Aimee, I'm under orders to resolve this issue, fast and with as little mess as possible. We will try and negotiate, I promise."

"Bullshit." She sat back, staring at the carpet.

Hammerson sighed. "Getting there first was to have been our ace-in-the-hole. They couldn't steal something, if we were already sitting on top of it, but …" He grimaced. "Things didn't go to plan."

"You already sent someone?" she asked.

Hammerson sat watching her for a few seconds. "Yes, we did. Someone who's been there before, someone unique, someone with extraordinary abilities, who could get there, and defend our position against everything and anything." He half turned away as he spoke, but was aware of her getting slowly to her feet.

He went on. "One man in, one man out – just one." He turned to her. "Alex Hunter."

Aimee was on her feet, but her legs looked about to buckle. Her mouth worked, but no words came for several seconds.

"Dead … dead …" She shook her head. "He's dead. *You told me*, he's dead."

Hammerson's eyes were rock steady. "Yes, and for all intents and purposes, he was." He lifted her glass of water, and walked towards her holding it out. "He should have been dead. His body was riddled with the Hades Bug you guys encountered in South America. But either the Israelis' medical technology, or his own system, managed to regenerate his body." He shrugged. "When he woke up, he didn't even know who he was."

Aimee's hand flashed out fast and slapped his face. He took it and turned back to look at her. She slapped him again, and again, slapping and punching him now. He closed his eyes, took it all, letting her fury burn itself out on his flesh. She screamed her anger and frustration, until his intercom buzzed, and a concerned voice cut through Aimee's fury.

"Everything okay, sir?"

He nodded. "We're all fine in here, Margie."

Aimee stood with shoulders hunched, fists balled and breathing hard. Her eyes were wet.

"You bastard, you let me think he was dead ... all those years." She wiped her face with a forearm. "Does he know about me ... about Joshua?"

Hammerson pulled a handkerchief from his pocket and wiped some blood from his lips. He still held her glass in his hand, now only a third full, most of its contents on the floor. He handed it to her.

She took it, glaring at him. "And you brought me in here to tell me that now?"

"No, Aimee." He motioned to her chair. "Please sit down."

"I'm fine." She remained standing, staring, her ice-blue eyes now red rimmed.

"I brought you here to tell you that we've lost contact with him. We need to initiate Plan B – send in another team. And speed is still our best hope of success." He held her gaze. "But this time we need someone who can talk to the Chinese, to their scientists – Zhang Li or Dr. Shenjung Xing – in a way they'll understand and accept. A type of scientific negotiator, if you like. We need experience, and a cool head, and most of all we need a guide." He smiled, he hoped, warmly. "There's only one person I know of who has all those qualifications, Aimee. And that's you."

Aimee's mouth hung open, and Hammerson continued.

"We need to show them, and explain to them, in their own language, that what's down there is not worth risking their lives over. Pull 'em back before it's too late." He smiled and nodded. "Save them from themselves. A quick in and out."

Her mouth snapped shut, lips clamped tight for several seconds. "Oh, no way, Jack. No fucking way in this world. I'm not insane."

He hated himself for the manipulation. "I know you want to keep Joshua safe." He looked into her eyes. "So do I. But, if there is a war between superpowers, just who is going to be safe ... anywhere?"

"You son of a bitch." She turned, her eyes watering. "My son ..."

"He will be safe. You'll be keeping him safe." He kept watching her. "Save him *please, Aimee*, guide the team down, find that submarine ... and maybe, Alex."

She finally sank into the chair. "He's still alive down there."

Hammerson turned away. "Yes."

She slumped, her face in her hands. "Oh god, oh god, oh god." She rubbed her face hard, and when she looked up, she was drained of color.

Hammerson came over and put a hand on her shoulder. "We learned a lot from last time. This time we'll be ready."

"No one can ever be ready for a trip to hell." She sighed. "You want me to go down there again – down beneath the dark ice."

"Yes." Hammerson's eyes were gun steady. "Today."

Aimee sat shaking her head, staring into the floor. "You never answered me." She lifted her eyes. "About whether Alex knows about Joshua."

There came a knock on the door, and Margie led Joshua into the office. The boy ran to Aimee, who immediately brightened, and he gushed about huge planes, jeeps, soldiers, and the great cheese they had on the macaroni. Suddenly, he stopped, looked into her eyes for a second or two, and then slowly turned to Hammerson.

Jack Hammerson leaned down. "Good to see you, Joshua."

The boy stared, his eyes uncannily like Alex's – not just the gray-green color, but the way they seemed to penetrate deep down to the soul.

"You sent him back down there."

Hammerson momentarily froze, before sitting back down slowly. But the boy's eyes held his. "Yes, Joshua. I did."

Aimee sat forward to look at his face. "Who, Joshua? Who do you mean?"

"The man who's always there, looking after me, guarding me." He turned to her. "My father." Joshua stared deep into her eyes, his own unwavering. "And you need to bring him home."

CHAPTER 21

McMurdo Base – Antarctic

Aimee crushed her eyes shut as the huge helicopter she rode in descended. Her stomach roiled as a shivery knot of fear coiled tight in her belly, and she dry-swallowed to keep the stinging bile from surging up into her throat.

She held tight to the image of Joshua, his huge gray-green eyes wide with excitement when earlier he'd asked her to bring him something back – a penguin, just a baby one – and then he'd moved on to asking about his dinner, as if she was just popping down to the store. She smiled as she thought about him, but felt tears in the corners of her eyes that immediately froze solid.

The mother in her screamed its rage at her stupidity for allowing herself to be convinced to come back to the ice. "*To stop a war,*" she whispered, her lips moving but no sound leaving them. *How can that not be a good thing for my son, for me, for everyone?* she thought, but it wasn't convincing enough to silence the maternal rage.

She used one bulky forearm to wipe her face and looked along the crowded cabin. Other than her, there were six huge people inside the cold helicopter. The heating had been turned off now to acclimatize the occupants, and from each, clouds of vapor puffed from mouths and nostrils as they grinned and joked. They were like a different species to her. Each was big, but made doubly so by the bulky snowsuits they wore. There was only one person she recognized – Casey Franks. The woman had let her eyes slide to

Aimee when they had boarded, and nodded once. *All HAWCS then.* Aimee was to be the only diplomat; they were the muscle.

Their leader was a tall man with a shaven head and skin the color of dark coffee. Captain Mitch Dempsey never seemed to blink and the way he moved told of immense strength held in check, and a quiet and confident authority. He had caught her looking at him a few hours back, and he'd casually saluted her with a finger, but then ignored her ... and then that was it. The HAWCs had been polite but had refused conversation, and after several attempts, she'd lapsed in and out of dozing as best she could in the loud, and now cold, craft.

The helicopter settled onto the packed ice and snow. Immediately, the door was slid open and a blast of icy air rushed in to sting her exposed skin. She buried her face into her collar, her eyes shut as she whispered: *I will see Joshua again soon, I will see Joshua again soon ...*

"Head's up, Dr. Weir." She looked up as a figure in goggles and thick hood held out a hand towards her – not one of the HAWCs. She nodded, hiked her kit to her shoulder, and grabbed the hand. When her feet touched the snow her heartbeat kicked up a few gears.

She squinted; McMurdo was bigger than she expected – prefabricated square box houses mixed with multi-story buildings ... and a lot of them. It was more a small town than a camp. Machine-like, the HAWCs leapt free, grabbing boxes and bags. They already knew where they were going and headed towards a smaller building a hundred feet farther into the falling snow.

The person helping her out ignored the HAWCs as if they didn't exist, and instead led her to a large square building with a path towards it cleared in the snow. As soon as they got within six feet of it, the door swung open, and they rushed in, someone dragging the heavy door closed behind them.

The man who'd led her into the building swept his hood back and stamped his feet. He pushed up goggles and grinned – teeth white against cold blasted red skin.

"Sergeant Bill Monroe. It's a pleasure to have you down with us, Dr. Weir." He tore off a glove and stuck out a hand.

Aimee leaned forward and shook herself, trying to dislodge the crystals of ice that were rapidly turning to liquid in the warmth of the hallway.

"Plee corr ee, Ai ..." She put a hand over her mouth; it was taking a few seconds for her lips to warm back up. "Please call me ... Aimee." She took off her own gloves and returned the handshake.

Sergeant Monroe pointed to a bear of a man with a bushy beard. "Big Ben Jackson, our go-to guy for everything from fixing a generator, to cooking roast beef."

"Doc." The huge man stuck out his hand, and Aimee gripped it, his fingers totally encircling her own.

Monroe then grabbed her by the arm. "Come and meet the rest of the team, and we can talk about what we need to do. Just need to make sure your other friends are settled in."

"Need me to tag along, Bill?" Jackson asked, his face becoming serious.

"I got this." He nodded at Aimee. "Get the doctor a hot drink and introduce her around. Back in five." His hood went back up, and goggles down, as he headed for the door.

CHAPTER 22

Aimee wrapped both hands around the mug of coffee and looked around the rec-room. It was also the meeting room, that apparently also managed to become the bar on Saturday evenings, and was likely to be used for a dozen other activities, as the darker weeks would roll on.

Those gathered were only a few of the many inhabitants at McMurdo. Even though she had been introduced, most of Monroe's core team were just ordinary military personnel and now just stole glances at her, before going back to chatting among themselves. Their hushed conversation continually touched on the strange soldiers gearing up in the supply room.

Big Ben Jackson threw his head back and laughed at something. Given his thick beard, he would have made a great movie lumberjack, Aimee thought. Chatting to Jackson was a wiry, nervous looking young man named John Dawkins, who had a chipped front tooth, and was their communications specialist. Coming towards her with the coffee pot again was Jennifer Hartigan, a pleasant faced medical officer, who looked to be roughly the same age as Aimee.

When Bill Monroe re-entered the room, the crowd immediately silenced. He walked towards Aimee, but first pointed at Jennifer's coffee pot.

"I'll take one of those, Jenn." He turned to smile at Aimee. "Everything okay?"

"Just like home." Aimee toasted him with her coffee.

"If home is an icebox," said Jennifer. "I've been here two years, and I dream of warm water and a sandy beach every single damn day."

John Dawkins scoffed. "She's from Great Bend in Kansas. The only beaches they have there are on the banks of a muddy river."

"It's still a beach, Dawk," she said with a good-humored scowl.

Aimee smiled at the banter. It reminded her of home and her own office and colleagues, but now that all seemed a million miles away.

"All right, people, we need to get down to business. We're already on the clock." Monroe leaned back against a pool table. "I've spoken to Colonel Jack Hammerson, and have been briefed at the highest level. What you are about to hear is classified and does not leave this room."

Nods and grunts of assent.

"You are all now aware that the Chinese have parked a guided missile destroyer in our front yard. In turn, we have a Seawolf class submarine eyeballing them. But to add even more spice to the mix, there are military vessel movements in the South China Sea. Our strategists indicate the Chinese navy might be preparing for seaborne engagement – one guess where that could be. Things are getting hot, and probably because of what's been happening just over the ridge at the Xuě Lóng Base ... or rather below it."

"They're mining, we knew that," Big Jackson said with a shrug. "That's a UN problem."

"Normally it would be. They're digging deep, going after rare earth minerals and anything else they can scoop up. But that's not why they're bringing in the military hardware, or why we're doing the same." Monroe looked along the faces. "Something a little more urgent has provoked our focused attention. In 2008 we trialed an experimental submarine, the *Sea Shadow* – a smaller, faster, and near invisible prototype submersible. It disappeared without a trace in the Southern Ocean, just on the edge of the trench."

Dawkins whistled. "Deep water there ... irretrievable, but we should have been able to at least locate it, even if we couldn't get to it."

"No trace." Monroe shook his head. "We looked for months, wasn't down there, wasn't anywhere."

"Haven't all our subs got an emergency beacon? They're hydro-automated – sub goes down, the alarm goes off," Jackson said.

"Yep, but we heard nothing." Monroe raised his brows. "That was until a few days ago. We detected the signal ... the *Sea Shadow*'s *unique* signal." He smiled without humor. "Coming from several miles below the rock and ice, in a designated no-go zone." He held up a hand. "Don't ask, because I don't know." He lowered his hand and sighed. "This is what we believe the Chinese are searching for." He shrugged. "Or maybe have already found."

"And now those bastards want to get it out so they can open it up," Jackson said evenly, thick brows knitted.

"Hey, maybe they've built a hidden submarine cave, you know, like the one that's hidden under that Chinese island," Dawkins added.

Aimee dropped her head, her own suspicions making her stomach knot once again.

Monroe shrugged. "Anything's possible. At this point, there is too much we don't know."

"Could there be survivors?" Jennifer asked.

"We don't know that either," Monroe said. "But there's a complication. The regular Chinese mining team has disappeared, and they think we had something to do with it."

"We? As in us? *McMurdo us?*" Jennifer's brows shot up.

Monroe shrugged. "Doesn't really matter now, the die is cast. But we," – he grinned – "*the McMurdo we,* have now been tasked with assisting in *deescalating* the situation. Us, Dr. Weir, and our friends currently receiving final orders in the other room."

"Friends? You mean the arsekickers, huh?" Jackson said and shook his head. "Is this gonna get nasty?"

Aimee sighed, keeping her head down. She felt sorry for them already.

"Hope not, but we've been ordered to assist in getting Dr. Weir into the Chinese base. Then, if need be, on down into their tunnel system, where we hope she can make contact with the searchers and convince them to give up their exploration." Monroe folded his arms and paced.

"And if they say no?" Jackson raised an eyebrow.

"Then that's why our friends are here. But we are *not* to engage. That's not our job." Monroe paused his pacing for a moment. "Look, people, we just have one job, and that's to establish a line of communication between Dr. Shenjung Xing, chief engineer and project leader, and Dr. Weir here. That's all we need to do. Then we all go home." He looked along their faces.

"So," Dawkins started, "all we need to do is enter the Chinese base, while not getting shot, travel down to where they have descended, which we believe is now several miles below the rock and ice, and find this Shenjung Xing. We need to do this without killing anyone, being killed, or if possible even firing a shot." He looked up, cynicism in the smile on his face. "That about it?"

Monroe grinned. "Oh yeah, the new Chinese soldiers that just arrived are PLA Special Forces."

"Jesus Christ, Bill. Those guys will kick our ass." Dawkins's mouth curled down. "They're not gonna let us just walk in there."

"Didn't say it was going to be easy. But our latest Intel leads us to believe they have already gone below ground, so the base should only contain a skeleton crew." He shrugged. "It's our chance, and we're going to take it."

"I'd feel better if someone told *them* not to shoot, as well." Jackson grinned. "When?"

"Within the hour." Bill Monroe looked at his watch. "We need to be there and back before any more big guns arrive on the water. Our job is to make sure they've got nothing to bump chests over. We can do that by getting to this Shenjung Xing."

"*If* we can get to him," Dawkins said softly.

Silence hung for several seconds, until there was a loud knock on the door that made Aimee jump. Monroe motioned for Dawkins to open it.

One after the other, the HAWCs entered. Captain Mitch Dempsey nodded to Monroe and Aimee, and then he and his team stood at ease in the center of the rec room. Their size and bulk eclipsed everything and everyone else inside. It was the first time Aimee had a chance to look at the people Jack Hammerson had chosen to accompany her – they were big, nearly all as big as Ben Jackson, except for Casey Franks, who nodded to Jennifer, and grinned, the scar on her cheek giving the smile the quality of an evil sneer.

Aimee saw that their bulky white suits were open and displayed underneath was the familiar caving suit she remembered, the suit she now wore herself. It was a combination of Kevlar thread and armor plating. The black, multiple terrain suits would stop a bullet, defraying their blunt impact, like a modern day suit of armor. *The Black Knights of the 21st century*, Aimee thought.

Monroe pointed to the coffee, but Dempsey shook his head. The McMurdo leader held out an arm. "Ladies and gentlemen, this here is Captain Dempsey of the Special Forces."

"Which Special Forces?" Dawkins asked, his arms folded.

Dempsey didn't blink, so Monroe went on. "*Ah*, he'll be leading the mission … under Dr. Weir's guidance." He leaned back against the table. "Captain."

"Thank you, Sergeant." Dempsey took a few seconds to eyeball each of the regular McMurdo soldiers. "By executive order, you are now all under my command." He paused, letting the words sink in. "There will not be a war today, or tomorrow. We will not permit it. We will enter the mining tunnels, contact the Chinese team, and allow Dr. Weir to negotiate their withdrawal without interference."

"Excuse me, Captain, but why would they listen to us? Or anyone with us?" Dawkins hiked his shoulders. "I mean, if they think we, that's us McMurdo guys, had something to do with their previous team going missing, what are we going to add?"

"Fair question." Dempsey nodded. "What are you going to add? Why exactly are *you* people going?" He pointed. "You, First Lieutenant John Dawkins, communications and computer specialist, are there because there is an emergency signal emanating from Area 24. You will be assisting us in tracking it." He pointed to the hulking Jackson. "And you, Second Lieutenant Ben Jackson, engineering specialist and ex-Ranger – your combat skills may be required. And you, Medical Officer Jennifer Hartigan? We hope we won't need you, but we may suffer some cuts and bruises. And the reality is, your field surgical expertise might be needed." He turned to look at each of their faces. "All of you have skills that we may require. That's why you're going."

Dawkins pulled at his chin. "Bill, *ah*, Sergeant Monroe, will you be going?"

Monroe shook his head. "No, not on this one, John. I've got work to do topside. It may get a little choppy up here as well."

"Great. So, *um*, is Dr. Weir or Captain Dempsey taking point?" Dawkins asked, but his eyes now stayed on the ground.

Dempsey nodded to Aimee. "Depends on the situation. We get us down, and provide cover. Dr. Weir takes it from there." He strode forward. "But to avoid confusion, *all* of my people are in charge. This is my team, and your new best friends. They tell you to do something, you do it."

Without turning, Dempsey held out an arm. "The friendly looking one to my left is Casey Franks."

Casey Franks gave a mock bow, the scar-pulled sneer permanently in place. On her neck, curling from under the suit, were angry red tattoos, and pink scars could also be seen. The trapezius muscles on her shoulders seemed to run up her neck to just under her ears. The tough female HAWC's expression only softened when she looked at Jennifer. Aimee worked hard to suppress a smile at the look on Dawkins's face.

Dempsey moved his arm slightly. "The big guy next to her is Hank Rinofsky."

Aimee had heard some of the team on the chopper refer to the giant HAWC as *Rhino*. Not just a play on his name, because the huge man had a lantern jaw and massive broken nose that gave it knuckle-like lump at its center.

"Then Misters Redman Hagel, Vince Blake, and Earl Parcellis." Each name was followed with a nod, or flat stare.

Redman Hagel grinned but also stared at Jennifer, raising his eyebrows. He was the youngest looking, and his short blond hair and light blue eyes gave him a pleasant, farmboy look. But there was something behind the eyes – a deadness, and a sliding shiftiness that urged caution. Next to him, Vince Blake was the shortest at about the same height as Casey Franks, with black hair, and a slight fold to his eyes, hinting at an Asian ancestry. Earl Parcellis looked Italian, with a wiry frame, tight shining curls and stubble that was already thick on his chin and disappearing on its way down his neck.

Each looked formidable, and next to the McMurdo soldiers, these were the guys you wanted to be close to if things went bad. Aimee looked again at the empty gaze of Hagel – perhaps most of them were, anyway.

She noticed that Dempsey kept the rank and other information about the team to the bare minimum. The HAWCs were an off-the-books group, and she bet as far as he was concerned, in twenty-four hours, they'd all just be memories when the mission had closed out.

Monroe straightened. "My team are good at what they do and all have climbing experience. They'll pull their own weight."

"Good." Dempsey nodded to Monroe. "Questions?"

"When would we leave?" Jennifer asked.

Dempsey looked at his watch. "In ... twenty-three minutes."

Jennifer's mouth dropped open, and Dempsey looked back along the group. "Anything else?"

The silence stretched, and the McMurdo soldiers seemed to be locked in their own thoughts. Dempsey began to turn away.

"That's it?" Aimee carefully placed her coffee down on the bench top and walked forward. "I mean, that's all you're going to say?"

Dempsey watched Aimee with half lidded eyes, but Casey Franks smiled her usual sneer-smile, excitement rising in her eyes.

"You'd like to add something, Dr. Weir? Something you feel would *assist* the group?" Dempsey's face was expressionless.

"You'll be taking these guys into a highly dangerous restricted zone under the ice. I know what's down there, and you've read the reports, so you do too." She thumbed over her shoulder. "But these poor saps sure don't. How is not telling them going to assist them?"

"We're saps now?" Dawkins asked, with a grin.

"*Poor* saps." Jennifer added.

Big Ben Jackson's scowl creased his forehead. "Are we missing something here?"

Monroe went to step forward, but Dempsey held up a hand.

Aimee folded her arms. "Well? You want to tell them or would you like me to?"

Dempsey smiled. "The floor is yours, Dr. Weir. Like I said, if you think it will help ... either the mission or their frame of mind." He stepped back, poured himself a coffee and watched her as he sipped.

Aimee gathered her thoughts; conscious that she needed to inform, to warn the McMurdo guys about what lay ahead, but also cautious about panicking them. Her lips compressed, and her throat tightened, as she wrestled with the memories. *Damnit*, she thought, there was no other way to roll it out, but as the unvarnished truth.

She sucked in a huge breath, filling her lungs, and then let it out slowly. "About five years ago, I was involved in an undocumented mission to travel into a newly opened crater in the ice. There was a missing plane, and the first team in had vanished. My friend was a member of that team." She swallowed and went on. "Well, anyway, in the course of our investigations, we detected what we thought was a huge reservoir of natural petroleum." She shook her head. "Wasn't petroleum. Oh no, it wasn't anything as simple as that."

Aimee paced now, pushing strands of shining, black hair back off her face. "There was no oil, and no empty caves or lifeless caverns below us." She shook her head at the memory. "There was life down there all right, and not just lichens, microbes, or even blind shrimp in shallow rock pools. No, no, no, there was a whole freaking world down there – warm, alive, primordial, and more deadly than anything on the surface. It was a place where we, and our team of apex killers, like these guys," – she thumbed over her shoulder at Dempsey and the HAWCs – "suddenly found ourselves just another part of the food chain ... and nowhere near the top. Of the several dozen people that went into that hole, only three of us made it out alive." She looked at the ground, her eyes watering. "So, we sealed it off and made it a restricted zone – Area 24." She exhaled. "And now, ladies and gentlemen, we're all going back down."

Jackson, Dawkins, and Jennifer Hartigan blinked with disbelief, and Aimee maintained eye contact with Mitch Dempsey.

"Yes, we've read the briefing notes," Dempsey said softly. "But we are prepared for all eventualities. There were mistakes made, and we learned from them – the first team expected to encounter nothing. We know that to be erroneous now, and have adjusted our methods and firepower accordingly."

"Yeah, I hope so." Aimee went back to staring at the ground, hugging herself.

"Wait a minute, exactly when were you going to tell us this?" Dawkins's neck strained. "And what *additional firepower* do we get?"

"You get our protection, fuck-knuckle. All you'll ever need." Casey Franks sneered at Dawkins. "Welcome to real soldiering, pussy."

"That's enough," Dempsey said evenly.

"And you expect our help?" Dawkins had stepped forward to jab a finger at Dempsey.

Hagel grinned and loomed closer to the McMurdo soldier. "Who said anything about a request, asshole?" He jammed a blunt finger into Dawkins's chest, pushing him back a step.

"Now wait a minute, mister." The towering soldier Jackson moved in, and went to grab Hagel's hand.

In a flash Hagel had spun to grip the giant's hand, and twisted it around, holding it in only one of his own hands, and forcing the bigger man to grimace in pain, and then forcing him to his knees. Hagel mimed drawing a knife and stabbing Jackson in the side of his neck – *a kill stroke*. He grinned. "Like we said, we're all the protection you'll ever need."

"*Enough*," Monroe raised his voice. "They're right, this is not a voluntary mission. This has orders from the highest level and is of critical importance to the nation – no, to *all* nations. Make no mistake, we must succeed, *as a team*."

Hagel pushed Jackson away, but continued standing over him.

"Back in line," Dempsey said to his HAWC. Hagel grinned a little more into Jackson's face, but complied.

"Sergeant Monroe is right. We will succeed, *together*." Dempsey motioned to the door. "Be ready to leave in fifteen minutes."

The HAWCs filed out, and Dempsey looked from Monroe, to each of the McMurdo soldiers.

"Make no mistake, people; we are all expendable in pursuit of the success of our mission." He paused, looking for any challenge. There was none. "You now have fourteen minutes."

CHAPTER 23

Xuě Lóng Base – Antarctic surface

Three PLA Special Forces commandos remained on the surface. The base cook, Lim Daiyu, the sole survivor they'd found so far, was still unconscious on a cot in the rear of the facility's sleeping quarters. They had decided to let the man sleep. At least that way they didn't have to listen to him wail about monsters and demons anymore.

PLA Operative Chen Zu yawned; the team was at ease now, tending over into boredom from the lack of activity. They had been unable to monitor Captain Yang for hours, as the fixed-line communications had been ripped from the shaft, and their wireless updates had at first become scratchy, before then hissing over to nothing but white-noise, the further the descent team moved from the elevator shaft and deeper into the tunnels.

All PLA soldiers had emergency walkie talkies, but though they were high powered, it was unlikely they would connect. Also each second of usage meant they reduced battery life. There was nothing they could do but wait.

He watched as his two comrades, Dijiang and Lanling, played a game, slapping down cards hard and fast, and roaring their approval or cursing at their luck, good and bad. Chen drummed his fingers; he was bored, but couldn't relax. Captain Yang being out of communication reach was expected and of no concern. However, what did gnaw at him was the *Kunming* going dark – the destroyer was only just off the coast, and seemed to suddenly vanish. As its primary role was to support them, it going offline was a mystery.

He drummed faster. He hoped it was just atmospheric ionization causing the disruption, but he desperately needed instruction. Yang had ordered them not to use the long range communications over the satellite link as the American base at McMurdo would undoubtedly be listening. If he disobeyed his captain's order, demotion, and then possibly missing front teeth, was the likely outcome.

He ground his molars, as his peers roared over the finish of their card game. He watched, trance-like, as Lanling began to reshuffle the deck, his hands moving fast and deftly flipping, slotting, and reslotting the cards, finishing with a fanning motion that zipped the entire deck together. The man was about to deal, when his eyes went wide, and then Chen felt his own nerves shock when one of the proximity alarms suddenly squealed and blinked its warning. All Chinese bases had alarms and sensors to detect anyone or anything coming close to the main structure.

It was the western quadrant alarm that flashed, and the motion sensitive cameras swiveled to zero in on the movement. Chen was on his feet, and the two seated soldiers had forgotten their cards and swung to the control panels, rapidly improving resolution and zooming in on the snow line.

Chen leaned in over their shoulders, and then snorted. He felt his heart rate ease back a few beats. A small group of penguins stood hunched over, facing into the wind and sporadic snow flurries, every now and then shaking themselves, or flapping stubby wings.

The alarm continued to flash and beep. He exhaled. "The penguins will continue to set off the alarms." He tapped Lanling on the shoulder. "Can you isolate them and remove their profiles from the sensors?"

The soldier grunted and worked at the console for several minutes, before sitting back and shaking his head. "This unit is not sophisticated enough to remove the distraction."

The alarm continued to beep at them. "Switch it off," Chen said.

"They're all interconnected." Dijiang shrugged. "We switch it off, we will lose all the external sensors."

Chen grimaced. "Then someone better go up and shoot them. That noise will make us crazy."

The two men ignored him for several moments, before Dijiang half turned. "You're the best shot."

Chen groaned, knowing neither of them was going to budge. He yelled over the alarm. "Then turn it off until I get back … or I might shoot you as well."

Lanling switched off the sensors, the alarm suddenly quietening. He zoomed in on the six small birds on the hilltop. "Only about two hundred yards." He spun in his chair. "Penguin and noodles for dinner?" He grinned.

"I hear they taste like fish shit," Dijiang said with a curled lip.

"I don't care if we make hats out of them," Chen growled. "Soon as they're gone, I want those alarms back on."

Chen cursed as he selected a rifle and swiveled the scope up and into place. He walked down the metal lined corridor, and then opened the airlock outer door, immediately having to hunch into the wind.

He grumbled. The breeze was up to fifty miles per hour now, and the fast moving snow stung like gravel when it hit his exposed skin. He pulled again at his hood, and pushed through the soft snow on the westward side of the building. He could just make out the several black and white dots, and he leaned against the building's edge to steady himself and sighted at the birds. They jumped into focus, and he readied his aim as he brought the crosshairs over the center of the largest penguin.

He snorted. "Dumb bird," he whispered with one eye screwed tight. The penguin continued to shake and flap its wings. He gently squeezed the trigger, and the top half of the penguin disappeared in a puff of black and white feathers. "*Hi-ya!*" He grinned, pulling his head back momentarily, but then sighting again at the birds.

He frowned around the scope. The bird he had just shot continued to stand, and its one remaining flipper-wing continued to shake and flap. "*Wha …?*"

Chen pulled his face away from the scope, just as the dart took him in the neck, piercing his fur-lined hood and embedding into his flesh. He reached up and felt the small projectile in his skin, but already his arm felt like lead, and a monstrous fatigue dragged him down into blackness.

"Robo-penguin strikes again." Casey Franks lowered the dart gun. She turned to Dawkins who lay beside her and grinned. "Let's go meet the neighbors."

The ten white-clothed shapes lifted from the snow, and rushed the base door. Big Ben Jackson brought up the rear, dragging the unconscious body of the Chinese soldier with him, and Hank Rinofsky ran at the shoulder of Aimee Weir.

They waited. The HAWC leader, Dempsey, held up a hand, three fingers splayed as he counted them down. He spun the wheel and pushed, the HAWCs rushing forward, guns up. Casey Franks and Vince Blake led them in – both still had tranq-darts loaded.

Blake spoke Cantonese and Mandarin fluently. Their priority was to assess how many were still above surface and incapacitate them quickly – non-lethally if possible, but by any means if necessary. Recriminations were for the politicians to argue over later.

Like a pair of bloodhounds, Franks and Blake went in low, fast, and silent as ghosts. Their task was to take down obvious targets. Casey knew that they needed a balance of speed, silence, and caution, as the Chinese usually wired their facilities with explosives, and if they thought their base was compromised they wouldn't hesitate to self-destruct.

Blake took off down the corridor to the right towards the sleeping quarters, and Casey headed into the control room. She found two men at consoles, and one spun towards her, his eyes momentarily going wide. He lunged for a rifle and she fired two darts. Both struck their targets – the throat of the guy going for the gun and the back of the neck of the other. Both men slumped to the floor, eyes rolled back.

She quickly met with Blake who shook his head, and then she headed back to the entrance and met with Dempsey in the darkened hallway.

"Two down. Clear," she said.

Dempsey nodded, gun up. He turned to the rest of the HAWCs. "Search." They scattered, seeking more inhabitants, performing a lower level examination.

At the control room, Dempsey waved over John Dawkins. The young man came forward cautiously, and the HAWC captain pointed.

"Disable this unit."

Dawkins looked briefly at the consoles, nodded, and then sat down to start flicking switches. The HAWCs came back in, announcing all clear.

Casey stood at ease, feeling relaxed, but her eyes darted from doors to alcoves and to anywhere else that could potentially launch a threat. Rinofsky knelt beside the downed guards. He grabbed one of them by the jaw, turning the man's head, and then peeled an eyelid back.

"Big bastards; not your usual PLA." He stood. "They'll sleep for a couple of hours."

"Secure them, and our penguin marksman from outside. I like my peace and quiet." Dempsey looked at Aimee, who seemed to be shivering. "You all right, Dr. Weir?"

She looked anxious rather than cold. "I'm fine."

Dempsey grinned. "It's okay to be a bit nervous."

"It's not that." She turned her head, sniffing. "There's something, a hint of a smell. Makes me feel a little unsettled, is all."

Dempsey sniffed. "Can't smell a thing. Just relax. He checked his watch. "Franks, take Dawkins and check the elevator. I want it …"

An alarm screamed.

"*Fuck.*" Casey backed into a wall, gun up. Dawkins cringed at his console, and like Casey, the other HAWCs spun, guns ready.

Aimee covered her ears. "What the hell is that?"

Hagel pointed at John Dawkins, still hunkered down at the console. "What the fuck did you just do?"

The young McMurdo soldier shook his head, his chip-toothed mouth working. Overhead, a mechanical Chinese voice started intoning from speakers throughout the base.

Dempsey spun to Blake. "What's he saying?"

The HAWCs face was white. "It's a countdown." He turned. "Detonation in 180 seconds, 179, 178 …"

*

Lim Daiyu carefully eased the door of the storeroom cupboard open a crack. Once again he had been forced to fold his body into a confined space in the face of a threat. He didn't recognize the people now entering the camp, but heard the voices and guessed they were American. He had seen them drag the limp body of one of the soldiers along the corridor – it didn't look like they were taking prisoners.

He had been a coward when the thing from the pit had risen up. He had hidden, and not tried to fight or save any of his friends. He crushed his eyes shut, willing courage into his trembling limbs. His eyes flicked open. This time he would not dishonor his family name.

When all of the foreigners were congregated in the main communication center, he stepped out of his hiding place and headed for the commander's office. Once inside he knew what he must do – it was the only piece of training he had shared with every member of the team – if there was ever an irresistible threat, and the base compromised, then protection of the camp's secrets was paramount.

He went to the wall and entered a code into a small metallic box. The door sprang open. Inside there was a single smaller box, under a Perspex lid. He flicked the lid up and pressed the single button underneath. A screen asked to *Proceed* or *Cancel*. Lim Daiyu became calm, and he prayed, not for his life or for the dead, but that the demon, the *Zhàyǔ*, would also be taken in the blast.

He pressed *Proceed*, and then sat down slowly, cross-legged, on the floor to wait.

CHAPTER 24

Captain Mitch Dempsey went from looking furious to roaring instructions in a heartbeat.

"Mission is *Go,* people – we are *going* down."

The HAWCs formed up at the door, but Jennifer Hartigan paused over one of the unconscious Chinese. "What about them?"

Dempsey waved her away. "Leave 'em. They wanna fry their camp, then let them enjoy the barbecue."

"But that's …" Jennifer bent to grab one of the men's jackets.

"*Move it, soldier!*" Dempsey's voice was so loud it shocked the medical officer into panicked action. The HAWCs shoved the McMurdo soldiers and Aimee towards the elevator shaft room.

Inside, Parcellis was already standing by, hand on the controls. They piled in, jammed tight.

Dempsey grimaced. "No roof – gonna get damned hot." He turned to Parcellis. "Punch it."

Dawkins's eyes were round in his head. "We're gonna be cooked, or crushed."

"Wait." The huge HAWC, Rinofsky, jumped back out and sprinted to the wall, grabbing the bent sheet of steel that had once been the roof of the cage. He leapt back in, dragging the heavy sheet of steel with him. "Go, go, go."

The cage started to descend, and Rinofsky lifted it above his head, grunting with the effort. Big Ben Jackson grabbed the other end, bracing himself. He looked to Rinofsky and the pair of huge men grinned at each other.

"Bet you drop it first, little fella," Jackson said.

"I'll take that bet. Loser buys first round," Rinofsky replied, his expression becoming grim, as the mechanical voice's numbers got shorter and fainter as they dropped.

"Ten seconds," Blake said.

"This is gonna hurt." Dawkins covered his head with his arms.

Hagel whooped. "Ladies and gentlemen, next stop hell, and it's gonna be *re-eeeal* hot."

"Brace," Dempsey roared, pushing people down, and then crouching.

The blast was thunderous, with a white light filling the shaft, immediately followed by the shock wave. Then came the heat. Aimee crouched into a ball, hood pulled down tight and hands over her face, but she still felt the temperature go from just above zero to well over a hundred in about a second. Then she felt, before she heard, the rumbling, like a stampede of horses getting closer.

Above her, Ben Jackson yelled: *"Incoming!"*

She opened her eyes a crack, and saw the tree-trunk legs of the two huge men buckle as enormous weight piled down on top of the sheet of steel they held aloft. There was the smell of burning wood and plastics, and an orange glow came from the edge of the iron roof as whatever had accumulated still burned.

More giant hammer blows on the sheet of steel, and Jackson groaned as the growing weight bore down on them. Casey Franks got to her feet, and lifted arms high, pushing at the steel from the center. Though the light was dim, Aimee could see that Casey's gloves smoked where she held onto their shield.

In another second, there was an almighty thump as something heavy struck the steel, and Casey and the men buckled, before the edges of the plate caught the wall, and were wedged tight. The plate was ripped from their hands, and was left behind. More heavy thumps sounded, but for now, the steel was a barrier holding tight, sealing off the shaft and holding back the tons of debris.

The entire group watched their glowing roof recede. Aimee said a tiny prayer of thanks, as their cage trundled on, dropping lower and getting farther and farther away from the inferno above. It was only when the soft glow at the steel plate's edge began to dim as the last embers burned themselves out that Aimee realized what it meant – *there was no going back now.*

*

There was a deep thump that they felt beneath their feet, seconds before they heard a sound like distant thunder. Dust rained down upon them, and Yang spun, looking furious.

The men grabbed at the walls as the echoes continued on for several seconds. More debris fell around them, and there came murmurs of a cave-in from the soldiers.

"Silence," Yang roared at them. He turned to Shenjung. "What are your imbecile engineers doing up there?"

"*My imbecile engineers?*" Shenjung frowned. "That was an explosion."

"Possibly." He pointed to his men. "You seven, go back and see what those idiots are doing." He dismissed them. "Double time; I do not want our group strung out."

Shenjung watched them sprint away. He prayed that Soong was not in trouble. He knew his small group, and knew none of them had explosives. He wanted to tell the captain, but Yang was already issuing orders to proceed.

*

"Well ain't that just fucking great?" Hagel paced back to the elevator, shining his light up into the blocked shaft. He turned back. "Now how the fuck do we get out of here?" He strode past the group, the light on his gun-barrel a pipe of illumination in the dust- and smoke-filled tunnel.

"Shut it, Hagel," Dempsey spoke over his shoulder to the young HAWC as he and Rinofsky looked at a screen of a small illuminated box.

Hagel coughed and spat. "I hope someone brought a shovel, because we better start digging now." His eyes were round with both fear and agitation, and Aimee watched him like she would a venomous snake.

Dempsey turned, his jaw jutting. "One more word outta you, mister." Dempsey glared, and Hagel's mouth clamped shut for a second before he threw a hand up and walked away, kicking a sheet of bent steel out of his way. It clanged away loudly down the choking tunnel.

Aimee wrapped her arms around herself, and walked towards the HAWC leader. "Captain, please tell me there is a Plan C for us Plan B team members? If I remember correctly, we were meant to keep the back door open."

"Chaos theory – shit happens." He shrugged. "We'll be fine, Dr. Weir." He went to walk away.

Aimee scoffed. "Fine? Captain, we needed a back door. I know you read the briefings. We could be walking into the lair of something that is far more dangerous than a squad of pissed off Chinese soldiers. We are not ..."

Dempsey quickly pulled his rifle from over his shoulder, and fired from his hip. Where Aimee expected to hear a report from a bullet being discharged, or even the spit of a compressed air round that the previous HAWC team had used, this time there was just a soft whine, as a thin orange beam of light went from Dempsey's gun to touch on the piece of steel plating that Hagel had kicked. Dempsey shut it off after a second, but kept his flashlight on it. Where the beam had touched the steel there was a pencil-thin hole cut right through it. The edges glowed molten.

He held the gun up. "Latest D.E.W. – Directed Energy Weapon technology. I'd like to introduce you to the M18X DEW rifle. Hot pressed boron carbide in a bullpup design, means longer barrel and powerplant all packed in behind the trigger." He turned it over, flicking open the rounded stock, revealing what looked like a glowing shard of glass. "Power is drawn from microfusion cells and processed through a single Erbium optical gain crystal. This bad boy will cut through anything." He half turned. "Mr. Rinofsky, front and center."

The big HAWC stepped forward and pulled a thicker version of the weapon Dempsey had from over his shoulder. He telescoped the barrel, and held it ready.

Dempsey nodded. "Just to make things interesting, our big friend here is packing a portable plasma cannon, with an optimized composite ceramic structure to contain the two thousand degree temperatures from a plasma pulse that will terminate anything that gets in front of it." He closed down his own rifle and cradled it in his arms. "Like I said, Dr. Weir, we're better prepared this time."

Aimee wanted to stay angry, but couldn't help feeling a little relieved. *We might just survive the day after all*, she thought.

"Movement," Hagel said, staring down as the small device in his hands gave off rapid proximity pulses.

Dempsey held up a fist. The HAWCs and the McMurdo soldiers froze. "Distance?"

Dawkins crowded in close, trying to see over Hagel's shoulder.

"Two hundred feet, coming fast," Hagel said, elbowing Dawkins back a step.

Aimee kept ambling forward, lost in her own thoughts, barely hearing the words or aware that everyone had stopped moving around her, until Casey Franks grabbed at her. Casey placed a finger to her lips, Aimee getting it immediately. She followed Franks as she shrunk back into a small depression in the wall of the tunnel.

Dempsey made a chopping motion, left and right, and the team went to either side of the tunnel, flattening themselves against the wall, or crouching, weapons ready. Lights went off, and the HAWCs went to infrared.

"If this shit goes bad, stay behind me," Franks whispered.

CHAPTER 25

Aimee crouched, concentrating on the tunnel. Without lights or night vision equipment, the darkness was absolute. After a few more seconds she heard the sound of voices, soft at first, and then the fall of boots on stone, coming fast, jogging. She waited, barely breathing. The voices became more distinct, Chinese, and then lights appeared.

Blake got to his feet. "*Wènhòu zhōngguó péngyǒu – wènhòu zhōngguó péngyǒu.*" His voice was loud in the tunnel.

Immediately the Chinese group froze, and though Aimee understood nothing of their language, she could sense their fear and surprise.

"*Shì lái bāng.*" Blake stepped out more, one of his hands up. "English?" he asked.

There was a single woman, about the same age as Aimee who pushed through the group. "I speak English."

Aimee saw that the men behind her didn't look like soldiers, but each of them had flashlights and many held them, club-like. It looked like fight or flight was kicking in – Blake needed to work fast.

"They're going to run," Aimee whispered.

Casey shrugged "Like where?"

They needed to take a chance or they'd lose them, she thought. Aimee got to her feet, also stepping out. "Hey, we're here to help. My name is Dr. Aimee Weir. I'm a scientist, just like you."

The woman spoke rapidly over her shoulder to the other men and women, before turning back, her eyes now cautious. "My name is Dr. Soong Chin Ling. We heard an explosion. Was that you?"

Aimee shook her head. "No, but it was someone in your camp. They detonated the base, and now the elevator shaft to the surface is now sealed."

Soong half turned, translating again. The words flung back and forth were fast and furious, until finally she turned back to Aimee.

"Because of you, we think," Soong said.

Dempsey's voice was low. "Dr. Weir, I suggest ..."

Aimee exhaled, ignoring the HAWC Captain. "Probably. We couldn't get them to understand we came for peaceful reasons. We need to find Shenjung Xing."

Soong's eyes narrowed. "How so?"

"We need to talk, explain things; is he among you?" Aimee grimaced as Soong Chin Ling remained mute. She felt the weight of Dempsey's focus on her. "Look, there's bigger issues at stake now. One of our submarines is missing."

"Dr. Weir ..." the note of warning in Dempsey's voice went up a notch.

She turned momentarily. "We're all in this together now ... trapped together." She spun back to Soong. "You have a naval vessel off the coast, so do we. Soon, more ships will join them. The situation is becoming tense ... dangerous. Whatever mining you are doing down here, right now, we don't give a damn. But you can't go lower down. You don't know what you'll find. It's off-limits for a reason. Your team, Shenjung Xing, everyone, is in grave danger."

Silence hung for a few moments, before Soong turned and translated slowly and carefully for her colleagues. She listened for a moment and then faced Aimee.

"They think you will trick us. There is no reason to trust you. If this is of such importance, why did you not tell Beijing?" Soong's face refused to soften.

Aimee groaned. "*Please!* Time is running out. We need to stop your people from going lower. You must come with us."

"No." Dempsey, cradling his gun, came and stood beside her. "Can't take 'em with us."

Soong snorted. "They would not go with you anyway. We will wait here."

"For what?" Aimee opened her arms. "Even if they started tunneling now, it would take days, weeks, to clear the shaft again." She looked at their packs. "You might have supplies for a day or two, then what?"

While Soong turned and spoke to her group, Aimee spun to Dempsey. "We can't let them stay, they'll die."

Dempsey's expression was blank. Blake came and stood at Aimee's other shoulder. "Forget it, Dr. Weir, they won't come. The distrust runs too deep."

"We damn well have to try," Aimee snapped back.

Blake was cradling his rifle, and half turned. "Boss, say the word, and I can transl ..."

The single bullet took him in the crease of his neck, just above his armored suit collar, and spun him around to lay flat on the cave floor.

"*Down!*"

Dempsey dived, pushing Aimee to the ground, but she knew enough to hit the deck, and roll to the side of the tunnel. Soong did the same, crouching with hands over her head. The Chinese engineers stood frozen and bewildered, turning one way, then the other, as the six tall PLA came up from the tunnel depths, moving fast and going into a V-attack formation.

"Hold," Dempsey hissed into his mic to the HAWCs, who had flattened to the floor or sides of the cave. And then: "Light 'em up."

Red laser dots picked individual targets, the small cherries appearing on the chests or foreheads of each of the PLA soldiers.

"Halt or die." Dempsey had a bead on the lead PLA.

Aimee looked to Blake, the man down and coughing. If ever they needed a translator, it was now. She wracked her brains for what fragments of the language she knew, with nothing suitable coming to mind.

The PLA soldiers whispered among themselves for a moment. Dempsey waited, and other than Blake's coughing, there was absolute silence and stillness from the HAWCs.

The lead soldier's gun was coming up, and she saw the man start to bunch the muscles in his thighs. *Don't even think about it*, Aimee silently pleaded.

In a split second, the PLA leapt and fired.

In response, there was the sound like a soft whine, and a pencil-thin beam of light touched the diving soldier, passing right through him. He was dead before he hit the ground.

Blake coughed blood and turned on his side. His words were croaked and strained, but the fluent Chinese filled the silent space.

After a moment, there came a few words in return. Blake groaned, exhaling his exasperation. "They think we have set a trap for them." He looked across to Aimee. "Hug the floor, it's going to get ugly."

"Works for me," Casey Franks said, and Aimee could imagine the grim smile on her face.

The silence stretched and the PLA soldiers didn't flinch. They waited, but with their command structure taken out, there was no one to issue new orders. So they did the only thing they knew how to do – *fight*. They came fast, yelling and their guns set to full automatic.

Rapid gunfire filled the tunnel, and Hagel, the most exposed, took a round in the chest, punching him backwards.

But the HAWCs were also trained to respond, quickly and efficiently, and the only way they knew how. Unfortunately for the PLA, the HAWCs were better at it, and better equipped. In seven seconds, the PLA were all lying dead, and there was just a whiff of burning skin floating in the air.

Casey Franks was first on her feet. "Look's like we just declared war on China. *Cool*."

"Stow it, Franks," Dempsey said, also now on his feet. "Parcellis, check on Blake." He half turned to the McMurdo team, searching for Jennifer. "Hartigan, see to Hagel, then check on the Chinese engineers. Franks, make sure we don't have any active shooters." He walked down the cave and crouched next to Aimee.

Aimee nodded. "I'm okay." She got to her feet, and crossed to where Parcellis was helping Blake sit forward.

"Lucky you were so close." Jennifer Hartigan joined Parcellis who had Blake's suit open as he examined the graze. He turned, showing her the injury. "The bullet was still hot; singed the wound closed – immediate self cauterization." Parcellis applied a med-patch – the swatch of synthetic skin contained antibiotics, steroids, and painkillers. "Good as new." He pulled the uniform back into place. "Well, hardly, but you know what I mean." He grinned and then turned.

"Hey, how you doin', Hagel?"

The young HAWC sat forward and spat onto the tunnel floor. He knocked on the armor plating over his chest. His fingers stopped at a chip in the ceramic plates.

"Feel like I've been mule-kicked, if Officer Hartigan could just take a look …"

"Yeah, yeah, you're fine," Parcellis slapped Blake on the back and got to his feet, pulling his friend with him.

"Five down, boss," Casey Franks spoke over her shoulder, as she stood glaring at the cowering engineers, as if hoping another PLA soldier would miraculously rise up to challenge her.

"I counted seven coming in." Dempsey growled and looked around. "Fuck, we lost two."

Franks turned. "Let me chase 'em down. They get back to their pals, and we're going to be fighting every step of our way."

Dempsey stared off into the dark. "Negative on that."

Aimee walked over and crouched beside Soong. "I'm so sorry."

Soong looked at the downed men. "Typical American negotiation."

Aimee winced. "You saw they left us no choice."

Soong lips turned down. "These men were not our friends, and I do not grieve for them. But there are a lot more soldiers down in the tunnels, and I think you are in big trouble when those two fleeing ones get back to their squad. Maybe they will negotiate with you in the same manner."

Dempsey appeared beside Aimee. "I suspect they will, and then more of them will die. Maybe some of us too, but they'll find out we don't die easily." He stared hard at her. "So my money is on them going down – all of them."

"You said you need to find Shenjung Xing," Soong said softly. "He is my friend, and he is with them. I would like to find him too."

"Well, you want to stop more deaths, keep your friend safe?" Dempsey said. "Then come with us, and tell them to talk first, rather than shoot. Their only chance."

Soong glanced over her shoulder at the huddle of engineers and scientists. "I do not think they will come with you. They will trust in their own government to save them." She turned back to look Aimee in the eye. "But I will check."

She walked back in among the group, and within a few seconds, agitated, rapid-fire dialogue bounced around the tunnel. Aimee shook her head, wondering how any of them could understand the other, with everyone talking at once. There were a few foot-stamps, and pushes in the chest before Soong returned with just two smaller men at her shoulders. She pointed to them: "Lee Pinying and Bo Xingmin will also come with you. The others will stay."

Aimee saw that one of the men with Soong had an intricate tattoo just showing above his collar. Hagel walked towards him, and at first the man cowered, but Hagel held up a hand. "It's okay, brother, just want to check out your cool ink." He peeled down his collar a few inches.

"Whoa, dig this." He stood back.

Just showing was the tip of an intricate dragon tattoo appearing from under the collar of the man's gray coveralls, the reds, yellows, and greens all swirling in a maelstrom of color and movement – wisdom, luck, and ferocity, Aimee bet he would have told her if given the chance.

"Cool stuff, man." Hagel swatted his shoulder, and then rolled up one of his sleeves showing his own tattoo of an eagle crushing a snake.

Rinofsky snorted with derision, and lifted half of his armored top – there was a blur of colors and designs. "Two days' work." He grinned and winked.

"Nice." Hagel nodded. "Who did it, a blind twelve year old?"

Rinofsky's grin broadened as he flipped Hagel the bird.

The engineer said something to Soong, who grunted. She took the pack off her shoulders and handed it to one of her engineers. "Shenjung Xing will listen to me." Her eyes were expressionless. "But the other men, the soldiers, are not the same. Their leader is very, *ah*, patriotic."

Aimee took that to mean the likelihood of negotiation with him was probably zero.

"We only need one to hear us." Dempsey turned to his team. "Franks, Parcellis, out at point."

Jennifer Hartigan pointed at the downed soldiers, and the huddle of very confused looking Chinese engineers. "What about them? Will someone stay and …"

"Not a chance," Hagel said, his lips turned down.

Aimee saw the look on Soong's face, and knew they needed her cooperation. "Captain, one of us should at least secure this position. Remain here to … supervise."

Dempsey shook his head. "Can't spare a single body, Dr. Weir." He stepped closer to her, but his voice was loud enough for Soong to overhear. "You know I can't make them come with us, and I'm not about to drag them under guard. Besides, hopefully we'll all be back soon, and working on a way out together." He smiled. "Think about it. They'll probably be safer here, than where we're going, right?"

Aimee looked to Soong momentarily, and then back to the HAWC captain. She exhaled, knowing the answer. "Yes."

"We'll leave 'em some extra water." Dempsey grunted and turned away. "Let's move."

*

The two surviving PLA soldiers, Han Biao and Fan Kai Ling, ran hard. Not that Han Biao was afraid of the Americans, but he knew that it was best to inform Captain Yang of their numbers and firepower, so they could make preparations, organize and ambush, and then wipe them all out.

He grinned as he ran. *They don't know just what they have done – rouse the dragon, as Captain Yang would surely say.*

"Stop!"

Han Biao skidded and turned to look back at his comrade. Fan Kai stood, legs planted and his fists clenched in the glare of Han's flashlight.

"What are we doing? We must fight them."

Han Biao frowned, and then shook his head. "No, we must stay ahead of them, tell Captain Yang, and then regroup. Together we can overwhelm them. We are many more than them."

"Stay ahead of them, or lead them to us?" Fan Kai glared. "We are PLA, not frightened children." His eyes narrowed. "Yang will call you a coward. Perhaps even shoot you for running away."

Dung eater, Han Biao thought. *How dare he call me a coward?* He grunted, thinking. "Then we should do both. You stay and slow them down. I will contact the captain via walkie talkie as I get closer to them, and bring back support." He bowed. "Good luck, brother." He turned and started to jog away into the dark. He had no intention of talking to anyone.

CHAPTER 26

Alex froze, listening, letting just his eyes move over the alien landscape. He pushed out with other senses, reaching out into the gloom, searching for traces of something that set his nerves on their very edge.

After a moment he relaxed, but the knot in his gut remained. He turned to find Cate, now a few dozen feet back and crouching beside a small plant. He watched her as she used the back of her hand to knock at its leaves, making them shrink back inside a sheath below the ground. She mouthed some words, and then smiled as if satisfied by her classification.

Alex turned back to the wall of drab green before him, inhaling the scents and hearing the tiny movements – *so much life*, he thought. He stepped back, craning his neck. Huge limbless trunks shot up into the air, and everywhere that should have had a fern or frond had something that looked similar, but instead its leaves were bulbs or polyps. Water dripped from everything, and some of the plants were covered in a greasy brown slime that was either a sign of rot, or some sort of natural coating – he couldn't even guess at its function. But the overwhelming impression was of a mad, living density.

Alex swung back to Cate again, feeling his impatience climb. He needed to get to the submarine and then find a way out as soon as he could. The signal from the pulser in his hand was loud and clear – his objective was located many miles away. He looked up at the odd treetops. He needed to get to some sort of higher ground. Where they were now made him feel buried.

He continued to look higher – what might have seemed like a night sky full of tiny blue stars was actually a cave roof ... and above that, miles of rock, ice, and snow. He half smiled – *What was I thinking? I'm already buried.*

The jungle was a solid wall before him, and the pulser only gave him an indication of which way to go. If he was off by even one degree, it could mean miles more hacking through the green knotted jungle. He didn't have time for mistakes. He turned slowly, stopping at one direction. His gut told him that was the way.

Alex placed his gloved hands on the trunks of two large trees barring his way, and exerting huge pressure. They pulled apart, creating an opening. He turned to Cate.

"Let's go. This way, quickly, but quietly."

*

Cate Canning grinned as she walked. "We're here, we're *really* here." She touched her face and winced. Her face felt raw and exposed where the goggles hadn't been covering it. Her skin stung, and she bet it would blister and peel. Plus she had a thumping headache. Otherwise, she felt pretty darn good.

She sucked in a breath, not only smelling but tasting the earth, saltwater, fungus, and rotting vegetation floating in the air.

She moved from plant to plant. "It's sort of quite beautiful when you get used to it."

"Beautiful?" Alex continued to stride on, but he half turned. "In the eye of the beholder maybe."

"And that's me." She slowed, looking around, and then holding her arms out. "We're in a forest." She continued to smile, undaunted. "Miles below the Antarctic." She sped up to him. "Did you just hear me? A freaking forest – *down here*."

"Yep." Alex paused but continued to look down at the small box. "And a deadly one."

Cate veered away to a large trunk and lifted her hand, but stopped short of touching it. "It's not actually wood, you know.

It's more like a fungal growth, or," – she spun – "a lichen." She pointed up at the huge tree shape's branching top that looked more like the tip of an asparagus.

"You know, I think I've seen something like these in the fossil record. It looks like a Prototaxite. Sort of makes sense, as they flourished in the warm, wet jungles of the Silurian and Devonian periods, about 400 million years ago." She walked around the three-foot-wide trunk, and then craned her neck to see up into its thirty-foot stubby canopy. "They were more like huge rolls of liverwort matting. They could survive with little light." She finally patted the hairy trunk. "And it's alive. Here, now – this is probably the *biggest* find of the century." She suddenly remembered the Pliosaur. "The *second* biggest find of the century."

She held out her arms, looking like she wanted to hug the thing. She turned, her face beaming. "If I died now, it would have been worth it."

"Be careful what you wish for." Alex turned away to peer out into the gloom.

Cate looked across at another of the liverwort tree trunks, letting her eyes move up its trunk. She frowned and approached. It had what looked like bore holes in the hairy surface. The first was about six feet up and the size of a baseball. All the dark holes glistened at their edges.

"That's weird, and interesting. Looks like something has been eating into it." She lifted her hand towards the hole and used a couple of her fingers to rub at the glistening patch around its outside.

"It's sticky, like webbing, slimy sap-web – " Something launched itself at her hand like a jack-in-a-box. Its red, bulbous head ended in a wet looking sucker. Cate jerked her hand back with a squeak, and the thing's head flopped down onto the surface of the lichen tree, feeling around the edge of its hole. It was like a lamprey eel, except the body was segmented like a wood louse, and no visible eyes were apparent. It lifted itself to wave its bulb-head in the air in her direction, small feelers rippling around its serrated mouth.

"I think it likes you," Alex said.

Cate blew air between her lips as it pulled itself back into its hole. She could just make out a hint of red, as the thing crouched just inside. She stepped back, and could now see that in each of the holes, there was the smooth red head just poised in their opening.

"Jesus." She made a fist of the hand that had touched the sticky web.

"Third find of the century, huh?" Alex grinned. "Best if you don't touch anything."

"Great, thanks for the heads up." Her jaw clenched. "Maybe you should have given me some warning, seeing I'm the one who's never been here." Cate wiped her hand on her leg.

Alex shook his head, and looked up at the hairy trunks. "Never seen this and haven't been here before. We were somewhere else entirely. But I know enough to be wary about anything and everything down here. You've got to remember that this place is as alien to us as we are to it." He looked at her. "It's a very primitive predator-prey environment, and we just dropped right into it."

"I know that. I've spent my entire life studying this type of environment." Cate noticed Alex's expression. "Okay, okay, it was fossilized, but still, I'm not a complete dummy."

"If I thought that, I'd leave you behind." He went to turn away.

"Hey, I saved your life, buster." Her raised voice carried through the silent forest. "And by the way; I can look after myself, and I'm far from being a quivering female." She snorted, her hands on her hips. "I made a choice, and I'm glad I did." She looked up and then out over the forest. "I can hear something." Turning her head, she concentrated. "Sounds like … movement." She pointed to the cliff wall. "From over there."

"I know … and that's where we're going." Alex motioned towards the interior and away from the cliff wall. "We've got a lot of ground to cover, and though we need to travel fast, we need to be cautious every single step of the way. Do not touch anything, do not make unnecessary sounds, and do not, under any circumstances, wander off."

Cate snorted.

"Do you understand?" Alex held her gaze.

She looked away. "Sure, sure, no problem."

*

Casey Franks was first through the broken tunnel wall, standing atop the tumbled boulders and using her gun-light to scan the darkness beyond. After a few more seconds she lowered her weapon.

"Clear."

Dempsey led the rest of the team in. Immediately, the hulking form of Hank Rinofsky walked a few paces forward and held out a small black box, and concentrated on its small screen. He waved it around and then pointed it downwards into the dark void.

"Speak to me, Rhino." Dempsey looked impatient.

Rinofsky whistled. "This mother is *deep*. Got a drop of nearly a mile, before it opens back up." He shook his head. "It's a goddamn labyrinth down there."

Franks yelled from out to the side. "Got steps here, boss."

Aimee saw that just along from them the ledge they all stood on ended at a set of steps cut into the rock face. They were steep, but passable.

Dempsey crossed over and crouched, holding up a flashlight. "Been used recently. But only used one way." He lifted his light higher, looking up into the darkness above him.

Aimee joined him, and saw that the steps went in both directions. "Do you think it could be another way out?" she asked, feeling little confidence.

"Unlikely," Dempsey said. "There was nothing on the surface to indicate an open vent or anything passable." He waved his flashlight around a little more. "Might be worth a look though. If we end up needing someone to dig us out, then closer to the surface, is closer to sunlight." He turned to yell over his shoulder. "Hagel, get up there and do a rec. You got twenty."

"Got it, boss." The young HAWC went up the steps like a mountain goat, and quickly vanished in the darkness above their heads.

Dempsey straightened. "Take five, people, going to be a long climb down." He sat with his back to a rock and unscrewed his canteen lid.

"All downhill, boss. Walk in the park," Rinofsky said with a grin.

"Maybe you should carry us then, ya big moose," Franks said, looking over the edge.

Aimee sipped water, and she offered the canteen to Soong, who shook her head.

"We might need that later. Best to conserve it."

"I don't think finding water will be our problem." She sipped. "But what's in it, might be." Soong looked perplexed, but Aimee didn't feel like explaining herself.

"Yo, boss, got some cave graffiti here." Parcellis aimed his light onto a huge flat wall.

"Does it say: *they went this way?*" Dempsey remained sitting on the ground. "Forget about it."

Aimee and Soong walked along the shelf of rock by themselves, and together they stood before the huge flat wall carved with the ancient glyphs.

"These are very old," Soong said. "Thousands of years. Shenjung would have been interested."

"Many thousands." Aimee felt her stomach knot. There were symbols, whorls, and strokes, some carved in, and some raised in relief. The pattern of writing style hinted at Mayan, Incan, Sumerian, and other ancient languages, and she knew it was perhaps the root of all of them. There were images of birds, snakes, something that could have been a big cat, and a bison type animal. Also, carved in great detail were the faces, with tongues lolling, some gritted teeth. Some had eyes wide and were staring, with looks of anger, and then some portrayed the unmistakable rictus of fear.

Soong turned to her. "You have seen them before?" she asked, and then pointed at one place on the wall. "This one."

The carving was of what looked like a nest of snakes with a giant eye at its center. "It is like one of the ancient demons from ancient Chinese mythology. We call it *Zhàyǔ*. It devours entire souls." Her expression grew dark. "And it lives in the dark of the underworld."

Aimee stared at the carving for a moment longer. "Not any more." Aimee looked away, not wanting to dwell on the thing in the carving, and hoping with every fiber of her being that the creature she had encountered in the past was long dead. She'd seen it die. She went to turn away, but Soong continued to stare.

The Chinese woman stepped even closer, and placed a hand on the carved coiling limbs. She turned to Aimee. "Did you know that our people were missing; the first team at the base? Long before you came, something had entered our camp, we think, from below."

Aimee stared at her for several moments, not wanting to hear the words.

Soong stepped back, but continued to stare at the glyph. "Something also destroyed our rock drill. Something that was already down here." She lowered her light. "And now we go looking for it."

"We'll be fine." Aimee felt a dark depression settling over her. "Let's get back to the group."

*

Redman Hagel felt his thighs burning – he liked the sensation – he liked pushing himself, and after jogging up nearly a thousand steps, sweat streamed and his legs screamed for a break. Now and then he'd send a pulse up ahead, similar to what Rhino had done on the shelf, and then read it as he continued to move. There was a cavern coming up. It appeared to have a ceiling – *about to hit the top*, he thought. According to his reader, there was still a shitload of rock, ice and snow still above them.

He came abreast of the floor. He paused, just letting his beam of light move over the geology for a few moments. Then he slowly lifted himself into the cavern. There was a wall built of stones, not mortared, but dry stacked. He pulled a few out, and leaned in, holding his flashlight up. It was a natural room, of sorts. Old rock carvings on the walls that meant nothing to him, but everywhere he looked there were bones … hundreds of them.

"What the fuck happened here?" He moved his light over the age-browned remnants of humanity, staring down at dark, brittle leg bones, ribs, and small skulls. They were intact, and by the look of the positioning of the bodies, they hadn't died violently. Some had arms wrapped around others, and many were lying out flat as if they had simply gone to sleep. "Ran out of room, so you just walled yourself in and stayed here until you died, huh? Good plan."

Hagel could see among the bodies that there were mineral outlines in the shape of large chisels, hammers, and picks.

"You were digging, but you stopped." He frowned. It didn't make sense. "Why would you stay?" Hagel did a quick survey of the room; there were no other openings. These people had climbed up here from somewhere down below. This wasn't their home, but it became their final resting place.

"You sealed yourselves in. What the fuck for? Were you running from something? Hiding?" He felt a chill on his neck. Something made these people decide this was as far as they'd go, and they would rather die than head back down.

He slid the pulser into a pouch at his waist. "No way, Jose." He started to head back down.

CHAPTER 27

Staff Sergeant Jim Harker knocked once and pushed right into General Marcus Chilton's office. "Banguuo, secure line – urgent." He shut the door behind him.

Chilton raised an eyebrow and pointed to a chair. He then pressed the secure line link. Harker held up a hand, mouthing: *I don't think he's alone.*

Chilton nodded. "General Marcus Chilton, go ahead, General Banguuo."

"I always thought you were a friend, and an intelligent man, General Chilton." There were no pleasantries, and that immediately sent a red flag up. Instead, the voice had a hard edge. "I always thought our mutual interests, and mutual power, meant all things would be discussed before anything ... precipitous, would be embarked upon."

"I'm not following you, General." Chilton stared straight ahead, waiting.

"And I do not follow you anymore. Our Xuě Lóng Base has been destroyed."

Chilton frowned, and pointed to Harker who immediately pulled a computer towards himself and rapidly began to access their link to the VELA satellite data.

Chilton waited for Banguuo to continue. "After our first team vanished, we sent in a new team to find out what happened. Now they are gone too."

Harker turned the screen around, showing satellite images of the Antarctic ice. There was just a blackened scab on the pristine snow where the Chinese base used to be. He shrugged.

Chilton exhaled, looking skyward for a moment. "General Banguuo, I promise you, this is news to me, and I can absolutely guarantee that we had nothing to do with it." He grimaced, knowing there was no way he could be sure of that.

"I see," Banguuo said. "Then who was it that sabotaged the *Kunming* destroyer in the Southern Ocean? A ghost maybe? A ghost that blows holes in our ship, and then swims towards your submarine?"

Chilton remained silent, until a new voice cut across the line.

"Maybe if *someone* were to destroy McMurdo, you would be more interested." This new voice was high with agitation.

Harker mouthed: *Chung Wanlin*. The minister of national defense. But it wasn't a surprise, as Chilton had expected that man would be standing beside his old friend.

"Mr. Wanlin, nice of you to speak up." Chilton's hand clenched into a fist. "But I would strongly suggest you back off that form of language, sir. You don't know where that might end."

"Our people are missing, we think dead. Our base is destroyed, our ship sabotaged. We hold you responsible." Wanlin's voice was cutting. "Our nation demands a response for these insults. You …"

It was Chilton's turn to cut across the Chinese minister. "General Banguuo, I know you have dispatched more naval hardware. I suggest we meet, urgently, so we can – "

"Too late." Wanlin's voice was like a screech. "You ask, where will this end? Perhaps you should have asked yourself that before you began your aggression."

"Listen here, there's something you need – " Chilton spoke through clenched teeth.

The line went dead.

"Goddamnit." He pushed back from the table.

"I don't like the sound of that," Harker said.

"Neither do I." Chilton's eyes narrowed. "Banguuo has been sidelined; that's bad news. That little prick Wanlin is a bureaucrat who wields power without knowing what the effects of that power will be."

He looked up at Harker. "We're committed, but we've got to move this up a level, whether we like it or not. Find out what naval assets we've got available. I want them down there, yesterday ... and get me Jack Hammerson."

*

Time: 26 hours 32 minutes 27 seconds until fleet convergence

Colonel Jack Hammerson disconnected the call from General Chilton and set a digital time banner on his computer for the US contingent of fourteen destroyers, including the new Zumwalt destroyer – a hundred feet longer than any other destroyer, and featuring radar deflective angles and a new type of gun that could shoot rocket-powered warheads up to a hundred miles. Added to this firepower, there would be eight cruisers, six Fast Attack submarines, and two Ballistic and Guided Missile submarines. All were expected to arrive in the Southern Ocean in a little over twenty-six hours, to face off against the massed Chinese vessels. The brass were taking this seriously, and the countdown had begun.

Hammerson sat for several seconds, thinking through the recent events and his next actions.

He fully expected the destroyer to be sabotaged; after all, he had planned it, and the Arcadian had executed it, perfectly. He swung in his seat, hitting keys on his computer. *The Hammer*, as he was known to friends and foes, was the leader of the HAWCs and not one to die wondering. He and his teams relished the hard jobs, and when the going got tough, he just got even tougher.

It was his job to anticipate what his adversary might do. In this regard, he fully expected the Chinese to hit back, *and to try and give us a little taste of what they think we're dishing out.* He smiled; General Marcus Chilton didn't need to tell him to move things up a level. He already had the third portion of his strategy in motion.

Hammerson's screen showed the lifeline of the huge HAWC, Sam Reid, now approaching his drop point on the Antarctic ice sheets. The lifeline was strong and calm. Sam would lead another small HAWC team in and secure McMurdo from any intrusion. He grinned, remembering the huge man's enthusiasm when he had told him of the mission.

Get the Bravo team to the pad, you're going in – and then the kicker – *and get down to Special Weapons, I've requisitioned a full MECH; we're going to take this one head-on, show 'em what real warfare tech looks like.*

Sam had clapped once, springing to his feet, the whine of the pneumatics of his external framework only just perceptible. The big man was still crippled from the lower vertebrae down, but you couldn't tell. Technology had allowed him to function normally – *better than normally.* Hammerson's grin widened. On arrival, Sam would be a two-legged tank.

Hammerson would certainly pay a dollar to see the look on Sergeant Bill Monroe's face when the big HAWC dropped in on McMurdo wearing the formidable body armor. Better yet, he'd give a month's pay to see the look in the PLAs' eyes, when they came face to face with American lethal determination combined with advanced warfare technology.

Hammerson turned back to his screen, sobering. There were three primary mission threads in play now: one, Alex Hunter, still dark; two, Dempsey's team, also now dark; and three, Sam's team, strong and enroute.

"Third time lucky," Hammerson said, sitting back with hands clasped behind his head.

CHAPTER 28

Aimee wiped a forearm up over her brow. The darkness, and the knowledge that perhaps something was lurking within that darkness, was stretching her nerves to the human limit, especially now that she also had to be constantly alert for a potential attack from the PLA.

It seemed like they had been descending into the cave system for hours. Their path led ever downward, the darkness absolute. Even though the carved steps were three feet wide, they all crept along with their backs to the rough-hewn wall. The cave wasn't dry anymore. A humid breeze gently rose up from the depths, and had encouraged all manner of mosses and lichens to grow over the stonework, making them dangerously slick in some places.

At first Aimee had often peered over the edge, but then needed to pull back and wait until her bouts of giddiness passed. There was nothing to see but a fathomless dark, anyway. A while back, Dempsey had stopped to momentarily lean out over the void himself. He'd reached into his slim pack and had drawn free a short stick, which he cracked and shook. It glowed a bright lemon yellow before he dropped it, watching it sail soundlessly into the dark. It didn't strike bottom, and continued on until it vanished completely.

"Deep," was all he said.

"Maybe too deep," Soong added.

"Do you think Captain Yang will give up?" Aimee asked.

"No," Soong replied without hesitation.

"I didn't think so," Dempsey said.

"You *must not* hurt my friend," Soong immediately replied.

"We won't," Aimed added, trying to give Dempsey a hard look that was probably lost in the darkness. "It's why we're here – to talk."

"Right," Dempsey said without conviction.

Rinofsky paused to read from a small box. "Seems like we're all still headed in the direction of the deep earth signal." He looked up. "And that's smack in the middle of Area 24."

"What a surprise," Dempsey said. "Then let's not be late for the party."

"Yo." Hagel clambered back down the steps behind them and jogged to the group. "Nothing up there, boss, no way out."

Dempsey's brow creased. "Why would they build steps to nowhere?"

"Not build, were *building* ... and they were still building them. Nothing left but weird brown skeletons." Hagel's lip curled.

"Fossilized," said Aimee.

"Whatever." Hagel shrugged. "Looks like they were trying to dig their way out, and then just stopped, sat down, and waited to die."

Dempsey snorted. "Ran out of food and water."

"Then why didn't they come back down? Down is easy," Hagel replied.

Dempsey shrugged. "Not our problem."

"Hey, Hagel, wanna know why *down is easy?*" Parcellis asked with a grin. "Because there is a *highway* to Hell, but only a *stairway* to Heaven."

"Shut up, asswipe," Hagel said.

After another hour of descending, the steps finally ended at a bridge of sorts. A three-foot-wide stone pathway across a chasm. On the other side there were two yawning cave openings, their forbidding blackness only a little more inviting than the bottomless chasm below them.

Dempsey stepped to the edge and leaned out. "The updraft's warm; I can smell saltwater." He stared down into the impenetrable depths and sniffed. "And soil ... I can smell earth." He turned to Aimee and grinned. "Looks like we're headed in the right direction – Pellucidar, right? Might be true after all."

Aimee's mouth fell open. "Oh great, you read the report, and didn't believe it."

"Impossible, it cannot be seawater. It must be some sort of geothermal pool disgorging mineral salts," Soong said.

"No, it's not." Aimee turned to her. "It's why we were sent here, and why I need to speak to Zhang Li or Shenjung. What your people are heading towards is an underground lake – huge, warm, and very much alive. And perhaps guarded."

"Guarded ... by Americans?" Soong whispered as she looked away.

Aimee sighed as she could see the distrust on her features.

Dempsey motioned to the bridge. "We need to follow the breadcrumbs. Dr. Weir, would you say it's safe to cross?"

Aimee looked out over the span of stone – old granite, hard, and had probably been in place for too many millennia to count.

"This is where the stairs end, so whoever made the carvings used the bridge. Also, same with the Chinese soldiers, so ..." She shrugged. "If we're careful, it should be fine."

"Good enough for me." Dempsey turned, singling out Rinofsky. "After you. If it holds, then we're all good. And once you're over, keep a lookout for our PLA friends."

Rinofsky snorted and pushed his rifle up over his shoulder. He stepped out, striding the three-foot wide path like a tightrope walker. He got to the middle and turned. "If I die, Captain, just promise me you'll make Franks carry me back up."

"Deal," Franks said. "But I'm only carrying your head, it's the only part of you that's never been used." She grinned.

"I promise to recover your weapons, Rhino." Dempsey folded his arms. "And that makes you next, Franks."

"You got it, Captain." Franks walked out onto the bridge, pirouetting, arms out.

Dempsey shook his head at her, then nodded at Blake to cross next.

Soong walked to the edge, the breeze lifting her hair. "It's so warm."

"Yes," Aimee said.

"Has to be geothermic." Soong's eyes were on the bridge. There was a little terror in them.

Aimee grimaced, feeling her own legs turning to rubber at the prospect of the cross. She hated heights, and hated that she hated them.

"Dr. Weir, Dr. Soong Chin Lang, and your two engineer friends, if you please." Dempsey must have seen something in their eyes, as he clicked his fingers. "Parcellis, lead them across. Hagel at the rear."

Parcellis immediately jumped up onto the bridge. "Dr. Weir, put your hand on my shoulder, just focus on the back of my head. Dr. Soong, you do the same, put your hand on Dr. Weir's shoulder, and ask your colleagues to do the same. We'll take it one step at a time."

Aimee did as he suggested, staring hard at the man's dark hair, noticing a mole on his neck, and the sheen of perspiration on the short-cropped bristles of hair. She shuffled, staring hard, until in another moment, Rinofsky grabbed her arm and eased her forward.

"Easy, huh?" He smiled, but held her upper arm for a moment, until she got her legs back. Soong still had her hand on Aimee's shoulder and Aimee turned to her. The two engineers behind her were still linked to her, one after the other.

"You okay?"

The Chinese scientist nodded, her face pale.

Hagel had walked off, ignoring them both. Dempsey yelled across the chasm. "Rhino, Parcellis, take a cave each. Give me a recon, two hundred feet. Send down some pulses."

The HAWCs nodded and disappeared, quickly being swallowed by an even denser form of darkness.

Dempsey then nodded to the last McMurdo soldiers, Jackson, Hartigan, and Dawkins, and once across, took one last look around the cavern before stepping up on the stone bridge himself.

Dempsey was the last one of them to begin to cross the stone bridge. Aimee turned away as Rinofsky rejoined them, followed by Parcellis. The McMurdo soldiers went into a huddle, and the HAWCs looked at the pulse reader that Rhino had in his hands. Standing apart were Soong and her two colleagues, and Aimee could feel the Chinese woman's eyes on her.

Aimee ran her fingers up through her hair, and then reached into a pocket for a band that she tied her hair up with. She turned back to watch Captain Dempsey finish his cross.

"Huh?" Aimee's mouth dropped open. There looked to be something clinging to the under-side of the bridge, something that must have been out of sight the whole time.

"*Hey!*" Aimee's voice raised a notch, and some of the HAWCs turned towards her.

As she stared, the thing scrabbled around the bridge and silently got to its feet behind Dempsey. It reached for its belt, retrieving two objects and closing on the HAWC captain.

"Look out!" Aimee yelled and pointed.

Dempsey reacted quickly, seeing Aimee's alarm, and then spinning. But the PLA soldier had his blade ready, and buried it into the neck of the HAWC leader. Dempsey used his great strength to continue to turn, the blade sticking out from the muscle bunch at his neck and shoulder. Aimee saw that in PLA soldier's other hand was a squat gray oval – a grenade – getting ready to be thrown among their group. The man was obviously intent on causing as much damage and trauma as he could – this was the ambush they feared. For an insane moment, all she worried about was what Dempsey would say to those who were supposed to be keeping lookout.

"Grenade!" Blake yelled. "Hit the deck!"

Dempsey's hand shot out and closed around the grenade. Time seemed to slow, and Aimee saw the PLA soldier in absolute clarity – every strand of hair, every crease on his face. She also saw that the determination in his eyes was matched by Dempsey.

"No shot." Casey Franks had her gun up like the rest and crabbed to the side. Her yell was echoed by the other HAWCs, the frustration in their words as Dempsey's larger body shielded his attacker.

Both men became locked in place as they looked into each other's eyes – they both knew where this was going to end, and the HAWC captain must have summed up the futility of his predicament. He knew what he needed to do and made the call.

Dempsey hugged the PLA soldier to him and then leapt into the abyss.

"*Fuck!*" Franks's yell was loud in the cavern, but was immediately drowned out by the colossal thump of the explosion that rose up from just fifty feet down into the chasm. They were all thrown off their feet, and then each lay flat, waiting and listening.

Then it came – the pop, the creak, and the splitting of rock. The grinding slide that turned into a roar.

"Take cover!" Franks yelled.

The roof above them simply slid down like a huge wine press, covering one of the tunnel mouths. The rockfall stopped as quickly as it started, but then sand rained down, and seemed pregnant with menace, as though millions of tons of loose rock was held back by just a few grains of sand only waiting for an excuse to crush them flat.

*

Alex froze, hearing and feeling the faint ghosts of the detonation as they pulsed through the stone.

"Did you hear that?" Cate asked. "Sounded like thunder. Does this place have its own weather?"

"No," Alex said without turning. "Not thunder, some sort of an explosive device."

"Explosive dev ...? Great, they're excavating." She caught up to him, grinning. "Look's like they're coming down to get us after all."

"Maybe, but that didn't sound like dynamite, more like the compression shock from a fragmentation device. Military."

Cate turned momentarily to where she believed the sound had come from. "Your people, you think?"

"Don't worry about it; let's keep moving." Alex hoped it wasn't his people – that noise would bring predators as sure as ringing a dinner bell.

*

The booming echoes pounded away along the huge crevasse. The waves of sound and vibrations reached out to every corner, tunnel, and crack in the rock, and finally down to the deepest places.

Silence fell, but only for a few seconds. The liquid sound that followed was heavy, sticky, and sliding, as something colossal heaved itself out of the brackish ooze to test the air. Its huge, muscular body had flattened, spreading over a vast distance, with its enormously strong limbs braced against the rock walls, the sensitive tips feeling the vibrations in the stone, reading them, and waiting momentarily as the final rock debris rained down around it. Boulders dropped and bounced harmlessly from its tough striated muscle hide.

And then came the rain of meat and warm liquid that finally followed from the two small, obliterated bodies. It tasted the morsels, and its skin flared with colors and shapes of delight – it remembered them.

Its enormous tentacle clubs, covered in suckers and hooks formed and reformed into myriad shapes – feline, reptilian, fish, and then human, faster and faster as excitement surged through its body. It began its climb to the higher caves. It surged upwards once again, its soft body flashing with color, a light display revealing its eagerness, and its hunger.

CHAPTER 29

No one moved. A fog of silt and dust hung in the air, and flashlight beams waved about like pipes of light from firefighters in a burning building.

"Clear." Rinofsky was the first to his feet – the ceiling now only a foot over his head.

"Fucking son of a bitch, that bastard was waiting for us." Casey Franks turned to Soong, enough fire in her eyes to scald the woman to cinders.

Aimee stood in front of her. "Forget it, Casey, it's over."

Soong remained expressionless. "He believed he was just doing his job."

"Yeah, stabbing people in the back." Franks jabbed a finger at Soong. "That's some job they're trained to do."

"As far as he was concerned, he killed the enemy leader, and sacrificed himself doing it. Would you do any different?" Soong turned away.

"Fuck, fuck, fuck." Rinofsky was looking down into the chasm, and then overhead at the hanging stone. "Now what?"

"Captain saved us … and the bridge." Hagel looked at the gap. "We can cross back if we need to."

'What the fuck for? It's blocked anyway." Casey spat dust to the cave floor.

"We go on," Aimee said.

"Someone make a call." Rinofsky looked across at the teams. "Who's got seniority?"

Casey Franks exhaled. "Goddamnit ... that'd be me."

"Hey, hey there, hold your horses, girl." Hagel grinned. "I vote for someone with a little more relevant mission experience here. I was on the Afghanistan caves mission." He shrugged. "I can take over."

Casey Franks's teeth looked to be grinding in her cheeks, but the scar pulling her face into a sneer made it hard to tell.

"Hey, asshole, the only one on the team with mission experience is Dr. Weir. Hagel, you went a few hundred feet into a cave one day, so as far as I'm concerned, you got jack shit. This ain't a democracy. I've got seniority, debate over." She glared, and Hagel returned the incendiary stare for a few seconds, before scoffing and turning away.

Casey watched him for another second or two before looking along the assembled faces as though seeking any other objections – there were none.

Aimee walked up close to the stocky female HAWC. "Okay then, let's get going."

"Goddamnit, Dempsey was a good man." Blake shook his head. "You know, we should at least ..."

"He's gone. If he were here, he'd say suck it up, and get your ass moving." Casey Franks's jaw jutted for a moment. "Listen up, people. We got good and bad news. The bad news is, we just lost a good man, and also one of the caves has now collapsed. The good news is, the rest of us are alive, and now we don't have to waste time checking two caves out." She looked to Rinofsky. "Lead us out, big guy."

*

Comrade Han Biao came back in, breathing heavily, his hands and face grazed by multiple wounds, and his body covered in gray rock dust. He snapped to attention when Wu Yang approached.

"Captain Yang." He saluted. "There has been a cave-in."

"A cave-in?" Yang tilted his head. "From an explosion, you mean. I know the sound of a Type 86 grenade when I hear it."

Yang's jaws clenched, and he leaned in. "Why was one of our grenades deployed?"

Han Biao stood rod-straight. "We were attacked ... by the Americans."

"Americans?"

"They must have come down from our base – many of them – following us." He swallowed. "I wanted to stay, but Fan Kai said you needed to be warned ... he stayed. Must have thrown a grenade."

"I send seven of my best PLA, and only one comes back." Yang's eyes were like obsidian chips in the flashlight's glare. "It would be too much to hope that the Americans are all dead."

Yang stared for a moment longer at Han Biao before turning to look along the granite-hard expressions of his men. "And now it seems we are trapped down here ... with them." He could only assume that the Americans were sent to stop him from getting to the submarine, and if they came in via the elevator shaft, then they must have overrun the base.

A serious problem, he thought. This was the time where command could slip, and fear caused stupidity and rebellion. Yang would not let that happen. The men would die on their feet, and never give up; he'd see to that. First he needed a common enemy – fear could kill, but fear could also unite.

"The Americans will try and stop our mission. They will try to kill us all – shoot us dead or bury us alive." He slowly looked at each. "They will *try*." He shook his head. "But they do not know who we are."

Yang spun. "Tell me!" he roared.

As one, came the reply: "*The mountain bows, the ocean splits before us; we are PLA Elite.*" The men shouted the words, the loudest coming from the giant Mungoi, the ogreish man's wide-spaced eyes furious in their fervor.

Yang held up a fist. "We fear no pain, fear no challenge, and fear no death." After a moment, he dropped his hand and looked up above his head into the cave roof as if seeing the light of day, miles above.

"We are too deep, there will be no rescue attempt." He waited, letting the words sink in. "We have been given a mission, and we will complete it." He looked back at his men, but let his eyes rest on Shenjung Xing.

"Mission success first, then, we obliterate the enemy." He pointed to the dust covered Han Biao. "You." Then he nodded to the endless black depths of the cave. "Lead us out, fearless warrior."

*

Hours passed, and the caves led ever downward. Shenjung Xing started to feel a coil of nausea from exhaustion, and wished now that he had spent a little more time exercising instead of researching.

Yang pushed them hard, and Shenjung guessed it was to ensure that physical exertion would leave little room for claustrophobia, dissention, or fear. Sweat streamed as the warmth rose upon the hour, and sometimes the walls closed in so much that he and the soldiers had to move sideways through massive fissures in the walls that looked ominously like they were about to close back up, crushing their insignificant bodies to paste between giant slabs of unyielding granite.

At times he felt like a rat running through a maze in the dark, and often they had to skirt around massive chasms that dropped away to fathomless dark depths. At one, Yang called a halt. The PLA captain went to the edge and crouched. He held up a hand, and the watching soldiers immediately quietened. He closed his eyes, and after a few seconds he half turned.

"Doctor Shenjung, come here, please."

Shenjung approached and crouched beside him.

"Listen," Yang said without turning.

Shenjung stared down into the depths, slowed his breathing, and concentrated. Then, *there it was*, the constant movement of liquid far down below them.

"Perhaps an underground river."

Yang grunted. "This is good news. Water comes from somewhere and goes somewhere." He stood. "Now we have two options – follow its source, or its destination. Either could be a way out. And a way to the sub."

"Maybe not," Shenjung said. "Its origination point might not be a place, but instead could be a thousand hairline cracks in the deep rock that allows seepage." He also got to his feet.

"Then we have an easy choice – its destination will be our goal." Yang put his hands on his hips, his chest out. "Following a river is easier than trying to push upstream anyway."

Shenjung sighed. "Its destination could be nothing more than a buried sea, and we …"

Yang quickly held a hand up to his face, then leaned closer. "Comrade Shenjung Xing, we need to keep the men's spirits high. Do you not agree?"

The man's sudden movement made Shenjung momentarily jerk backwards. But Shenjung knew that hopelessness and fear would be a bigger threat to them than falling into a hole.

"Yes, yes, you are probably right. Perhaps it will lead to the surface somewhere."

Shenjung looked back down into the shadowy depths. *We are heading ever downward*, he thought. *And far away from the light.* He turned to look up at the roof of the cave above him, feeling the oppressive weight of the millions upon millions of tons of stone. He hoped Soong made it out.

"Yes," he said at last. "Water moving that fast will be a powerful erosion factor – and water usually finds its way out."

Yang grunted. "Then let us find that river. Our mission depends on it."

And perhaps all our lives, thought Shenjung.

CHAPTER 30

"Take five." Casey Franks used a forearm to wipe her brow, and then motioned for Aimee to follow her.

The cavern they were now in was dust-dry and the size of a football field. The HAWCs immediately sat and sipped water, sparingly, but no one ate – all resources were finite now. Casey continued to walk Aimee a few paces away, and Soong stood watching with arms folded, looking edgy around the McMurdo soldiers and the HAWCs.

Casey blew air through compressed lips and stepped in closer to Aimee. "I'm flying blind here. We keep tracking the sub, and blow the shit out of anything that gets in front of us. But then what? I have no idea how to climb us back out." She grimaced. "I can incapacitate an armed combatant in three seconds, can pilot a chopper, a tank, and even disable a nuke if I have to, but down here, that asshole Hagel is right; I'm outta my depth." She raised her eyebrows. "Your report – you've been down here. You made it out. What am I supposed to do?"

Aimee ran one hand up through her slick hair. "What we do is survive." She knew that their options were to wander around in the caves until their food, water, and lights ran out, and then just sit down and wait to die. Or maybe die horribly, but quickly, somewhere lower down. She looked past Casey to the lounging HAWCs, all armed and formidable. Casey was the same. If she gave them a choice, it'd be to face the horrors, to fight, and then perhaps prevail. None would choose lying down and dying in the darkness.

"We found a way out before. It's sealed now, but only by ice and snow. Hammerson knows where that is." She exhaled. "First we need to find our way down to the sea." She worked at sounding confident. "You've read the reports, you know what to expect. But we *can* make it."

"Yeah, I've read the reports. I didn't believe them." Franks raised an eyebrow. "The monster under the ice, *huh*?"

"You guys better wise up." Aimee sighed. "I've been there, and I've survived. You like to fight. Well, you'll damn well get your chance." She gave Casey a crooked half smile. "High risk of death, for the chance at life. Good deal, huh?"

Franks smiled back, the scar on her cheek making it look like a permanent sneer. "Fight or die. Yeah, I'll take that."

Aimee looked over Casey's shoulder. "The caves are still sloping downwards. That's where we need to go. Once we find the sea, if we're anywhere near where I last was, I can find our way to the tunnels that lead close to the surface. Then we need to get a message out for them to dig down to us."

Casey put a thumb in her belt. "Hey, on the bright side, if those warships face off up there, this may be the safest place to be."

"Maybe." Aimee reached out to grasp Casey's shoulder, and pulled her a little closer. "Just remember, as we get nearer to the water, we may encounter the predator mimic."

"The what?" Jennifer tilted her head. "The predator what?"

"Great," Franks said. She half turned to Jennifer, but kept her eyes on Aimee. "It's nothing."

"No, it's not, Lieutenant." Aimee straightened. "And if we're going lower, then I think everyone has a right to know what we might have to deal with down here."

"It's not gonna help," Casey said, folding her arms and looking away.

"What isn't?" Dawkins said, coming closer, trailed by Big Ben Jackson.

Aimee could feel their eyes boring into her. Even the other HAWCs were watching. What she had told them at McMurdo could never prepare them for what may still be down here, lurking in the darkness. She didn't want to frighten them, but maybe if that fear led to caution, then maybe, just maybe, it was a good thing. She drew in a breath.

"Back up at the base, I told you that I had been down here before. Of the several dozen people that went into the caves, only three of us made it out alive. What I never told you was what tracked us, and killed nearly all of us." She folded her arms tight on her body, her eyes rooted to the cave floor as she spoke.

"The thing was an apex predator of extraordinary size and intelligence. It doesn't exist anywhere on the surface, and hasn't for millions of years. It was similar to the orthocone cephalopods …"

"Cephala-*what*? Hey, I missed my last science class, Doc. What the hell is that?" Dawkins glanced from Aimee to Ben Jackson, and then back.

Aimee faced Dawkins, her gaze level. "A cephalopod is from the Mollusca family – octopuses, squid, cuttlefish, and Nautiloids. They're old, been here for nearly half a billion years, give or take. This thing is like that, an orthocone, one of the oldest from our fossil record, but they were nothing like this thing. Down here it'd grown big … *very big*."

"How big can it be, if it can fit in here?" Jackson glanced sideways.

Aimee tried to remain dispassionate, and let the scientist in her take over. "Ben, we can't fit into anywhere smaller than our skulls. But this thing is boneless and made up of pure striated muscle mass. It's enormously powerful, and can also flatten its cell structure down to be able to fit its tentacle tips in just about anywhere." She grimaced, but quickly corrected herself. "And size? Maybe blue whale, maybe bigger."

"Oh fucking great," Dawkins said. His mouth stayed hung open and his chipped tooth was now showing. "And it's down here, now?"

Aimee looked at him, her eyes unblinking. "We thought we killed it, but all I really know is that we buried it. So I just don't know for sure."

"Oh god." Jennifer turned to glare at Casey. "What did you get us into?"

Casey's expression was flat. "Hey, I'm here." She held up her gun. "And we're also damn dangerous predators."

"Dr. Weir." Big Ben Jackson cleared his throat. "You said it was a *mimic*; what did you mean by that?"

"Yes, I did." Aimee nodded. "Perhaps another evolutionary adaption to allow it to get close to its prey. It has the ability to mold parts of itself into shapes; even human shapes. It tricked some of our team, got close to them, and then attacked. So don't trust everything you see in the dark."

Casey scoffed. "Hey lady, down here, it's *all* dark."

Aimee stared hard, and Casey held up a hand. "Okay, okay, we got it." She went to turn away, but Aimee grabbed her elbow.

"One more thing; stay out of the water."

"The water? I thought you said it hunted in the caves." Casey frowned.

"No, this is something else," Aimee said softly.

"Something ... *hey*." Casey spun to Soong who had appeared silently behind her and touched her shoulder. "What is it?"

"Excuse me." The woman bit her lip. "But my colleagues, Lee Pinying and Bo Xingmin ... they are not here anymore."

"Not here?" Casey then tilted her head back. "Oh for fuck's sake. Is it too much to ask that we at least *try* and stay together?" She looked over Soong's head. "Rhino, Hagel, Parcellis, find our Chinese friends; they've gone for a walk."

*

"That PLA soldier, he was one of us, but didn't care if we were killed in the blast or not." Bo Pinyin slowed as he spoke, fiddling with his pants. His shirt was already open, his tattooed chest wet from perspiration.

"No, not one of us." Lee shook his head. "To them we are nothing. But remember, if the Americans are successfully ambushed by the PLA, we tell them that we were taken hostage by them." He half turned. "And hurry, they are getting too far in front. I do not like this place." Lee held up his lantern light. "And I can barely hear them anymore." He turned back to the darkness, his brow creased. "Hurry up!"

Bo Pinyin was standing over a small opening in the cave floor and wall, his fly open and a solid stream of urine disappearing into the crack. He grinned in the light.

"Maybe it will drip down on Captain Yang's head?"

Lee turned away. "Just hurry." He wished he'd never come. The job was a lucrative contract, but now it seemed there wasn't enough money in all of China to make it worthwhile. Behind him his colleague grunted, and Lee turned back to rouse on him again. "Hey ..."

Lee was at first disgusted by the man thrusting his hips into a crack in the cave wall. He looked like he was trying to violently fuck the wall, but his face was warped with agony and horror.

"What are you doing?" Lee approached – one, two steps, and then three. He held up his lantern light. Bo was grunting and pounding himself right into the wall. Lee reached out for him, but just as his hand alighted on his shoulder, there came a weird sensation of suction against his calf. He looked down and saw his foot spanned the crack that Bo had urinated into, but now something was rising from it to encircle his boot and leg. At its very tip there was a small dark orb, and Lee knew immediately that it saw him as clearly as he saw it.

"*Yi, look!*" Lee quickly turned to his friend, but strangely Bo wasn't there anymore. He yelped and tugged, but the thing suckered on tighter, and then something dug into his flesh.

He screamed now, the pain becoming infinitely worse as the thing wormed its way further up his leg, and dug in deeper to the meat of his thigh. Then it started to drag him down. Lee's scream quickly turned to a long howl of agony.

*

Rhino and Parcellis checked their weapons, as Hagel leaned against a wall, chuckling. "Hey, Franks, seriously? After hearing the doc's Halloween stories, you want to split us up?"

"Get moving, or I'll make you go alone, wise guy." Casey went to turn away, just as the hideous scream ripped through the darkness, making even the toughened HAWCs cringe.

"What the fuck was that?" Dawkins looked about to panic and Aimee grabbed him by the sleeve, hanging on tight. She looked to Casey.

The female HAWC swung back to Rhino, Hagel, and Parcellis, and motioned with her head to the cave mouth. "Double time."

The three HAWCs didn't blink, but instead spun and sprinted into the darkness. Jennifer babbled, and Dawkins's eyes were wide and shining. Only Ben Jackson stood like a colossus in the mouth of the cave, legs braced.

Casey paced, her gun cradled in her arms. It was only a few more minutes before the three HAWCs came back to the huddled group. Rhino lifted one of the missing men's lantern lights, still glowing.

"Nothing; there's nothing, no sign of them."

Soong's fists were balled at her chest. "They ran off? I don't believe it."

Hagel pointed at the lantern. "Without a light? I don't believe it either. That little tattoo guy was sticking to us like glue."

"Then what?" Jennifer said. She spun to Casey. "The PLA?"

"Maybe," Casey said.

"We *must* look for them immediately," Soong said quickly.

Casey shook her head, looking off into darkness. "No, we don't."

Soong went quickly to grab at Aimee's arm. "Please, Dr. Weir. We must find my colleagues."

Aimee gently pulled her arm free, and rested a hand on Soong's shoulder, looking into the Chinese woman's face. "They're gone." She stepped away from the woman and turned to Casey. "We need to move."

Hagel hooted. "Oh yeah, that is one stone-cold bitch."

Casey Franks looked into Aimee's eyes for a second or two, perhaps reading what was there, before turning away. "Move out. Double time."

CHAPTER 31

The languid stream moved like oil as it traveled away into the seemingly endless dark cave. Captain Wu Yang walked out into the water to his knees, and dipped a hand, cupping some water and lifting it, shining his flashlight into it and examining it closely. He sniffed, then squinted – there seemed to be tiny dust motes floating in the liquid – rock particles maybe. He flicked his hand, and waded out further to his thighs, shining his flashlight down into the water.

"So, if need be, at least we will not die of thirst." He turned back to his team. "But for now, do not drink. Only what's in your canteens." He wiped his hands, carefully walking from the water and over to where Shenjung Xing stood slightly apart from the soldiers.

"So, Comrade Shenjung, we follow the river, and hope it comes out at the coast or surfaces somewhere shallow enough for us to break through, yes?"

Shenjung looked from the water to the PLA captain, and then shrugged. "All options present the same chance of success or failure." He turned back towards the dark, slow moving liquid. "But I agree that following the stream might take us to an area where we can potentially breach."

Yang grunted. "We follow the river." He looked at his signal locator. "Good; this is also the direction the beacon is emanating from, so maybe this is where the American submarine became wedged under the ice." He lifted his flashlight, squinting into the darkness. "If the cave narrows any more, we will need to take to the water." He turned, pointing to several of his men. "Switch off your lights. Lead and rear lights only – we need to preserve our resources now."

Yang clicked his fingers. "Han Biao, Liu Yandong, take the scouting position, one hundred feet. *Go.*"

The two men half bowed and Shenjung watched as they jogged out along the black sandy bank. Yang turned to Shenjung, his voice lowered.

"Doctor, I estimate we have food for another forty-eight hours. We can survive without that for much longer. Water is now not a problem. But our batteries will soon be exhausted, and our lights will then yellow and fade. We can extend their life by conservation of usage, but ..." He turned to the winding watercourse in the pitch cave, before returning to look at Shenjung with a humorless smile. "Darkness has a way of breaking the strongest of us, Doctor. It would be best if we found our way out long before the lights go out."

Yang heard the faint scream come at them in a wave from somewhere far back, or was it far ahead? Flashlight beams came on, and flicked back and forth, before Yang barked at his men to shut them down.

"Nothing. Rocks settling, or water. *Nothing.*" He glared, and then turned to Shenjung. The scientist nodded once, but then looked away.

Yang turned back to the darkness, straining to hear anything more. He licked dry lips; he knew a man's cry of fear when he heard it. Maybe one of the engineers was following them and slipped into a crevasse. He concentrated, but save for the faintest movement of water, there was silence.

He turned back to the soldiers. "*Hoy!*" They assembled and he led them down the river cave.

*

PLA commandos Han Biao and Liu Yandong jogged along the riverbank and then out of sight around the bend in the cave.

"Slow now," Liu said as he began to walk.

"But Captain Yang said a hundred feet; we are only about half that," Han Biao responded, not caring for Liu's tone.

"Yang isn't here. They take a break while we run in the dark. You run if you want." Liu held up the only flashlight, moving the beam over the bank and walls.

Beneath their boots, the black sand scrunched and squeaked, and stuck to the iron lace holes in their boots. Beside them the water made little sound except for the occasional plink or gurgle as a tiny wave splashed up against the cave sides.

Liu shined the light on the far wall and it wetly reflected his beam back at them. "This stream has probably been traveling like this, far below the ground, for millions of years. It has probably never seen the sun." He pointed the light at Han. "Do you think we will find our way out?"

Han held a hand up to block his colleague's light. "If the water can find a way out, then we can too." He turned away, rubbing at a spot on his shoulder where the toughened uniform material was torn from the previous cave-in. He rolled his shoulder, feeling the abrasion there, and knowing he carried several more cuts and contusions underneath his clothes. When they next rested, he would need to attend to his wounds. If his wounds became infected and he became too ill to walk, he doubted Yang would suggest he be carried.

Liu nodded. "I hope so." He dropped the circle light from Han Biao. "I would hate to have to eat you when we ran out of food."

Han Biao grinned. "I think we will all be eating Changlong, he is the fattest of all of us."

Liu stared back along the watercourse. After a moment, his words were softer. "Maybe we should have tried to dig our way back out of the tunnel at the cave-in. At least we'd know where we were then."

Han Biao sighed, and then shook his head. "I think it collapsed for dozens of feet, and some of the rocks were big as trucks. You would need dynamite, and after a cave-in like that, who would dare use explosives? We will either find a new way out, or …"

"We eat Changlong." Liu scoffed softly. "Or we go mad in the dark." He turned away. "Let's go."

Up ahead the tunnel curved and their riverbank ended, making the opposite side of the watercourse the one with the dry bank. The men stopped and Liu walked a few feet into the water and held the flashlight out and down. "I don't think it's too deep. We will need to cross." He motioned with the light. "Go across and scout around the bend."

Han Biao thought briefly about arguing over who should cross, but he knew that sooner or later they all would need to, so he immediately waded into the ink-black water, heading for the opposite bank.

The river wasn't broad, no more than thirty feet across, and even though the ambient temperature was quite warm, Han Biao didn't relish the idea of getting soaked. But, his next step plunged him to his chest, and the icy water flowed up and around him, with just a blanket of warmth on his face. He cursed, hearing Liu bray with laughter.

At least the coolness bathed his numerous cuts and abrasions, and hopefully the pristine cave water washed them clean of any debris that had stuck to the wounds. He held his hands up and bounced now, his buoyancy allowing jumps across the languid current, as his feet squished in a slimy mud at the bottom.

In another few moments, he had left the water and strode up on the far bank, stamping his wet boots. He could see that this shoreline was unbroken for as long as the light could reach.

"It continues on. We will travel from here now." Han Biao sat and unlaced his boots, pulling one off and upending it.

Liu quickly waded across, avoiding the hole that Han Biao had stepped into. In a moment he came up the bank, and sat next to his friend.

"We wait for them." Liu switched off his light.

Han Biao nodded, and sat shivering from the cold, and then held himself in check, not wanting Captain Yang to see him show any discomfort.

In another moment, they could see the lights of the group approaching. He reached up to scratch at a tingling itch at one of the larger abrasions on his chest.

Good, he thought – *first sign of healing.*

*

Minutes before, minuscule fragments of Han Biao's clothing, skin, and blood had been washed ahead of him down the river, and within an environment that was near devoid of life, and food, every scrap was eagerly sought and pursued. From beneath the mud, from out of cracks in the submerged cave wall and floor, tiny thread-like heads pushed out to sample the water, waving back and forth momentarily, tracking its source, before launching themselves, sperm like, their tiny tails flicking madly towards Han Biao. Above the water, the man felt nothing, as his body, and every scrape, cut, and graze on it, became a source of great interest to the worms.

*

"That's water ... running water." Casey turned back to Aimee, Soong, and the soldiers. "And there's more humidity."

"Yes, I can smell it; we must be close," Aimee said. She was the only one allowed to use a flashlight, and she kept it pointed at the ground. The HAWCs had switched to night-scopes, and the McMurdo team walked in the dark, following Aimee's beam. The tunnels were narrowing now, and they only permitted single file movement. Around the group, the darkness was becoming a living thing, and Aimee could feel the weight of the stone around her as if it lay heavily on her shoulders.

The stocky female HAWC led them on, followed by Soong and Aimee, then Parcellis, Hagel, Blake, Dawkins, and Jennifer Hartigan. Bringing up the rear, were the hulking forms of Ben Jackson and Hank Rinofsky. Both Jackson and Rhino were having a difficult time with the caves narrowing and the pace was slowing with both having to move side-on to navigate. Aimee knew that if the space shrunk any more, then Rinofsky and Jackson would either have to find another way, or they'd all have to double back.

From time to time, Aimee would look over her shoulder. It was an eerie sensation, because although the team was strung out with several feet between each of them, all she saw was the intermittent red dots over the eyes of the HAWCs. She knew they saw her, but unless she lifted the flashlight to them, they were invisible.

We're ghosts in the land of the dead, she thought glumly, and shook her head. *What am I doing here?* She swallowed down a lump in her throat. *I'm sorry, Joshua, I made a terrible mistake.*

The image of his beautiful face floated in the darkness, and she drew comfort from it. She saw him laughing, playing, eating, even arguing – all the small moments of their life together. She had raised him from nothing, and all by herself. She was his everything, and he was hers. She sniffed, seeing his tiny face sleeping, the features so relaxed, so innocent, and so … helpless. *What the hell was I thinking?* she thought miserably, and dragged a forearm across her eyes, wiping away tears, but also grinding dust into them, making them worse.

She heard her son's voice then: "You need to bring him home."

I'll try, she whispered, and, with her head down, she walked on, step after step.

From time to time, the group passed over fissures in the stone – sometimes they needed to step across them in the floor, and other times the wall beside them was torn, as if titanic hands had ripped the stone asunder.

Casey held up a fist, causing Aimee to nearly stumble into Soong. The female HAWC stood frozen for many seconds. Aimee crept up closer, collapsing Soong into the HAWC.

"What is it?"

"Listen," Casey whispered.

Aimee concentrated, and then held her breath. There was a soft rapid dripping, somewhere off in the darkness. Other than that there was nothing, there wasn't even breathing, as everyone seemed to be holding their breath.

"I think …"

Casey's fist was still up, but she flicked a finger to quiet Aimee.

Aimee concentrated again, and then she heard it, or rather, *stopped* hearing it.

"The dripping … it's stopped."

"Yeah," Casey said softly. "It's been doing that as if it's shutting off and on." She half turned. "Or something is getting in and out of water. Any ideas?"

Aimee felt a coiling in her stomach, but pushed it down and shook her head. "Could be a lot of things. But at this depth, the water seepage should be consistent."

"Seasonality, variable sinking points, chemical blockages," Soong said, looking at each woman. "But this happens over longer extended periods – months and years, not minutes."

Casey's eyes slid from Soong back to Aimee. "Or something or someone passing underneath the flow?" She waited for a response.

Aimee just shrugged, not wanting to advance any theories that would panic anyone ... *yet*.

Casey pulled her M18X rifle from over her shoulder, and waved them on. "Eyes on, people. Don't want to run into our PLA friends." She turned to raise an eyebrow at Aimee. "Or anything else."

CHAPTER 32

"Do you know what one of my favorite books was, when I was a kid?" Cate Canning stood with hands on hips, smiling dreamily. "*At the Earth's Core*." She turned slowly, sighing. Alex ignored her.

"It was written by Edgar Rice Burroughs, just over one hundred years ago. It's about a hidden world within our world."

"*Hm-hmm*." Alex stopped to use his scanner once again.

"Do you know how the scientists first got there?" She knew he probably wouldn't know, so continued. "They used a machine they called the 'Iron Mole' to drill down through the crust. Guess from where?" She waited this time.

"I'm guessing, the South Pole," Alex said without looking up.

"Exactly. Is this not fiction becoming true?"

"I preferred his Tarzan series myself." Alex half smiled, but motioned to the deeper forest. "C'mon, this way."

They threaded their way through the hairy trunks of the Prototaxites and pulpy looking plants pushing back at them at waist level. But as they moved further from the shoreline, the flora changed, becoming more dense and, if possible, even stranger.

Cate pointed as she walked, giving Alex a running commentary. "Glossopteris, or some sort of gymnosperm, anyway. *Hmm*, but the leaves are all wrong." She paused to look up at the twilight ceiling. "You know, it's like a Valdivian rainforest, but it survives with little light. All these plants are relics from the Pangaean supercontinent. They share common characteristics from relic forests, but have adapted, just like ferns and mosses, to a permanent low-light environment."

She strode across a large pile of what looked like dried sphagnum moss. "Hundreds of millions of years ago, ferns learned how to share genetic material to allow them to survive in extremely low-light environments. I think the plants here have done the same. They're now getting most of their nutrients from the soil."

"Not just from the soil." Alex pointed to a weird looking tree trunk that had what appeared to be a huge spiny bug wrapped tight in sticky tendrils. "Seems they're quite happy to eat a bit of meat now and then."

Cate snorted and walked closer to the glistening mass. "Blood and bone – we feed it to our roses."

"Looks like it's self serve down here." Alex's head whipped around. "Hey, hold up."

"Huh?" Cate turned, and seeing his face, spun to also stare into the dark forest. "What is it?"

"Movement," Alex said. "Back up."

Cate eased back, one foot carefully behind the other. Her rear foot sank into a mat of the sphagnum moss, eliciting a hiss, and then something shot from underneath it. It moved like a snake, but with small spindly legs flicking madly. Cate leapt backwards.

"Shit!"

"*Quiet!*" Alex turned, frowning. "It was just a snake."

"It had legs. You know, it could have been a *dinilysia*. That was one of the snake's earliest ancestors." She kicked over the moss-mound, revealing a clutch of small eggs. She knelt down and reached into the pile, lifting one and squeezing it slightly. "Soft shell." She shook her head. "I would kill to bring one of these back."

Alex grunted. "Good to know we won't starve."

Cate looked horrified. "Over my dead body."

Alex half smiled. "You go a few days without food, you'll eat 'em, and eat 'em raw." He motioned to the forest. "Come on ... and watch where you step, Professor."

Cate exhaled, loitering for a moment before getting to her feet. "You know what?" She grinned. "My bucket list is now officially empty."

Alex half turned. "Mine still has *get out alive* in it, and about now, it's close to the top." He turned away. "Let's follow the path."

"Yeah, right, *the path*," Cate said, scoffing. "You do know this is a game trail?"

"I know … but I'm kinda hoping it's an old and unused one right now," Alex said without turning.

They walked in silence for another fifteen minutes, Cate stopping from time to time to examine something on a trunk, or among the forest floor debris. She wiped her brow.

"It's so hot down here. Must be geothermal activity."

"Yeah."

Cate followed Alex, her head craned to the ceiling again. "The blue glow makes it look like late sunset. The sun has just gone down, but the last blush of light remains – *beautiful*. It's some sort of bioluminescence – either floral or faunal."

"Glow worms." Alex looked up. "Billons and billions of them."

Cate snorted. "I should probably just shut up. But you know what? If you shared a bit more, it would save me from having to flap my lips all the time." She increased her pace to catch up. "And how the hell doesn't anyone know about this place?"

Alex stopped and turned. "Because if they did, there'd be a thousand of you on the ice, and a hundred of you below it. This is a designated restricted zone – off limits to everyone. It's no greenhouse, or petting zoo, or nature sanctuary, where you walk behind safety barriers. I lost an entire team down here, and it is the most deadly place on Earth, bar none."

"Under," Cate said. "Not on Earth, but under it."

Alex half smiled, but it held little humor. "You need to take this very seriously, Professor Canning. Just about every second creature down here will either eat you, try to eat you, or at least do a good job of making a damned mess out of you."

"Oh, we're back to Professor Canning now, are we?" She waited, hands on hips, but Alex didn't bite. She exhaled loudly. "Okay, okay." Then titled her head. "It's just, I've studied this all my life." She waved a hand around. "But it's always been echoes of the real thing that vanished millions of years ago. I can't count the number of times I sat alone, wondering what some of these things would be like if they were alive today – what color would they be? What would they sound like, smell like? And now ..." She grinned, arms out.

"I know all I need to know. We stay away from them, we stay alive." Alex checked his tracker. "Come on."

They marched on, and soon the land dipped and became spongy beneath their feet. Water squelched up with every step they took, and the plants lifted themselves up even higher on long mangrove-like root legs. The smell of damp and rot was all-pervading.

Cate bent and swished her hand through a puddle. "It's almost hot." She sniffed her fingers. "Fresh, but very brackish."

"Careful," Alex said. Their pace slowed, as they needed to weave around ponds that held greenish water of unknown depths. In one, an insect the size of a cherry flew lazily over the surface, to suddenly be speared from the oil-still surface and then vanish below its green algal blanket.

Cate watched, transfixed for a second or two, before going and kneeling beside one of the larger ponds. Bubbles popped and the surface swirled with languid movement below. She grabbed the stem of a fern frond to wipe it across the water's surface, so she could see into its depths.

"*Ha.*" She dipped the frond in like a giant paddle, dragging it back towards herself. She hauled her prize up onto the soggy bank.

The foot-long black creature flipped and flopped, looking glossy black under the blue light of the bioluminescent glow from the ceiling.

"Pollywog," she said and grinned up at Alex.

"Is that what I think it is?" he asked.

"Yep, *that*, is a tadpole ... a huge, monstrous tadpole." She cursed. "*Arg*, why didn't I bring a camera? I'm an idiot." She got to her feet. "When I was a kid, I had a stream down at the far edge of our yard that had frogs, eels, and tortoises living in it. I spent hours just lying on the bank watching them." She used the frond like a broom to sweep the tadpole back towards the water. "I bet that's a Beelzebufo ampinga larvae. Called the *devil frog* – long extinct on the surface, but it had jaws like a bear trap and grew to nearly two feet in length. Could've eaten a small dog."

She dropped the frond. "Hmm, but why can't we hear them? Frogs are some of the noisiest creatures on the planet. Something that big should be near deafening."

"That, like most things down here, has learned to be quiet. So should you." Alex pointed off into the distance where there was a rise to a rocky plateau – it was miles away. "I think there's a waterfall way back there. That's where the fresh water is coming from, and I'm betting they all empty into the sea around here. There'll be a stream we can follow. The signal seems to be coming from the far cliffs."

Cate continued to look out over the pond. She inhaled deeply, drawing in all the scents of brackish water, decay, damp mosses, and rich earth. *I'm in a prehistoric jungle miles below the earth's surface.* She smiled at the insane thought. From when she was a little girl, poking sticks into frog ponds, or turning over stones in tidal pools, this was what drew her to her profession like a magnet. It was what she had dreamed of – *no, not this* – this was beyond anything she could have dreamed. Her smile widened and she looked over her shoulder at Alex, the man's dangerously handsome features now twisted in either contemplation or concern. But she wasn't concerned; down here felt like she had landed right in heaven. She knew she would never, ever get this chance again.

Alex turned to her, catching her looking at him. "At least we get to move out of this coastal jungle." He raised his eyebrows. "But no more diversions until we get there. We're not here for a picnic, got it?"

"Nope." She turned back to the pond. "No more."

Alex turned. "What? Tired, need a break?

"Not at all. In fact, I'm totally invigorated." Cate waved an arm about. "See this? *All of this?* It's my life's work. So, no, I'm not asking for a picnic, just a minute or two now and then, and maybe you can share a little more of what you know." Alex ignored her, and she folded her arms. "You wouldn't even be down here if not for me."

Alex turned, his expression hardening for a moment. "Maybe. Look, I know we have different objectives. But as soon as we find the submarine, then you can spend a little time on exploration – provided it's safe. Okay?

"No, Alex." She smiled flatly. "*This* is both my objective *and* my passion. All my life I've dreamed of this, ever since I was that kid lying on a muddy bank somewhere. How can I pass it by?" She shrugged. "I can't. You go find your missing submarine; it's your job. But for me, my job is this ... *paradise*." She waved an arm about again. "You go, I'll be fine. Swing past on the way back."

"Oh for Chrissake." Alex rubbed a hand up through sweat-slicked hair. "Cate, down here is nothing like you've ever known. It's not the Everglades, it's not the Congo, or even the Amazon, and it sure as hell isn't a paradise. It's hell for human beings – everything down here wants to eat you. I can't begin to ..."

She held up a hand. "I know, I know." She shrugged. "I'll be careful."

Alex stared at her for a few moments. He pulled one of his Ka-bar knives from a sheath at his back, and handed the seven-inch black blade to her.

"I can't promise I'll be back. So stay silent, keep your head down, and ... good luck." He turned and left.

Cate stood open-mouthed for a moment, not really expecting him to simply leave. "Wow." She stuck the blade on her belt. "Thanks, and you still owe me a drink."

He was already gone.

*

Cate had used the knife to sharpen the stalk of a dried frond into a multi-purpose spear, walking stick, and probe, and used it to carefully move through the thickening fronds. Perspiration ran down her face and stung her eyes. She had pulled the wetsuit down and tied its arms around her waist. Her white t-shirt was already stained and stuck slickly to her from the rivulets of sweat that streamed from her.

She stopped and lifted her canteen to her lips. It was only a third full. Not good, as she was losing a lot of fluid. She'd need to find water soon, as drinking the brackish pond-soup was out of the question. She felt confident, as she'd been in jungles before, and one thing a place like this wasn't short of was drinkable water – *you just need to know where to look.* She pushed through another frond barrier and grinned.

"Oh wow."

There was a small lake, around a hundred feet across, with an algae-covered island about forty feet out at its center. Heavy fronds overhung the water's edge, and there was the soft purr of insect wings beating furiously as they hovered over the surface.

"I'm in heaven," she whispered and squatted on the bank, pulling herself into a small ball and gripping her knees. A smile of wonder on her lips, she was content to just stay idle and watch as a scene straight from prehistory played out in real time, just for her.

She stayed motionless, letting her eyes move along the bank. On the far side, there was a fallen tree trunk, and a shiver of movement caught her attention. Crawling along its top was a reptile – no, not a reptile – the breath caught in her throat. It was something far more fantastic.

The creature turned in her direction, staring with ruby-red eyes. It was about six feet long and had a stiff sail along its back. It was mottled green and brown, and expertly camouflaged. Its hide wasn't scaled, but instead was pebbled and leathery, and it ended in a box-like head that looked like it was made of solid bone. Powerful jaws hung open, and were studded with needle-like teeth.

"*Dimetrodon*," she whispered. "But you guys were as big as rhinos. Are you a juvenile?"

She squinted, concentrating. The creature didn't look young. "Perhaps you've shrunk."

Dwarfism maybe, she thought. The same thing happened to mammoths when they were trapped on islands. Over many millennia, they grew smaller to fit their environments. The last vestiges of the great beasts were in Crete, where the population was all under four feet tall, she remembered. *This is an entire world down here, but a small one.*

Giants in the water, but maybe everything else had shrunk to accommodate their smaller landmass. "A world of tiny dinosaurs." She grinned, feeling safer by the second. "But big frogs. Hey, I can live with that."

The *Dimetrodon* slipped away. *Damn*, she thought, watching for a few moments for it to reappear. Eventually, she turned back to the pond. The water was dark and didn't look inviting in any way, but she longed to see what was below the surface. There was occasional movement as the pondweed swirled, meaning something was moving beneath the algal blanket.

Cate tried to imagine what sort of creatures there could be, her imagination fired by the previous monstrous tadpole. There'd been bony fish around for hundreds of millions of years, and primitive air-breathing lungfish and their lobe-finned variants since the Paleozoic period.

The pond surface swirled and flipped only half a dozen feet from the bank where she crouched. She desperately wanted to get a glimpse of what was in the water. After all, she had ditched Alex Hunter to observe this world, so …

She lifted her sharpened stick, looking at its end, thinking, justifying. *She could spear one – just one – all in the name of science*, she convinced herself. She got slowly to her feet and walked carefully down the bank.

She placed one foot in the water, and paused, looking up to check her surroundings. She frowned. The small island at the pond's center seemed closer – now only about twenty feet from the bank. She watched it for a moment. A large bug alighted on it, and then flew away. Everything was still and quiet. *An optical illusion or I'm just tired*, she thought.

Cate placed another foot in the water, and stared down, frowning again. It was no use, the darkness made even the shallow water difficult to see. She pulled her flashlight, flicked it on, and pointed the beam down. She crouched.

Life, lots of it. Things whirled and whizzed past her circle of light. There were crustaceans, but unlike anything she had ever seen living or from any fossil record. Long bodies, spines on their backs, and jagged claws held out stiffly before them. A tiny eel wriggled past, and then something like a salamander with a wedge-shaped head momentarily investigated the light before twisting away.

Cate stood slightly bent over and leaned out further. From the new angle she could see something bumping along in the shallows.

She moved quickly, spear poised, but then smiled and turned to toss the spear up onto the bank behind her. She bent over to scoop up the creature.

"Hello, beautiful." She grunted from the weight and turned the foot-and-a-half long thing around to look into its face. It was some sort of tortoise, with a bony head and heavily clawed toes. Its shell was oval and the huge plates overlapped almost like giant scales that had been welded together into its armor.

"Hmm, *Pleurosternon*, maybe, or something new?" The thing hissed in her hands, its beak snapping at the air. "Easy there, fella. I'm not going to eat you." She looked at the patterning on its back – more like wood grain than the usual tortoise coloring. Tortoise were long-lived creatures, and as everything else here had a nice coating of moss and algae, the tortoise's shell should too.

"How did you avoid getting covered?" She put it down on the bank, and flipped it over, eliciting another round of furious hissing as the thing bicycled its legs in the air.

"Oh, hell."

The answer became clear – because it hadn't lived long enough – *yet*. The creature was a juvenile. The pond water surged slightly up on the bank in front of her. Cate's head whipped up, alert now. The small island was even closer, only a dozen feet from the bank ... *and from her*.

She flipped the baby tortoise back into the water, and rose slowly to her feet.

"Sorry mama, no harm no foul." She started to back away from the water. Alex Hunter's words run again in her ears: *Everything down here wants to eat you, eat you, eat you ...*

Cate reached down for her spear. "Okay, we're *a-aaall* good here. Saying goodbye now."

She held the spear out in front of her as she backed away. One foot after another, easing back until her next footfall came down on something soft that wriggled furiously under her foot. She shrieked and leapt to the side, landing hard on her ass and elbow.

CHAPTER 33

Cate's sudden movement was like a trigger – the thing that looked like a small island burst from the water, moving at a colossal speed for something so large. The *Carbonemys* turtle was about eighteen feet across, and its broad bony head was easily three feet wide, with a sharp curving beak, angled down like a single large dagger tooth. That horned mouth was open and its angry hiss was like a truck coming into a hard breaking stop.

Cate's eyes were wide, and she felt an electric jolt of pure terror run through her to flood her system with adrenalin, making everything seem to happen in slow motion. In a blink, she knew her puny stick was kindling compared to the armor-plated behemoth that bore down on her. Its neck extended, a column of leathery muscle reaching for her, with its head angling down for her legs, and she knew it would crush them like twigs before she was dragged into the water.

Her mind, now supercharged with fear, collected strange data and images from around her – the buzzing of some sort of gnat at her ear, a drop of water splattered onto her nose, the polypy fronds that closed by themselves when she grazed them, and then the huge turtle, now up on the bank before her, revealing that it had a stump where one of its front legs should be.

Who took that? she wondered, as a familiar voice – *her mother's?* – whispered softly: *shut your eyes, darling.*

As her lids began to close, there was a blur from the corner of her eye, and something like a black cannon ball struck the tortoise's extended neck. The behemoth's mouth snapped shut with an audible *clack*, and incredibly the huge beast was spun sideways. Before she could even draw another breath, the blur was back, scooping her up and carrying her like she weighed nothing.

Cate blinked, not able to speak as fern fronds closed over her, leaving the lake and its mistress long behind. She was let go then, and she lay on the marshy ground for several seconds, her mouth working. Adrenalin still coursed through her system, making her limbs feel like they had singing wires within them. She sucked in a few deep breaths, aware her heartbeat was a racing staccato. Nausea suddenly gripped her and she doubled over, throwing up onto the squelchy ground.

Cate wiped her mouth and turned. "You … you …"

"Take it easy, you're in shock."

Alex crouched down beside her. She spat, wiped her mouth and got to her feet.

Her head spun with dizziness, but she felt more anger than relief. She waited for the, *I told you so.*

Alex came up beside her. "You okay?"

"Listen, before you say anything …" Cate began.

"It's my fault," Alex said.

"Huh?" Cate's eyebrows shot up. "What?"

"No one can ever be ready for this place. It's not our world. We are nothing down here." He half smiled. "Nothing but warm meals." He looked back in the direction of the pond for a second or two, before fixing her with his unblinking gaze. "We were lucky this time."

"Lucky?" Cate wiped her hands on her legs.

"There are far worse things down here. You have no idea." He put a hand on her shoulder. "Are you okay?"

She exhaled, pushing the hair back from her face. It was covered with grit and slime. "Yeah, yeah, I'm fine."

"Good. We need to get out of this swamp."

Cate looked back in the direction of the lake. Suddenly it didn't seem like paradise anymore. "I agree. We need to find drier ground."

Alex turned. "That's the plan, and the signal's coming from that way." He smiled and motioned for her to follow.

*

Aimee followed in close behind Soong and Casey, feeling her nerves becoming wire-tight as she strained to hear anything unusual. Though she and Casey were fairly tall women, both standing about five foot ten, Casey was twice as broad and more muscular and it gave her a stocky appearance. They were both dwarfed by the male HAWCs. Except for Blake, each man was over six foot. But it was Aimee who seemed to be the one walking like she was made of lead – scuffing a toe, crunching a piece of rock, or grazing a cave wall. She felt she was the loudest among all of them. The training these men and women undertook for stealth movement was showing now, as the huge ghosts edged through the ever-tightening cave.

The walls were becoming slick, the moisture undeniable, and tiny amounts of algae and flat lichens were patterning the stone. As a petro-biologist, Aimee knew that they'd be the basis of a food chain. And she knew exactly how far the links of that chain grew.

Aimee edged past a narrow fissure, and heard the sound of something liquid deep inside. She briefly turned to shine her light into its depths, and momentarily caught her breath as it looked as if there was movement within the crack. But when she moved her light around, there were just the slick walls in a fissure that narrowed to no more than eight inches wide. She placed her face into the crack and inhaled deeply. No telltale ammonia scent, and besides, not even she could have fit in there.

She continued on a few paces, and then heard a grunt behind her. Must be Parcellis. She smiled – at least she wasn't the only one to walk into something, she thought, and turned. But there was nothing there, not even the twin dots of the night vision equipment the HAWCs wore.

The grunt came again, further back, this time with cursing, and then shouts.

"What the fuck?" Casey climbed over Soong, and barged into Aimee but couldn't get past, so she pushed Aimee back along the narrow tunnel until they came to an alcove that she was roughly jammed into. Casey bullocked on, Aimee now following close behind. Lights came on and goggles were pushed up, as peak illumination was the priority.

Another ten feet back, Aimee saw Earl Parcellis leaning hard up against the wall – *no*, she thought, *not leaning at all*. The soldier was wedged into the small crack she had just passed over. His face was wracked with pain, and his arms were out to the sides as he braced himself. It wasn't clear what he was doing until there was a sharp tug on his body, and then came the sound of something ripping, followed by the revolting sound of bones cracking.

Jennifer Hartigan came up fast, crawling, burrowing, and edging past the HAWCs to grab at one of his arms. "He's suffering some sort of seizure. Help me to hold him."

Parcellis roared a curse that ended as a howl of pain. He seemed to be yanked another few inches and his body started to fold into the crack.

"It stinks," Hagel yelled.

Seizure my ass, Aimee thought, as her eyes watered from the reek of ammonia.

The trapped HAWC gritted his teeth, threw his head back, and screamed his agony in a sound that Aimee found truly frightening coming from a man who knew how to deal with pain in all its forms. Redman Hagel lunged forward to grab his other arm, just as another sharp tug dragged more of Parcellis into the fissure.

It was impossible, Aimee thought. He couldn't possibly fit – his equipment alone made him many times the size of the opening in the stone.

Another yank, and more crunching of bone. Jennifer was screaming now. "He's stuck on something." She shook her head. "*Its – got – hold of him*."

With another almighty tug, a crackle-crunch of material, and perhaps flesh ripping, the tough HAWC simply ... folded in on himself.

Casey threw herself to the ground, getting underneath the deformed shape of Parcellis, and pointed her rifle into the crack.

"*Fuck it* – no shot, no shot!" She half turned. "Hold him; don't you dare let him go. Hold *hiiiim*!"

Hagel and Jennifer still gripped Parcellis's arms, and Aimee came to hang on as well. Blake reached past Hagel, and took hold of a forearm, now one of the last bits of the man still showing, besides his head.

Parcellis was silent now, the blood on his lips looked black against his ghastly white face. Aimee knew that no one of his size could fit into that crack without significant trauma – his own crushed body would suffocate him. There was a final tug, and then they were all jerked together to collide with the crack in the stone.

Impossibly, he was inside now, and Aimee saw his fear-filled, glazed eyes fix on her momentarily, before he was ripped away into the narrow darkness.

"Fuck you!" Casey screamed as she fired into the crack. Blake and Hagel joined in, the others not able to get close. The laser's concentrated light beams fizzed as they burned stone, and anything else they could touch.

Aimee put a hand over her mouth and nose, as the lasers scorched the traces of blood and gore on the fissure's inner walls. Deeper inside it took on a hellish orange hue, and the extra light showed them just how narrow the fissure was, and made it seem impossible for the large man to have disappeared. However, the bloody debris on the ground just inside was testament to how he was made to fit, and the immense forces that were brought to bear on his mutilated body.

"*Rhino, cannon!*" Casey yelled, and the big HAWC strode over the top of everyone, telescoping out his weapons, and jamming its end into the crack.

"Fire in the hole." Rhino pulled the trigger, and immediately Aimee felt intense heat on her face and shut her eyes as the world flared white. She lifted an arm to ward off the burning, and held her breath from the stench. Water streamed from her screwed-shut eyes.

"Hold fire." Casey's head dropped to the cave floor. "He's gone." She exhaled long and slow, and then punched her armor-plated fist into the cave floor, once, twice, and a third time, sending chips of rock flying. She got slowly to her feet.

Aimee slid to the ground, sitting with her back to the wall. "Did you see *anything*?" She felt her stomach lurch, and old memories raced back at her in a tidal wave of horror. "*Anything at all?*" Aimee asked, but already knew.

"I don't know, but we hit it. I know a protein burn when I smell it," Casey said.

"No, I think that was bits of Parcellis we hit." Jennifer shook her head, cringing.

"Maybe, and that'd be a good thing. But I know what human flesh smells like, and there was something else mixed within that burn."

"Something had him. Something had hold of him, and was strong enough to fucking pull …" Dawkins looked from Casey to the hand-span wide crack in the wall. "Pull a grown man into that?"

"Do you think we hurt it?" Soong's voice was tiny at the rear.

Casey shook her head. "Fucked if I know. Can't have missed it though – filled the crack, top to bottom. How can it be that big? It's freaking tiny in there."

"No," Aimee said, and turned away. "No, we didn't hurt it. We simply educated it." She sighed wearily. The burning odor of rock, sand, flesh, and the ammonia stink hung around them. She knew what that meant.

Casey stared at her for a second or two.

Jennifer stood back a few steps. "It was stuck to him … his back, and just reeled him in." She looked up at them, grimacing. "I don't understand how it could pull him in – the human body just wouldn't fit; Big Ben couldn't have dragged him in there, and he's twice the size of that opening."

Hagel pointed at Aimee's face. "The briefing said this mimic predator could compress itself. But you said it was dead." His finger waggled at her, his expression suspicious. "Well, at least we now know what happened to those other chinks."

"Shut it, Hagel," Casey barked.

"It's picking us off, one at a time." Rhino looked down at Aimee. "Dr. Weir, what do you mean, we educated it?"

Aimee winced. "This thing, it learns, and quickly." She nodded to the dark cave. "We just … need to be away from here."

Casey looked back at the crack in the wall, then to each of the HAWCs and the McMurdo team. Her eyes became alert. "Hey, where's the Chinese chick?"

There was head turning, and furious movement, and Aimee felt a sickening lurch in her stomach.

"Yo." Dawkins's voice floated out of the dark. "She's back here."

Hagel snorted, his eyes wide. "Like where the fuck is she gonna go?" He looked up. "Leave her."

"Last chance, Hagel," Casey snapped at him.

"I don't like this." It was Blake, gun up, and pointing to the rear of the tunnel. "We're sitting ducks."

Aimee could feel the tension and fear. Her own body felt like the nerves in her hummed from being stretched to breaking point. She looked at Casey, trying to impart her urgency to the woman.

"Okay." Casey exhaled, looking one last time back to the fissure in the wall, shining her light inside. She grimaced, and held up a hand. Aimee could see there was a boiling fury in her eyes.

There was just the constant drip of water from somewhere far away in the dark. After another second, the dripping stopped. Casey spun.

"Soldiers, let's get the fuck out of here. Move it." She pushed past Aimee to take the lead, and started to jog.

Aimee noticed she left her barrel light on.

CHAPTER 34

Time: 20 hours 12 minutes 37 seconds until fleet convergence

They pushed into a larger, open chamber, and Casey held up a hand, slowing out at front and moving her light around.

"Give me a perimeter, and check for movement." The words came out through clamped teeth.

Big Ben Jackson looked in shock, and John Dawkins slid down a wall to sit with his hands over his face. But the HAWCs went to work, spreading out, jogging from one cave opening to the next, stopping and checking even the minutest fissures in the cavern walls. They each pointed barrel-lights in first, followed by sensors, checking the data, and then quickly moving on to the next.

Their professionalism impressed Aimee, and she relaxed a fraction, turning to Casey. The tough female HAWC leaned back against a wall, sucking in air, her face still furious. She was staring at the ground, mouthing silent obscenities. Aimee grimaced as she watched Casey suddenly bring a fist up to bang it hard against her forehead.

"*Godfuckingdammitalltohell.*" She bounced off the cave wall and turned her face to Aimee. "That was it, wasn't it?"

"I don't know, I didn't see it." Aimee's mind raced. "But probably."

"Don't bullshit me, Dr. Weir. I saw the look on your face." Casey grabbed at Aimee's chest with a gloved hand. "I read the report. Hagel was right; it said it was dead. But it's still here and it fucking found us *real* quick."

"Found me." Aimee pushed her back. "We saw the original creature attacked, and then buried. But it's here, it's always been here, waiting for me ... all these years." Aimee felt her own sanity slipping from the sheer terror. She giggled. "It's Moby Dick, and I'm Ahab."

"Oh, pull yourself together." Casey's eyes burned.

"Well, Mrs. Ahab, news flash – it ain't dead, but Parcellis sure is." Hagel loomed in close, his face red. "Hunter said he saw it die. The big hero fucks up, and now we're all gonna get it in the neck."

Casey spun at him, obviously preferring Hagel as the target of her aggression. "*Hey*, she's right. The report said they saw it attacked, not die, so get out of the lady's face, meathead." Casey's lower jaw jutted as she spoke.

"Tell that to Parcellis. We came down here expecting to kick some Chinese commando butt, and within hours we're down two good soldiers – and one of 'em fucking got pulled into a hole the size of a letterbox. I tell you something, I sure ain't fucking checking out like that."

"Back off, mister." Casey's voice carried a clear threat.

Hagel bared his teeth. "Bad Intel kills ... *boss*." He spun away.

Casey watched him for another moment before turning back to Aimee, sighing. "He's right, dammit." She half smiled. "Hey, I'd sure like to read that report again. Didn't pay much attention first time round."

"Sorry," Aimee said, but she wasn't sure why she was apologizing.

"*Ah*, it is what it is. We're here now, and whining ain't going to make it any better." Casey shrugged. "So, what are we missing?"

"You can't fight it in here. It's an ambush predator, adapted for hunting in the caves." Aimee tried to remember what she knew. "This is its home turf."

"I never understood that bit. I thought this thing was like a sea creature. We're still miles from any water," Casey said.

"It still is, sort of. Like a cephalopod, but this thing is not the same as the cephalopods we know. Evolutionary biologists have been hypothesizing for years about the inevitability of these creatures being able to colonize land." She shrugged. "This thing is probably semi-aquatic, or might only ever need to get back to water to lay its eggs."

"Great." Casey exhaled through her teeth. "But it can dry out, right?"

Aimee shrugged. "I don't know. Did you smell that stink? It's covered in an ammonia gel that acts like a water-retaining lubricant. They exude it." She smiled weakly. "The good news is, we'll probably smell it long before we see it."

"That's something. What else?" Casey waited, and the others began to crowd around. She lifted her head to the big soldiers. "Rhino, Jackson, watch the tunnels." She turned back to Aimee. "Go on, Doc."

"Well, it tracks movement – our vibrations, and has excellent vision. This thing is *the* apex predator down here ... as far as we know."

"As far as we know? Are you telling me, there could be something sitting higher in the food chain?"

Hagel snorted, his face red. "Where do we fit in this food chain?"

"In these caves, we're the mice in a maze," Aimee said.

"More like rats in a trap." Hagel was breathing hard. "This is bullshit, man. Further into that crack you couldn't fit a fucking hamster – it was goddamn only a few inches wide. I read the report, that thing that attacked you last time was the size of a freaking battleship. No way it could fit in there."

Hagel spun, his eyes wide. "I didn't see it, did you?" He stepped closer to Blake. "Did you, Blake? Did you see it?"

Blake shrugged and then started to fiddle with his gun.

"Hagel, this thing is boneless, and can squeeze in anywhere." Aimee turned to the jabbering man. "It's also immensely powerful, and if it wants to get in somewhere, and can't squeeze in, it could probably tear its way in."

Hagel shook his head. "Maybe it was something else." He turned to Casey. "Did you see it? I didn't, neither did Blake. Rhino, did you ..."

"I fucking well saw something," Casey yelled into his face. "Parcellis could bench press three hundred pounds, and he didn't drag *himself* in there, so just bite it off and swallow it down, soldier."

"We need to get moving ... downwards," Aimee said.

"Oh no, no, no – not down. If it was that *thing*, it came from down there. We'll be walking right into its fucking living room." Hagel's face looked hot and wet as he lunged forward. "We need to find another way up." He held a hand out to Aimee, and then gripped her sleeve. "You know a way out, you got out before. You said in your ..."

Casey sprung forward and pushed him in the chest, causing the bigger man to stagger back. She stood side on, hands bunched, and Hagel stared, his eyes blazing with murderous intent. He took a step towards her.

Casey waited. Her face was in its permanent sneer, but her eyes were cold. "Any time."

Seconds stretched.

"Back off, Hagel," Rinofsky said, his deep voice barely above a whisper.

Hagel's teeth ground for a moment longer, and then he violently punched one fist into his other open hand, holding them up and twisting as if the pain was a pressure valve releasing excess aggression. He turned away, cursing loudly into the dark.

"Hey!" Casey's voice boomed. "I ain't finished with you yet. Listen up, mister. You fall in under my command, or you find your own way home." Her eyes held an implacable determination, and the scar-smile made her stare all the more ominous.

All the HAWCs seemed up on their toes. Casey's hands were on her hips, but the fingers of one rested lightly on the hilt of a blade.

"*You – fucking – fall in*," she roared.

In the glare of the flashlights, Hagel's face went the color of boiled beet. There was a fire behind his eyes and his teeth were bared. His eyes bulged momentarily before his words hissed from behind clamped teeth.

"Sir, yes, sir." He came to attention.

"*Louder!*" Casey yelled back, pressing her authority.

"Shut up," Jennifer screamed. "Just shut up." Her voice became small. "It'll hear us."

"It's okay, it's okay." Casey turned away from Hagel and reached out to Jennifer, putting an arm around her shoulders, and then pulling her closer. "I'm here with you," she whispered.

"Actually, it won't hear us," Aimee said. "They don't have any hearing ability at all."

"Good. How can we use that?" Rhino asked, now reading from his scanner.

Aimee shook her head. "I don't know. It can't hear us, but it can feel us and see us and smell us. We learned much later that it has outstanding vision, plus a rudimentary visual organ on the tip of each tentacle like a starfish. It has numerous other sensory organs, and can even taste us with those suckers."

"It touches you and it tastes you. Oh, for fuck's sake. Someone wake me up from this bad-ass nightmare," Hagel said from out in the dark.

"I don't know if this is the same thing we encountered, or another one of them. But I do know it was a very accomplished ambush hunter. It didn't need to squeeze all of itself into the cracks and fissures, it only needed to get the tips of its feeding clubs in there. There are hooks on them. Big, sharp, used to impale flash."

"That's enough," Jennifer said quietly, gently pulling out Casey's embrace.

Casey exhaled. "Give me something, Rhino."

Rhino had moved to a large cave exit, and held up the small device. "Got a path, boss. No blockage."

"Please, not down," Jennifer breathed.

Aimee exhaled. "Listen up. It knows we're here. It's fed now, but will be wanting more. We can't stay." She looked along the faces, seeing some determination, but mostly anxiety and downright fear. "It will be relentless until it has taken all of us." She looked to Casey. "We must keep going. Keep ahead of it."

"Down," Hagel said and laughed, mirthlessly.

Casey bristled again, but Aimee stepped in towards him.

"Yes, down. Where it probably lives. But it's already up here now, so what's the difference?" she said evenly. "I survived, and now you guys have better weapons and know what it is we're dealing with."

Rhino's words were slow. "But you had something we don't." His eyes looked dead. "You had the Arcadian."

Aimee stared at the big man, wanting to object, to reassure him. But in the end, she knew he was right.

"Well then," Aimee said. "Let's go find him."

CHAPTER 35

Alex stopped to unzip and then pull his suit down to the waist. Turning slowly, he saw Cate lagging behind and staring up at the column-like trunk of some sort of huge fungi. She smiled and nodded, and he understood exactly what was captivating her – the place they were in was beautiful, wondrous, and also terrifying. Everything he saw was larger than it should be, or its alien shapes defied being compared to anything that existed on the surface. If someone invented a time machine, and they stepped out in one of the most prehistoric of ages, this is what it would be like.

Alex remembered feeling exactly like Cate did now. He too had marveled at this world. But now, the only enjoyment he could draw from his time in this subterranean hell was that it had given him the opportunity to first meet Aimee. Everything else here was colored dark, as he knew that behind all the wonders lurked monsters, *real monsters*.

He watched Cate smiling and nodding at some other thing she had found. She could be a pain in the ass, but he couldn't help liking her – strong willed, intelligent, resourceful, and with a sharp sense of humor – exactly the attributes that had first drawn him to Aimee. He looked up to the cave ceiling hundreds of feet above them, thinking of her. *At least this time you're safe at home*, he thought.

Looking back to his companion, he noticed that Cate had pulled her wetsuit back up, even though he guessed her body streamed with perspiration like his own. She turned to him, and raised an eyebrow.

"That's some wetsuit."

He looked down at his pulled down suit – the tough looking material was more than a wetsuit, but also had armor plating woven into its Kevlar fibers. But for all its protective characteristics, it was designed more to retain heat in a cold climate, and wasn't ideal for eighty degree heat and humidity.

She shook her head. "It's a good look, Hercules, but I wouldn't take it off if I was you."

Alex shrugged. "I'm losing too much fluid through perspiration."

"Me too, but look." Cate pointed a gloved hand at the weird stump of a plant. Then to the stem of another – the growths held spikes, bristles, or reaching tendrils. "See the tips of these thorns? That glistening drop on each is probably venom, and given these things and humans have probably never met each other, I've got to assume that it's something we've never had to deal with."

Alex grunted, and looked at a stump that had four-inch thorns. "Big defenses against big eaters."

"Big herbivores, means big predators," Cate replied.

"You got that right." Alex pulled the suit back up.

They walked in silence for many minutes, Cate stopping to investigate a frond here, or something crawling in the bracken there. She jogged to catch up to him.

"Can you slow down a tad? My legs aren't as long as yours, you know."

Alex glanced at her. "No, sorry, you *must* try and keep up. Every minute we're down here increases our chances of being detected." He lifted his pace, making her need to trot now.

"Must be hard, huh? I mean on your loved ones," she said, slightly out of breath.

Alex didn't turn. "Yeah, hard."

"Have you any? I mean, loved ones, back home? Family like?" she asked.

Alex stopped and turned. Cate almost crashed into him, before taking a step back. He didn't know why, but the question angered him, maybe it was because he wasn't sure himself.

She held up a hand. "Forget I asked. I get it. None of my business."

"It's okay." Alex turned back, and continued. "I just don't know the answer to that anymore."

"Yeah, me either." She skipped over a brackish puddle, trying to keep pace. "Hey, you said something back there." She walked on, waiting, but when Alex ignored her, she went on.

"You said, *every minute we're down here increases our chances of being detected*. I got the impression you didn't think that was a good thing." She increased her pace to be within one stride of him. "Detected by who ... or what?"

Alex stopped so suddenly that Cate bounced off him. He spun to stop her falling, but also held up a hand to quiet her protests. He turned his head slowly. She waited, seconds stretching.

He had a familiar sensation deep inside, like when you had tried to remember something, but couldn't, and then hours later the answer just popped into your head. Except now, what had suddenly manifested was his mind telling him that they weren't alone.

"What is it?" she whispered.

"Someone," Alex said, concentrating.

Cate followed his gaze, but probably saw and heard nothing. "You heard something?"

Alex continued to stare.

"Is it the Chinese team?" She breathed out the words.

"I don't know, but it feels different."

"*Feels different*; what does that mean?" She looked up into his face.

"It's in the same direction as the signal, so maybe ..." He inhaled deeply through his nose. "Not good."

"What? Come on, I'm right here. This is my field, I can help." She tugged at his arm.

Alex looked down at her. "There are things down here beyond anyone's field, things that have not been studied by anyone, anytime." He looked at her – her expression was a mix of annoyance and frustration. "But perhaps we're the ones being studied."

She blew air through her lips. "Don't treat me like an idiot. Okay, I admit, I was wrong back there. I've studied many prehistoric aquatic habitats, and should have known better. But we should be safer now that we're well away from the water."

"That means nothing down here." Alex shook his head, taking a few steps.

She folded her arms. "You said, *every minute we're down here increases our chances of being found.* You haven't explained that yet, and every second you don't explain it, leaves me at a disadvantage. I know you're hiding something."

Alex exhaled and turned. "What exist down here, are not things from some fossil room at the museum. These things are real. These are the things from legend." He had to trust her, he needed her judgement and expertise. "Have you ever heard of the Kraken legend?"

Cate frowned. "*Pfft*, sure, who hasn't? The Norse legend of the many-armed beast from the depths. Pulled ships under and all that."

He nodded. "When we first came, we had no idea what was really down here. Had no idea about this creature, the Kraken, or massive cephalopod anomaly, call it whatever you like. The bottom line is, I lost a good team mainly because we underestimated our enemy."

"Enemy? This thing isn't a combatant. If there is something like that down here, its just an animal, working on instinct."

He half smiled. "It was working on instinct all right. But it was far smarter than anyone suspected. And something else." He looked into her face. "I got the feeling it enjoyed what it did. I could sense it." He stopped and scanned the dark blue jungle around them.

"Impossible," Cate said quickly.

"Why not? Killer whales, cats, some primates, they all take great delight in tormenting their prey prior to killing it. Aimee ... *ah*, a friend of mine, told me how smart these things are. Normal cephalopods are only limited by their short life spans. But this thing, this thing might be hundreds or even thousands of years old."

Cate shook her head. "Unlikely."

"Yeah well, I thought we killed it." Alex shrugged. "Maybe we did and maybe we didn't. And maybe there was more than one." He turned back to the jungle. "It gave off an ammonia stink." His face was grim. "And I can damn well smell it now."

"You can?" Cate sniffed and then stared off into the gloom for another moment. "Hey, you know, thinking about it, there is some recent paleontological evidence that might be a precedent. A few years back, a researcher submitted some findings at a Geological Society meeting for evidence of the Kraken. Putting flesh on the bones of the legend, if you like. He had found some strange marks on the fossilized bones of another great creature of the time, called an Ichthyosaur – a forty-five-foot sea dinosaur of the Triassic period."

Cate tapped her chin as she seemed to pull the details from her memory. "When they arranged the Ichthyosaur vertebrae, they noticed an odd patterning on the bones." She stopped tapping and looked up. "Sucker marks. The scoring on the bones of the dinosaur resembled the sucker marks that would have been left behind by the tentacle of a giant cephalopod. One that would have been over a hundred feet long." She tilted her head. "But, not everyone agreed with the report's findings."

"That researcher was more right than he knew," Alex said.

Cate inhaled again, but shook her head. "I smell nothing ... but okay, I'll keep an open mind."

Alex nodded, turning away. Just over the top of the plants, there was a cliff face that ended at the water line, its base covered by a stand of what looked like huge straight trunks or columns. He looked down at his signal locator, and then back up at the cliffs where they met the water.

"The signal's coming from over there," he said.

"The cliffs?" She got on her toes.

"Looks like it. But I think it's more than a cliff. I think it's a structure."

As Cate watched, his expression clouded. "Strange," he said. "I can still sense something ... familiar."

"The Kraken?" Cate frowned.

"No. Some ... one." He tilted his head, trying to form an image; not believing what his instincts were telling him.

"Who?" Cate crowded in closer to him.

"We have to move – *fast*." Alex started to jog.

CHAPTER 36

Captain Wu Yang and his team had to cross the underground stream, again and again. At times, it was shallow, the water being of crystal clarity. But other times, the stream bed fell away beneath their feet and they needed to paddle, the shadowy impenetrable depths unknown, perhaps just over their heads, or many fathoms deep.

In another hour they came to a broad, dark beach, and Captain Yang called a halt. Han Biao and Liu Yandong sat together, each pulling up rounded stones to perch on, as the black sand seemed to stick to anything metallic. Han Biao had scolded Liu for sipping water from the cave stream, admonishing him for his lack of caution. But the bigger man had just shrugged it off.

"Tastes fine, and better to save what we have," Liu said. "Who knows what will be around the bend."

Han Biao grunted. Liu was right, but he would neither eat nor drink anything until Captain Yang allowed them to nibble on their rations. He felt the captain had it in for him already, and insubordination would be the last straw.

Han Biao scratched at his arms, and Liu pointed. "You have a rash ... on your neck."

He reached up and touched his neck. It felt smooth, not painful, but he had a tingling itch. It was nothing compared to his arm, which crawled madly with the irritation. He could feel the lumps there.

"Must have been something in the water I'm allergic to. Itches, very bad."

"Urine," Liu said. "My grandmother always said that if you have been stung by something to use your urine. Pat on, let it dry." He shrugged.

Han Biao nodded. It was a good idea, as they had little first aid with them, and he knew that urine had many medicinal properties. "Maybe I will." He looked around. "Okay." It was a home remedy, but right about now the insane itch made him ready to try anything.

He got to his feet and wandered a few paces down the bank and then in towards the cave wall. Shadows swallowed him almost immediately, as the men sat in groups around a few of the lit flashlights – the small dots were a comforting glow in the utter darkness.

He grimaced. The tickling itch on his neck had turned to a crawling sensation just like on his arm. And now the rest of his body decided it wanted to join in. Even his throat start to burn and he had a strong desire to cough – a bad idea in the quiet of the caves. Yang would be furious if he made a commotion. Maybe he had caught a cold. *What a time to get sick*, he thought depressingly.

Han Biao stepped further into the shadows and unbuckled his belt. He reached in for his penis, his cold hands shrinking him, and needing a tug to pull it free of the zip. He sighed, feeling like crap. He was trained to ignore discomfort, still, that didn't mean he and his comrade brothers didn't experience it.

He started to urinate, and there came a strange sensation. It felt as if lumps were passing along the length of his penis. He reached one hand forward in a cup shape to capture some of the warm liquid in preparation for smearing it on himself, in the places where he felt the insane tickling the most. He cupped a handful of urine and raised it to his shirtsleeve – there were already holes and rents in the tough fabric from the cave-in, so getting to his flesh was easy. He splashed it over the largest of his abrasions and then rubbed the liquid up and down in long strokes. It felt like there were grains of rice under his hand.

"*Hoy?*" The tickling on his skin was now amplified by a new sensation – his skin crawled both inside and out now. Han Biao looked quickly over his shoulder. Captain Yang sat with a small group. He had been most specific about there being no use of their lights, but his fear and curiosity was screaming. He would chance a quick look. He lifted the elbow shaped light from his belt and snapped it on, pointing the beam into his cupped hand to both stifle the flare of the white light, and also see what was in his hand.

His mouth dropped open in confusion. He hurriedly changed the angle of his light, not caring now who saw his use of the precious batteries.

"*Ack!*" His lips pulled back in revulsion. The remaining fluid in his hand was pink, tinged with blood. But this was not the main source of his concern. Within the cherry colored liquid, there wriggled a mass of black thread-like worms, each thrashing madly like sperm seeking an egg. There was a small scratch on the meat of his palm, and his eyes bulged as he saw that the worms were spearing what he assumed was their heads into the wound, and then thrashing ever harder.

"*Yi!*" He flicked his hand, and then had a horrifying thought. He pulled at his shirt, craning to look at his shoulder where he had smeared the mass. The red oily liquid was covering his body, the worms now coating his torso. What was worse, was that the wounds on his arms and shoulders had far too many of the worms to have just come from his urine – they must have already been there – coming from inside.

Han Biao felt the tickling now in his belly, and even at the back of his mouth. He dropped his hand and turned to the group.

"Captain-*nnnnn!*" He staggered forward, his arms out. "Captain Yang, in my wounds … they got into my wounds."

The men were all on their feet in a second, guns now up and pointed, seeking an enemy or intruder to defend against.

He staggered towards them. "Captain, they're inside me. I can feel them … they're eating me."

Yang strode quickly towards him, his face twisted in fury. "Silence."

He had a pistol in his hand, and with the other he held it up flat in front of Biao's face, halting him. With the barrel of his gun, he edged open Biao's shirt. His lips compressed.

"From the water. They got in my wounds," Han Biao said, not being able to help his words turning to a wail.

"Come quick," Yang said, and turned to walk further up the dark beach and away from the men.

Han Biao staggered after him, feeling the insane itch from his ears to his anus. His limbs started to go numb, and suddenly his pants felt loose at his waist.

His gut roiled, and he sobbed, grabbing hold of his belt to keep his pants up. He staggered after Yang, just focusing on the man's back, as his rapidly fear-fragmenting mind was beginning to leave him. He fell to his knees.

Yang nodded, edging into an alcove. "In here, I have something that will help."

Han Biao walked forward on his knees. He felt a weakness in his limbs like he had never felt before in his life. He looked down at his pathetic frame – his clothes bagged on him, and holding up a hand he saw that he was nearly shriveled down to bone, but there was furious movement beneath his skin. The remaining meat was literally being eaten from within him right before his eyes.

He looked up at his captain, and into the muzzle of the gun. The black dot at the end of the barrel flared, and then there was nothing.

*

Liu Yandong's eyes were wide as Captain Yang walked back to the group, holstering his sidearm.

"Infected," he said, and looked up at his men, arms hung loosely at his side. "Is anyone else injured, sick?"

The men quickly checked themselves, murmuring. Liu did the same, but if he had any injuries, he would not dare share them with the captain. After a minute, the group professed themselves fit, and Yang grunted, and went to turn away, before stopping and quickly turning back.

"Or did anyone drink from the stream?"

Liu Yandong had been staring at the body of his friend, but the question snapped him back. He licked his lips and swallowed, feeling a small tickle in his throat. He had some gnawing in his belly, but that was just from hunger. Besides, there was no way he was going to say anything.

Yang turned to him. "Liu Yandong, lead us out again. Rest time is over."

Liu gave a rapid half bow. *"Yao."* And he jogged out ahead of the men, relieved to be away from Yang's penetrating stare.

He gritted his teeth, trying not to look at the body of his colleague as he neared it. But from the corner of his eye, he detected movement. Was his comrade still alive? He veered towards the cave wall for a better look. Sure enough, the body was moving. Maybe Yang's shot only wounded him? He wished he could use his light, as Biao now looked tiny, shrunken, lying on the dark sand.

Liu slowed. There – there *was* movement – Han Biao's body jerked and jumped. But the activity was strange, boneless, and not how he would have expected a man to be if he was alive or even writhing in pain. Something wasn't right. Liu stopped walking and stared. He grimaced, his eyes going wide in horror. Han Biao's body suddenly collapsed in on itself, but the clothing was not quite empty. There was a rippling beneath the fabric as though there were small animals fighting inside.

Láizì dìyù de shēngwù, he whispered. It was a line from an ancient story he read as a child; a village fell into a sinkhole, and the villagers had to descend to hell, where on the way, demons tormented them, and cursed them with plagues of flies, and beetles, and worms. Liu momentarily crushed his eyes shut and turned away. He forged on, keeping his head down. *That's where we really are*, he thought – *in hell*. They all died in the cave-in, and now they were lost souls making their way down to the Underworld.

CHAPTER 37

Aimee and Casey knelt at the rim of a hole in the cave floor. There was a warm breeze lifting from the impenetrably dark depths that smelled of salt, moisture, and rotting vegetation. Aimee lay down and closed her eyes, straining to hear anything that might indicate movement. After a moment she sat back. There was nothing and no hint of the acrid scent that usually heralded the stink of the creatures' approach.

"It's a chute." Aimee got to one knee. "And probably the quickest way down."

"Well, that's where the signal is coming from, so …" Casey pulled out a glow stick, bent it, and let it drop. The flaring yellow stick sailed down into the darkness, bouncing a few times against rocky outcrops before disappearing around some sort of bend.

"Not too bad, and it's rough. Plenty of handholds." She stood and looked around the cave, pointing to a stalagmite rising from the cave floor. "Going to have to tie off just the same."

Hagel looked from the stalagmite to the hole. "Means we'll use the rope up – no one to untie it. One-time deal."

"Open to alternate suggestions," Dawkins said from the rear.

"Yeah, like not use the rope, and we just scale down." He glanced at Aimee, and then over his shoulder to the non-HAWCs, his eyes alighting on the slender Soong. "You'll be fine."

"You know what? One of us falls and dies, no problem." Casey's eyes were level. "One of us falls and breaks a leg, well now, that's a disadvantage I don't want to have to deal with. Unless it's you." The scar on her cheek made it hard to tell whether her expression was just her permanent sneer, or something more hopeful.

Aimee felt that Casey was digging in, simply because she was pissed off. "I don't need to tell you guys how to manage risk. We've each got rope, but no pitons, cams, or rope locks. So as far as climbing or caving is concerned, the rope is all we got. We need it," Aimee said. "Long way to go yet – down, and then, hopefully, back up."

"Okay." Casey grunted. "We use the rope for non-climbers. I'll go first, and secure the rope. Have a little look-see down there." She pointed to the huge form of Rinofsky. "Rhino, you're last and on gear recovery."

"Got it, boss."

Casey turned to Vince Blake. "Tie off your rope, Lieutenant."

Blake crossed to the stalagmite, and looped his rope, carrying back the loops of soft cord and dropping it down into the hole. It only reached about two thirds of the way.

"Good enough," Casey said. "I'll go down this length and, if need be, use my own rope. Hopefully, the rock will be broken up enough that we don't need it."

"Good luck," Aimee said.

The stocky HAWC snorted. "You bet. Break a leg, huh?" She grin-sneered at Aimee, and then her eyes slid to Hagel. She winked. The man looked back at her, deadpan.

Casey pushed her rifle up over her shoulder, and then pulled a flashlight – its handle split in half and opened into a loop that she pulled over her forehead. She then looped the rope around her groin and ass, turned, and stepped back, dropping down quickly, the rope *zizzing* between her gloved hands, one up and one down.

The group crowded around the hole, watching as Casey hopped her way down. At about fifty feet, the rope slackened as she obviously had stepped onto something or reached the end of her rope.

Her beam of light illuminated the cave as she continued down. After another few minutes the light went out or disappeared around a bend.

Seconds passed, a minute, then more.

Aimee got down on her belly again. "Okay down there?"

They waited. Silence. The rope stayed slack.

"Yo, boss." Rhino leaned out.

A bobbing light, far down appeared. "All good." Casey's voice repeated ever softer in an echo. "Plenty of ledges on the way down. Comin' back up."

The rope began to jerk, and in another few moments Casey was hefting herself over the side of the hole. She sucked in a single deep breath, and rolled her shoulders.

Aimee shook her head. That climb would have near totaled her, but the female HAWC barely broke a sweat.

"Steep to begin with, and no handholds. But then it breaks up and gets a lot rougher – lots of boulders and jutting ledges, before it bends slightly and the angle eases off. More a scramble over loose debris then." Casey wiped her gloved hands together, dislodging some wet cave-slime. "It's damper, and looks like it keeps going and going, all the way down." She grinned at Aimee. "Maybe to that underground sea of yours, huh?"

Casey stepped back from the edge, and stared off into the tunnels behind the group for a moment. She snapped back. "Okay, people, form up. Let's get this party started."

*

Hank Rinofsky stood back and watched the team descend. Rhino kept one hand on the rope, just monitoring its tension. He continually turned his head, using his scope now to switch between thermal, night vision, and then back to light intense as he checked for anything above the grunts and heavy breathing of the team as they vanished into the chute.

When it came his turn, Rhino hovered at the lip for a few moments, contemplating his own descent. First he needed to untie and retrieve the rope. He laid his hand on the soft but extremely strong cord. From away in the darkness, there came a tiny sound from the cave they had just left. He paused, reaching up to switch his scope back to infrared, and then thermal – there was nothing.

"Hey, little tattoo guy, that you?" His voice was soft, but still carried in the dark silence. He squinted, trying to remember the word for hello that Blake had taught him. "*Nín hǎo?*"

He waited, but there was nothing but a prickling sensation on the back of his neck. "*Nín hǎo?*" This time softer, and again he listened for a response.

His hand went quickly to the rope. He knew he was skilled enough to climb down without it, and Franks wanted all the gear recovered. He picked up the knot, and then froze – there was a wet sliding noise and then a soft thumping, like something bouncing.

He pulled his huge weapon from over his shoulder. *Come on, you motherfucker*, he thought, as he braced huge legs.

The bouncing continued, and when it started to slow, it then sounded like it was being kicked along, sped up again to bounce some more. He waited, the grip on his gun so hard his knuckles were probably bone-white under his armored gloves. From out of the dark cave they'd just exited, came what he at first took to be a football. It ricocheted off the walls to bounce several more times, and then it rolled wetly to a stop.

Big Hank Rinofsky stared, open-mouthed. It was a human head, slightly flattened and the stump of neck ragged. In the few seconds he stared, time seemed to elongate – he took in every detail: the blood, the Asian features twisted in horror and pain, and on one side of the neck a dragon tattoo, with the reds, greens, and yellows still flaring hotly beneath the blood.

Little tattoo guy, that you? his mind yelled. Rhino snapped into action, raising his weapon and firing into the cave. His laser pulse cut into the dark, but hit nothing but stone. There was the smell of hot plasma in the air, and Rhino shut it off. He held his position. He could hear or see nothing, but every sense in his body screamed at him to run.

"Fuck this, I'm seeing things." He left the rope tied off, and grabbed it, dropping down into the chute, jumping and bouncing down to the first landing fifty feet below. He quickly unhooked himself, and spun, pointing his gun back up the pipe, using the barrel-mounted light to scan its edges.

He stepped back a pace, and was about to turn away, when beside him, the rope wriggled, and then started to be pulled up. He watched it, his mouth open for a few more seconds.

"You've gotta be shitting me." Rhino backed up, his gun ready. The massive HAWC was scared of no man, but this ... this was something far different. He turned, almost sprinting, as he retreated over the tumbled boulders to catch up to the group.

CHAPTER 38

McMurdo Base, the surface

Sam Reid waited in the snow. It was heavier now, the wind having eased back so it fell in sheets, long curtains of white that piled up, obscuring much of the McMurdo Base, and also turning the soft mounds into growing hills around him.

Jack Hammerson had kept them up to date on the small boats that had arrived on the Antarctic shoreline, dispatched by the *Kunming*, to immediately birth a half dozen high-speed snow skis that had powered furiously over the ice and snow towards them.

A few miles out, they had stopped, and Sam knew what that meant. Their visitors had taken to foot. Stealth was their objective now, and therefore the attack was imminent.

Sam stretched, growing bored. He flicked ice crystals from his face as he stood waiting, like a colossus in the snow. He was six feet, eight inches tall and as wide as two men. He was by far the most powerful HAWC in Jack Hammerson's arsenal, bar Alex Hunter, but Sam liked to think his strength and skill was natural, so that put him in front.

He rolled massive shoulders, not feeling the bitter cold inside the Advanced Combat Suit's military grade exoskeleton. On Sam, the synaptic electronics were a molded framework that was built on, and into, his body. A metal bracing belt fit around his waist, and comprised a power-pack and supportive base for the banded ribbing up the back, with needle-like nodes pressed into his spinal cord, basically making the suit's mechanics part of his nervous system.

The titanium hyper-alloy composite exoskeleton framework was enhanced for full combat mode, with molded ceramic armor plating that had a density nearly off the Mohs hardness scale. Sam, the HAWC, was now a mobile heavy weapon.

His scanners beeped, letting him know that his visitors were now at the perimeter's line of snow mounds, and were probably taking up flanking positions and readying their attack. He deployed the helmet shield and a full-face mask telescoped up and over his face in an armadillo plating structure, just leaving a clear panel for vision.

A digital readout above Sam's brow showed him the time they had left until the two navies were head to head: 16 hours, 21 minutes, and 45 seconds, 44, 43 … Events were accelerating.

He grinned, ready. What would they make of him? A giant, made more giant by the suit. He turned slowly, switching to thermal. He could see the white-clad bodies, flaring red, each easing forward, undoubtedly seeing him, but unsure if he was really a man or not. He counted twelve, and detected lots of metal – *lots of weapons*.

Sam spoke calmly. "Targets acquired. Status?"

"Ready, all grids," came a soft reply.

"On my word."

First, the olive branch, he thought. He held up one huge hand, and switched to external speaker.

"This base is designated territory of the United States of America. You will not advance any further." He translated: "*Zhège jīdì pī zhǐdìng měilìjiān hézhòngguó de lǐngtǔ. Nǐ bù huì tíchū rènhé jìnyībù de.*"

Sam waited, but the men continued to edge towards him. Last chance, he thought. "*Go home, boys!*"

The first few bullets that struck him came out of the snow line and were noiseless – standard automatic rifles, each with a sound baffler, and each hit his chest with a dull thud that barely marked the armor plating of his suit.

The next was something more – a high velocity slug that hit his face dead center, compressing the armor and punching his head back. *Sniper rifle, big caliber, M99 probably*, Sam thought, *and it fucking hurt.* He felt blood on his lips, and he growled through gritted teeth.

He roared into his mic. "Take 'em down." Sam lifted his huge arm, and along the forearm a barrel was attached. He pointed at one of the three figures coming at him fast, and immediately a shotgun blast roared from the barrel. Boom after boom, the rubber-nosed slugs found the approaching PLA soldiers and kicked them off their feet. Without body armor, the big rubberized slugs would break bones, or render even a big man unconscious.

Three men went down, and the approaching soldiers immediately split their attack. Several more men looped rapidly towards Sam, zigzagging, and others peeled off left and right to try and enter the camp from behind him.

"Okay, three down, three more coming to party, that leaves six trying to gate crash from behind. Take 'em out, people."

The snow moved, and HAWCs materialized close to the attacking soldiers. Even bigger and faster warriors suddenly confronted the PLA commandos. Very few shots were fired, as hand-to-hand engagement was executed quickly and efficiently.

Sam grunted, and held his arms wide, as the men sprinted at him. Handgun fire pelted into his torso. Finally, Sam moved – the suit's hydraulics moving his muscles at a blistering speed. First, he shot forward, faster than any normal man, to lower a shoulder and strike one of the white-clad PLA commandos square in the chest. The soft flesh and bone was no match for the two-legged truck that ran into him, and the man bounced away to lay still.

Sam then spun, finding his next target, and flinging out an arm that caught a second man across the back, smashing him into snowdrift. The third and final soldier put his head down, and sprinted hard, ignoring Sam and instead heading towards the line of snow-covered buildings of the McMurdo base. His head was tucked down, and his hands were working furiously on something clutched to his chest. Sam had a sinking feeling and exploded into action, running the man down, grabbing him and lifting him in the air.

The man turned and screamed something, and Sam immediately saw the package in his hands. Numbers were already counting down, and he could see the soda can-sized cylinders of different colored fluids – it was a chemical incendiary device, and a large one.

"Bomb!" he screamed, and like a hammer thrower, he began to spin with the man in one arm and when he had enough centrifugal force, he released the PLA soldier. The ACS suit gave Sam's already phenomenal strength a super powered boost, and the man was flung into the air to travel fifty feet up and over the rise, falling behind a large snow bank.

"Fire in the – "

The immediate explosion that erupted staggered the huge HAWC, and even though he raised an arm and planted trunk-like legs, the hydraulic pistons struggled to maintain his balance.

Sam had crushed his eyes shut, and when he opened them, he was shocked to see that most of the snow around them had melted from the heat. *Sonofabitch*, he thought, imagining the devastation that it would have inflicted on the base's population.

"Sound off."

His HAWC team rose up among the sludge and debris, each counting off, most holding one or more PLA bodies, now looped at the wrists and ankles. In the closest McMurdo cabin, Sergeant Bill Monroe stood in a doorway, grinning and giving Sam a thumbs up.

Sam nodded to him, and then sent an information squirt to Jack Hammerson.

"Storm passed, McMurdo is still ours."

"Acknowledged." There was no joy, surprise, or even satisfaction in Hammerson's voice. The older warrior was just moving his pieces on the board, and there were more moves yet to come. "Proceed to next engagement. Over."

"On my way." Sam turned back to his team and circled a finger in the air. The HAWCs began to drag their captors into the McMurdo camp. Sam turned back to the snow drifts, smiling. *Time to pay our Brit friends a little visit.*

The mountainous HAWC, encased in the armored suit, began to plow through the snow to the Ellsworth base, picking up speed as he went.

*

"It was premature." General Banguuo's eyes followed Chung Wanlin as the smaller man paced, his face near purple. "Sending a PLA team to McMurdo was premature, obviously anticipated, and now neutralized."

The minister stopped and spun, his eyes narrowed. "At least I had the courage to act." He grinned, but it was more like a death's-head grimace. "It is true, I am not a soldier ... but are you?"

Banguuo smiled and got slowly to his feet. The general was a veteran of border skirmishes, and was a formidable man compared to the slight bureaucrat. "Be careful you do not leave this room with your expensive teeth in your pocket, dear minister." He came slowly around his desk, his eyes drilling into Wanlin.

Wanlin started to back towards the door. "I will inform the general secretary ..."

"The general secretary has been fully briefed ... *by me.*" Banguuo kept the man pinned with his gaze. "Your bullishness has forced us into a situation that neither we, nor the Americans, wish to find ourselves in."

Banguuo stood over Wanlin. "The cost of a war right now would break us. The cost of a war with America, could *annihilate us.*" The general pushed down an urge to beat the man senseless. He inhaled deeply, and then let it out slow. "But now, if we just turn around and go home, the loss of face in front of our greatest rival and competitor would be unthinkable."

Wanlin straightened slightly. "We would never back down."

"No, no, we cannot. Thanks to you, we have the tiger by the tail, and dare not let go." Banguuo turned to walk to his window. "The aircraft carrier will be there soon." He turned. "Pray they blink before we do."

CHAPTER 39

Comrade Liu Yandong continued to work his way along the dark river bank. He silently prayed that there were no more crossings necessary, as he didn't think his nerves could bear it. The pressure, the darkness, and the lack of food – he *hoped* – were all making his stomach jump and twist. The cave stream had gotten wider, and in turn the shoreline had shrunk. In addition, the water appeared to be slowing. It could only mean one thing – an obstruction.

Liu rounded the bend and his shoulders slumped. It was as he suspected. The river cave ended with a wall of tumbled rocks, totally blocking any further progress. He moved his flashlight over the wall; some of the boulders were no more than the size of a bread loaf, but others were car sized. There was no army on earth that could shift them without moving equipment. He approached the stones and looked up. The barrier went all the way to the ceiling, not even leaving a gap at the top, and the rocks were slime coated, and in some places looked welded together from the countless ages they had rested upon one another. This was an ancient fall.

He breathed out his frustration and waited, knowing that Captain Yang was a man who often shot the messenger. He grimaced as he felt his stomach roil again, and then felt the pain drop lower, to force pressure on his bowels. He needed to shit ... *now*.

Liu looked around quickly. The rest of the squad was still a few hundred feet back – he had time. There were a few small places close to the cave walls and he strode into one, already loosening his belt. He dug a small hole in the dark sand, switched off his light and squatted over it.

There was no explosive gas as he expected, but instead a thick stream that fell heavily to the sand. As well, there was little stink, more just an odor he had experienced once when he had been on his father's farm. His father had slaughtered a pig, and the air had filled with a hot, coppery, offal smell.

His anus itched madly afterwards, and as he had no paper, he had no choice but to pull his pants back up, grimacing at the unpleasant wetness between his cheeks.

He looked back down the cave, and only just made out the glow of the approaching group. They'd be around the bend soon. Liu tightened his belt, his gut feeling slightly better, and went to step away when a tiny sound caused him to pause. A sticky wetness, a movement like dying fish flip-flopping in a puddle. He turned back, knowing where the sound was coming from, and with a rising sense of fear, he lifted his flashlight and flicked it on, pointing it down at where he had moved his bowels.

"*Ah no, no, no.*" Liu backed up, feeling his stomach contents threaten to explode up and over his lips. The brown red mush puddle was a mass of glossy black threads, some no thicker than hair, but others pencil thick. The things were shiny, eyeless, but coiling and twisting, sliding through his feces as if searching for the warm flesh that they had just been expelled from.

"*Eeyaa!*" He looked back down the cave tunnel and saw the outline of his squad now appearing. His first instinct was to tell his leader, Captain Yang, but he remembered how he had dealt with Han Biao. *Infected*, was all Yang said, treating the man like a dog, and calmly putting a bullet in his brain.

His throat tickled now, and the crawling coiled within him from the back of his nose and inner ears right down to feet. *Infected, infected, infected.*

He made a soft mewling in his throat, knowing that he now had limited choices. Getting out was not his concern anymore, but all his life he had abided by a code of honor. He would not go out like a dog.

He hated them, then. The things inside him that had invaded his body and had won the battle without him even knowing there was a fight. Anger and frustration energized him. He wanted to kill them all ... and he would.

He dropped his pack, quickly searching for the small tin of cooking kerosene. He found it, and then fumbled again in his kit, finding his second item. He straightened.

Liu crushed his eyes shut, held an image of his parents standing there, waving, proud of him for attaining his rank in the Special Forces.

No, he would not die like a dog. He would die like a true soldier. He held the image of his parents as he unscrewed the tin's lid, and in a single motion, brought it to his lips and drained the liquid.

He grimaced as the scalding chemical made its way down his throat and into his belly, stripping the lining as it went. Before he lost his nerve, he opened his mouth, held the lighter to his lips and spun the wheel.

*

"Stay back." Yang held up a hand. His men stopped their forward rush immediately. All eyes were on the bucking body, flames shooting from the wide-open mouth and nose. The orange and blue tongues had leaked down over the neck and across the head, and the short-cropped hair of Liu Yandong had singed away, adding to the oily smoke rising to collect under the cave ceiling.

Yang walked forward alone, his flashlight in one hand and revolver in the other. He saw the puddle of squirming excrement, and also the frying worms that exited the dead man's mouth to curl up on the dark sand.

He grunted and holstered his weapon. He clicked his fingers and pointed at two of his soldiers. "Bury that, it will suffocate us if it burns much more." He half turned and then looked back.

The men rushed forward to kick the black sand over the body, extinguishing the flames within a dark mound. Yang sauntered towards the cave wall of tumbled boulders, Liu Yandong already forgotten. He put his hands on his hips, surveying the blockage, before turning.

"Professor."

"That man," – Shenjung looked panicked – "*those men*, something infected them, from the water. It must be avoided."

"And how do we do that? Fly across it?" Yang's gaze turned quizzical. "Are you sick?"

"Huh? I am not," Shenjung replied, feeling his torso.

Yang shrugged. "No, you're not, and neither am I. Han Biao died because his wounds got infected. Liu, because he drank from the stream, when he was warned not to."

"Liu committed suicide. Horrible."

"Horrible?" Yang exhaled evenly through his nose. "No, *brave*. He was a true PLA warrior in his soul. We never surrender, we fight on, past fear, past pain, past all adversity." He half turned, raising his voice. "Liu chose to fight his inner demons – to the end." He raised a fist, lifting his voice. "When we face adversity, when we come to a barrier, we do not tremble or wail. We show them that we are harder, stronger ... *even than stone*."

Yang had his fist still in the air, and held his smile. In the darkest corners of his mind, he wondered if *he* became infected, whether he would end himself like Liu, or whether he would run screaming into the darkness. In that instant, he resolved that his men would never know. While he remained brave, or at least looked it, then they would hold together as well.

A demonstration of his resolve then. He looked from the men to the tumble of huge boulders, and then pointed. "Blow it up."

"What? *No!*" Shenjung Xing waved his hands. "This is not a good idea. The blast could bring the entire cave down on us."

There was silence as the soldiers' eyes slid from the scientist back to their captain.

Yang stayed calm. "And what would you have us do, Professor? Go back to ... where? Maybe wait here until we all have a belly full of worms? Or perhaps simply sit down here and wait until the wall erodes away by itself?" He scoffed.

"There must be another way. The risks ..." Shenjung pleaded.

"Yes, the risks. There are *always* risks. And men like us are not afraid to face them, so men like you can sleep safe at night." He turned and clicked his fingers. "Proceed." Yang started to walk quickly back down the dark cave. When he and Shenjung were a hundred paces back, he stopped and turned.

His soldiers scrambled over the tumbled boulders, planting fragmentation grenades into crevices at a strategic position of the wall. They turned, waiting.

Yang nodded, and the men danced from grenade to grenade pulling the pins and then scrambling down, having mere seconds to try and get to safety. Yang backed everyone around the corner.

The explosion was near deafening in the enclosed space, and the shock wave thumped past the men who were crowded in close to the wall of the tunnel. The monstrous echo was like a titanic drumbeat pulsing away down the cave. They waited, no one moving. Seconds passed, and the echoes had now fallen away to silence.

Yang was first out, waving a hand in front of himself to try and dispel the floating rock dust. He coughed. There was the sound of rocks falling into water, but the air was so choked with dust that visibility was down to a few feet.

"Hold." Yang knew the dust would settle soon. He turned to the stream and lifted his flashlight. Through the gritty mist he could see its black sinuous surface was no more like an oily sheet of glass, but was now moving, and fast. He smiled, *open, I win*, he thought.

He was about to order the men forward, when he paused. There was a creaking sound, like the splintering of wooden boards. He stepped out, holding up his light. The air was clearing, but he still couldn't make out the end of the tunnel. He turned, sighted on one of his men, and then motioned with his head. "Go and look."

The young soldier nodded once and sprinted forward. He was soon swallowed in the foggy dust. Yang waited.

"Clear." The voice floated back. "More tunnel, sir."

Yang looked at Shenjung, feeling both relieved and vindicated. The professor was frowning as he looked at the stream. The water sizzled, popped, and jumped and he stared hard at its surface. At first he assumed it was something underneath pushing upwards, but the more the air cleared, the more he saw that instead, it was something dropping down from above. He lifted his flashlight beam to the ceiling of the cave. A dark crack had opened, *no*, was still opening, and unzipping down the length of the tunnel.

Shenjung pointed at the ceiling, and Yang screamed a single word. *"Run!"*

He turned and sprinted towards the newly cleared cave end with Shenjung and his men following him instantly. They clambered over the broken stones, and the water, now free, jumped and swirled as it kept pace with them. There came a huge splash from behind them, and some of his men yelled with fear. Yang didn't turn, knowing it was probably a rock falling from the ceiling. There came more pounding splashes, then the roar of a giant and the sound of boiling, rushing liquid.

Yang leapt over another boulder, sprinting hard. There must have been another cave stream directly over this one. The explosion had ruptured its bottom, and the streams were about to merge – right on top of them. He put his head down and ran harder.

The growing roar was a living thing that shook the cave around them. The water was an oncoming train, and its speed was about the same. They never had any hope of outrunning it.

Seconds later, Yang and his men were like rats in a drain, snatched up and flushed away in the current. They tumbled down a dark pipe towards a destination that was out of their control.

The water boiled around Yang, pummeling him, throwing him from cave wall to ceiling and then to floor. He tried to keep his eyes and mouth jammed tight, praying that none of the horrifying worms would find their way inside him.

In the inky black water, he struck another body, hard. He went to snatch at it but it was already gone, and in the next instant a massive surge threw him so violently into a cave wall, that he was momentarily stunned.

His lungs were going into spasms, and involuntarily, he opened his mouth wide to drag in a huge breath of air. But instead, the gritty coldness that surged down his throat and into his lungs brought him back instantly. He screamed out the last air in his lungs, and spewed the bile in his gut along with the water. The next thing he knew he was falling through space – *falling, falling*.

It is over, he thought, just before the impact.

CHAPTER 40

The thumping explosion was felt milliseconds before it was heard. *Grenades*, Casey thought, reacting first, yelling out to her team and diving. She took Aimee and Soong with her as she crashed to the wall of the cave chute they were descending in. Dust and debris rained down on them as the shock waves pulsed through the stone, and then raced past them.

They stayed down, hugging the rock for a second or two more, before Casey lifted her head.

"Gimme a source, big guy." She spat and blinked away grit, and then shined her light up at the ceiling.

Rinofsky held up the scanner, first one way, and then the next. "Speed of the tremor wave, and echo duration, gives us a source of about two klicks southeast. With a downward inclination of twenty-five degrees." Rhino pointed. "Down and that way." He looked at Casey. "Got to be our Chinese friends."

Casey stood slowly. "Looks like they decided to clear some blockage, huh? Great idea under freaking miles of stone."

Dawkins coughed and wiped his mouth, spitting and grinning, and displaying his chipped tooth again. He got to his feet. "Maybe they ran into something they could only fight with explosives."

"Well," Casey said, and dragged Soong to her feet. "Whatever it was, I wonder if they achieved little more than a free burial." She must have noticed Soong's disapproving expression, and shrugged. "*Ah*, whatever."

Aimee dragged a sleeve across her eyes. "We're probably moving parallel to them. Maybe we can intersect if we find a conjoining tunnel. Provided they made it through."

Casey held her flashlight in the air. "Interesting, look ..." She nudged Aimee. "The dust, it's moving."

Aimee watched the floating specks within her own beam. The tiny motes should have been settling straight down to the cave floor, but instead they gently floated towards the dark end of the cave tunnel.

"Air movement," Aimee said.

"Gotta be a good thing, right?" Casey's brows were up.

"Better than a dead end, boss," Rinofsky said, smacking Hagel on the shoulder, and raising a puff of chalky dust.

"Got that right. Let's move 'em out." Casey turned to Hagel. "Lieutenant, take point, fifty paces out."

Hagel hesitated for a moment, and then spun and jogged off into the dark.

Aimee grimaced. "We shouldn't split up."

Casey half grinned. "Nah, he enjoys his own company."

*

They eased around through a narrowing in the cave, and Aimee saw the glow from Hagel's light. The man stood silently, pointing his beam to the floor.

He lifted an arm and pointed to their flashlights. "I don't think you'll need those anymore." He switched his own off, and then stood aside, holding out an arm and half bowing, like a maître d' showing guests to their table.

Casey kept her light on, and moved past the young HAWC. "*Holy – fucking – hell.*" She immediately pushed her gun up over her shoulder and stood with hands on her hips, grinning. "It's all true."

Their cave ended, and they found themselves high up on a cliff wall. The hint of light that Hagel had first seen gradually turned to a twilight blue from the ceiling – a ceiling that traveled away for as far as their eyes could make out.

"Glow worms," Aimee said. "Permanent twilight, but be careful with loud noises, or they shut down."

Rinofsky snorted, elbowing Ben Jackson in the ribs. "I didn't believe it could be real. I mean, I read it, but never thought ..." He shook his head. "*It's so goddamn huge.* This ain't no cave." He grinned. "It's a world."

"A world beneath the world," Jackson said softly.

Aimee pointed. "That's the sea in the distance." Before the colossal cave curved away with its own horizon dipping from view, there was the glint on a flat surface that hinted at water. Aimee stepped forward to peer over the edge. "We weren't here before. I don't remember there being a jungle. We never traveled over the other side of the sea. I guess this is what was over there."

"Well, it sure wasn't in Hunter's report," Hagel said sourly.

Casey used a scope to look out over the landscape. "Nothing on visual. Blake, where's our signal source?"

Blake read from his scanner. "Got it, loud and clear – five miles due east." He looked up and frowned. "But that would put it near the water at that far rock face, or maybe, *in* the rock face."

Casey exhaled through compressed lips. "Must be on the shoreline, then ... still hidden." She turned. "What, you thought it was going to be easy?" She lifted her scope again, moving it over the jungle. "If our Chinese friends survived, I'm betting that's where they're gonna end up."

Rinofsky also waved a small box over the edge. "*Whoowee*, I've got so many life signs, I might as well be pointing this at the San Diego Zoo."

"Great." Casey turned to Aimee. "Good to be home?"

Aimee shook her head, her eyes focused on the water in the distance. Casey leaned out over the edge, and then whistled. "That is one helluva long way down."

Hagel stood beside her, also leaning out. "Stuck up on a cliff wall."

Franks looked up. "Make that, *in* a cliff wall."

They were about half the way up the sheer wall of granite, with about a thousand feet to the jungle below. Further along the wall waterfalls fell slowly, most turning to mist before they ever struck the ground. Some had huge torrents pouring out and turning into rivers that wound their way towards the sea in the distance.

"Grab my belt." Franks began to lean out even further, and Hagel hung on so she could gain an extra few feet.

Aimee watched as Hagel's lips curled just a fraction, and saw Rinofsky look hard at him from under lowered brows.

"Okay," Casey said, and Hagel pulled her back.

"Going to be tough, but doable." She walked a few feet into the cave mouth and into the center of the group. "This wall is Swiss cheese. It's riddled with holes and caves. It's a sheer cliff, but with all the pockmarks in it, I reckon we can lower someone down to the next cave. Some places we can scale down." She bobbed her head. "I'm sure we can ease the non-climbers down a bit."

Jennifer Hartigan briefly stepped forward, before quickly stepping back. "I don't think I can do that."

Hagel nodded and confected a concerned look. "Good idea, you wait here for rescue team." He lifted his brows in surprise. "Hey, I just remembered; *we* are the rescue team."

"You can do it," Aimee told her. "I'm scared witless of heights, but I'd be more worried about staying behind if I was you." She turned to Casey. "Have we got enough rope?"

Big Ben Jackson shook his head. "I got nothing. Dawks, Jennifer?"

Both Dawkins and Jennifer shrugged.

"We've got a hundred feet, from each of us," Casey said. "That gives us four hundred; maybe just enough."

"Ah, boss, make that three hundred." Rinofsky grimaced. "I never recovered mine."

"What?" Casey's brows went up. "You can fucking climb like a mountain goat. How the hell did you not recover that loop?"

Rinofsky hiked massive shoulders, looking pained. Aimee could tell he was concealing something.

Franks ground her teeth. "I ought to make you go back and get it. Why didn't you climb back up like you were ordered? And why the fuck didn't you even tell me?"

"Ah, shit." Rinofsky stared off into the dark momentarily. "There was ..." He grimaced. "There was something, *ah*, there was something that had hold of it. And I saw ..."

In two paces Casey was in front of him, grabbing his arm and turning the huge man around, her eyes blazing. She grabbed his suit front and dragged him further into the cave and away from the others. She hung on, pulling him close, near nose-to-nose.

"Listen mister, you came back from the chute white as a fucking sheet. What the fuck happened back there?"

Rhino shook his head. "Bad shit."

Casey gabbed him with both hands and shook. "Soldier, *what ... did ... you ... fucking ... see*?"

Rhino yanked himself from Casey's hands, and held fists up on each side of his head.

"I dunno, I dunno what I saw. Something ... nothing." He looked up, his expression pained. "When I got to the bottom of the chute, I think there was someone still up at the rim." He shook his head again. "They were just fucking with me."

"Someone? *Someone* was just *fucking* with you? What the hell does that mean?" Her voice seethed with fury.

"Jesus." He grimaced. "They pulled the rope up, slow like. And ..." He grinned, confused. "And they rolled a freaking head down at me."

There was a snigger from out of the dark. "Did you just say, *they rolled a head at you*?" Hagel, now listening, brayed with laughter. "Goddamn, now I've heard everything."

Casey ignored Hagel to stare for several more seconds into Rhino's face. "Ah, for fuck's sake, you big moose. You thought this was best kept to yourself?" Casey's teeth were bared as she stared up into the face nearly a foot above her. "Someone is jerking you round, and you run like a school kid? I oughta make you ..."

She walked off a few paces before coming back in and glaring up at him. The big HAWC's face was twisted in agitation. At last she just shook her head.

"Fuck it, we're outta here." She looked at each member. "We need to be down, and fast."

Aimee took another peek over the edge and blanched.

Casey half smiled. "Now's the time to stomach some risks." She showed her teeth. "Because we don't really have a fucking choice."

She turned to walk back to the edge and then leaned out. "Unfortunately, the first part looks like it's a real kicker with few handholds, then a straight drop for about eighty feet down to the next cave. Means we're gonna lose a third of our rope straight up." Casey eased back. "Blake." She turned. "Find me a tie off."

Blake quickly removed a rope from his pack, and found a jagged tooth of granite jutting from the cave floor. He tied it off and then tossed the end over the cliff edge. He then stripped off his backpack, and placed it on the cave edge, just under the rope.

Casey looked down, judging distances for a few seconds. She picked up the rope and yanked it a few times. She didn't bother tying herself off, but instead turned and gripped the rope tightly, her heels now over the edge.

"Rhino, make sure people who need to be secured, are secured."

The big man nodded. "Got it."

Casey eased out. "Give me five to check the next cave and make sure there are no surprises." She grinned. "And if there are, well, you all try another route." She winked at Jennifer and began to walk backwards.

The group surged forward and some of them got down on their bellies to watch Casey descend. Aimee crushed her eyes shut, feeling her stomach flip and her head spin. *Heights* – she hated them. She blinked again and tried to focus just on Casey and not the hundreds of feet drop that she'd also be expected to scale down any minute.

Aimee brought one arm up to wipe her forehead. In another few seconds, Casey was already close to the end of the rope, and started to use her legs to push herself one way and then the other until she began to swing and run across the face of the wall. Just watching it made Aimee feel ill, but in another moment, the female HAWC stretched out and caught hold of the side of a new cave, and then pulled herself in.

Casey reappeared to lean out and give them a thumbs-up. Rinofsky stepped forward, and then turned to Ben Jackson, the equally big McMurdo soldier.

"That means you're up next, big guy. We'll need your long arms down there."

Jackson simply nodded and walked to the edge, picking up the rope, turning, and then walking backwards. The rope popped and strained, and Rinofsky laid a hand on it, feeling the tension.

"All good." He sized up the remaining team members. Still to go was the wiry Dawkins, Blake, Soong, Aimee, and Jennifer, and …

"Hey!" Rhino yelled as Hagel leaned out, and then disappeared around the outside of their cave. Aimee looked across to see the young HAWC just using his fingers and toes to scale the sheer face. He looked back and grinned.

"Haven't got all day, losers. See you down there."

"Break a leg," Dawkins whispered, his mouth turned down, his chipped tooth resting on his bottom lip. They watched Hagel clamber out and across as if he was only a few feet from his back lawn.

Rhino gave him a minute, and then motioned to Jennifer. The woman grimaced, and Rhino removed a length of material from his pack, and tied one end of the material around the rope in a looping knot. "This is an arbor knot." He tied the other end around Jennifer's wrist. "You should be able to climb down by yourself, but if you slip," – he tugged on the material and it immediately tightened and gripped the rope – "then this will catch you. You *can't* fall. You'll be fine, okay?"

She nodded jerkily. Rhino grabbed her and looked into her face. "Just concentrate on the rope, the rock wall, and Lieutenant Franks … and nothing else. Got it?"

Jennifer nodded and he pushed her out. It took ages, but she eventually made it level with Casey. Then it was Soong's turn and then Aimee's.

"You're up, Doc." Rhino held out one big hand.

Aimee exhaled and got to her feet, but felt her legs wobble. Rinofsky looped the slipknot over her wrist. He placed large hands on her shoulders and looked into her face.

"Just on the rope, just on the wall, and just on me – nothing else."

And then she was over the edge – one hand after the other, concentrating on the rock face. She noticed the fine grain in the rock, the spots of lichen and mosses like tiny corals embedded in tiny cracks. In a damp pocket, there was something that looked like lice that scurried in and out of the moisture. She focused on the rock wall as she descended, one hand after the other, over and over. There was a piece of crystal embedded in the rock, or maybe it was diamond. A crazy thought of stopping to dig it out entered her head. *Forget it, keep going, and don't stop, don't stop, don't stop,* she kept repeating.

Her shoulders screamed and her hands were becoming slick. Aimee chanced a look back up – Rhino was just a dot above her now, but he had started to swing her. Her stomach flipped as she yawed against the cliff face.

"Reach out ... nearly got you."

"*Huh?*" Aimee spun her head. Casey was only a few feet away, reaching out. Aimee pushed with her legs, one way and then the next, until Casey grabbed her and dragged her in.

Casey slapped her on the back, and Aimee staggered away from the edge to sit down. Jennifer held out a water bottle that she took gratefully.

In another few minutes Blake swung in, followed by Rhino.

Ben Jackson stuck his head out. "Yo, Dawkins, hustle it up."

John Dawkins, the smallest, was the last to go. He nimbly started down the rope.

Jackson grinned as he continued to watch his smaller friend. "Hurry up, Dawks ... no time for sightseeing."

Still fifty feet up from the new cave mouth, the McMurdo soldier just seemed to hang for a moment, his head tilted upwards as if watching something. Then, while they watched, he lifted back up a few feet.

"What the hell?" Casey leaned out further.

"What's he think he's doing?" Big Ben Jackson turned to the group and then leaned out past Casey. "Dawkins, *John*, you okay up there, buddy?"

The man just hung on, his neck craned as he stared up the rope.

Jackson shook his head. "Something's up, he wouldn't freeze. He knows how to climb, and he ain't scared of heights."

Aimee hung onto Jackson's arm and peered around him. Unbelievably, Dawkins started to rise.

"Is he climbing back up?" Jennifer rose up on her toes, trying her best to see.

"Fuck no, not again," Rinofsky said softly.

Casey Franks turned to glare at him for a second, before watching the McMurdo soldier rise slowly on the rope.

"Is it the Chinese?" Jennifer asked.

Casey edged out further, lifting an arm and looking like she planned to try and make a leap for the tip of the rope.

"Don't." Blake grabbed her and held on.

Dawkins suddenly seemed jolted into action, and began to climb down as fast as the rope was being reeled in. But in a few moments he came to the end, and hung on, looking across at the sheer granite wall, searching for something to grab onto. There was nothing, and no choice but to let himself be pulled to the upper cave mouth.

Dawkins soon reached the lip and stuck there, staring for several seconds, seeming to look deep into the cave, and then he simply pushed backwards, into space, and just … fell.

The soldier didn't make a sound, but as his body passed them, gathering speed, the split second glimpse of his face showed wide eyes and teeth grit in a rictus of pure terror.

They watched his body plummet to the ground. Casey blinked several times, her mouth open. "He fucking jumped?" She shook her head. "Why the fuck would he jump?" She backed up, her fists balled.

Aimee saw that Hank Rinofsky had turned away, one fist held up to his mouth. She looked back down at the jungle that had swallowed Dawkins's body. There was no trace. After another moment, she turned away.

"He jumped because he decided it was better than facing what he saw in the cave." Aimee felt ill. The cold knot was in her stomach again. "God help us."

"Dawks is no coward." Ben Jackson grimaced as he stared down into the vegetation hundreds of feet below. "No way would he kill himself."

"Yes, he would. Anyone would … *anyone*." Aimee folded her arms tight against her body, and shut her eyes. "You guys read the report, but didn't actually learn a damned thing, did you?"

She turned to look at Casey. "This is no dumb animal. It's playing with us. It's probably known mankind for years, maybe hundreds or thousands of years. The people who used to live here had a name for it. They called it the *Qwo-to-oan*."

"I think I heard of that," Hagel said.

"We need to wake up, real quick," Aimee said, looking at each of them. "Because this thing is big, smart, and we're right in its home."

"Jesus Christ." Hagel glared at Casey Franks. "We're fucked."

"Shut the hell up." Casey glared right back.

"Oh, okay, we're all fine then." Hagel's face twisted as he walked away shaking his head.

Casey's face was furious, but it relaxed and she exhaled long and loud. "So, this is our job. This is what we do. We've had to deal with worst case scenarios before." She looked along their faces. "And this is one of them."

"I musta missed that briefing," Ben Jackson said. He sighed and shook his head. "Fuck it, we're all in the same boat now."

The group, bar Hagel, crowded in tight, all eyes focused on Casey Franks. Aimee looked over their heads and into the cave depths. There was no light, and no end to its impenetrable darkness. For all she knew there was something back in there, edging forward, sliding silently, its leviathan strength compressed, coiled, and waiting to flex out and then snatch them up.

"Let's get out of here," she said softly.

Casey looked from the group to Aimee, and then into the tunnel depths. She nodded. "Blake, tie us off again. This time, I go last."

CHAPTER 41

"Stinks down here." Blake had his gun up, scanning the dense undergrowth.

"Creepy as hell," Hagel added, sighting along his rifle in the other direction.

"I heard that, brother," Blake said. He'd been in plenty of jungles before, from Colombia to the Congo, but this was like nothing he'd ever seen. Strange boughs, gnarled and twisted, dripping with slick mosses, all looked less like trees and more like some sort of elongated mold growths. Others were just hairy trunks rising three stories in the air, with bulbous pads like tongues on their ends. The only real characteristic they shared was that where they touched the ground, they all looked like they were trying to break free, lift their roots out, and then go marching, triffid-like, off on their own.

But the thing that bothered Blake the most was the silence. Jungles weren't quiet, unless something *made them* go quiet. He sensed life all around them, but nothing chirped, croaked, or whistled. It was like a dead forest, but not. His gut told him that the predator knew they were there and was watching them – he hated it.

Blake half turned. "You know, a lot of civilizations, old and new, think that hell is under our feet. Looks like they were right," Blake said, his gun moving along another quadrant of the jungle.

"No way, man. This is home from now on. Get used to it. Cause we ain't got enough rope to climb out anymore," Hagel added.

Blake shook his head, keeping his eyes on the silent jungle. "We needed it to get everyone down. What would you have done, smartass?"

Hagel put his gun on his shoulder, and turned. "We were given a job by Hammerson – find that sub. That's our priority. We could have scaled down without the rope." He bobbed his head. "I'd have left the civs behind. Send a rescue party back for them later."

"Yeah right, what rescue party? You mean leave 'em to die." Blake knew Hagel meant every word he said.

"Look, Blake, all I'm saying is, butchy boy is burning through our resources far too quick." He shrugged. "We could also track down the PLA, take their resources. Improve our chances."

Blake scoffed. "We're doin' okay so far. I suggest you lighten up, as you're starting to piss me off." Blake looked squarely at the younger HAWC. "Hey, why don't you share your views with Franks? I'm sure she'll enjoy having a chat – just the two of you."

"I'm not scared of Franks. She's just …"

Rhino appeared out of the undergrowth. "Can't find Dawkins."

"*Huh?* I don't get it." Blake's brows went up. "That kid fell straight down. We all saw it." He looked up, calculating. "Should be around here, and as he was no superman, I don't see him walking away."

Rhino shrugged. "I'm telling you there's nothing, not even an impact mark. Guy never hit the ground." He tilted his head to the towering tops of the growths that had odd, stubby heads, looking like massive undersea tubeworms. "Maybe he's caught up in the canopy of one of these suckers?"

"Maybe," Blake said, unconvinced.

"Yeah, maybe." Hagel grinned. "And maybe we only imagined he fell. Maybe we're all asleep and this is a dream." He chuckled. "Assholes." He pushed his rifle up over his shoulder and walked off to rejoin the group.

Rhino watched Hagel for a moment before turning back to Blake. "I'm telling you, it's like he never hit the ground." He grimaced. "This place is all fucked up."

"You think?" Blake exhaled. "Hold it together, big guy. We'll all be fine if we all just keep clear heads."

"Clear heads." Rhino pushed his weapon up over his shoulder. "Yeah, sure."

*

Aimee was lost in her own thoughts. *How did I get here again?* she wondered as she pushed aside stubby fronds. *Some people are just programmed to make bad decisions,* she answered. She looked up towards the roof of the giant cavern – tiny blue lights twinkled like stars – bioluminescent glow worms. Attached to the ceiling, huge multibranched trees of lichens hung down hundreds of feet, almost looking like a mirror image of the ground. Things flew in and out of the lichens. Some looked like mere dots, but others she knew were probably the size of small airplanes. *Up there, it's another world, in yet another world.* She smiled at the paradox.

She sighed. Another few miles or so above that clinging ceiling was another world again, her world, frozen, and perhaps now engaged in a tense nuclear standoff … or worse. A sudden image of Joshua screaming as he was caught in a nuclear inferno ripped across her mind, and she shook her head to clear it away.

Idiot, she whispered with enough venom to lash her own conscience. Jack Hammerson had said he wanted a scientific negotiator with experience, someone who could be their guide. She had been vain enough to suck up his flattery, but now thought that if she was the best they had, they were all doomed. She ground her teeth. Some people will continue to make stupid decisions until one eventually kills them.

Aimee stumbled from fatigue, and tried to remember when it was she last really rested – *too long ago.*

She exhaled long and slow, looking over her shoulder to the cliffs they had just scaled down. The thing she feared the most was in there – a thing that could squeeze its monstrous boneless bulk down, and then spring at them from any crevasse, cave, or dark space. It could mimic their form, seeming to be like one of them until it was close enough for you to realize you had made a horrible mistake, and by then it *was* too late, as it was in reach and able to grab you, and steal you away, to ... she grimaced, not wanting to finish the thought.

They were leaving the caves behind, *but in the open, are we any better off?* she wondered. She slowed and watched as Hagel remonstrated with Casey. She was half a head shorter than Hagel, but Aimee bet the female HAWC was a dozen times more deadly. She caught up to Ben Jackson, and the equally big Rhino, who was looking over his shoulder at the small device he had in his hands. He pointed at the screen, showing the McMurdo soldier what he was looking at. Aimee craned to see.

"Signal here is long and strong, and about 4.4 klicks." Rhino turned and recalibrated the device and pointed it into the distance. "This cave is too big for a signal bounce – has its own horizon, and beyond."

Blake and Casey also joined them, Blake holding out a different small box. He whistled softly.

"What is it?" Aimee asked, looking down at the small screen as a wave pulsed out and showed up a smattering of dots, some large and some pinpricks.

"Standard movement tracker," Blake said, looking up and then along at the walls of jungle around them. "This place is near tomb silent, but there's a helluva lot of movement out there. Too much for the tracker to fully untangle, but basically, we're surrounded by things as small as a mouse and as big as a freakin' bus." He pointed. "About a hundred feet that way, there's something the size of a truck right now."

Casey leaned back. "Moving away from us, thank Christ."

Soong peered down at the screen and walked off a few paces with Blake and Rhino, just as Jennifer came into the group, her arms wrapped around herself. Casey tilted her head towards the dark haired medic. "How you holdin' up, Jenn?"

Jennifer shrugged. "I'd rather be back in the rec room, with a cold beer, getting ready to shoot some pool."

Casey grinned and reached out to grasp one of her shoulders. "I heard that. Maybe when this is over, you and I can catch up. Share a beer and rack up a few."

Jennifer's cheek dimpled. "I'd like that."

Aimee smiled as the two walked off. *You go girl*, she thought with a half smile.

Within an hour, they came to a small depression, like a fifty foot bowl in the soft lichen mats. Casey held up a hand.

"Rest. Thirty minutes, sleep if you can. Might be the last opportunity we get."

"We should keep going," Hagel said, continuing to walk.

"*We* could continue, but the group needs rest," Casey said, turning away.

Hagel paused, his eyes going from Casey to each of the HAWCs, trying to gain support – he got nothing. Casey turned back to him.

"I'll do first watch. Then seeing you've got so much energy, you can take over in thirty minutes. Happy now?"

Hagel smiled, but there was little humor in the lift of his lips. He turned and muttered all the way over to a pile of rocks where he sat down, back against it, and covered his eyes.

"Wake me in thirty, mommy."

The group collapsed, the HAWCs lifting the belts and straps of packs and weapons off their shoulders and laying prone. Aimee lay down, and Soong lay close to her.

"This is not a good place," Soong said.

"No." Aimee had few words of comfort for her, so she just smiled, and reached out to squeeze her arm. "Rest now."

Aimee turned away and shut her eyes. What seemed like seconds later, she was being shaken awake.

She sat up and saw Hagel talking rapidly to Casey and pointing off into the undergrowth. He stood over her, giving her grief, the man as usual not amused by something out in the jungle. *Give it a rest, twerp*, she thought and went to sit forward. She groaned, sore all over.

"Hey, who's fucking around?" Rhino was on his feet, walking in a circle, kicking plants and debris out of his way. "Where the fuck is my cannon?"

Casey Franks turned away from Hagel to glare. "You better find that weapon, mister."

Rhino looked at each of them, trying to detect someone stifling a laugh. He turned his attention to Hagel. "What the fuck happened to it?"

Hagel waved him away. "I was scouting and didn't see nothin'. When did you last have it – the caves? Betting that's where it still is."

"No, asshole, I had it right here." Rhino pointed at the ground.

Blake also spun one way and the next. "Holy shit, where's mine?"

"Oh, for fuck's sake." Casey marched over, and looked from Blake to Rhino, and then to Hagel. "You were on watch, what the hell happened?"

"Like I said," Hagel spoke slowly. "I saw nothin'." He shrugged. "I just went to scout for a few minutes, is all. But there was no sound, no movement – *nuuu-thing*."

Aimee pointed at the lichen matting behind Rhino. "Look."

There was a small, flattened path in the plants. Its edges glistened like a snail trial, and Aimee bent closer and sniffed.

"Ammonia." She straightened. "We had a visit."

"What?" Casey's eyes bulged. "Here? It came in here?"

"Bullshit," said Blake. "Why didn't it grab us all, when we were out cold?" He pointed with his thumb. "And all while this jackass was off the reservation."

Aimee wrapped her arms around herself, thinking. "Because it didn't want to."

"Huh?" Blake's lip curled in confusion.

"It didn't want to." She looked up. "It's having too much fun. You asked me what I meant by us *educating it*. Well, it learned real quick that these things," – she pointed at the HAWCs' remaining guns – "cause it pain."

"So, it's taking them from us," Ben Jackson said, running a hand through his hair.

She grimaced, looking around. "It's here, somewhere, probably watching us right now."

The silence stretched as they turned, looking over their shoulders. Soong instinctively edged in closer to the group.

"That's bullshit," Casey finally said, her face red and furious.

"Nah, it's not." Hagel had his gun now cradled in his arms. "It's what I was trying to tell you, Franks. You better come take a look at this." He turned and waved them on, heading into the jungle.

"Gear up, we're out of here," Casey said, following.

*

"Remember our young scout who did the high-dive?" Hagel looked slightly amused.

"You found Dawkins?" Casey's brows shot up.

"Maybe." Hagel shrugged, a touch of a sneer in his smile. "You be the judge."

He came to a fallen bough and crouched behind it. Casey did the same beside him. Hagel looked to Casey, grinning. "Ten o'clock, five up."

She turned to the small clearing ahead. In among the twisted branches and oversized vines, there was a tree stump as thick as her waist. Five feet up, its top was near flat, creating a small tabletop. On it there was a smaller object. From the distance, it gleamed wetly.

She put a scope to her eye. "Jesus Christ." Her teeth came together, and her lips curled in a snarl.

It was a skull, wet, streaked red, and also white where bone showed through the last vestiges of flesh.

Casey quickly turned to speak over her shoulder. "Keep 'em back, Rhino."

The big HAWC held out massive arms to push the remaining McMurdo soldiers, plus Soong and Aimee back a pace.

Casey turned towards the grisly trophy and grimaced. The skull had a chipped front tooth.

"Could be Dawkins; got that same boyish smile." Hagel sniggered. "I'm not thinking the fall did that to him ... what do you think?"

"That's him." Casey tried to keep her breathing calm, but a range of emotions washed over her. Anger gave way to frustration, and then settled in as confusion. Who or whatever it was, it was dogging them, one step ahead all the time. She had never felt more out of her depth. *Fuck that Dempsey*, she thought. *Getting himself killed, he was supposed to be making the decisions.* She licked dry lips. *What would Alex or Sam do?* she wondered.

"Hey, you still here?" Hagel whispered.

"Yeah," she said, and knew exactly what Alex would say. He'd tell her to fight her adversary at a time and place of her choosing, not its. She pulled back. In the caves, Rhino had been right about one thing – someone or something sure was fucking with them.

"You think it's the Chinese, or like the Doc says, it's that fucking monster thing playing with us?" He leaned closer. "What do you think? Can't fight what we can't see."

"What I think, is from now on, we need eyes in the back of our heads." She got to her feet, staying low. "We detour around it, and keep permanent watch. You're still on point."

"Nice time to be losing weapons, huh, *boss*?" Hagel grinned as he pulled back.

CHAPTER 42

Time: 12 hours 05 minutes 12 seconds until fleet convergence

Sam Reid slowed as he topped the rise, gazing down onto the Ellsworth base. It was much like he expected – a few prefabricated igloos joined by some boxes. Not much shelter for the coming cold, but the occupants were here to do science, not enjoy a winter holiday, he guessed.

Just out to the side, there stood the mini-submersible's launch silo, snow covered and empty now. Sam shook his head. *Only Alex Hunter would try something so crazy*, he thought.

He powered down the slope, heading for the main building. Just as he reached for the handle it was pulled inward by a small bearded man. He first looked straight ahead, directly into Sam's armored chest, then his eyes moved slowly up, towards Sam's head. Sam telescoped the facial shielding back into his collar and leaned forward.

"You ordered pizza? *Hey* ..." The man's eyes rolled and he fell back. Sam shot out an arm to grab him. "I gotcha." He helped him upright again. "I'm Sam Reid, and I'm here to help."

The still speechless man led him inside, and at the main room, Sam had to duck down and turn sideways to enter. The Ellsworth group of scientists sat in a circle, their backs to multiple consoles and control panels. They all sat mute with folded arms, or tugging at straggly beards. For the most part, their gazes were firmly fixed on the ground, each man lost in his own thoughts. The sudden appearance of Sam had every mouth dropping open. They seemed in shock.

Only one man stayed at his console with his back turned as he typed away. He was furiously shaking his head. "I told you, I told *all* of you, that letting that Yank hijack our probe would crash *Orca*." He banged at more keys, continuing to mutter.

"Uh, Bentley?" One of the team members still had his eyes on Sam, but reached out an arm to tug the mutterer's sleeve. The man ignored it, and kept up his cursing complaints.

"Did anyone back me up? No-*ooo*." Bentley straightened in his seat. "I'm not one to say, *I told you so* … but, I bleedin' well *told you so*." He threw his hands up, and spun. "Worst – day – of my – fucking life." He froze, staring.

Sam in the MECH suit probably stood close to seven feet tall. In the warmth of the cabin the snow had melted on him, and the liquid runoff on his external armor carried with it some blood.

One of the scientists cleared his throat. "Hello. We are from earth. Please don't kill us."

Sam grinned and held up one huge hand. "Me too. I'm First Lieutenant Samuel Reid, Special Forces. I'm here to help and for your protection."

"No thanks," Bentley said, wiping a long, thin nose. "We're not a military base … and certainly not a US one. We're not obligated to work with you."

Sam smiled, knowing that their major funder, GBR, was owned by the US military. He'd hold that revelation back for now. "You already did, by sending one of our operatives under the ice." He pointed over his shoulder with a thumb. "From out there. I'm here for an update."

The man who had led him in edged around in front of him. "I'm Dr. Sulley, and from left to right, are doctors Timms, Schmidt, and Bentley."

The scientists nodded cautiously, and only Bentley's mouth remained turned down. "Like I said, worst day of my life, and it's not getting any better."

Sulley scoffed. "Give it a rest, Bent. You're still young, I'm sure you'll have plenty worse days to come." He chuckled softly, but held up a hand when Bentley shot a volcanic glare on him.

Bentley turned back to Sam, folding his arms. "I'd introduce you to our team leader, but the Yank, your friend, took her down in the probe."

Sam's brows rose near imperceptibly. He doubted this would have been Alex's choice. "Where are they now?"

Schmidt frowned. "Wait a minute, Lieutenant, what did you mean you were *here for our protection*? What does that mean?"

Sam hesitated for only a second. "Look, time is short, and what I tell you now is classified. Less than an hour ago, the McMurdo base was attacked by Chinese Special Forces. We successfully ... *subdued them*. There is also a Chinese destroyer off the Antarctic coast, and more warships on the way – theirs and ours." He looked at each man. "There is a possibility they may come here next. Gentlemen, things are getting real hot down on the ice."

"What? Why?" Timms got to his feet. "What did we miss?"

"Actually, it was what you didn't miss that started all this." Sam smiled, and tried to radiate calm to the men. "That tiny signal you first detected coming from under the ice, well, it's a missing submarine – ours. The Chinese want it. But we don't intend to let them get it."

Timms scoffed. "Oh fuck off, that underlying signal we thought was just a background distortion? Are you're telling us it was a submarine, under the ice?" He put his hands to his temples. "Boom, head explosion."

Sulley's lips had been pressed tight. "Hey, Lieutenant Reid, *ah*, why would the Chinese come here?"

Sam grinned and pointed to the wall in front of the probe launcher. "Seems we are now in a partnership to get down there first." He laughed at the looks they gave each other.

Bentley rubbed his hands up through his hair and muttered curses.

"So, where are they now?" Sam asked. "We don't have much time."

Bentley sat back and then turned around to his console. "Dead, most likely."

Sam felt the first flame of anger, but swallowed it down. "That's not what I asked you."

Sulley grimaced. "Sorry, but it's probably true, Lieutenant. *Orca*, the probe, was never designed to carry passengers. Our data showed us that the drop to the water's surface was 220 feet. The impact force would have been like a car crash. *Orca* survived and launched, but we doubt anything biological would have survived."

Sam titled his head. "But the probe survived ... and was sending you signals?"

"Sure, signals, environmental and visual data," Sulley said.

"Show me. Show me everything." Sam came closer.

"Sure." Sulley spun, his hands flying over the keyboards, twisting dials and then retrieving video and other data from the submersible's short voyage.

"*Orca* was designed to see, hear, and taste the subterranean environment." Sulley spoke over his shoulder as he called up the probe's images. "You know, he has the same amount of inbuilt capabilities as an orbiting satellite – probably more." He turned and grinned. "We did that."

Sam nodded. "And the probe was undamaged?"

"Well, mostly," Sulley said. "It didn't operate as expected, maneuverability went a bit wonky, and then we lost it at the end." He sighed. "Lost it, or had it taken, more like it. There was something else down there, something very big and very pissed off."

He reran the footage and Sam watched closely. The film started in near total blackness as the probe launched into the subterranean sea. The resolution was adjusted, and then improved, to show specks of light floating around them. At the periphery, Sam could see larger shapes pass in and out of the cone of light.

"Goes on like this for a while." Sulley sped it up, the duration counter at the bottom of the screen spinning numbers. "Here." He slowed it to normal speed again.

In another second or two, the submersible seemed to slide sideways in the water.

"And this is where it gets freaky," Timms said, standing behind Sulley.

Orca suddenly changed direction, nose up, rushing to the surface. It breached, and Sam's brows went up. The cavern was enormous and bathed in a soft blue twilight. Sulley leaned around in front of him, pointing to the floor at their feet.

"That's 2.55 miles right below us. Incredible, *huh*?"

"Incredible," Sam repeated, his eyes glued to the small screen.

"A-*aaand*, enter the leviathan," Bentley said ominously.

A few dozen feet out from *Orca*, a striped island appeared and then glided closer. The underwater shot showed a massive head turning side-on, and a gigantic round eye that studied them intently for a second or two, before the thing glided off to the right.

"Holy shit." Sam leaned back. "What the hell was that?"

"Don't know," Bentley said. "Big predator. Our computer estimated it to be about sixty feet in length." He chuckled. "Guess you just can't plan for everything."

The probe then dived, sharply, suddenly speeding up and continuing on down into the dark depths, until a darker cave, lined with conical teeth, rushed up to meet it. The film blacked out.

"Jesus." Sam exhaled. "That's it?"

"Yes and no. *Orca* is pretty tough, and he's still operational. But we think it's busted up pretty bad, and maybe, just maybe, it has beached itself somewhere. My instincts tell me that *Orca* can hear us, but doesn't have the power to respond." Bentley eased back in his chair.

Sam sat staring at the dark screen for several more seconds. "Sulley, show me the thing again ... where it came to the surface."

Sulley's fingers rippled over the keyboard as he rapidly skipped the footage backwards, until the twilight blue surface was in frame. "Here we go."

"Slow it down." Sam leaned in close, watching as the thing glided in front of the camera. Its huge orb of an eye hung in-frame. "Freeze that." He squinted. "Can you increase magnification, and tidy it up?"

"Sure." Sulley enlarged the image. The eye filled the screen, but was now blurry. The scientist then tapped keys, using a resolution algorithm in the software to sharpen the focus. His mouth dropped open.

"Oh my god." He leaned back. "Hey, you guys check this out."

Sam folded his arms. "What's a mere 220 foot drop to a HAWC?" He grinned at the screen.

In the center of the massive eye, in its soulless black pupil, was a reflection. It showed the glow of *Orca*'s nose-cone light, and just visible behind it were two diver-masked heads, one looking directly at them, and another facing away.

"They're alive." Timms clapped his hands. "Hey, Bentley, best day of your life, right?" He whooped.

Bentley gave him a brief, tight-lipped smile. "That doesn't really mean anything ... now. *Orca* was wrecked by that *thing*. If Cate and the Yank were hanging onto it, what do you think happened to them?"

"You're not really a glass half full kinda guy, are you?" Sam got to his feet, filling the room. He hated hearing Bentley's snide tone, but hated even more that the man was probably right. Whatever that thing was, being in the water with it was a death sentence – even for someone like the Arcadian. He drew in a deep breath and pushed the morbid thoughts away, staring down at the man.

"You know who one of my favorite military leaders is, Dr. Bentley? It's this funny looking little Brit guy called Winston Churchill. Gave a rousing little speech one day about never surrendering."

Timms saluted, and put on a mock voice. "We shall fight on the beaches, we shall fight in the fields and in the streets, we shall fight in the hills; *we shall never surrender*."

Sam leaned forward, Bentley shrinking back. "I'd like to see a little of that fighting spirit now." He straightened. "Alex Hunter wouldn't surrender, doesn't know how. It's not in his DNA. To him, it's fight or die." His eyes bored into Bentley's. "Tell me, why can't that probe operate?"

"Maybe it can, in parts," Schmidt answered quickly. "Probably busted up real bad, and the battery is at only ten percent strength – that's bad. But we still have contact, so that's good."

Sam folded massive arms, thinking. He began to pace for a moment, the floor creaking underneath him. He stopped and turned. "You're running all of the applications and processes concurrently, aren't you?"

Sulley nodded. "Yeah, most of them. Some we rest, but others are constant background apps. We need them to be that way, so ..."

"Shut them down," Sam said evenly.

There were confused looks and Schmidt sat stroking his beard for a second or two. He suddenly spun to do some quick calculations on his screen. He turned back, eyebrows raised.

"You know, we haven't tried that. I mean, chemical analysis alone used about ten percent of the battery. Shutting down all non-essentials, might, *just might*, give us enough kick to get vision back and also pull us into the water."

Nods and murmurs from Timms and Sulley.

Bentley folded his arms tight. "Great, if we can shut down anything of scientific value we *just might* have the world's most expensive underwater camera."

"Better than nothing. What have you got now?" Sam waited.

Schmidt looked across to Timms. "Do it."

Timms nodded, his fingers dancing over his console. "Shutting down magnetic resonance imaging, shutting down gyroscope," – panels went from green to red on his screen – "shutting down environmental sampling, biological sampling, chemical analysis, depth telemetry, sonar ..."

"No, leave that one for now," Schmidt said. "We'll also need ears once we're in the water." He shrugged. "Got to see *and hear* what's coming."

Timms continued switching off applications for a few more seconds before sitting back. "Batteries now up at forty percent – good as it's going to get."

Schmidt turned to Sulley. "Okay Sull, punch it."

Sulley eased back on a joystick. "Reverse propulsion at one quarter."

They waited. Timms shook his head. "Nothing."

Sulley eased it back some more. "Reverse at one third power." He turned to Timms who shook his head, his eyes on his own screen.

"Now at fifty percent."

Timms grimaced. "*Nada*, but the battery drain is beginning to hurt us."

Schmidt nodded to the screen. "Do it. Might as well be dead where it is now."

Sulley frowned as he pulled back on the small stick. "RP at 70%, 75%, 80% ..." His teeth were bared, as if he were bearing the physical strain of the submersible himself.

The visual feed screen suddenly showed a sliver of light as the thing jerked back a quarter inch.

"Whoa! Gentlemen, we have movement." Timms clapped once, and then there was suddenly a rush of a twilight blue glow filling the screen.

Sulley exhaled, grinning. He turned to Sam. "And we are now in open water."

*

Hagel froze, just letting his eyes move over the foliage. Did he just hear something, or was his mind just fucking with him again in this weird ass place? He was sure he'd heard something soft and heavy, like someone dragging a sack over wet grass. He turned slowly. Maybe he was just spooking himself?

There was nothing now – no cricket chirrup, no birdcall, or even the rustle of a breeze in this fucked up ghost jungle. If not for the odd drip of water, and his own breathing, he might have thought he'd gone deaf.

Hagel was following a trail of sorts, but the ground was squashy soft, covered in thick moss and lichen. There were soupy looking puddles everywhere, and everything stunk like bad mushrooms. He continued on, carefully placing one foot in front of the other. He could just make out the others about fifty feet back. Franks was keeping them relatively silent, but still the sound of their movement carried.

Hagel came to a bend in the trail at an enormous fallen tree – its trunk easily five feet around. He paused, listening. There was more dripping. He pulled his scope down over his eyes, switching from light enhance in the twilight atmosphere to thermal. There was a ton of background heat, but mostly everything was cold as the grave. He scanned slowly, stopping as something just off to the left showed a flare of warmth. He approached and noticed a spattering on the ground. Closer now, he saw more spattering on the trunks of the trees. He let his eyes travel upwards, higher to the broad fronds towering overhead, and then switched his scope to distance enhance.

"Fuck me."

He gritted his teeth and began to back up when he paused, turning to the line of the jungle. He frowned, seeing a natural tunnel formation within the undergrowth. There was something in there.

"Oh you gotta be shittin' me."

He retreated silently and quickly. He soon found Franks and held up a hand flat – the group halted. He motioned for just Franks to follow, and then the pair burrowed back through the undergrowth.

Hagel worked along the trail again, cautiously, and then found the huge tree, which he leaned against. Franks eased in beside him.

"I think we just found the rest of Dawkins." He motioned with his head towards the treetops.

Casey Franks used her hand scope to scan the canopy. About fifty feet up there was a body, or rather a torso, stripped naked, no head or arms, but still dripping blood.

Hagel watched her as she gazed at the body. A low growl started deep in her throat.

"It's dogging us," she said.

"Yep, that's what I figure." He nudged her. "And that's not all. Look in there ..." He pointed one grimy, gloved finger to the tunnel in the undergrowth.

Casey moved her scope, flicking it to light enhance to improve the illumination within the dark space. Hanging just inside was one of their laser rifles.

"Blake's," she said. "Suicide trap."

"This is too fucked up," Hagel said. "Gotta be the Chinese. No fucking animal is going to do this."

"Yeah, maybe." She pulled back.

Hagel watched her go, and then turned back to the jungle. His scalp prickled. He had the feeling something was watching, waiting, just past the first line of ferns, willing him to enter the undergrowth cave.

"Not today, motherfucker." He backed away, gun up.

CHAPTER 43

Shenjung Xing felt himself grabbed and dragged through warm water. He blinked, his eyes gritty and stinging, but still not focusing properly. His stomach convulsed, and coughing, he emptied about two pints of water from his gut, before he was cast up onto an embankment.

"Good, get it all out." Captain Yang stood over him.

Shenjung moaned and rubbed at his eyes, wiping out grit. He blinked, restoring his sight this time.

"Where …?" He sat up, and saw some of the soldiers nearby. There were ten, about half of Yang's original squad. Only one other was on his feet, the giant, Mungoi.

Yang turned to sit beside him, picked up a twig, and looked out over the river as it wended its way out of sight. "My men are gone." He nodded, still watching the water. "The flow is strong, and if they were unconscious they would have been swept away." He flicked the twig into the water. "More food for the worms."

Shenjung suddenly remembered and turned over, jamming fingers down his throat, and gagging up more water and bile.

Yang laughed. "Too late now, Doctor." He slapped Shenjung's back. "But I think we are okay; the water was moving too fast for them to get to us."

Shenjung flopped onto his back, wiping one hand over his sticky mouth. "Where are we? Did we make it out?"

"Out of the caves? Yes. But *out-out* ..." Yang motioned to the cliff wall, towering a half mile behind them, which then kept rising to touch a ceiling. "No, we are still in a cave. We fell, washed from up there." He motioned upwards.

Shenjung followed his hand. A hundred feet up from the ground, a torrent of water poured forth, slowing now that the deluge was being exhausted.

"The missing men, will we look for them?" Shenjung asked.

Yang glanced again at the surging water. "No." He got to his feet, and reached into a pouch to pull out his signal tracker. "Each man has a device like this one. If they are alive, they'll know where we are going, and they will join us. We cannot spend any more time down here."

"And if they are hurt?" Shenjung asked.

"Then they have a new home." Yang checked his tracker.

Shenjung pushed wet hair back off his face. He knew there was nothing he could say which would change the PLA captain's mind. He got unsteadily to his feet, wiped his face, and then looked around.

"So big, so ... fantastic. It's a forest, under the Earth." He turned slowly.

"And now, all Chinese territory," Yang said. "The Antarctic Treaty covers the continent's surface. But down here is no one's territory. So it all belongs to us." Yang lifted his head high. "I claim this land in the name of the People's Republic of China." He saluted, and then turned to grin at him. "Good day's work, huh?"

"Maybe you can be king." Shenjung turned away.

Yang leaned back, looking skyward. "Yes, and my new kingdom even has light."

Shenjung looked up at the twinkling stars in the dark blue heavens above them. "No, this is an illusion," he said softly. "We're still trapped in a cave ... just a bigger one. I wish to see the light, real sunlight, one more time, Captain."

Yang grunted. "Enough dreaming." He read from his tracker. "We're not far from the source of the signal." He looked up again briefly. "At least we can preserve our batteries on our way to the sub."

"Small gifts," Shenjung responded.

Yang turned to bark at his men. They got to their feet, some slowly. Their suits were sodden and ripped. Many were hunched with fatigue.

"Mungoi will lead us out." He pointed to where the far cave wall stopped at an endless dark sea. "That way."

Shenjung looked skyward one more time. *Sunlight, fresh air, and my Soong. Please be up there safe and waiting for me*, he silently prayed, and then followed the soldiers.

*

"Something."

Yang nodded to his scout, and turned to wave his remaining men down. He drew his revolver and followed.

Hung Balin was his latest scout. He was a good soldier – solid, trustworthy, even if not so brilliant. Already one of the previous scouts had gone missing. Perhaps he'd wandered too far ahead and got lost in the chaotic tangle of weird plants, some with poisonous looking barbs, stinging sap, or vines that refused to let go.

Though the jungle around them was deathly silent, Yang couldn't escape the feeling that they were being watched, followed by something that was always close by, sliding silently and just out of sight.

"Hung, what did you see?" Yang eased up closer to the man, crouching now, and slowing as his soldier did.

The soldier turned, but there was a hint of confusion in his eyes. "I saw something ... I couldn't see clearly at first. But then it became a person ... one of the engineers, I think."

Yang frowned. "Impossible. One of those we left in the higher caves? How did they get down here so quickly?"

Hung shook his head and continued to burrow through the undergrowth as Yang followed. It started to make sense – *this* is who had been following them – the engineers. They had been too scared to join them, but also too scared to be by themselves. Yang's chin jutted. They'd certainly feel his wrath when he caught them, he thought.

Hung led him to an opening in the undergrowth, with a small muddy pond at its center. The place was no more than twenty feet around, and almost totally overgrown to give the appearance of a dark green cave. The soldier turned and placed a finger to his lips. He waved Yang on and crept forward.

A man was standing perfectly still on the other side of the pond. He wore the familiar gray coveralls of the engineers, and was in the water. Yang frowned, *no, not in the water*. It looked like he was *on top* of the water.

"One of our engineers, but he doesn't move or acknowledge me. Maybe he is in shock," Hung said softly.

Yang snorted. "Go and get him, bring him back for questioning. I want to know how he got here and where the others are."

Hung nodded sharply, his expression brightening as if he were happy to have some concrete orders to carry out. He got to his feet as Yang started to ease backwards.

Captain Yang turned away and only took a few paces, when he heard a grunt and the thud of an impact. Looking back quickly, he saw Hung and the engineer in some sort of embrace. He groaned, thinking that either his soldier was overreaching in his orders to bring the man in, or perhaps the befuddled engineer was fighting back out of fear.

While he watched, he saw Hung, who outweighed the smaller engineer by at least fifty pounds, struggle for a moment more. There came a tiny sound that could have been a whimper of pain or fear, and then the larger PLA soldier was yanked from his feet to disappear into the thick foliage.

"Huh?" Yang blinked, not understanding what he was seeing. How could that little fart of a man overpower and drag away the bigger Hung? He spat in disgust and crawled forward quickly, following both men into the deeper undergrowth.

The stink was the first thing that assailed him – the stink, the slime that covered everything, and the fresh path through the foliage. He followed quickly and then when it opened out, he stood.

His soldier, Hung, was there, or what was left of him. He also guessed he might have found his other missing scout, as there were too many body parts for just one man. Hanging in the trees like some sort of macabre decorations were strips of flesh, arms, legs, and the trunk of a torso, impaled on a sharp branch. Blood dripped down onto the ground where it mixed with the mud to create a bubbling red-brown soup.

Yang felt his testicles shrivel and he tightened his fingers around his gun. *What had that little freak done to his men?* The stench in the small clearing made his eyes water. It smelled of ammonia, blood, bowel contents and crushed plants. He lifted an arm across his mouth and nose.

A flicker of movement in the corner of his eye caused him to spin, his gun up and heart hammering. The engineer stood silently in the shadow of a huge tree trunk. His expression was totally devoid of emotion, as if the mutilation laid out before him didn't exist.

"What have you done?" Yang whispered.

The figure edged forward, strangely, in a gliding manner like that of a ghost. The engineer looked wet, glistening, his eyes unfocused. He glided another few inches closer.

Yang took a step back. "Oh no, you don't." He took another step. "This is a trick." He eased back another few paces, and then turned and ran.

CHAPTER 44

Alex Hunter lifted his pace, forgetting about Cate, forgetting about anything that might have been lurking in the blue-lit undergrowth. He now knew that the Chinese were in the cave system – they'd be going for the *Sea Shadow*. He *must* get there first.

He also felt a growing awareness of something far more familiar – he had sensed the presence of a HAWC team for hours. He should have known that Hammerson wouldn't just send him in alone.

Strangely, he sensed another connection that both exhilarated and confused him. *It couldn't be*, he thought. She wouldn't … *he wouldn't*. Alex pummeled the undergrowth. Hammerson wouldn't dare send her. Anger flared and he swung out an arm, smashing a tree trunk from his path. She wouldn't come, she wouldn't leave Joshua by himself. It was impossible.

He's not by himself. You know she has someone else with her now. The whispered voice in his head sounded amused at his torment. Alex gritted his teeth, accelerating. Another trunk bared his way, and he lowered a shoulder, striking it hard, making the stump splinter away into the undergrowth. He tried to shut out the voice, its words, not wanting to acknowledge the truth.

Maybe now, he even calls him … father. A corrosive laugh. *Joshua doesn't need you, doesn't even know you. No one does anymore. You've been a ghost for years.*

Alex ricocheted off another huge tree trunk, not concentrating on his track. He placed a hand to his bloody face, wiping the stinging liquid from his eyes, blinded for a moment, and not seeing the sinuous scaled head rising up in the undergrowth.

The giant snake shot forward, striking Alex from the side, and gripping his body in its alligator sized mouth around the torso and one arm. The massive diamond shaped head was two feet across and was attached to a dark scaled body that still trailed forty feet into the foliage.

Alex was carried backwards from the impact to slam hard into one of the hairy Prototaxite trunks, dropping polypy fronds down on top of him. Though the ancient snake was incredibly powerful, its inwardly curved teeth were relatively small, and used for gripping rather than venom delivery. Alex's suit stopped the fangs from penetrating his flesh, but the danger was from the enormous body now piling in the undergrowth. If it managed to coil around his chest, the muscular body would easily crush the air from his lungs.

Easily distracted means easily killed. The voice was contemptuous this time.

Alex felt an enormous pressure building from the creature's mouth, but also inside his own head – *frustration, impatience, and raw fury* – he had no time for this. He reached up with his free arm and grabbed one side of the huge mouth, lifting and opening the huge jaws, and then ripped his other arm free. The black, glass-like eye displayed no surprise, nor fear, or even concern, it only reflected back Alex's own twisted features in those soulless depths.

Alex pulled back one arm, his teeth bared, and then punched down with all the strength he could gather. His fist exploded through the snake's eye, and on into its skull to then embed in the brain. Its mouth immediately sprung open, and the huge body and tail thrashed behind it as Alex held the head aloft to momentarily snarl into its dying face before throwing it aside and charging on again.

Faster, he needed to move faster. He reached out, his senses ballooning forward in a wave. He felt the multiple bodies, their hearts racing, the tangy smells of sweat and blood mixed with fear. The Chinese, they were far ahead; beating him to the submarine.

Kill them all. They were your orders.

"Kill them all," he repeated. His anger was boiling within him, his body now so hot. Even in the humid air, the moisture on his suit was rising from him as steam. He pushed his senses out again, but before he could get a lock on any one person he detected something else – a huge presence, a monstrosity with a malevolent intelligence, moving quickly and silently, rolling and tumbling, and flowing like liquid. He sensed its hunger, but also something more – its enjoyment.

Your old friend is still here. It's been waiting for you. The voice became caustic. *Don't run away this time.*

"*Wait!*" He barely heard Cate as she yelled after him. She was a long way back now, sprinting hard, but never hoping to keep up with him. She at least had the benefit of being able to move along the tunnel he was bullocking through the growth.

Alex put his head down. He was a dark blur smashing through the jungle – one monster pursuing another.

*

Captain Yang moved his men into the stand of gnarled and ancient looking trees. He pointed to each man, and then had them positioned where he wanted. Some in the canopy, some concealed in among low foliage, and some even pulling mats of lichen up over themselves. He grunted his satisfaction. His PLA were masters of natural camouflage.

His rear scouts had picked up the approach of the Americans a while back, and he eagerly awaited their arrival. He and his men seethed with hatred and a desire for vengeance. He had told them of the taken scouts, and of their bodies found mutilated, portions of them hung like grisly trophies in trees or impaled on low branches. The Americans were playing a gruesome trick on them; they were evil, and he would treat them accordingly.

"We should talk to them. I know Americans, and they would not have done this." Shenjung tugged at his sleeve, but Yang pulled his arm free.

"You know nothing. American war games are both physical and psychological."

"War games?" Shenjung shook his head. "No, you are the one making war. I must warn you, I will be compelled to report any … crimes."

Yang studied the man for several seconds, seeing the waver of fear in his eyes. He leaned in close to his face.

"Comrade Shenjung, you are not at home in your comfortable office anymore. Down here, all authority resides with me. Down here I am both law and punishment. For them, *and* you. Conceal yourself; that is an order." He pushed the man into the undergrowth.

Yang then walked to stand in the center of a flattened area of the jungle, with his back turned to the trail. He would be the bait at the end of a fifty-foot killing zone.

He concentrated – the silence in this strange world was unnerving, but now, it meant the slightest sound was magnified. The Americans were coming, close now. He smiled, unholstered his gun, stuck it in his belt, and then unzipped his fly. He waited a few moments until they were there, and began to urinate, slowly, making the stream last. He began to sing softly.

*

Rinofsky saw that Hagel had stopped, holding up a fist. He and the group halted, and waited as Hagel then turned to lift a single finger, and then waved them down.

The group crouched low and only Casey Franks eased up to join him. Hagel remained silent, just using two fingers to point at his eyes and then into the jungle at about ten o'clock. Casey followed his prompt, and then nodded, and then turned to point at Big Ben Jackson and Rhino and then out to two o'clock. She then sent Hagel and Blake out to nine.

Rhino and Jackson were first into position, staring at the PLA soldier ahead. Jackson leaned in close to Rhino.

"That's horrible," he whispered.

"Keep it down." Rinofsky scowled, but then spoke out of the side of his mouth, leaving his eyes on the target. "So where've you been pissing; in your water bottle?"

Jackson grinned. "I meant his voice, it's horrible."

Rinofsky groaned and put a finger to his lips. At the end of a small clearing, the Chinese soldier was standing by himself, taking a casual piss as if he was in his own bathroom. A soft tune lifted from him, as he seemed to be enjoying his ablutions.

"Stay here ... and stay alert." Rhino moved along the brush line, and then waited. Across from him, he saw Blake appear, and nod to him, and then hold up a hand. Blake pointed to the other end of the clearing. Casey Franks had stepped out, gun cradled in her arms as she watched the soldier finish up.

Casey stood slightly side-on, legs planted. "Hey," she said.

The man kept singing, and then jiggled a bit as if he was hiking up his zipper.

"Hey, water boy." Casey kept her eyes directly on him. "Turn around, real slow."

The man did neither. Casey half turned. "Blake, tell this guy to drop his cock, and turn around. Tell him that we're friends, or some other bullshit."

Blake talked softly, his voice carrying easily in the stillness. He was halfway through speaking when the soldier began to turn. In his hand was something other than his penis.

The small gun spat twice, and then the trees started to rain soldiers. From the canopy overhead, PLA Special Forces dropped down around them. Big Ben Jackson turned, and though he was a formidable soldier, he faced a man even taller than he. The big broad face creased in a gap-toothed grin, and then a leg as thick as a tree trunk shot out in a pile driver blow to strike him in the chest and fling him back into the trees.

Rhino moved to engage. The big HAWC and the bigger Chinese soldier traded rapid blows, and each blocked many. The huge HAWC was far superior to Jackson, and let fly with a single lunge punch that sounded like a mallet on clay. The Chinese giant staggered, but shook a head the size of a watermelon and then gap-grinned again.

He came at Rhino in a spin, a person that big having no right to be so quick and nimble. Rhino blocked the first kick, but a backhanded blow was already rounding on him. The fist that connected with his temple was the size of a dinner plate, and his oversized hands had calluses that were rock hard across the knuckles and palm edges.

Rhino went down on one knee, his head swimming. No one had ever hit him that hard in his life. He knew he was as good as dead. Once you lost focus in combat, for even a split second, the killing blow soon came. In the seconds between consciousness and oblivion, he remembered what Hammerson had said to him when he was recruited – HAWCs didn't die of old age. Rhino now knew; *HAWCs died like this.*

CHAPTER 45

The first bullet punched into Casey's right pectoral, spinning her and making the second one miss. In her armored suit, she knew only a head-shot could have been counted on to take her down for good. As it was, the impact would deaden her shoulder, but she ignored it as she had long learned to live with pain.

She rolled and came up fast, seeing Blake and Rhino engaging in combat, and the big McMurdo soldier, Jackson, already on the ground and struggling to breathe. The PLA seemed to be appearing from everywhere, and she had walked them right into it. *Fucking amateur hour*, she thought.

Her HAWCs she wasn't worried about, but she knew she had left Aimee and Soong without cover. The pissing soldier who had shot her was coming at her fast. He was big, with eyes that were black as coal. There was no hint of anything other than determination to finish her off.

"Fuck you." She spun, sweeping one of her legs around, taking him off his feet, and sending his gun flying. A punch to her ear suddenly told her that she wasn't fighting just one man. She dived and rolled and came up in front of the first PLA soldier, who was now back on his feet. He was half a head taller, and trained to solid muscle.

She backed to the side, trying to keep both of her attackers in view. Casey excelled at unarmed combat, and in a number of different disciplines, all blended into a style created just for the

HAWCs, termed RADET – Rapid Debilitation Technique. Most maneuvers were lethal, and she had been trained for fighting multiple opponents.

But for each kick or punch she and her combatants threw, the other would block it, and would in turn direct ever more furious punches, strikes, and kicks back towards the other. Casey gritted her teeth, becoming ever more infuriated. Unwaveringly, the two soldiers betrayed nothing – no surprise, fear, pain – they never grunted, made a noise, or changed their expression. It was like she fought robots.

Seems they've picked up their training, she thought. Though her focus was supreme, she became aware of a whistle, and then it was like the combat changed up a level. The PLA to her left kicked out, pushing her back. She blocked it, but immediately felt a jarring impact to her spine. The blow wasn't meant to do anything other than knock her forward again into the flying boot of the first guy.

Casey saw stars, her head swimming for a few seconds, before she came up with a blade in her hand, blinking away watering eyes and a streaming bloody nose.

When her world cleared, she found she was alone. Her opponents had left the field. Jackson was rubbing his neck and helping a groggy Rhino to his feet. Blake was walking back towards her, also wiping blood from his lip.

"They're gone. There was whistle, and they just vanished."

Casey grimaced from the pain, and felt her nose and eye socket. It was raw and hurt like a bitch, but the eye orbital wasn't shattered. "A signal. Something changed, or they ..." She spun. "Shit." She sprinted back to where they had left Aimee, Soong, and Jennifer.

Jennifer was face down on the boggy ground. Casey knelt and flipped her over. Thankfully the woman was breathing and her eyes opened slowly.

"Wha ...?"

The others crowded around.

"Easy. You okay?" Casey sat her up, ripping her canteen from her pouch and tipping it into the McMurdo woman's mouth.

Jennifer nodded. "They came ... from the jungle." She looked up, her mind seeming to clear. "Where are they?" She spun one way and then the other. "Aimee and Soong, they took them."

Casey gritted her teeth. Hagel jogged back in.

"They're gone."

Casey looked up at him. He didn't have a scratch. Her eyes blazed, but she kept her mouth shut ... for now. She turned.

"Rhino!" She turned to the big man, who still looked groggy. "Get your head back in the game. We're going after them, now."

"No, we're not." Hagel stood his ground, looking down on Casey as she held Jennifer's shoulder. He shook his head.

"You just made bad decision number one hundred and ten. As far as I'm concerned you're done." He leaned his rifle against a trunk. "You fucking walked us right into it."

Hagel looked up at Rhino, and then to Blake. "They could have mowed us all down. Just as well they decided to pull back, or we'd be food for whatever goddamn thing it is that's ghosting us down here."

Casey rose slowly to her feet, feeling her adrenalin start to pump.

Rhino winced. "Hagel, c'mon, man. This is not the time."

"Not the time to be ambushed." Hagel snorted. "We're fucking HAWCs. No one, but *no one*, gets the jump on us." He grinned, turning to Rhino. "Unless we have an incompetent leading us."

"Ah, fuck." Rhino looked skyward.

"You want to be the daddy now? That it, Hagel?" Casey sneered, but her brow dropped.

"Maybe I should be," he said evenly.

Before anyone could blink Casey had her Glock pointed between the man's eyes. "Insubordination in field, only one way to deal with that."

"*Boss.*" Rhino grimaced.

"All mouth, just what I thought." Hagel didn't blink as he stared back into the gun's muzzle. "Takes more than a gun to be a leader." He leaned forward slightly. "Certainly not a job for a coward." He grinned.

Casey chuckled. "Oh boy." She stared down at the ground for a moment, before letting her gun drop. She then lifted her rifle from her shoulders and let that drop beside it. Next went her knives. "Time for some education."

Ben Jackson put one large hand to his head. "Now? You're gonna do this *now*?"

Hagel turned back, a grim smile on his face. He started to pull and drop his own weapons. "No weapons, no rank, no report."

"Just you, me, and your big fucking mouth ... that's gonna be full of broken teeth in about ten seconds," Casey said, keeping her gaze leveled at the young HAWC. "I'm going to enjoy this, you little freak."

Casey got into a crouch, and began to circle. Hagel did the same.

"Are you two mad?" Jennifer Hartigan was on her feet. She turned to Rinofsky. "Stop them. Make them stop."

He shook his head. "Bad blood, got to be sorted."

Hagel came in fast. He feinted one way, and then threw two flat-handed strikes at Casey's face. She blocked them both, and returned her own, her fist flicking out, and Hagel just pulling back by fractions. Both swung, dodged, and kicked out, but this was only the prelude, the sizing up, and it soon ended.

They engaged. The two HAWCs came together in an explosion of furious blows. Every part of their body, every hard or sharp edge, was a formidable weapon. Each HAWC warrior was trained to be an ultimate combatant – fearless in attack, and near impervious to pain.

The sound of reinforced knuckles against armor plates was as loud as the punches were hard. Both fighters knew that a full strike of that force to a vulnerable area would be devastating or even lethal. Regardless, neither of them pulled their punches.

The pair broke apart momentarily. Both were now streaming perspiration and blood. They sucked in the humid air of the jungle. Casey's scar lifted her face into its usual sneer. She knew that both of them were fast, well trained, and could give and take a killer punch. But she felt calm, her heartbeat barely rising over resting normal. She knew she could withstand whatever Hagel dished out. Her heart was like iron, and so was her jaw.

She looked Hagel up and down, assessing him again. He was younger, bigger at just on six two, and weighing in at around 220 pounds. His physique was iron hard through training and a tough Special Forces existence. Casey was four inches shorter and many pounds lighter. But anyone who had seen her stripped down attested to a body that had obviously navigated years of pain. She had bullet holes, a zipper stitching of old scars, burns, and flaring tattoos, all over muscles that bulged without an ounce of fat. Pain was her friend, and fighting was an equation. When facing a skilled opponent, for her it came down to two elements of that equation: who could take the most pain, and who had the most experience. She smiled, because that would be her.

She decided on her next move. Hagel's reach was longer, so she needed to be behind that reach. To do that meant taking a risk, and she took it. Casey lunged straight at Hagel. He threw his arms up, but then flicked out one fist to lash across her jaw. It connected, hard. A lesser opponent would have been rocked back on their heels, or maybe even felled.

Casey expected it, planned for it, and took the impact on her jaw. As Hagel's arm continued on its swing, she had what she wanted – she was close to her goal, and under his reach. In a lightening fast strike, she struck out at his throat. Her hand was open, and she caught his larynx between her thumb and forefingers. His windpipe collapsed, the cartilage closing off.

The bigger man coughed and staggered back; only his training kept him focused, as his hands never dropped. But Casey knew now his oxygen was cut off, in seconds, his overstrained body would burn through his reserves, and first his head would begin to pound and then his vision would swim. Once that occurred, no matter how hyper-trained you were, oxygen panic would start to short-circuit the system.

Casey nodded into the man's eyes, letting him know it was over. Either he surrendered, or she would enjoy putting him down.

Hagel made his choice and came at her, his teeth showing through split lips, his eyes manic and white, framed by slick bloody features. Such was the depths of the man's hatred for her. He staggered as he came. Casey dodged his clumsy attack, and used his own bodyweight to throw him over one of her legs.

Hagel landed on the ground with Casey immediately on top of him. She started to pound down, blow after blow, her reinforced knuckle plates smashing bone and shredding flesh.

"Enough." Rhino tried to drag her off, but she wasn't done. Her bloodlust not yet sated.

The two gunshots were loud in the near tomb silence of the jungle. The bioluminescent light overhead immediately went out.

Casey froze ... the seconds ticked by, and then gradually, the bioluminescent creatures on the roof of the massive cave overcame their timidity and started to glow once again. The twilight gloom returned.

Jennifer stood holding Casey's Glock, the barrel pointed in the air.

Underneath Casey, Hagel gasped like a fish out of water. She quickly reached down and gripped his throat at the area of the compression, squeezed, and then tugged hard, pulling the cartilage back into place. It'd hurt like a bitch, and would swell back up, but at least he'd be able to breathe. Hagel dragged in two huge breaths and then groaned.

"Oh shit," Rhino said.

Around them it was as if the jungle had fallen into a vacuum. Casey slowly stood up from the man's chest, wiping the blood and gore from her hands on her pants. She waited.

Rinofsky's face was lit by a small box he had pulled from his belt. He held it up and turned slowly. He frowned down at the small tracker.

"Boss ..."

"What've you got?" Casey asked evenly.

"Movement, boss ... plenty of it," Rhino said without looking up.

Blake led Jennifer in closer, and Jackson joined them, looking at the small device in Rhino's hand.

"Incoming?" Casey walked away from Hagel's prone form and took the gun from Jennifer's hand. As she holstered the weapon, she noticed that the McMurdo medic had blanched at her frightful appearance.

Casey half smiled, and turned away to collect her knives and rifle from the ground.

"I'm right here, Rhino, talk to me."

"Multiple signatures, too many to fully register. They're big and small, but get this, they're all moving away. Disappearing off the grid."

Casey grunted. "They're going to ground." She turned slowly, and scanned the dark, dripping growth surrounding them. "Making noise down here, and you might as well have just rung the dinner bell." She growled. "Fucking distraction." She turned back to where Hagel lay. "I should have just shot you, you bag of ..."

The man was gone.

"What the fuck?" Casey spun. "Where'd that asshole go?"

Jennifer put a hand over her nose. "That smell is back. Just like in the caves." She started to back up, looking like she was going to bolt.

"Grab her." Casey pointed and Blake lunged at the woman, gripping her arm.

Casey quickly went to where Hagel had been laying. The mosses and lichen mats were flattened, and so was a glistening path leading into the underbrush.

"Hagel," Jennifer screamed. "Hagel!" She strained against Blake's hands, her eyes wide. "We have to go after him."

"That's just what it wants," Casey said softly, scanning the jungle with her gun up.

"I don't like this." Ben Jackson backed in towards them.

Casey looked from the grass to the shrinking group. "He's gone. He wouldn't walk out and leave his rifle." She nodded towards it. "Rhino, get the weapon. We're out of here."

"I heard that," Rhino said, picking up the gun, his eyes on the jungle. "Go after Dr. Weir, boss?"

"No, we head for the signal." She pointed. "It's where the Chinese will be going. Maybe we can get the jump on them. We stay fast and stay tight." She turned and vanished into the jungle, the others at her heels.

CHAPTER 46

Time: 08 hours 07 minutes 12 seconds until fleet convergence

"I'm sorry," Soong whispered to Aimee, whose hands were tied together in front of her. A length of rope tethered her to the giant Chinese soldier in front.

Aimee snorted. "I don't exactly remember, but when was it that we had you tied up?" She scoffed. "Must be a cultural thing, huh?"

Soong shook her head. "I trust you, but they do not. I told Captain Yang that you didn't take their men, that it was something else, something down here already. And that you know what it is." She stared hard at Aimee. "They could have killed all of you … I stopped them."

Aimee snorted. "Do you have any idea what they're triggering by going after the American submarine? Do you really think that they're going to be allowed to walk out of here with the technology?" She shook her head. "Not that any of us is going to walk out of here."

Soong sped up slightly, leaving Aimee behind.

"There could be war," Aimee said forcefully to Soong's hunched shoulders.

The Chinese woman half turned. "You can talk to my friend."

"Shenjung Xing? Damn right I'll talk to him, that's why I'm here," Aimee said, but Soong had threaded her way around the giant Mungoi, who turned to grin and tug a little harder on her rope.

Yang led them towards a small camp, or rather an area of flattened foliage in among the tangled jungle.

Soong ran to Shenjung Xing. Aimee recognized the scientist immediately from Hammerson's profile picture. The pair embraced warmly. Shenjung reached up to tenderly brush strands of hair from her face, and Aimee now knew why Soong had so eagerly wanted to come with them. Soong spoke rapidly, and Shenjung's face creased into a frown. His eyes lifted to Aimee.

"Untie her." He spoke loudly, but Yang ignored him. Mungoi continued to stand like a colossus, hanging on to Aimee's leash like she was a pet dog.

Aimee held up her bound wrists. "Do you mind?" She spoke directly to Yang. "I'm not going to run off into the jungle by myself, and I think you know why."

Yang shook his head, and turned back to his conversation with one of his men. Aimee let her breath hiss out from between clenched teeth. She turned to Shenjung.

"You know what? We came down here for you. To warn you that there is a potential global conflict happening over our heads. I was sent as a diplomat ... a spokesperson. If you ever managed to find your way out, which is unlikely, you'll find something a lot different than diplomats waiting for you."

Yang, overhearing, finally turned, his lips a thin line. "We are not afraid of you. This century belongs to China, Dr. Weir." He looked Aimee up and down for a second or two, and smirked. "And we cannot go back, because Dr. Soong Chin Ling has informed us that you blew up our base." His face was like stone. "She also tells me that you may know another way out. I agreed not to kill your people, because she convinced me that you would help us find that path back out. But if you won't, then I am more than happy to finish my job."

Aimee stared for a moment. "Listen, that wasn't us. That was your own people that set your base to self-destruct. And by the way, one of your men ambushed and killed our captain."

Yang's lips pursed. "Only your captain? Shame."

Aimee growled under her breath. She turned back to Shenjung. "You fools, you're in danger. I know your soldiers are going missing, so are ours. You sense it out there; *I know you do*. It's the other thing I needed to warn you about – what *really* lives down here."

"Lives down here?" Shenjung looked from Aimee to Soong. Behind them, Yang edged closer.

"There's a reason this place is off-limits. It's unsafe." Aimee waited. Yang's eyes narrowed, but they slid to Soong.

Soong's brows were knitted. "There is something, in the caves. And now, maybe down here with us."

"No *maybe* about it." Aimee tugged on her rope. "It's big, smart, and hungry ... and we're right in its goddamn backyard." She nodded to their weapons. "And you guys might as well have pea shooters for all the good they'll do."

"We are not that easily tricked," Yang said evenly. "We have seen nothing." He looked away quickly.

Shenjung's head snapped around to Yang. "But you did! The scouts went missing, to turn up massacred. And then just hours back ..."

"*I saw nothing!*" Yang's voice boomed. He pointed a fist at Aimee. "Nothing but what the Americans wanted me to see."

"Oh, bullshit," Aimee spat the words back at him, and tugged angrily on the rope. "You're going to walk everyone right into the jaws of death, literally."

Yang's lip curled. "An American trick, denied by an American spy, sent to divert us." Yang held up a hand. "We will complete our mission, secure the site of the derelict submarine, and then Dr. Weir will show us the way out."

Anger began to burn within Aimee, and it blew apart any diplomacy she had planned. "Your mission?" Her jaw jutted, and she lifted her head. "You think you can take ownership of American property?" She smiled at the way his head turned to her a fraction. "That's right, that *derelict submarine* is the *Sea Shadow*. You try and even set foot on it, and there'll be war ... and one you can't win."

Yang sauntered closer. "You still think you can win a war with us?" He threw his head back and barked out a single laugh. "Our cyber-technologists will shut down your launch programs before they even start." He leered at her. "By the time you figure out what went wrong, your country will be ash."

Aimee lunged at him. "You fucking ..."

Yang's backhand knocked her down. Shenjung and Soong rushed to her, shielding her, but Aimee pushed them away, and wiped her mouth.

"You weak sonofabitch, you're as good as dead, and don't even know it. One by one, either in the next few minutes or hours, the thing down here will catch you, rip you to shreds, and you won't be able to do anything about it. You can't even hide, because it will find you, dig you out, and rip walls apart to get at you."

She felt exhausted, beaten. "Forget the submarine. We need to be gone from here, and we need much better defenses. At least combine your forces with the HAWCs. That way we might, *just might*, be able to make it."

Yang tilted his head. "So it's our supplies, ammunition, and protection you need? If you think we will assist your team, you are wrong."

Aimee's head dropped for a moment. "We're all going to die." She looked up slowly, turning to Soong. "Make sure you stay in the center of the group, don't lag behind. Predators always pick off the stragglers first."

Aimee exhaled in exasperation. She suddenly realized that she had failed. She followed the thought – if she failed, then there was no turning the Chinese back from trying to get to the submarine. The future was set, and there would be justification for conflict – *war*. Millions would die, and she was here, and Joshua up there. She felt a cramp in her stomach at the thought of him being alone.

"Ho!" Yang pointed, and the team marched on.

*

The gunshots jerked Alex back to his senses. They were close, and he recognized the sound of the handgun – a Glock 22, plastic casing, feather light with a lot of punch, and an excellent weapon for wet environments. It was a jungle weapon and also part of the HAWC arsenal.

He slowed as he burst into a clearing and skidded to a stop. The trees were flattened, some of them with trunks a half dozen feet across, and others sunk deep into the soft ground as if something heavy had pushed into the jungle and rested there. There was a coating of ammoniac slime over everything that hung in the air like a stinging mist. Alex eased back into the tree line, wary. He knew that the nightmare predator that stalked, and probably attacked, his people was the most successful and inventive monstrosity that he had ever faced. His best chance of survival – *everyone's best chance of survival* – was to simply avoid it.

Alex let the vines fall in front of him, and remained motionless. Aimee had once told him that cephalopods had acute vision that was triggered by movement. He just let his eyes travel over the foliage of the hundred feet of crushed plants, and the canopy and edges, looking for anything, no matter how camouflaged, that might have hinted at its presence.

Alex's enhanced vision could pick up details at a granular level and also allowed perfect sight in night-black environments that was well beyond normal human vision. He could also "see" thermal variations. If something was warmer or colder than its surroundings, he would know it.

After another moment he stepped out and walked a few paces into the clearing. There was something black and glistening red, incongruous among the mud browns and drab greens. He quickly moved to it, snatching it up. He recognized it – he wore the same thing. It was an armored HAWC suit, its ceramic plating and Kevlar weave tough enough to withstand a shotgun blast, but here it was torn apart like paper. It was coated with streaks of blood and gore. The creature had taken at least one of the HAWCs, had peeled them out of the suit, and he could guess what happened after that. He dropped the armor, its obliterated remnants making it impossible to even guess who it had belonged to.

Alex wiped his hands. They were sticky, as the blood hadn't fully coagulated – it was minutes fresh. Both his team and the thing were close by.

Come on guys, Hammerson would have made you read the reports, he whispered. *You know what you're up against.* Alex reached out again – he could still sense the huge presence, but it was further out now, and moving away. He grabbed for his signal finder, quickly checking the readout and then cursing. The predator was headed in the same direction he needed to go ... and the direction he bet his HAWCs had gone.

"Damnit, it's tracking them."

"Alex."

He turned at Cate's voice, and stepped in front of the bloody debris. "Stay there."

She froze, wheezing, her face beet red. "What is it?" She gasped. "I can smell ... *phew* ... cat pee."

"Ammonia; it exudes it. Allows it to leave the water without drying out."

"This thing – is it your Kraken?"

"My Kraken?" Alex turned to face the cliffs. "Yeah, my Kraken," he whispered. He imagined the beast pursuing the HAWCs, or maybe traveling parallel to their position, staying just out of sight. Its huge, boneless body keeping compressed and low, flowing around and over the trees and foliage like a slimy, muscular wave as it kept them in sight, staying close to its food ... or its new toys.

Cate looked from the massive depression in the foliage, and then up at him, her eyes round. "This big? There's nothing like this in the fossil record."

"Yes, there is. According to one of the scientists who was with us, it was called an orthocone."

Cate frowned, looking around again. "*Cameroceras*, orthoconic cephalopods, I know them. They were the apex predator of their time. But that was during the Ordovician period, hundreds of millions of years ago. And they only grew to about thirty feet, *max*." She waved an arm around at the flattened trees. "This thing must have been ..." Her lips compressed. "Hundreds of feet." Her brow creased even further. "And it had a large conical shell, like some sort of mollusk."

Alex kept his eyes on the jungle. "Seems it had plenty of time to evolve. It's still the apex predator, but it's developed a whole bunch of new skills." He looked around. "It only used the shell in the water, and could leave it behind when it wanted to pursue us into the caves. It was able to flatten its body, get into the smallest of crevices, flowing almost like liquid. And it was a mimic – a *very* good mimic." He looked at her.

She was frowning as she listened, but nodded. "Many creatures, and certainly many cephalopods, can mimic their surroundings, or even other animal shapes ... in a fashion."

"Not like this thing," Alex responded. "It could create near perfect images of our people. Once it had ingested them, it could ... become them."

"That's impossible." She turned away, arms folded.

"That's what I would have said ... before." He sighed and looked past her towards the dark sea. "Maybe it felt it only needed the shell in the water. Maybe your leviathan friends out there caused it to retain its armor. Got a weakness, after all." He wondered how he could use this, but quickly gave up. "We've got to hurry, there were gunshots." Alex looked down at her, wishing he could leave her behind, but knowing that would spell her death. Urgency now coiled within him. "Cate, we need to try and catch up ... with my team."

Cate nodded and her mouth curled down. "Boy oh boy, what I wouldn't give to catch a glimpse of this thing."

"No," Alex said softly. "If it was close enough for us to see, we'd be dead, or just become part of its cat and mouse torture game. We're going to stay as far away from this thing as we can." He grabbed hold of her shoulders. "But if we do see it, I'm just hoping it's long before it sees us."

*

"Warm bodies ... with plenty of nonbiological elements. Gotta be our PLA friends." Rhino held up the reader, turning slightly. "Multiple signatures, all about the same size, and all stationary."

Jackson grunted. "Not gonna let these guys get the jump on me again."

Rhino leaned back. "Don't feel too bad. These guys are robots – trained to be lethal since they were kids. We can take 'em, but that might mean permanent take-down. Not a great option while they've got Dr. Weir." He exhaled. "And the last thing we want to be doing is starting a war that we were sent to stop in the first place."

Casey came back in and crouched. Blake and Jennifer joined them. "Fifty feet, directly in front. They're not moving."

"Ambush?" Jackson asked.

"If it's an ambush, it's a strange one." Casey's lip curled. "Nah, unlikely. We've seen the concealment techniques these guys have used. They wouldn't just be hanging it out there in the open." She looked around. "Better scan for claymores, or anything else they could use for booby traps."

"I don't think so, boss," Rhino said. "That big guy coulda taken me out clean. He didn't. I don't think that's what they wanted."

"Maybe they want to talk," Blake said. "Let me go in."

"Not a fucking chance," Casey spat back.

"*Attention, HAWC Special Forces operative Casey Franks!*'

"What the fuck." Casey's head jerked around.

"*HAWC Special Forces operative Casey Franks, operative Hank Rinofsky, operative Vincent Blake, soldiers Jennifer Hartigan and Benjamin Jackson. Come forward. We will not harm you.*"

Casey turned to the group, her teeth clamped tight.

"No secrets in hell, huh?" Rhino said to Blake.

The voice drifted back to them again. "You are outgunned, outnumbered, and we have your chief scientist. Lower your weapons, we just wish to talk."

All eyes were on Casey. She got to her feet. "Jackson, you come with me. Jennifer, stay put. Rhino, Blake, left and right flank." She looked up at Jackson. "Stay on my shoulder, and stay cool."

Rhino grinned at the big McMurdo soldier. "You just got a promotion, big fella ... coz you're expendable."

Jackson grinned back. "That's the nicest thing anyone ever said to me."

Casey cradled her gun and pushed through the broad fronds and hair-like foliage of the blue tinged jungle.

CHAPTER 47

Casey stood just inside the line of hanging vines, watching the two men in the clearing. Rising up behind them, nearly invisible in the gloom, was the cliff wall, and the source of the signal. Somewhere at its base, or even inside, their goal resided.

So close, she thought. She looked back at the men. There was the brutal, black-eyed soldier, their leader – she assumed – one of the men she had briefly fought only just before. Behind him was the giant she had seen take down Jackson and Rinofsky. The massive soldier didn't look human, and she assumed he was afflicted by something like acromegaly, the gigantism syndrome. His features were big and broad to the point of being ogreish. But instead of the lumbering gait she would have expected from someone like that, he moved fluidly, athletically. She knew he'd be a problem.

Peeking out behind him was Aimee Weir. By the way Aimee held her shoulders, she guessed her hands were tied.

"Show time." Casey grit her teeth and stepped forward.

She knew that though Aimee wasn't being used as a shield, her proximity meant going in shooting was not an option. She also bet that the other PLA solders were close by, and a single word from their leader would bring them from the trees and trapdoors.

The soldier in front of her stood at ease, his hands clasped behind his back. He brought a hand around, making Casey brace, but it was empty. He motioned her forward.

"HAWC Casey Franks."

Casey waited, watching.

"What now," Jackson whispered.

"Now? Now, we join the party." Casey continued in, her gun cradled.

The soldier smiled, but the lift of his lips never reached his blank eyes. "I am Captain Wu Yang of the PLA Special Forces, Dragon Brigade. You are Casey Franks of the American Special Forces, HAWCs." He half turned. "Your chief scientist speaks very highly of you. She tells me we need you and your team's expertise to survive." He chuckled and looked around. "In this strange and savage place."

"You bet you do," Casey said.

"I think I do." He nodded. "But I do not think I need you, though I do think we need your armaments. However, I am generous. Hand over your weapons and join us. It makes sense for us to combine under my leadership. I outrank you, Lieutenant."

"Not in my army, pal." Casey didn't flinch.

Yang smiled grimly. "We could have killed you all. Many times. Please don't make me regret that decision."

"We're just gonna find what we came here to find, and we'll take Dr. Weir back. No one gets hurt, no one wastes time, energy, or ammunition. Then we all go home."

"Go home?" His expression hardened. "I believe you shut that door ... and killed our people." His arms dropped to his sides. He spoke a few words in Chinese, and the giant turned to put a large hand on Aimee's shoulder and pull her forward.

Yang took hold of Aimee and looked into her face for a few seconds. "I know you Americans, very well. You value the individual, where we in China have learned to value the whole. One life is worth nothing." He gripped Aimee by the hair, dragging her head to one side.

Aimee grimaced, but never made a sound.

"I won't ask you again." His eyes slid back to Casey.

Casey's jaws clenched briefly. "We all know where this is going. Let's just get to it."

Yang turned. "Last time."

Casey didn't want a firefight, not while Aimee was so close. She needed to make some space. "I coulda kicked your ass – still might."

She needed more time; her eyes traveled to the giant. "How about I chop Dumbo down to size first."

Yang stared for a moment, perhaps not believing what he was hearing from the woman. His face broke into a grin and then he started to laugh. He half turned to speak a few words to the giant. In return the big man's eyes widened momentarily, before he too started to laugh, the sound like two buzzsaw blades grating together.

Jackson leaned forward. "Maybe I should take that guy on, you know, because ..."

Casey half turned, snarling. "Because you're a man, huh? Listen, boy scout, he already handed you your ass once. I can take him, you haven't got a chance."

The huge PLA soldier leaned down towards Yang and spoke in a deep slow voice. Yang listened, grunted and then nodded. "His name is Mungoi. Maybe if you defeat him in unarmed combat, I might let you live. If not ..." He grinned. "You won't be here to know about it."

Yang let Aimee's hair go and clapped his hands once. "Trial by combat. Yes, this is appropriate for warriors. You have my permission to kill him, if you can." He turned and spoke rapidly to Mungoi, and the huge man grinned, his eyes sliding to Casey. "And he has my permission to kill you."

Yang clicked his fingers, and his men came from the trees. Several escorted Blake, Rinofsky, and Jennifer.

"Ah, *fuck*." Casey felt her spirits sink.

Yang ordered them tied up, the same with Jackson. All their weapons and provisions were taken and piled before them. "You really must update your concealment techniques." He smiled without humor. "Good, now we are all here as witnesses. If at any time, Casey Franks, you wish to retire before you are beaten, I'm sure Mungoi will be happy to fight your replacement." He chortled, and spoke again to the giant PLA soldier. Mungoi nodded vigorously. Yang turned back to Casey. "Perhaps he could fight you all at once, if you're feeling a bit nervous."

Casey balled her fists. Never had she wanted to break someone in half so bad. She wanted to rip through the big dummy, and then wipe the floor with Yang. Her problem was, her people were unarmed, and Yang's soldiers were fully armed. She doubted that she would be spared even if she were victorious.

She had no choice, and deep inside, she didn't want one. She just wanted to fight.

*

Alex could sense the huge presence close by, but couldn't get a fix on where it was. It felt like it was in front of him, behind him, and all around him. Maybe it was just the terrain, maybe this might have been the killing field or foraging ground for the creature before, and that's what made its presence loom so large.

He also sensed the bodies up ahead. People, and he knew now it was his team, as there was one he could feel more strongly than all others. His heart rate kicked up a notch, not from any sort of adrenalin kick, but from the thought of seeing her again. Aimee, Aimee Weir, it could only be her.

Alex was torn between his excitement at her being so close, and also his outrage at her decision to leave Joshua behind. He needed to understand why she had abandoned their son ... *for this*. Alex bulldozed through some clinging vines. For the first time in years, he felt something strange – a nervousness that he found both worrying and exhilarating.

There was a grunt from behind, and Cate called out. He ground his teeth and spun, indecision momentarily wracking him. He needed speed, but with the thing lurking somewhere close by, leaving Cate behind was out of the question.

Alex sprinted back to her, and lifted her. "Keep your head down, it's here."

Cate looked shocked, and then tucked her head into the crook of his neck. Alex turned and accelerated, holding one elbow up in front of them, and smashing through the foliage – faster, and then faster again.

His neck tingled. Just out of sight, something heavy slid through the undergrowth. Plants were pushed aside or flattened as it kept pace, or perhaps only part of it needed to follow them. Alex felt like they were small prey, being hunted down ... or worse, they were being herded exactly where it wanted.

*

"Bring the pain." Casey advanced.

Mungoi made fists and brought one trunk-like leg forward and stamped it down hard. He then went through a few karate katas, a detailed pattern of combat movements. For a big man, he was fluid, and controlled – not what Casey wanted to see.

She knew how to fight bigger opponents. She was tall for a woman, but in her game, some of the players were more than a head taller. This guy happened to be twice that, but the basic rules still applied: big guys were blind to overhand bomb-punches – they never expected to be hit down upon. She would leap in the air and punch down at him. She would also go to his body, use front kicks, and try and get inside his huge reach. But it was a risk. His arms were as thick as her thighs. If he got hold of her it'd be all over. Finally, if possible, she would need to get him on the ground. Once there, everything was even.

Casey knew her training was superior, and she would be much faster. It'd have to be enough. She sucked in a huge breath, and breathed out evenly through her nose. She felt calm, she felt good. She attacked.

She darted in, and immediately ducked under a swinging arm that created a breeze over her head. She punched out twice, hard and fast into his kidneys. Mungoi didn't flinch. The man had a layer of fat and slab-like muscle running around his torso.

She came back again, this time feinting one way, and then coming back lightening quick to shoot out a kick with her armored boot, straight at his knee. His legs might have been able to support thousands of pounds, but the kneecap, if forced back on itself, was surprisingly weak.

Her leg flicked out, but before she could complete her full motion, Mungoi braced himself, her boot bouncing off the bent forward limb, and then a backhand blow caught her on the ear. She staggered.

The huge PLA soldier's fist was half as big as her head, and had raised knuckles like knobs of rock. Her head rang like a bell, and her ear immediately felt wet. She shook her head to clear it, and was relieved to feel she hadn't lost balance and could still hear. That meant the eardrum wasn't perforated, and it was probably just the cartilage and flesh that had been smashed.

Mungoi advanced, and Casey backed up. She edged to one side, then the next. But every time she shifted, so did he. The bigger man was boxing her in.

Fuck it, Casey thought. *The big asshole is trying to reduce my field of movement. Can't let him corner me, or I've had it.*

She then saw her opening. Mungoi kept his arms low, exposing his head and neck – she needed to come in over the top. She mentally went through her movements: spring forward, jink left, then leap high and bring the two large knuckles of her right fist down hard against his temple where the skull bone was thinnest.

Casey looked into the giant's eyes, grinned, and then flew at him. She side-stepped left away from his lunging blow, and then leapt high – everything went to plan, except for the lightening fast blow that knocked her from the air, and also the wind from her lungs.

Casey landed hard, but rolled fast, and just as she sprung back to her feet, a massive boot flew in a back-kick to strike her spine. She felt the impact from her kidneys to her fingertips. And then he was on her.

Mungoi lifted Casey up a few feet by the rear collar of her armored suit and punched the back of her head. She thumped down onto the ground. He kicked her ribs, cracking several, and then reached down to lift her again, punching her in the gut. The breath whooshed from her lungs, and her shocked diaphragm refused to draw another breath in – she was winded, and becoming dizzy.

Blake and Rinofsky strained at their ropes, yelling in fury. Jennifer had stopped watching, her face turned away, while Jackson worked furiously at his bonds. Aimee simply watched, her fists balled.

Mungoi held onto the shattered HAWC, and briefly grinned at the bound Americans. Casey felt him change his grip, holding her now by the neck and lifting, her feet coming free of the ground. He turned her one way then the other, studying her like a shooter looks at a downed partridge, examining his future meal. The huge

PLA soldier then looked down at the ground, searching for a few seconds. He found what he sought, and threw Casey to the dirt like an old sack. He said a few words to Yang, and then waited for his captain's response.

"Last chance, Lieutenant Casey Franks," Yang said.

Casey turned and tried to sit up but couldn't. The pain in her body was near unbearable and she could only manage to turn her bloody face towards the PLA captain, and rasp out a few hoarse words: "Fuck you."

Yang shrugged, and nodded to Mungoi, a small smile on his lips.

Mungoi reached down and picked up a damp log. It was big, six feet long and about two wide. The big man strained under its weight, grunting as he lifted it. He turned it around, holding the stump end over Casey's face. He lifted it pile driver style, holding it momentarily.

"*Do it-tttt!*" Casey screamed the words up at the giant.

The log came down.

CHAPTER 48

Alex launched himself from the tree line to appear before the colossal soldier, so fast it probably seemed he simply materialized. He caught the huge stump in mid-drop and stood, legs spread over Casey.

"*Yeah!*" Rinofsky yelled, straining at his bonds.

Alex had never seen a human being so large, and the strength in the giant's arms was insanely strong. Casey groaned underneath him, and the giant tried to wrench the log free, obviously wanting to continue the job of crushing the downed soldier.

Alex took it all in: his captured HAWCs, Casey broken at his feet, and Aimee pale and bound. He looked back at the giant, the man's wide-spaced eyes moved from surprise to glaring with anger. He bared huge yellow teeth, and then jerked hard on the log, trying to tear it from Alex's grip.

Casey groaned beneath him, and Alex felt the urge to do more than just disarm the man, and there was nothing now constraining him. He wrenched the log from the soldier's hands, and smashed it into the large head, once, twice, and then three times, the third blow splitting his face from brow to chin.

The giant blinked in confusion as the gash ran red. Alex held the log in one hand, and grabbed the huge soldier's collar, pulling his face down and close to his own. He stared into the wide spaced eyes, almost nose to nose, and Alex had no words for him, just a low growl. Alex could see something deep in the man's black eyes, pain, confusion ... and fear.

Behind Alex, someone was yelling orders, and one of the other PLA ran at them. Alex heard the sound of a blade coming free of a sheath, and Alex spun, throwing the log at the man with enough force to knock him backwards; the sound of cracking and splintering came from inside the man's body, not the wood.

Alex then turned back to the giant, his hands gripping the front of his uniform. The soldier had reached up to encircle Alex's neck with hands that fully wrapped around his throat. His forearms bulged with the pressure he exerted, and his gap-toothed grin appeared once again, but this time his huge mouth was full of blood from his facial wounds.

The huge man's powerful arms and hands strained, as he dragged Alex closer. His bloody mouth began to open, and Alex guessed he planned to take a piece from his face, probably his nose. In close quarters combat, debilitating the bridge of the nose, around the upper septum, made the eyes water uncontrollably – it would blind him.

The bloody mouth opened wider as the giant dragged Alex closer. Alex straightened his arms, pushing the big man back, one inch, two, a foot, and then he paused momentarily to grin into the broad face, before yanking him forward, fast, headbutting him so hard the huge soldier fell back like a tree trunk, out cold before he even hit the ground.

Alex looked down at Casey. The female HAWC was barely conscious. *"On your feet, soldier!"*

Panicked orders were screamed from all around him, and he turned to see a senior officer looking bewildered and Aimee, *Aimee Weir*, staring, and sinking down to be in a sitting position on the ground, her face white.

The senior Chinese officer reacted fast, pulling his revolver and firing. The bullet struck Alex's shoulder, knocking him to the ground. The PLA captain then moved quickly, dragging Aimee to her feet, and grinding the muzzle of his gun into her temple.

But instead of rising, Alex stayed down, and he turned to the near impenetrable mad tangle of plant life. He stared just beyond the hanging foliage, beyond the physical wall of the jungle, and he knew it was too late, *it* was coming. He could sense its approach like the feeling of static in the air when a huge storm front is building.

He couldn't see it yet, but he followed his instincts until he came to a darker alcove among the hanging fronds. A figure silently appeared.

Blake also stared for several seconds. "I don't fucking believe it." His voice sounded incredulous. "Hagel ... *fucking Hagel*. That's impossible."

To the group it looked like the young HAWC – same uniform, height, and features. Just a hint of a wet sheen glistened over his face and body. But Alex saw past the camouflage. He saw the deadness emanating from it – there was no mammalian warmth, just the coldness of a creature that belonged deep in an ocean trench or even deeper in his nightmares.

Alex spoke without turning. "Franks, when I give the word, get the others free. For now, *don't, move, a muscle*."

Casey nodded slowly, her eyes fixed on Hagel. Blood covered her face, and her wounds probably stung like a bitch, but she remained calm and immobile. Alex just hoped the bindings of his team would also keep them in place, because he knew the one sure thing to trigger an attack was movement.

The PLA captain let go of Aimee and began to scream orders to his giant soldier, Mungoi. The huge man got groggily to his feet, as guns came up, but it was like the silence of the strange jungle became more intense, building energy, as if they had all been dropped into the eye of a cyclone.

"Oh, god, no." Aimee started to back away from the figure that stood motionless in the dark. Soong reached out to grab her, and used a small knife to slit the bonds at her wrists.

The Chinese captain raised his gun again and fired twice into the Hagel figure. There was no response, or even any apparent wounds. To the senior soldier, he couldn't have been sure if he missed, or whether the greasy looking HAWC had body armor. He turned and yelled at his huge warrior, and urged the man on.

Mungoi spat blood, and then wiped one arm up and down over his split face. His glare went momentarily to Alex, who he really wanted to rain hell on, and then back to Hagel. He grunted, his unnaturally large jaw jutting. He staggered forward, his bear like arms outstretched and fingers flexing. When he had only taken a few steps, Hagel shot forward – not leaping forward, or running or diving, but instead it was if he were on a spring, a projectile being fired at the huge soldier.

Hagel smacked into Mungoi, knocking him back a few feet. The dull, wet thud was loud in the small clearing. The huge soldier didn't go down, Alex knew he couldn't have if he tried. He seemed glued to the figure. Mungoi brought one arm up and put it between himself and Hagel, and pushed. His split face went from shock to horror, as up close, he must have realized what he was really attached to.

Mungoi strained with all his colossal strength, but sticky strands of the substance the creature exuded engulfed his arm as well. The pretense of the Hagel figure was dropped as the creature's attacking club revealed itself. The human shape dissolved into a six-foot pad covered in baseball-sized suckers. Mungoi struggled even harder, his expression bordering on madness, but then his face went momentarily slack, before he began to howl in pain.

Alex knew exactly what was happening – the second part of the snare was now being used. Hook-like tusks emerged from the center of the suckers that appeared over the front of the pad. Mungoi thrashed in agony, as the eight-inch daggers entered his body, and the curved hook held his flesh tight. Now that he was locked tight to the pad, he began to move forward.

Mungoi braced his colossal legs, but Alex could now see the fleshy column trailing from the back of the once Hagel-like figure, and into the jungle behind them. This appendage was one of two tentacle clubs of a monstrous creature. Its long tentacles now flexed impossible muscle that the insignificant Mungoi had no hope of resisting. In the next second, the huge Chinese PLA soldier was yanked off his feet and into the foliage.

There was silence for a few seconds, and the group stared in disbelief and horror. Then, Hagel reappeared. As before, his form was perfect as that of the silent, motionless soldier, standing just inside the jungle's edge.

The Chinese officer reacted, screaming orders, his face blood-red from fury. His men attacked the figure, charging and firing with everything they had. But as soon as they got within a half dozen feet, more tentacles emerged from the slimy jungle. These were not the mimic clubs, but the tips of the other appendages, these ones just used for fighting, grasping, and feeding. They lifted and coiled, swatted, and crushed the small human bodies like insects.

The captain's face drained of color, and he started to back up.

Alex turned to Casey Franks. "Now, move it – untie them, and then head to the cliff wall." He was up and sprinting, snatching up Aimee, quickly going to Jennifer Hartigan, and ripping her bonds from her wrists. He pushed them both towards the far side of the jungle.

"To the cliff wall." He then spun. "Cate ... Cate Canning." He yelled over the fury and chaos in the clearing, the sound of the screaming soldiers either fighting to the death, dying in agony, or worse – being hauled away like netted fish to be consumed alive.

Cate appeared from the jungle line. Alex pointed. "Go around that way."

Cate looked from Alex to the maelstrom of madness in the clearing. Her mouth dropped open and her eyes glassed over. She was transfixed, as surely as if she was captured by the creature herself.

"*Cate!*" Alex roared her name. She jumped and turned, shocked into action. She then nodded and threaded her way through the far side of the jungle.

"Fuck me." Jackson's hands were now freed, but he stood transfixed too, his expression blank. He began to back up, looking above their heads.

There was a sensation of coldness against Alex's spine. He didn't need to turn to know that the creature, the monstrous orthocone mimic, was rising up as he and Casey finished ripping rope from the last bound men.

"Run." He herded them to the jungle, and then turned to witness his nemesis. He felt a thrill of horror run through his body like an electric current. A mottled green and black mountain was rising up over the jungle. At its top was a huge pulsating sack with unblinking goat-like eyes the size of train tunnels. Beside it, tentacles rose and fell, undulating and almost graceful in their sinuous movements. In some of them, small human bodies screamed and wriggled, but were soon handed down beneath the mountain to where Alex knew the giant mouth resided – the massive maw, behind a horned beak that would crush and render flesh and bone down to pulp.

Alex backed away, careful now not to make too many darting movements. Though his instinct was to sprint and propel himself far from this place. He knew *he* might have been able to outrun it, certainly he would outpace his team, but then they would be overtaken by the questing tentacles that could unfurl a hundred feet, or pursue them through and over the jungle using its boneless form to flow like a river of pure hunger.

Alex eased back into the jungle where Aimee was standing, waiting, refusing to leave, her expression a mix of anger, confusion, and a thousand questions.

Alex grabbed her hand, dragging her. "Not now; soon." They were out of the clearing and running. His team and some of the Chinese sprinted beside him, bashing soft, wet fronds out of the way, and sidestepping fallen trunks and hairy, column-like boughs.

Behind them, they could hear its approach. It was fast, crushing everything before it as it flowed over or through any obstacles. There was no need for stealth now, just a need for furious running. The cave wall loomed up before them, its top now lost in the dark blue gloom above them, and its far edge just touching the edge of the vast underground sea.

"There." Alex pointed as he let go of Aimee. He half turned. "Stay away from the water." He accelerated, leaving the others behind.

There was an opening in the cave wall, multiple openings, but one in particular demanded his attention – it wasn't created by geology or erosion, it was a carved entrance.

Alex sprinted inside, quickly checking for danger, and then came back to urge them on, grabbing people and pulling them through. He felt the hair on his neck rise, as the glistening mountain surged towards them.

"Don't look back. Get inside, *faster, faster*!" Alex watched the thing bear down on them, fascinated and repelled at the same time. Its mottled hide now pulsated with color as its excitement grew. In one of its tentacles, Mungoi thrashed and struggled, pounding against a monstrous muscular limb he had no hope of escaping.

"Get back. Everyone away from the cave mouth, now." Alex backed up, holding his arms wide like a barrier. Outside the blue tinged light from the glow worms was shut off, and he spun.

"Blake, Rhino, take the lead and scout ahead. We need to get as far from this opening as we can."

"Won't make any difference," Aimee said. "This thing will either tear the cave wall open, or just squeeze in. All we can do is stay ahead of it."

Alex knew she was right, and thankfully, she was one of the few keeping a clear head. "Move." Alex pushed Shenjung, Soong, and Cate, urging them further in. The few remaining flashlights came on, and the group moved deeper into the smaller tunnel, staying calm, even though apprehension came off them in waves.

"Faster." They ran along some flat and even ground – too flat for natural geology. Alex could see the remains of tiles beneath his feet. They rounded a corner and found themselves in an alcove, and they slowed to a halt.

From behind them there came an enormous thump as something hit the mouth of the cave. Dust rained down, and Alex alone edged out to look back at the opening. The weak light that had been seeping in had now been totally extinguished, but even in the blackness, Alex could make out the tip of a questing tentacle as it silently eased its way in.

Alex knew the power of the thing, and Aimee was right – the creature had the ability to stretch and flatten itself to be able to squeeze into impossibly small places. Down here, it had grown large, but it had also evolved an ability to hunt within the narrow, twisting labyrinths of the cave systems.

He half turned, still backing up. "It's coming in."

Alex looked around at the cave structure, noting its areas of strength and weakness, and wasn't happy with what he saw. The powerfully long tentacles could tear the side of the cave open, inching in, and then flexing with a striated muscular strength that could rip apart iron sheets like paper. A rock wall would be like clay to it.

They needed to be further ...

The scream jerked his head around. He saw Shenjung and Soong engaged in a tug of war. One of the tentacles had stretched out, rope thin now, and the tip had snagged Shenjung's sleeve. While Alex watched the coils started to wrap around his forearm and then thicken. Shenjung dug his heels in, his eyes wider than seemed humanly possible. Soong held on to him, but already his feet began to slip.

Alex had seconds. When the hooks in the tentacles engaged, then the man would be jerked from the cave like a cork from a bottle. Alex sprinted and dived, grabbing Shenjung around the waist. But the tentacle didn't break or release its grip, instead it simply stretched. Alex turned and gripped the now wrist-thick limb and yanked hard – too easily it released the Chinese scientist, but then like a writhing viper, the thing whipped back to coil around Alex's arm.

Alex pushed the Chinese couple away, and then used his enormous strength to pull back. The elasticized flesh refused to break. There came a burning pain as the suckers engaged, and then the first sensation of sharpness.

Aimee ran towards him, but he held up a hand. *"Get back!"*

Alex drew a small knife and hacked at the limb but when he pressed down, the flesh would give a bit, and not allow the blade to bite. He felt the thing began to pull at him; he needed to brace himself, and he turned and tried to walk back further into the cave. Each step was impossibly hard, and the thing simply brought more and more power to bear on him, canceling out his effort. He knew it had been playing with him. The force on his arm increased, and he began to slide backwards. The tusk began to dig through his cave suit. The game was obviously over.

Then a sharp pain ripped through Alex's head, and suddenly the pressure on his arm was gone. He brought his hands up to his ears, grimacing.

Aimee was beside him in a second. "What is it?"

"Something ... a sound." Alex moaned. It felt like an icepick being jammed into the center of his brain. He went to his knees, and then buried his forehead to the ground, groaning.

Aimee followed him down. She looked up, then around. "I can't hear anything."

"Ultrasonic." He lifted his head, his eyes streaming, and blood at his nostrils. Behind him the questing tentacles had begun to quickly withdraw.

After another few seconds they were gone, the sound shut off, and with it went the pain. Alex eased back up, and took his hands away, blinking.

"The sound, it's gone." He looked around. "And so is the creature."

Aimee helped him to his feet. "This is no ordinary cave." She turned. "And maybe whatever that sound was, scared the orthocone away."

"Maybe." Alex looked down at his arm. There was a ring cut from the tough material of his suit, and his skin was raised and raw. He lifted his head. "And maybe it just knows another way in."

CHAPTER 49

Aimee let go of Alex and looked up at his face. He hadn't changed. He had the same brutally handsome features, the same eyes that saw deep inside her. He returned the gaze, his expression suddenly hardening.

"You shouldn't damn well be here," he said.

Her mouth momentarily dropped open. "You're right, I shouldn't." She folded her arms, her jaw set. "And neither should you. After all you're dead, remember?" She pushed him hard in the chest. "Or at least that's what you wanted *me* to think."

"That wasn't in my control." Alex rounded on her. "You have bigger priorities than this." He waved an arm around. "Or me."

"You dare ..." Her teeth clamped. "You have no idea what I have done to be here."

He leaned towards her, lowering his voice. "You left Joshua unguarded. That's what you've done."

She felt the anger boil over. "*I* left Joshua? *You* goddamn left us both." She couldn't help her voice rising, and could feel the stares of the group. "You left us both, when we needed you most."

"No, I didn't." Alex pulled back. "And you had *someone*."

He knew, she thought. *How?* Aimee tilted her head, stepping in closer. "You've been watching us ... or did that Jack Hammerson run tabs on me and keep you in the loop?"

He began to turn away, but she grabbed his arm and tugged him around. "Peter looked after us when I needed support. He was a father figure to Joshua, but never his true father. Where were you?" She stepped right up to him. "*Where were you?*"

Alex put a hand out and eased her back a step. "You should have married him. Joshua needs that permanency ... so do you."

That was it. Aimee swung at him. "You son of a bitch."

The blow caught Alex on the shoulder and bounced off. Aimee felt her hand throb with pain, but her anger wouldn't subside. She wanted to hit him again, hurt him.

"Yo." Casey Franks sauntered over, followed by Rhino and Blake. "What kept you, boss?" Her bloodied face was pulled up into its usual sneer. Her eyes went from Aimee to Alex, as she stepped in between them.

Alex shrugged, looking relieved at the distraction. "A mile or so of ice and rock, a sea serpent or two, miles of jungle." He smiled flatly. "The usual." Alex held out a fist to her.

"All in a day's work." Casey bumped knuckles. "Good to see you."

Alex did the same to his other HAWCs, who grinned like they'd just been given a reprieve from death row. He looked down again at the HAWC woman's battered face. "How you doing?"

Casey grinned back. "Me? Fine, I was ugly to start with."

Rhino put a large hand and on her shoulder. "But it's what's inside that counts, right, Franks?"

Alex laughed. "For most people." He nodded towards the group standing in the dark. "Let's see what we've got." He took a few paces towards them, but paused to look back at Aimee.

"We'll finish this later."

You bet we will, she thought.

*

"Come forward," Alex said, his voice echoing in the smaller cavern.

All eyes shifted from Alex to Captain Wu Yang. He and his remaining men stayed in the shadows. Around them the cavern was heavily overgrown with hanging lichen and mosses, things that had grown over many millennia to obscure walls that seemed unnaturally flat. Beneath their feet a layer of dirt couldn't conceal ancient tiles. Unlike most of the caves leading down, this one smelled damp, earthen, and of something Alex could only just detect – the hint of metal rusting somewhere far away in the dark.

"Now," Alex said.

Captain Wu Yang was the first to step from the shadows, his gaze unflinching. Alex noticed his gun was still in his holster. He had two remaining soldiers with him. The captain squared his shoulders and folded his arms. There would be no apology from this man, nor would Alex have expected one. As far as he was concerned, he was just doing the job ordered by his country.

Yang made no move for his gun, but his soldiers still had their rifles cradled. Alex's team now had no armaments, other than knives.

"Lower your weapons." Alex had his HAWCs spread to either side of him, and he could feel the waves of fury radiating from them. The power imbalance would not be tolerated for long.

Yang didn't flinch, and his men didn't move. Alex knew they understood him.

"Hey assholes, you heard the man." Casey walked forward, eyes blazing. She looked like she wanted to settle a few scores right here, right now.

Alex grabbed her shoulder and pulled her back. He turned again to Yang. "Lower them or I'll take them from you." He stared from under lowered brows. "And I *will* hurt you." Alex looked over his shoulder to the cave entrance. "Then I think I'll throw you all outside to play with our new friend."

Yang's eyes remained fixed on Alex, but he could almost hear his mind ticking over, perhaps remembering what he had seen this new American soldier do to his giant, Mungoi. He turned and spoke a few words. His men didn't hesitate to comply; they placed their weapons on the ground – rifles, handguns, and knives.

Alex looked each of them in the eyes. "If you want to live, you will take orders from me." He waited until there came a near imperceptible nod from Wu Yang.

Alex continued to hold the man's gaze. "Now, I'll take the grenades."

The soldiers looked to Yang who frowned and shrugged.

Alex chuckled, but with zero humor. "I know PLA each have a Type-86 grenade. They're minifrags full of nice ballbearings and with a wide burst radius. Hand them over, now." Alex curled his fingers. "Quickly." He tilted his head, seeing the walkie talkies on their belts. "And take those off … I'll have them as well."

"Who are you?" Yang asked.

"The Arcadian." Casey smile-sneered at the Chinese captain. "And unless you want your head ripped off, I'd do as he says."

"Arcadian? *Captain Alex Hunter.*" Familiarity momentarily crossed the captain's features, his eyes going from Alex to Aimee, before closing down.

"You know me." Alex stepped closer to the man. He could sense that Yang knew both him *and* Aimee. He was holding something back from them.

Yang smirked, but turned to speak softly to his men, and then they each pulled the rounded explosives from their pouches and walked forward to drop them into Alex's hand. The same for the walkie talkies. Alex quickly checked the grenades and then slid them all into his own pockets and pouches. He looked at the three walkie talkies.

"Hiyunton Model H280s. They'll do." Alex turned to give one to Aimee. He gave one back to Yang, and kept the other himself. "Now, we're all one big happy connected family."

Yang took the single device, his expression implacable. Alex stared back hard for a moment. "Good choice." He turned away. "Everyone, fall in."

The HAWCs and McMurdo soldiers approached. Alex looked over their heads and pointed at Yang, also to Soong and Shenjung. "You too. This affects us all."

The group crowded around. There was a sense of relief and optimistic anticipation, probably just because of his arrival. At this point Alex knew it was probably misplaced.

"Equipment and weapons check. What have we got left?"

The soldiers checked pockets and pouches. Yang and his team stood waiting.

Casey spoke first. "Got a flashlight, and one small Ka-bar." She turned to stab a finger at Yang. "The rest is fucking piled out in the clearing where these guys stripped it from us." She glared.

"Same," said Rinofsky, then Blake.

"Nothing left," said Ben Jackson and Jennifer Hartigan. Aimee also shook her head. Cate had a knife, a small flashlight and some water.

"Worse than I thought." Alex looked to Yang's weapon pile. "You've got a handgun and two rifles. Keep the handgun, but hand over the rifles."

Yang's eyes bulged. "You leave us with nothing."

"You have a handgun, knives, and your experience. Now, pick up your weapons; we will all need to fight before this day is done."

Cursing, the Chinese soldiers snatched up their knives. Alex turned away. "Franks, Rinofsky, take the rest."

His two HAWCs eagerly grabbed the Chinese weapons and then checked them.

"Okay, me, I've got knives, a signal locator, and now, grenades." He tossed one of the grenades to Casey, and the signal locator to Rhino. "We have flashlights, which is good, but we'll need to conserve battery life. We don't have food and water, but if need be we can find that in a jungle … if we have to go back outside." He motioned to the rifles. "But, this is not enough to survive down here for long."

"Boss." Rhino shook his head, his face lit by the small screen of the locator. "Just fired this thing up. That signal is right around here." He looked up. "I mean, it's here; *right in here,* somewhere."

Alex nodded, looking around. "And there's something else in here. I don't think we're alone. That creature was either scared of, or called off by, something or someone."

Silence stretched as the group looked around in the dark cave-like tunnel. Every crack or corner now took on more menace.

Alex held up a hand, raising his voice only slightly. "Listen, right now, we have some urgent priorities if we're to survive. Two scouting teams. Jackson, Rhino, Yang are team one. Blake, take the two PLA soldiers. Scout ahead, see what we've got coming up. Keep your eyes open." He turned. "Franks, on rear guard. The rest, gather your strength before we follow them in."

Alex edged to the corner and looked back to the entrance. The blue glow had returned, and the creature was gone – for now.

CHAPTER 50

Aimee lifted her flashlight to examine their surroundings, joining the other small glowing circles that danced around within the tunnel. The tiles beneath her feet were worn, but at the edges were hints of the original colors. Blue, green, and flashing reflective mica sparkled in their flashlights. The walls had magnificent carved frescoes leaning out at them with smiling, leering, and tongue-lolling faces in the broad style Aimee recognized too well. Above her, corbelled archways of fierce creatures interspaced with large oval stone heads with benevolent stares watched over them.

She let her beam momentarily trail towards Alex, before quickly moving it away. But her eyes remained.

The man made anger burn inside her. After all these years, the first thing he did was to scold her? *How dare he!* She bristled the more she dwelled on it. She continued to watch him. Her head held onto the indignation, but in her core, there was still a feeling of attraction and familiarity that was as intoxicating as it had ever been. She wanted to scream at him, curse him, and make him say sorry for lying to her, and all that sat uneasily beside a deep desire to rekindle something she had only felt in her dreams for many years. She pushed her thoughts away and focused on the tiles.

"This is unbelievable."

"*Jesus.*" Aimee jerked her light around, directly onto the woman's face.

The woman squinted, smiled, and held out her hand. "Hi, Cate Canning, *Dr. Cate Canning*, evolutionary biologist and team leader on Project Ellsworth. It's, *ah*, a government funded study of the buried lake." She pointed at the ceiling. "From somewhere wa-*aay* up there. I hitched a ride ..." She half smiled, shrugging. "Seemed like a good idea at the time."

"Dr. Aimee Weir, petrobiologist and suicidal fool." She shook Cate's hand. "Still think it was a good idea?"

"Ask me again, when we're topside," Cate said, panning her light over the flooring, and then raising it higher. She turned to smile again at Aimee. "*If* ... I mean, *if* we get out."

"We'll get out," Aimee projected more confidence than she felt.

Cate turned her light towards Alex, who noticed them looking and nodded. "Well, if anyone can get us out, it'll be that guy." Her eyes slid to Aimee. "Saw you watching him before. You should see him with his shirt off."

Aimee turned a little too quickly. "What?"

Cate momentarily pulled back at Aimee's reaction, and Aimee immediately regretted it.

"*Uh oh*, you two know each other, huh?"

"No, yes, forget it ... long time ago." Aimee waved it away.

"Good." Cate's eyebrows flicked up momentarily and she grinned.

Aimee sighed, feeling a twinge of something inside that she hated. *You are not jealous*, she told herself.

Cate wandered further into the dark tunnel and Aimee followed her. "Amazing," Cate said, her light moving up and down. "Just, damned, amazing."

Aimee knew what she was experiencing; she had felt the same sense of wonder when they first found the buried city. And here, even after countless centuries, the architecture was still striking. Interspaced Doric columns and large trapezoidal stones fitted together without a hair's breadth between them. Vestiges of color clung to some of the images, and even the mosses and mineralized waters now staining them in all manner of rainbow hues couldn't fully mask their magnificence.

"It's just like Tikal, the Mayan temple ruins ... and just as old, I'd say." Cate turned. "I've been there. It's called the Temple of the Two Headed Snake, built by King Yaxkin Caan Chac in 470AD."

"No, it's older than that," said Aimee. "Much, much older. This place was a memory before Tikal was even a dream." She turned to find Alex coming up behind them, and she pointed to the carvings. "Just like Aztlan."

He nodded. "So, maybe some of them did make it down here after all," Alex said softly. "We always wondered."

"Aztlan? What the hell is Aztlan?" Cate asked, stepping in closer to the pair.

"Something much older than the Mayans," Aimee said, shining her light onto the glyphic images. "These guys predated the Aztecs, Egyptians, Mayans, and even the Sumerians, by thousands of years. In fact, as they were originally a seafaring people, they may have created those other races, seeded them."

"Buried beneath the Antarctic ice?" Cate scoffed. "I know what you're inferring ... Aztlan, is Atlantis, right?" She looked at Aimee from under her brows. "Please tell me you're not really saying that?"

"I'm not," Aimee said. "This down here is nothing like Atlantis. This is just the remnants of that. It's real name is – *was* – Aztlan, and that great city, perhaps the first great city on the planet, is above us, buried just under snow and ice. A civilization that flourished when this continent was mostly ice-free." She walked to the wall, placing a hand on one of the moss-covered images. "When the final ice age took hold, many escaped, perhaps becoming one or all the world's first great races. But others stayed behind, and became trapped in the dark. Some obviously came down here, and ..." She shrugged. "And then, I don't know."

Aimee moved her light to the next image. It was of a coiling mass, with a huge eye at its center. "But I can guess."

*

"Yo, boss." Rhino led Jackson and Yang back to the group.

Alex noticed that Shenjung and Soong didn't move to welcome Yang, but stayed with Cate and Jennifer Hartigan, who talked quietly with Casey Franks.

"What've you got?" he asked when they stopped before him.

"Multiple caves, and more. This place is enormous – buildings, rooms, a freaking city. Or what's left of it." Rhino stopped, the equally huge Jackson beside him. "Something bad happened here, maybe an earthquake – a lot of damage. Seems long deserted, but ..." He shrugged. "You kinda get the feeling, that, *I dunno*, there's someone still here."

"Impossible," Cate said.

"More like, improbable," Aimee said. "These guys were born survivors."

"Well, we found more of the weird markings on the walls that we saw in the upper caves." Rhino pointed at one of the ancient carvings of a warrior. "Not like these, they were more recent, but they were rougher, crude, like they were done by someone a lot less skilled. Like what Hagel said he found with a bunch of skeletons in a dead-end cave that was higher up. He said it was as if they were trying to tunnel towards the surface. They never made it."

"They went in both directions," Alex said. "Some tried for the light, maybe others for the eternal twilight of this place."

"Well, down here worked out well, didn't it?" Casey said, joining them.

"It did for a while," Aimee said. "About 12,000 years ago, when the land iced-over and trapped them, enough of them came down to be able to create all this." Aimee waved an arm around. "They re-established, but then something happened, and their civilization collapsed." She looked towards the mouth of the cave. "No sunlight, and no hope with that thing out there."

"Why didn't they just head back up?" Jackson asked.

"Because this would be preferable," Cate said. "They make it to the surface, and all they're going to find is a frozen desert. Imagine what they would have thought of that blinding white and freezing world after thousands of years in the warmth and dark? They'd see it as hell."

"Yeah, well, with that thing down here, I'd take that over this place any day." Rhino frowned. "But Aimee's right; these guys must have survived just fine for a while. Before slipping back or something."

"Slipping back to the stone age," Cate said. "There is something called the Olduvai theory. It postulates civilization always sliding backwards, regressing after a certain period." She shrugged. "It's inevitable – war, disease, natural disaster, using up resources, all can lead to great powers simply collapsing, fragmenting, and the people scattering, leaving the great cities deserted or in ruins. Like this place." She looked around. "And I can tell you, as an evolutionary biologist, 12,000 years is about 50,000 generations – more than enough time to force adaptations … *evolutionary adaptations*." She smiled. "Maybe they flourished, again, but didn't need the things that the first arrivals did."

Rhino raised his eyebrows. "Like what, no roof over their heads?"

"Seriously?" Cate gave him a look. "Look up, soldier. Here, everywhere you go, there's a roof over your head."

Jackson sniggered. "*Boom*. She wins that round, big fella."

Rhino grinned. "Well, let's see what …"

"That's enough, Rinofsky," Alex said. "Any other observations?" He looked from Rhino to Jackson, and then to Yang, who stood brooding a few paces back.

"Well, yeah, you couldn't help feeling that someone was there … just out of sight," Jackson said. "Spooky."

"We were being watched." Yang lifted his head and Rhino nodded. "I could feel it."

Alex looked at the men, knowing they were probably right – he felt it himself. He could sense there was more in the tunnels than lichen-covered statues. Even now, he could feel that somewhere in the dark, there were eyes upon them.

"We need to move." He turned slowly, trying to see into every crevice and dark corner. "Being in here is no guarantee of our safety."

"Got that right," Rhino said. "We lost Parcellis in a freaking crack in the wall, no bigger than …" He stopped when he saw Alex's expression.

"We all know what we're up against." Alex looked to the group who were now all watching him. "We need to fully investigate this place. If there's a way out, we need to find it …" He looked hard at Yang. "And, we need to find *our* submarine."

"A way out? Yeah, works for me," Jackson said.

There was no bioluminescence in the tunnels, and without the flashlights, the darkness would have been absolute. Alex turned slowly, concentrating. The silence was so thick, it was as if it was suspended in the humidity. But there was something ... he sensed activity, or furtive movement all around them. He turned back to Rhino.

"Where's Blake? He should have been back by now."

Rhino frowned. "Yeah, damned right. He was ahead of us ... should have been back first."

Yang bullocked his way past the taller Jackson. "And where are my men?"

"How would we know?" Rhino put his hand on the Chinese captain's chest.

Yang knocked it away, and glowered at Alex. "So, I agree for you to lead, and we immediately lose people. This is leadership, American style?"

"Get a load of this guy, would ya?" Rhino shook his head.

"That's enough," Alex said. He turned to Yang. "Listen, our man is missing as well. I get the feeling this place is huge, but we'll find them. Probably just exploring further than they expected."

"Or my men are dead; killed by one of your assassins." Yang's features were set hard.

Rhino chuckled. "Assassin? Blake's gonna love that one." He leaned over Yang, putting a large, blunt finger in his chest. "Then where's our *assassin*; why hasn't he returned either?"

"Hiding," Yang said, turning to stand square on to Rhino.

"Someone cracking under pressure are they?" Casey muscled in, getting between Yang and Rhino.

"Lighten up, *all of you*." Alex pulled them apart. "We're all wire-tight right now. But we've got to stick together." He stared hard in the direction the men had disappeared, straining to hear or get a sense of them. His neck tingled from a feeling of imminent danger that refused to materialize. "We stay alive, find the sub. But first ... we look for our missing men. Everyone stay close," he said, looking towards Jennifer and the two Chinese scientists. "Rhino, you and I will take point, Jackson, at rear." He looked at

Casey, and then nodded at Yang. She understood immediately, and got close to him.

Alex waved them on. "Let's go."

"I'm also at front," Aimee said quickly.

"So am I," said Cate, pushing past the others.

"Hey?" Casey grabbed for her, but Alex waved her back. He wanted Franks on Yang. He had a feeling that taking orders from an American hadn't been in the man's job description. And if he got a chance, he might take the opportunity to rebalance the power dynamics by putting a bullet in the back of Alex's head.

CHAPTER 51

Yang felt the female HAWC at his shoulder. She was of no threat to him; he knew he could disable or kill her whenever he wished. His primary threat was the leader of this Special Forces group. But he was also his biggest opportunity.

He bristled at the thought of his missing men, and now needed to rely on Soong Chin Ling and Shenjung Xing for support. He had reservations about their patriotism, but he knew a quiet word reminding the pair of what lay in store for them back home, if they failed to remember where their true allegiances lay, would bring them back into line.

Yang inhaled the humid air of the tunnel, and watched the back of Alex Hunter. Following close to him was Dr. Aimee Weir. Perhaps this was why Yang had been chosen to lead the mission. It was payback or an opportunity for redemption for the failed mission to procure the child – Joshua Weir.

Their own top secret Advanced Soldier Program had stalled, stuck in a cul-de-sac of producing giants like Mungoi, but not being able to complement their strength with intellect. Their soldiers were little more than two-legged battering rams and what they needed was something better.

Yang continued to watch Alex Hunter. Where they were stalled, the Americans had succeeded with this man who was known as the Arcadian. With his own eyes Yang had witnessed the ease with which Hunter had defeated Mungoi, making the big PLA soldier, their most advanced breed, seem like an outdated model within seconds.

He felt his spirits lift. If this was an opportunity for redemption, he would seize it with both hands. He would secure the submarine for his country, and also the body of the Arcadian. He turned again, and smiled at the stocky female HAWC. She sneered in return. His smile broadened – he was right where he needed to be – on his way to the submarine, and now embedded within the enemy camp.

He sped up as he remembered an ancient proverb: *patience is power*. He could wait, and he would be ready to act.

*

Soong and Shenjung followed next, just in front of Jennifer, and Yang trawled behind them, with Casey on his shoulder.

"This way." Rhino led them up a mound of broken rock that suddenly turned into age-worn steps. Even now it was clear that these had not been rough-hewn risers, but once were carved of something shining and smooth. The stumps of broken balustrades were of a dark stone that was ebony black, and could have been the finest polished marble. The stairs themselves were soft, carpeted by thick mosses that squelched as they stepped up on them.

They next crossed a wide balcony and then entered a curved tunnel. Overhead there were once polished lintel stones, each with their own intricate carving of a face with a different expression, now all with beards of lichen that they needed to duck beneath.

Alex stopped before one wall, looking along its length, feeling the sense of misery and dismay in the images portrayed. He exhaled slowly and then waited for Aimee to catch up. He motioned with a nod. Aimee followed his gaze and shined her flashlight along the carved relief, exhaling softly.

"An old friend," she said.

"More like the ancient enemy," Alex responded.

The coiled mass with an unblinking eye at its center dominated the wall. The Aztlantic carving style was a mix of raised glyphs, faces, but now the once benevolent visages were twisted in horror, fear, or pain.

Alex tilted his head back, staring upwards, feeling like he was seeing through the miles of stone to the ancient city he knew was buried just below the snow and dark ice. Many years ago, he had encountered a similar tableau to the one on the wall, but the scenes then were of the land, sunlight, and happier times. Now, down here, a darkness had not only permeated the lives of these forgotten people, but had even influenced their art.

"Wow." Cate joined them, her mouth hanging open as she stared at the glyphs. "Amazing, isn't it? It's like the pre-Columbian stone artisan work, but different somehow. Not more primitive, just ... different." Cate walked quickly to the wall, laying her hands on some of the images. "I wish I could understand them."

"Possibly the most ancient formal language ever known. A linguist who was with us, Professor Matt Kearns, said the Aztlantian words might even be the skeleton key – the root language for all languages."

"And those who stayed in the city above, just sat there and froze in the dark." Cate exhaled through compressed lips.

"No." Aimee turned to Cate. "We found evidence in the city above, where the orthocone managed to find its way in, snaking in through cracks and holes, and snatching the remaining inhabitants in the dark. It would have been a nightmare."

Rhino grimaced. "Like with Parcellis. This thing can get in anywhere, and it's smart, been fucking with us the whole time." He lifted his light to the coiling mass. "I bet that's what happened to them."

"We don't know that for sure," Alex said. "The creatures, these Kraken species, have made a home here for countless millions of years. And the Aztlantians must have been here for centuries as well. These structures take time to plan and build. They could never have created them if they were being constantly attacked. Somehow, they learned to coexist."

"Maybe you're right on that part." Cate stepped back from the wall, shining her light along its entire length. "Everything, every image; it's all about the beast."

Aimee sighed. "The mighty Aztlan people, rulers of the world, before even the Egyptians lifted their pyramids, or the Persians built Persepolis. Who worshiped the sun, and the wind, and the sea, and were suddenly forced to believe in only one god, this thing, this monster in the dark."

"Not just their god, it became their *everything*." Alex hurried them on.

Aimee wandered along the wall, shining her light up and down. "Maybe they struck a bargain?"

Rhino grunted. "Striking a bargain usually means they had something to offer each other. Safety for the people down here, sure, but what would the monster get out of it? Other than free food, I mean."

"Let's keep moving." Alex led them along the tomb-dark corridor. The air was thick with damp, and other than their breathing, there was near total silence.

"Look." Rhino shined his light at the ground. At the edge of a puddle of murky water, there were boot marks in the moss. "HAWC boot; Blake's, heading this way."

Alex nodded. "All going in one direction – and no one coming back. Means if they're anywhere, it's still up ahead." He turned to his HAWCs. "Be ready; they may have walked into a trap."

Alex slowed the pace, wary now, and reached out with his senses. He could feel the void long before he saw it.

"It's opening out."

"How can you tell?" Jackson asked. "We lost all the sensors."

Alex kept staring directly ahead. "The echo isn't as compressed as it was only a moment ago, and it's taking longer to bounce back to us. In here, its bounce is muted by the low ceiling – not anymore."

"Got it." Jackson didn't sound convinced.

"Wait here." Alex switched off his flashlight and vanished into the darkness.

He moved lightly along the corridor, his flashlight off, as his eyes were perfectly dark-adapted – another side effect of the Arcadian treatment. He stopped when he was around a bend and away from the group. He stood silently, listening and waiting, trying to draw forth a sense of his surroundings. The heavy stones blocked many of his senses, but he was sure he could detect life … and not that of the monstrous creature that waited outside for them. He hoped it was Blake. The man was a good HAWC, and not one to easily walk into an ambush.

Alex moved on, quickly now, further along the corridor until a soft light started to permeate the darkness. He exited the tunnel, and found himself in a huge room, like a cathedral, many hundreds of feet across. The ceiling was high enough overhead that it had its own bioluminescent biology fixed to it. Along all four walls there were small alcoves, like window-sized pigeonholes. He guessed there might have been more levels higher up.

He closed his eyes and slowed his breathing, concentrating – there was the essence of life again, but nothing close by. He turned to the passage he had just exited.

"Yo, come on in."

*

Aimee was first in, followed by Cate, and then the rest of the group. Aimee wandered out towards the center. She saw that Shenjung and Soong remained joined at the hip, as though frightened one or the other was going to be snatched away.

"Oh my god," Cate said.

Aimee followed her gaze with her own light. There was a giant carving in the far wall – more than a carving – instead a mighty statue that seemed to be breaking out from the very rock. It was a human figure, in a dress-like tunic, holding a huge stone sword. The long ages had colored it green with many varieties of moss and lichen. Only two spots remained clear of the mossy covering – the eyes. Both gleamed in the beams of light.

"Is that gold?" Jennifer asked.

"Probably," said Aimee. "Antarctica is a very old continent, and has rich deposits of the metal. Makes sense for them to mine it."

"Many ancient races found it something they could work quite readily," Cate said.

"A treasure," said Yang, lifting a small pair of field glasses to his eyes.

Casey's lip curled. "That's all you're taking away from this? Maybe you can lug some home – I heard it's not that heavy."

Yang lowered the glasses and turned front on to her. "Idiot. You see, but do not understand. It is a sign of an advanced civilization. They were able to mine the metal, smelt it, and then work it into such an ornate design." He waved a hand up at the huge being. "This statue alone would have taken decades to create. If something catastrophic happened to them, it either happened very slowly, or very quickly. We need to learn from this."

Casey sneered. "Yeah, you've seen what's outside, right?"

"He's right," Aimee said softly. "Everything we learn is important now. Keep your eyes, and minds, open."

"Whatever." Casey turned away.

Cate craned her neck, shining her light above them. "This room is like a church. The roof is arched, and looks carved. This civilization must have been monumental for centuries." She turned. "Was it like this in the city above?"

"No," said Aimee. "It was well beyond this. It was magnificent, and would have rivaled anything in Egypt or ancient Persia. But, the creature found them, or they found it while digging in their basements. They broke through into the caves while excavating. Found the labyrinths leading down to the sea. The creature rose up and pursued them into their most private places. They tried to appease it for a while, feed it. But it grew ever more hungry, and eventually stopped waiting to be fed, and decided to feed itself." Aimee sighed. "From what we were able to translate, we found out that finally they decided to fight. Sent an army down to make war on it, led by two brave warrior brothers."

"They were sent to hell to make war on the devil," Alex said. "Of the two thousand warriors that went down, only one man returned."

Aimee sighed. "And then the climate changed and the cold and dark set in for good. They had two monsters to contend with – the never ending cold, and the monster from the depths." She shivered.

"They came down to where the monster lived then?" Jackson asked.

"No choice." Alex turned. "They were buried alive. A hundred feet of ice and snow eventually covered the city – no sun means no food. We found evidence of cannibalism. Those that stayed were going mad, or were getting picked off in the dark."

"*Ugh*, makes me sick just thinking of it." Cate grimaced. "Being alone in the dark, and having this thing snake its way in, silent, invisible, its cold touch meaning a horrible death. Eaten alive."

Aimee nodded. "Some got out, others didn't. Looks like many chose to risk coming here – taking a slim chance at life, or dying in the darkness." She turned back to the massive statue. "Looks like it worked out fine, at least for a while."

Shenjung and Soong edged closer. The Chinese engineer cleared his throat. "It may not have been the creature," he said. "Consider what causes civilizations to collapse: war, but there was no competing clan down here, unless they split into factions, which is unlikely. Climate, again unlikely, as this environment has been static for millions of years. Interbreeding, causing genetic weaknesses, is a possibility. Maybe even mutation."

"That's a great thought – evolution, or devolution." Jackson grimaced.

"Let's find our people, and then search for a way out," Alex said. "Spread out, look for traces – two by twos, and stay in sight of each other."

CHAPTER 52

"Do you think we will ever see the sunlight again?" Soong asked softly.

Shenjung smiled down at her. "I can see it now."

She titled her head and laughed. "*Now* you become romantic?" She grabbed his hand.

"Why not? Down here, in this dark place, it is exactly what we need." He squeezed her hand back, becoming serious. "I hope we will see the sunlight again. But what I hope and what I believe might be two different things." He turned, seeing Yang watching them. "He doesn't trust us."

"I don't think he ever did," Soong replied. "And I do not trust Yang either." She looked up at him. "All our team, we left in the upper tunnels, do you think …?"

Shenjung shook his head. "Do not dwell on it. We must stay strong, survive together, and be prepared for anything." He saw that Yang still stared, and steered Soong a little further away. "And that means, if it comes down to a choice, I trust the Americans more than I do Yang."

Soong peeked over her shoulder at the PLA captain. "Yes, and I believe soon, he will want us to choose sides. I will not choose his."

He sighed. "And if we do not, then even if we find a way out, we will never be able to go home. Are you prepared for that?"

*

Aimee and Cate broke off, walking towards a far wall, deep in conversation. Alex pointed to Franks and motioned with his head for her to follow them. She nodded.

He watched as the teams spread out, and then turned to peer up at the huge statue. He walked to its base and began to climb. In only a few minutes he had reached one of the shoulders, and stood upright. The ceiling was still another fifty or so feet above his head, and he looked across to the face. The golden eyes glowed with hints of blue, reflecting the weak bioluminescent light from above. The statue's expression was frozen in a permanent stare. He followed its gaze.

At the far end of the room, about fifty feet up, there was another carving in the wall. The tentacled horror he had become used to. Maybe that's how it started for them – the warriors fighting the creature, he thought, and this was a monument to them.

Alex noticed that at the center of the coiling mass, there was another opening. As soon as his eyes alighted on it, something moved inside, darted back into the shadows. He had an impression of a humanoid shape and colorless flesh, but with dangling appendages.

So, he thought. You *are* watching.

"Boss, got something here." Rhino waved an arm up at him over near one of the huge walls.

Alex climbed down and jogged towards him. Jackson and Yang were leaning over a spot on the ground.

Rhino crouched. "Ground's all messed up. Something violent happened here." He turned about. "No prints leading away, and no doorways ... that I can see." He stood and turned to the wall, giving it a push. "Can't see any pivot points."

Alex leaned in close to the stone, running his fingers along the edges of some of the blocks. They had sat for so long that they had fused together. "I think it's solid now. Don't think they went through here."

"They didn't fly away," Jackson said.

Alex looked to the huge McMurdo soldier, and then up. He remembered the small darting figure he had seen above them. He spun to the group. "*Everyone back from the walls!*" His voice boomed in the large room. As soon as the words left his mouth, there came a gagging sound, and they turned to see Jennifer

Hartigan rising up, a rope around her neck and under one arm. More ropes came down, lassoing towards Yang, and then Cate.

Ben Jackson caught a tether as it tried to loop over his large head. He grabbed it and yanked hard. In turn, it was yanked back even harder and the loop slid tight around his wrist.

"Ah fuck." He started to rise up. "A little help here."

Rhino rushed to him, and grabbed the cord. Immediately another dropped down and also circled Jackson's neck.

"*Farg-gggh*," was all the big man could rasp out.

"Use your knives, get to the center." Alex yelled instructions, but there was nothing but the chaos of flickering lights and shouting people. He saw in an instant what the alcoves were now used for – they were staging portals for capturing prey. Whether this was their original purpose or something later adapted by the descendants of the once great race, he would never know.

In each of the window-sized alcoves, multiple figures hauled on the ropes they had dropped down. Alex frowned as he tried to make sense of what he was seeing. They were smaller than normal, and were bone-white humanoids, but their faces were like nothing he could recognize. They seemed smooth-skinned, and there were dangling tendrils starting from halfway down the face. Their eyes were just vertical slits, like those of a goat ... or octopus.

Yang easily stepped back, avoiding the tethers, not helping or hindering, just standing and watching. Alex was furious at his lack of support, but ignored the man, and pulled free his smallest Ka-bar blade. He spun it in his hand until he held the dark steel, and then launched it towards one of the humanoids dragging on Jackson's rope. The blade flew through the air so fast it was near invisible, and then embedded in the center of one of the hideous faces. The figure disappeared, soundlessly, and Jackson dropped a few feet. The figure was soon replaced by another, and the big soldier began to be pulled up once again.

Alex took a step towards Jackson, but spun back at the sound of Aimee yelling. She had her arms wrapped around Cate's waist, as the woman was also lifted, kicking, into the air.

He was momentarily torn, but in another second, both women were several feet up. He decided – then put his head down and sprinted. He pulled his last blade from it sheath, holding it backwards, and then leaping. In one powerful movement, he grabbed and slashed the rope at Cate's neck, dropping her and Aimee to the ground. He landed on his feet, and called to Casey Franks, who was there to grab both women and drag them backwards, not bothering to check on their health until they were out of danger.

"*Boss!*" Rhino now had hold of Jackson, whose eyes bulged as his oxygen was cut off. Above them a large group of the humanoids tugged on the ropes, and both men were being lifted.

Too many of them, Alex thought. *Must be how Blake and the two PLA soldiers were overwhelmed.* He ran again, jumping up and catching hold of Rhino around the waist. The big HAWC still had hold of Jackson, who now had Alex clinging to his legs. The added weight made the soldier's eyes bulge ever more furiously from his head as his neck was being crushed.

Alex began to quickly clamber up Rhino, but stopped when Jennifer's scream dragged his head around. She was already halfway up the wall, twisting and struggling like a fish on a line. He knew if he went after Jennifer, then Jackson would be lost. He couldn't be everywhere and his frustration was knotting inside him.

"Yang!" The man ignored him. "*Goddamnit*, Franks!"

He saw Casey run at the woman, and Alex then scrambled up the big soldier's body, once again ripping a knife free and hacking through the ropes holding him. They fell in a heap on the ground. He turned to see Casey jump in the air at Jennifer, spearing toward her, arm and hand stretching out. Her fingertips grazed the woman's boot, as she slammed hard into the wall. But she was too late, in another second Jennifer had been dragged into one of the windows and had vanished.

"Shit." Alex bared his teeth and lifted both men to their feet as if they weighed nothing.

He yelled into their faces. "Get 'em all back." He ran at Franks, who was now trying to scale one of the ropes. He was underneath her in a second, and pulled her back down. The female HAWC's face was creased with fury, and Alex pushed her back.

"Defensive position. That's an order."

Her teeth were grit and her eyes were defiant as they went from Alex to the landing Jennifer had just been hauled onto.

"Franks." Alex's hand came down hard on her shoulder. Casey nodded, and headed back to the group, the HAWCs now herding the others back.

More ropes came down, trying to snag them, and Alex didn't wait anymore. He dived for one of the looping cords that flew down to try and encircle him. He gripped it and began to climb, rapidly ascending. When he got near the top, the beings must have suddenly decided that Alex untethered wasn't something they wanted to deal with and the rope was let go.

He fell backwards, plummeting the sixty feet to the ground. He spun in mid air, and landed hard, but on his feet. He immediately stood straight, the rope piling beside him.

"Holy shit. *Awesome*," said Jackson, his voice still painfully coarse. He coughed and looked back up. "Did you see anything up there? Jennifer?"

"I saw people," Alex said. "I think." He backed up, keeping a watch on the windows. For now, they looked empty. "Pull in tight." The group gathered in. He turned to Aimee, and reached out to her. "Are you okay?"

Aimee nodded. Cate rubbed at the red mark around her neck, scowling. "Hey," she croaked. "I'm fine too. Thank you for asking."

Casey shined her light upwards, but the beam didn't reach the higher balconies. "We need to get up there. They took Jennifer, and no two guesses as to where Blake and Yang's guys went."

Rhino turned slowly. "Down here, we're fish in a barrel." He turned to Alex. "How many you figure, boss?"

"Dozens ... and probably a lot more we *didn't* see." Alex backed up a few more steps. "We're going to have to climb. Go after them." He turned. "Everyone okay with that?"

Soong and Shenjung looked dubious. Soong spoke quickly to her partner who shook his head, and then turned. "We can stay here."

"That's not a good idea." Aimee went and took the small Chinese woman's hand. "We can haul you up." She turned to Alex. "Can't we?"

"Sure can," he said. "And Aimee's right. They'll be back. Ropes might not be the only thing they drop down."

The pair looked at each other, and then dropped their eyes. Alex took that as consent and went to the coils of rope still lying on the ground. He checked it quickly and then looped it over his shoulder and headed to the wall. He picked up speed and then leapt a dozen feet to the top of a stone column. It only took him a few minutes to scale to where the pale beings had disappeared.

Easing over the edge, he saw he was in a long balcony or windowed corridor. As he had earlier suspected, it was another level. He crouched, waiting and listening. There was stillness and silence. He stood, quickly tying off the rope and tossing one end over.

"Franks, you're up."

Casey didn't hesitate, and scaled the rope quickly, arm over arm as Rhino held it straight. In no time she threw a leg in through the window and clambered in.

Alex looked down. "Rhino, rig a loop-step. Aimee, you're next."

Rhino immediately set to creating a small loop in the end of the rope, and showed Aimee how to put her foot through, and then hang on. Alex hauled her up in seconds. Followed then by Cate, Soong, and then Shenjung.

Jackson was next, the big man climbing slowly as he struggled with his own weight.

Rhino cupped hands around his mouth. "Too many donuts, hey, brother?"

Jackson climbed in, and then shot out his long arm, single finger flipping the bird.

Up next was Yang, and then Rhino, the big HAWC coming up with an ease and speed that told of someone who did this for a living. He stepped over the window edge, barely breathing hard. He held onto the rope. "Leave this, boss?"

"Take it. We need all the tools we can get our hands on." Alex called the group in close. "We move fast and silent. I'll take point."

Alex moved in near silence in the dark, slowing from time to time to listen and try and sense anything that might have indicated an ambush. When he came to bends or corners he would stop and try and reach out, just using his senses. There was always the background hum of life, but for the most part, it wasn't nearby.

The ornate architecture became more decrepit. Whoever was residing in the old buried city hadn't been maintaining the tunnels for centuries. Perhaps the skills or the desire had been long lost. There was one change that seemed to be more gradual and evolutionary – the images carved into the walls became less articulate, as if the work wasn't undertaken by craftsmen, but instead now by simple cave artists. The pictoglyphs themselves stopped being about multiple deities, warriors, and kings, and morphed into being about one thing only – the coiled mass of the creature outside the cave, the Kraken. Alex shook his head. *It became their everything.*

At a T-shaped juncture he slowed and then stopped. He could sense the crush of bodies ahead long before he saw them. Both sides of the hidden corridor end were jammed tight. Those beings were waiting for his group to round the corner, to catch them in some sort of crossfire.

Alex eased back, and then waited for the group to catch up. He held up a hand to Rhino, who then shot out an arm, stopping everyone.

"Around the bend, an ambush. We have a choice: go back, and find another way, or crash through it."

"Punch it," said Franks.

"How did I know you were going to say that?" said Rhino. He grinned at Alex. "Do it."

Jackson nodded. "Let's get it over with."

Alex turned to Yang. "You get a vote too."

The Chinese captain didn't flinch. "They have my people. We go forward."

"I'll go first," Alex said. "We hit them hard and fast. Preserve ammunition – knives and knuckles."

"Wait," Cate said. "The best weapon you have is your flashlight. They attacked us in the darkness, and I'm betting they see just fine. I think these guys have got to be dark-adapted. Living in permanent twilight and darkness means they will have evolved masses of enlarged photoreceptor cells. Even weak light should hurt them."

Alex nodded. "Good, get your lights out. Franks, Rhino – left corridor. Jacksons, Yang – the right one. On my word."

The soldiers crept forward until they were just a few feet from the corner. Alex held a hand up, and they waited. He closed his eyes momentarily, and could hear the multiple breaths, feel the warmth of the crush of bodies emanating from the junction. There were many of them, staying silent, waiting.

Alex counted down on his fingers … 3-2-1 … then dropped his fist. Lights came on, and the soldiers roared as they rushed forward.

CHAPTER 53

Time: 04 hours 01 minutes 08 seconds until fleet convergence

The Seawolf class submarine, the USS *Texas*, had finally surfaced. There was no need anymore for the cat and mouse game of only a few hours ago.

Commander Eric Carmack in the conning tower smiled ruefully and lowered his field glasses, as he watched the wall of steel maneuver into place. The People's Liberation Army Naval Force had now assembled five more Luyang III class destroyers to add to the *Kunming*'s presence. Each of the sleek vessels bristled with weaponry. There were also two submarines just below the surface and, imposingly, an aircraft carrier, called the *Liaoning*. This last one was a veritable mountain on the water.

Carmack exhaled, knowing that way up on the deck of this floating monstrosity they had a dozen Shenyang J-15 carrier based fighter craft. The planes were fast and furious darts known as *Flying Sharks*. Bad news.

"Armed to the teeth and ready for war." He handed the glasses to his COB, Alan Hensen.

Hensen took them, scanned the vessels, and then turned to look over his shoulder at the horizon. "Our muscle is still hours away. Gonna get real crowded here soon."

Carmack grunted, leaning forward on his forearms. This morning there'd been only two vessels of war on the water. Soon there'd be two mighty fleets – two horned bulls, squaring off against each other, both pawing the ground, and breathing fire.

"Think they'll try anything while they've got us outgunned and outnumbered?" Hensen asked.

Commander Eric Carmack was the ranking naval officer and was given control of the approaching fleet. He knew that the naval war machinery arrayed, for and against, was formidable, and even deep diving would give little protection against the technology that could be brought to bear. He also knew that the modern Chinese ships had computer assisted guidance systems in their depth charges – good ones – *of course they were*, because the tech plans were hacked straight from one of the US secret military R&D databases.

He smiled; perhaps in the future there would be no need for armed head-to-head conflict, as everything would be fought in the cyberspace. Maybe that'd be better, but who knew.

He exhaled a breath that danced away from his lips like a small frozen ghost. Carmack looked down into the iron-gray water; it was cold, and deadly. His job was to make sure his men and women didn't end up in it, and if it came to it, to make damn well sure the other guys did.

"Unlikely," he said, clasping his fingers together. "We can shoot over the horizon, they know that, and already our satellites are probably staring right down the noses of their officers."

"Good," Hensen said. "Sanity prevails."

"Sanity?" Carmack shrugged. "In war, sanity is in short supply. Right about now, I'm betting there's a lot of nervous fingers on a lot of launch buttons over there. Someone gets excited or has a rush of blood, and a lot of people will die. Then, like a goddamn disease, the infection would spread to both our mainlands." He turned to Hensen, leaning on one arm. "Then onto their allies, and then ... fiery death on a global scale."

Carmack turned back to look at the Chinese ships. They were so close he could see the individual officers on the bridge, glasses up, watching him. He waved. If it came to it, the Chinese were too close to miss. Unfortunately, so were they.

*

General Chilton turned to the blinking phone – *that phone* – the red one that was a direct line through to the Oval Office. Jim Harker stood up, and motioned towards the door.

Chilton nodded. When President Paul Banning, the Commander in Chief, called, it was never just to ask how his golf swing was looking. And today, the potential for conflict in the Southern Ocean was a clear and present danger.

He waited until the door was closed, sat down, and lifted the receiver. Encrypters and randomizers immediately went to work ensuring that their communication would be invulnerable to all attempted intrusion.

"Mr. President." Chilton stared at the picture on his wall. It showed the USS *Nimitz* coming over the horizon at dawn; it always lifted his spirits.

"Marcus, the secretary of defense has just informed me that I may need to prepare for some time in the mole hole. Yesterday, I'm planning my holidays, and today I need to be secured beneath a million tons of concrete and steel because we could be going to war. You told me you had this under control; just what the hell is happening down there?"

Chilton smiled. He knew the president had read the briefings. But it was ever the way, that as soon as the rubber looked about to hit the road, then the questions, doubts, and nerves set in.

"Sir, the Chinese have assembled a small fleet in the Southern Ocean, just as we expected and planned for. I'm afraid things may get worse before they get better."

"That goddamned sub. In future, we should have a remote self destruct on all prototypes." The president exhaled long and slow. "How the hell do they think they're going to benefit from this, let alone be able to get it out, and then get it past us?"

"They're obviously going to claim international salvage rights," Chilton said.

"Oh c'mon, Marcus, that's bullshit, and you know it. Even I know it doesn't apply to military vessels."

"You're right, sir. In fact, at the International Convention on Salvage in London of 1989, we all agreed that the uniform international rules regarding salvage operations, of which we and the Chinese attended and were signatory to, was that in *no way* would these rights apply to warships."

"So they haven't got a leg to stand on." The president sounded relieved.

"Correct, but they're relying on an earlier set of rules," Chilton said, and then quoted what he had just read. "Those from the Brussels agreement of 1910. They state that the law of salvage applies to anyone who recovers a ship or cargo after peril or loss at sea, and after a period of two years. They are entitled to a reward commensurate with the value of the property saved, *or to the property itself*."

"Jesus Christ, that's a joke, they know warships are a red line," the president said quickly.

"We know it, and they know it. But all they want is time and a distraction. We'll need to take them to the International Maritime courts. Of course we'll win, but by then, they'll have pulled the *Sea Shadow* to bits. Bottom line, sir, is that the Chinese are poor initiators, but great imitators – in a decade they'll have reproduced enough *Sea Shadow* type vessels to sneak in off the coast of most of our major cities. These are gifts we just cannot afford to give away."

Chilton heard the president groan.

"Well, Marcus, what do we do here? I do not want to go down in history as the guy that started a war with China."

"For now, sir, we do nothing but wait. Our assets are enroute, and will be there within a few hours. In the meantime, the Chinese will be making some aggressive displays to try and scare us off. But we don't back down, we don't even blink. We don't need to. We're the 300 pound gorilla here, sir."

"So, we stare 'em down." The president clicked his tongue. "I need more options, Marcus. You said it might get worse before it gets better. If that's the case, then you bring me those options, ASAP. I want more choices than backing down or sinking ships, understood?"

"Yes, sir. At this time we have deployed two teams under the Antarctic ice. Both under Jack Hammerson's oversight." Chilton leaned towards his computer screen to see if there were any updates from Hammerson – there were none.

"That's good. Progress?" The president asked.

"Some, but not all what we want to hear. We have lost contact with both teams, but we believe at least one of them is down under the ice making progress towards the submarine. That's all I know for now, sir." Chilton knew Banning would want more, but he didn't have it.

"*You believe?* Can't exactly take that to the bank, can I, General?" The president's voice sounded strained.

"Our teams just need time to secure or destroy the vessel. I trust Hammerson and his people. It's still the best option for a non-conflict outcome we have," Chilton responded calmly.

"Sounds more like the only option." The chair squeaked as if the president sat back. "Okay, Marcus, we stay cool for now, but you keep me informed of anything else; priority one. We're all on the edge of the abyss here."

"Yes, sir." As the head of the US Armed Forces, Chilton knew it better than anyone.

"At 1800 hours, I will authorize the raising of the security level from DEFCON-3 to DEFCON-2. I pray your team wins the day, Marcus. God help us all." The president disconnected.

General Marcus Chilton swung back to the picture on his wall. He breathed easily, calmly. He always stayed cool; that's why they called him *chilli*. He also stayed cool because he prepared for anything and everything. He had his primary Chinese targets chosen, and they were following every ship, submarine and aircraft they had via satellite. The first launch flare confirmation he got, he'd unleash hell.

His eyes slid to a time banner on his computer screen – 04 hours, 01 minutes, 08 seconds until his war fleet arrived. *God help us all*, President Benning had said. He sat back. "Amen to that."

*

Joshua had the two superhero figures, one in each hand. Iron Man to his left, and the Hulk in the other. He was sitting on the floor in Margie's office in the big building where Mommy had talked to the gray-haired man with all the lines on his face. *Jack*, he remembered. The man smiled a lot, but Joshua knew that he didn't tell the truth all the time. He had to see past his words, and pull the truth directly from inside his head. Doing this gave both of them a headache, but the more he tried it, the easier it got ... at least for him.

The door opened again, and Jack came out. He handed something to Margie at her big desk, and then looked down and waved and saluted. Joshua grinned, and returned the salute, Hulk and all.

He held the man's eyes. "When is Mommy coming back?"

Jack crouched and ruffled his hair. "Soon, I hope. She just has to finish some important work for us."

Joshua continued to stare, reading the man. "You don't know where they are, and you think they might be lost."

Jack continued to smile, but inwardly he winced from the pain in his head that Joshua knew he was feeling. He could also sense that he was momentarily frightened. *No, that wasn't right.* The man didn't scare, but he sure didn't like it.

Jack ruffled his hair again, and stood. "I promise you, Joshua, as soon as I hear something I'll let you know. Mommy will be fine." He turned then to Margie, a brief look passing between them, and then he was back in his office.

Joshua looked at Margie, and sensed the waves of sympathy rising from her. She thought Mommy was lost too.

He liked Margie. He smiled at her. "She's fine."

She was alive, he knew it, and so was his father. He couldn't wait to meet him, to talk to him. Peter was nice, but Peter wasn't like him. Where Alex Hunter was *just* like him.

He lifted the posable plastic figures in each hand. He turned to Hulk, and made words for him.

"Don't worry, Mommy is happy and safe, and coming home soon."

He nodded and grinned and lifted Iron Man. His smile fell away and he stared, his brows coming together. The words came again, but they weren't his own this time.

"They won't make it out alive. The thing, the monster, knows they are there now. It wants them ... to eat them both."

Joshua continued to stare, his eyes shining wet for a moment more as his teeth ground together.

"Joshua?" It might have been Margie's voice.

He stared, unblinking, and his tiny fingers closed on the hard plastic figurine. Iron Man crushed into shards.

CHAPTER 54

Alex was the first one around and was immediately confronted by a wall of pale, hairless bodies. The lights illuminated the horde in a frozen glaring snapshot, and for a split second, even he was momentarily taken aback. The figures were powerfully built but smaller than normal, no more than four-and-a-half feet at their tallest, and their bodies were chalk white. In their hands were all manner of stabbing and cutting weapons.

But what had shocked Alex the most were their faces ... or lack of faces. They were claylike, near featureless, with tendrils dangling from the middle of their heads. No mouth could be seen, and though they must have been startled by the sudden appearance of the tall humans and their blinding lights, not a word or sound was made.

Startled, they still came at Alex like a wave. Cutting and stabbing tools speared forth and chopped down. Alex felt numerous rents to his flesh, and despite his HAWC suit repelling most, he knew he'd still be running blood.

The muscular creatures displayed a sort of simian strength and agility, and at first Alex just pushed them back, or brushed them aside, but they kept coming in greater and greater numbers. He then threw them back into the darkness, and finally, the sheer numbers coupled with the ferocity meant he could not pull his punches anymore, so he exploded into them.

Alex grabbed an axe-like weapon from one creature, and his other hand clenched into a fist, as he threw himself at the writhing, furious mass. He cleaved heads and limbs, smashed bones, and crushed all before him as they came. Behind him, he heard the sound of his team, forcing back even more. The beings' blood, warm and sticky, now coated the floor, ran from the walls, and also dripped from Alex and his soldiers.

As quick as it started, the humanoids ceased their attack and sped back down their dark corridor, dragging away their dead and injured, but leaving weapons behind. Alex took off after them, diving and grabbing at one of the fleeing creatures. He disarmed it, and held it up.

"*Jesus Christ,* what the hell are you?" He came back into the group holding the struggling thing up by the neck.

"What the fuck are they?" Casey's mouth turned down in disgust.

Rhino stooped to lift one of the weapons that looked like an axe, crafted from heavy-toothed jawbone, then stopped to stare at the being. "Holy crap."

"That's not human," Jackson said, taking the jawbone axe from Rhino and hefting it.

"Take it easy," Cate said, peering around Rhino. "It might have been once."

Alex held the wriggling thing by the neck, its feet up off the ground. "Maybe." He lowered it and then grabbed the dangling tentacles on the face. He lifted.

"Like I thought, a mask." He pulled it back.

Franks scoffed. "Oh yeah, like that's any better."

Alex frowned, looking at the thing that now stood listless as though resigned to its fate. "Aimee, Cate, I'd like your scientific expertise here." He turned it towards them.

The being's face could barely be called human, even protohuman. It was so pale, the skin was near transparent, and the entire head was egg-smooth. The nose was non-existent, being just two slits in the center of the face, but it was the eyes that were truly alien. They were the size of chicken eggs and black as oil, shiny, and more like those of a spider.

"*Agh*, deformed," Yang said. "You should kill it."

"*Ho-leeey* shit," said Jackson.

"Dark adapted. I bet it sees in an entire range of spectrums," Aimee said.

"Wow." Cate ducked down to look into the eyes. She turned. "Get that light away. Aimee's right, dark environment evolution. No wonder the light freaked them out; it's got almost total pupil to sclera ratio."

Rhino also bent lower as the thing wriggled again in Alex's grip, now trying to reach around and bite his hand. He pointed, and the thing's jaws snapped at his finger. He snatched his hand back. "What's with that mouth?"

"Hold him, her, whatever," Cate said. Alex gripped the thing tighter, and it calmed again in his hand, surrendering.

"Her, by the look of that chest," Jackson said.

Cate carefully reached forward, gripping the chin and holding it tight. With her other hand she peeled the lips apart.

"Fuck me," said Rhino. "What the hell are they for?"

The teeth in the small mouth looked to be just a single pair, one on the top jaw and one at the bottom. They were large triangular wedges growing from both gums, to scissor over one another.

"That's not normal," Cate said.

"No shit," said Casey.

"No, I mean, it's not natural, even for this female. I can see that the tongue and larynx look well formed – she should be able to talk. And by feeling the jawline and looking at the growth of the teeth at the gumline, I can tell it's a female only just out of her teens. But the teeth themselves have been altered, perhaps filed, to be like this."

"If it can talk, make it talk." Yang leaned in close, his face twisted in disgust.

"It's like a beak," Alex said. "Same association for the mask – the ultimate worship – make yourself like your idol ... or god." He turned to Rhino. "Use the rope, bind her."

"It's like tattooing or scarification in primitive tribes," Rhino said, taking hold of her and looping the rope around her wrists and neck.

"Easy," Aimee said. "We humans do what we need to do to survive. The great Aztlan race collapsed and regressed. An ever-hungry god became their religion and their idol, and they in turn tried to become like it. So, they reverted back to something primordial to survive in this primordial place."

Yang continued to stare, but still looked like he had smelled something bad. "The freak *must* talk."

"Well, it's freaky anyway," Rhino said, finishing his work, and holding the rope like a leash. The small being looked down at her bound hands, and then stood silently, her large black eyes unreadable.

Yang pushed in close. *"Where are my men?"*

Casey moved fast to intervene, grabbing Yang and spinning him so she could stare into his face. "Back off. You're not in charge anymore."

Yang glared at her, and his fists balled. Casey returned the cold stare, her face twisted into its usual sneer. "Just to be clear, I still want to kill you."

Yang's lips momentarily twisted before he turned to briefly lunge again at the small creature. This time, it bared its beak-like teeth at Yang, and then opened its mouth wider. Alex felt the splitting scream deep in the core of his brain. He doubled over, his hands pressed to his ears.

Aimee rushed to him, and knelt. "What is it?"

Alex lifted his head, his eyes tightly closed from the pain. "The sound." He opened his eyes to slits and looked across to the being, who then snapped its mouth shut with an audible clack of teeth. The sound was immediately shut off.

Alex breathed deeply, feeling the white-hot needle of pain withdraw. "It came from her."

"We heard nothing." Aimee looked from Alex to the humanoid. "Just like in the cave mouth. It's the subsonic wavelength again, a defensive mechanism."

Alex got to his feet. "Now we know where the sound came from. But I don't think it was designed to cause pain ... more like a call to its own kind ... or to something else." He straightened. "We need to be on guard."

Alex looked off into the darkness, and saw Yang watching them silently. The PLA captain turned to walk away a few paces into the dark. Shenjung and Soong were talking quietly, standing away from the being.

Alex ducked down, looking into the small pale being's face. "You're safe." She recoiled from him slightly. "I'm sure we're as freaky to her, as she is to us." He smiled. "We mean you no harm ... if you mean us no harm." He repeated the words in his mind, trying to project them, the silence from the being making him think they might communicate by other means. She stood there as impenetrable as ever.

"It's unnatural. The silence freaks me out," Franks said.

"Like everything else down here," Jackson added. "Guess they learned that being quiet is something that keeps you alive."

Alex stood, and pointed to himself, then the others. Then he pointed at her, and made looping motions around her neck, and then walked away. "Where did you take them ... our friends?" he said slowly.

Cate snorted. "You can say it as slow as you like, Alex, but she isn't going to understand."

The girl lifted her dark orbs to Alex, and he felt a sudden throbbing in his brain. She turned and started off down the dark tunnel, only stopping when she reached the end of her leash.

"You were saying?" Casey asked with a grin.

"Give her some slack." Alex motioned forward and she set off again. "Keep the flashlights on, and watch side corridors and also overhead. Don't want anyone having a noose dropped around their necks."

Alex let the small being lead him. The tunnel narrowed, with huge age-patinated stone blocks having fallen from the ceiling or collapsed in from the walls. Alex stopped the girl at one of the fallen blocks, and looked up into the cavernous dark from where it had fallen. The rock fall was ancient, but the size of the boulders meant that if there were another cave-in, they would never be able to dig themselves out.

Aimee laid her hand on the wall. "This building, this entire city, is carved from the surrounding cliff face."

"Like the ancient Jordanian city of Petra, the Rose City," Cate said. "It's carved straight into the side of a mountain. But this," – she slowly panned her light around – "this far exceeds its complexity, and size."

"It's a maze," said Rhino.

"Makes for good defensive fortifications," Casey said. "Against everything except earthquakes."

"Something sure hit it," Jackson said. "But why is it a wreck on just this side?"

"Good question." Alex turned back to the stygian depths of the tunnel ahead. He noticed that the small female being was staring off into the darkness. He laid a hand gently on her shoulder. "Hey, let's go." She turned to stare up at him with those glassy black orbs for a moment, before leading him again.

Alex sensed the change in air density long before the tunnel ended. "There's something up ahead."

The small female being led Alex around more fallen blocks and then out onto a ledge, perhaps once a balcony. She stopped and pointed. Alex lifted a hand, keeping the group back, as he surveyed the new surroundings. After a moment, he stepped to the side and waved them on.

They had passed through the cliff wall. Or the wall itself was only a partition of one underground world to the next. There was another huge cavern, this one even hotter than the one they had left. It was also luminescently lit, but this world was dominated by a body of water, nothing like what they had encountered with the previous underground sea. It was more a lake, miles across. Steam, like a low mist, hung over its surface, and on some of the banks, mangrove-like plants stepped out into the water on stilt-like legs. At its center, bubbles popped and small eddies swirled as submerged gas pockets were released from their muddy prisons.

"So much for the grand city," Jackson said. "It ends here."

"Look down," Alex said, pointing to huge blocks half submerged. "That rubble? I think this *was* part of the city, but somehow it collapsed into here."

"Maybe it's like a giant sinkhole," Soong said. "These things happen in China a lot. There are big land-drops that can swallow entire villages. Maybe this one opened under the city, swallowed it entirely."

"Long, long time ago," Rhino said. "This collapse is damn old."

"Maybe it wasn't just the land falling in, but maybe something else trying to break its way in. I got a bad feeling this is something's backyard. Check out ten o'clock." Alex stared out at the far shoreline as a veil of mist lifted.

Jackson squinted into the distance as the fog cleared slightly. His mouth hung open, and he adjusted the jawbone axe still stuck in his belt. "No fucking way."

"This is why we're here," Rhino said softly.

Lining one of the far shorelines were ships, dozens and dozens of huge vessels. Some were small skiffs, and some were huge. There was even the skeleton of a WW2 bomber plane, many of its panels missing, and one wing sagging onto the bank.

Some of the boats had the three masts of centuries-old sailing clippers, ragged remnants hanging limply from the moss-covered wood. There were rusting iron hulks of cargo ships, and even a fishing trawler. They were all lined up, side by side, like a child's collection.

"There's an old goddamn warship – side cannons." Rhino stepped forward. "Remains of a Union Jack still hanging on the bow." He slowly read the name. "S-A-P-P-H-O – *The Sappho*."

"It's almost dream-like." Aimee breathed the words. "The mist, the ships. You know, this reminds me of something, from childhood." Aimee frowned as if searching her memory. "*That's it*, the cove on Never-never Land, with all the ancient shipwrecks, lost in time."

"Now crewed by ghosts," said Cate softly.

"No," Alex said, feeling a sense of elation. "These guys weren't shipwrecked ... they were brought here." He lifted an arm to point. "Just like our sub."

He couldn't stop the grin spreading across his face. *They'd found it*, the *Sea Shadow*. There, among the decaying hulks, was the submarine, smaller than normal, dented and crushed in the center, but still looking largely intact.

"The *Shadow*, right damn there." Rhino turned briefly to high-five Jackson. "But how the hell did these little freaks get them all down?"

"No, no, they didn't do it. Look," Aimee pointed to a different place on the lake's edge. There were two piles of round white objects.

Alex ground his teeth. "Skulls, human skulls."

"They're fucking cannibals," Jackson said, looking down at the small female being standing ghostly quiet beside them. "No wonder they file their teeth."

"Maybe, but I don't think they're the only suspect," said Cate. "Cephalopods are smart, very smart. A sign of intelligence is constructive play, and it's been observed in modern octopus time and time again. Even in the wild, they will stack the remains of their prey into piles and then continue to rearrange them differently on different days. They play with them, like a child would play with its blocks."

"Oh for fuck's sake," Franks spat. "They're not blocks, they're freakin' human heads."

"Bingo, good news," said Rhino. "That little inlet on our three o'clock ... I have Blake, Jennifer, and our PLA buddies."

Tied to stakes at the water's edge were the four missing members of the group. They were in the lake to their knees, and Alex could see they'd been beaten. They had blood running from multiple wounds that could have been bite marks. The blood dripped into the water.

Alex looked down at the small female humanoid, feeling a sudden rush of disgust and anger. She was already looking at him, as though seeing how he would react to the captives. She turned her unreadable eyes away from him.

Casey was on the brink of the ledge. "They're hurt." She spun. "What did you little freaks do?" She went to grab at the small female, and Alex pushed her back.

"Save it, Lieutenant. We're the intruders here." He knew exactly what Casey felt, but needed them focused for what came next. "We got bigger things to worry about."

"I don't understand ... how?" Rhino ran a hand up over his cropped hair. "The ships, they came from outside. Are we saying this thing can get out?"

"Yes, in and out," Aimee said. "Last time we were here we found evidence of abyssal shrimp – they're crustaceans only found in cold and deep ocean water. Not in these tropical temp, underground seas. Somewhere, somehow, there's a vent between here and there."

"Best news I've heard all day. If *it* can get out, maybe *we* can too," Casey said.

"First things first, we get our people." Alex looked up and around at the cave walls. The cliffside was like a bombed building. There were far too many smaller caves, and ancient room cavities open to the air. "Damn, these little guys could be anywhere, and I'm betting our people aren't tied there just for fun."

"You're right. Got to be a sacrifice," Cate said evenly. "We wondered how these ... people, learned to live in harmony with the creature. I think now we know how."

"Doubt it. Didn't save the Aztlantians above. They tried human sacrifice but the cephalopod just ate its way through most of their virgins, and then their slaves. Then it decided it wanted to come and get the rest itself," Aimee said. "This thing is smart, dexterous, and has senses well beyond our own. The only reason it doesn't compete with mankind for top spot is that it usually doesn't live that long." She snorted softly. "But down here that rule doesn't apply. This thing could be centuries old, maybe more."

"And it could be as smart as we are," Cate added.

"Could we try and communicate with it?" Soong asked, reaching to hold Shenjung's hand.

Yang scoffed. "Would the butcher listen to the sheep? We are food and toys, and nothing more. It is in there, the lake, waiting for us now."

The group turned back to the ancient, black body of water, looking over its mist-covered surface, wondering what lay beneath that dark liquid veneer. Knowing there could be huge eyes on them even now.

"I can't sense it's in there," Alex said, leaning out. "But I'm betting it was or will be soon. We only have two rifles, a pistol and a few grenades. Rhino, Casey, you're the best shots; you stay at high ground and give us cover. Jackson, Yang, you come too; rescue your own people." Alex straightened. "The rest of you stay down ... and watch your six. Don't want more of these guys sneaking up on you."

Alex looked back down at the people tied to the stakes at the water's edge. They were about twenty feet apart. First Blake, then

Jennifer, followed by the two Chinese soldiers. They had all been stripped to the waist, and blood ran down their torsos. All were slumped forward either from fatigue or pain.

Alex pulled Jackson and Yang in closer. "This is our staging point. We move fast, cut them loose, and come straight back here. Hopefully they'll be able to walk, but if not, we carry or drag them. Yang, do your men. Jackson, you get Jennifer and I'll get Blake." He looked each man in the eye. "Set?"

They nodded. Alex looked quickly back at his destination. The mist had started to thicken again, the ships now hidden behind the drifting curtain and the far end of the lake were beginning to vanish. Alex went to turn away, but paused. "And watch the water." He thought through his next few minutes and held up a hand. "Three, two, one ..."

CHAPTER 55

They ran, staying low and jumping over tumbled blocks larger than cars, maneuvering in and out of pathways between even bigger boulders. Alex went past one of the piles of jawless skulls, noticing that there were larger ones, human, some brown with age, and looking perhaps thousands of years old. There were also smaller skulls, with filed teeth like the humanoid they had captured. It seemed the sacrificial candidates were also drawn from the local population.

They stopped behind a mound of rubble. A low sprawling cover of green polyps hugged its surface, making it look like a giant dead animal with matted fur. Alex counted down again, and then they charged. As he ran with the others, he watched the water, but couldn't sense anything lurking below its surface. Also, above them, the cliff sides were empty. Still, there was a sensation of life all around them, but for now, it remained hidden.

Alex was first to Blake, and lifted his head. "Hey there, buddy." The man had multiple wounds that could have been spear piercings or bites from the beak-like dentistry of the small beings.

"Am I … glad to … see you," Blake said groggily.

"We're getting you out of here. Be ready, soldier."

Blake nodded slowly, and Alex quickly sliced through the binding around his hands, and then the straps holding him to the rusting iron rings on the ancient post. Alex noticed that the rings Blake was bound to still had remnants of dried flesh hanging from them – *well used*, he thought.

Blake fell forward into the water, and the liquid quickly revived him. He got up, staggered, and then Alex grabbed his arm.

"Can you walk?" Alex held on.

"I'll damn well try." Blake shook his head once, trying to throw off both water and his stupor. He began to stagger beside Alex, picking up speed.

Alex turned to see Jackson half carrying Jennifer towards them. Yang and one of his already freed soldiers were cutting the bonds of the third.

Once back at the staging point, Alex pulled Blake down with him, and gave him a sip from his canteen. "Do you remember what happened?" Alex asked.

Blake nodded. "Yeah, they beat the shit out of us. And the little fuckers bit me, bit all of us. It was as if they were tasting us." He felt the shredded skin on his neck. "Too many of them. Tied us up and left us."

Jackson came in with Jennifer, who looked shaken but alert. She gratefully took Jackson's offered water. "Thank god you came. I think they were waiting for the tide to come in or something."

Jackson looked at Alex. "Yeah, something like that."

Alex lifted his head to look back to the water. "What the hell is keeping ..." He bared his teeth, the words hissing from between them. *"That sonofa ..."*

Yang had untied both his men now, but instead of them making their way back to their staging place, they were moving along the bank ... towards the ships.

"Motherf ... is he doing what I think he's doing?" Jackson said, his mouth open in a disbelieving grin.

"He's going for the submarine." Alex's eyes narrowed, a hate welling up inside him that he could only barely contain.

"And then what?" Jackson asked.

Alex continued to stare. "Then he holds his ground, and waits to die, or for us to die." Alex's brows came together. "Or maybe he doesn't have to do anything. I'm no engineer, but that powerful distress signal could possibly be adapted. He can tell anyone who's listening that he has found the submarine and is in control of it. At a minimum it would be a propaganda coup for the Chinese government."

"What do you need us to do?" Blake asked.

Alex got to his feet. "Yang's orders were to take the sub, and mine were to stop him. Let's get back, quickly."

Alex and Jackson quickly dragged their injured team members back up through the tumbled boulders to where their group waited on the ledge.

"Fucking Yang." Casey Franks had the gun to her shoulder.

"Save it," Alex said. He turned to look up at the cliffs behind them, and then overhead. There were no small bodies dropping nooses, but the sensation of life was growing with every passing second.

The small being still lashed to Rhino edged to the end of her leash to reach out to him. Her small pale fingers curled on Alex's forearm. She pointed to her mask, which Aimee still held.

Alex looked deep into her black eyes, and then nodded. "Aimee, give it to her."

Aimee handed it over, and the pale creature immediately pulled it over her head and face.

"That's an improvement," Casey said.

"She knows something," Alex said.

The group fell silent, and hunkered down, watching and waiting. Alex pulled out the walkie talkie and turned to the three men sprinting across the rocks, now becoming indistinct in the shrouds of mist.

*

Yang dashed across the moss-slicked boulders, his two men trailing just behind. He always knew he would succeed in his mission. He knew his intellect was vastly superior and more formidable than the engineered American soldier, Alex Hunter.

The two small pings at his belt confused him momentarily, until he remembered his walkie talkie. He smiled as he reached for it, looking forward to the dialogue.

"You'll never make it," Hunter said.

Yang grinned. "But I'm nearly there." His grin widened. "I think it is you who will not make it. Maybe I will watch from within the *Sea Shadow* as your skull is added to the pile."

There was silence for a few seconds, until the American's voice returned, now low and lethal. "Don't make me come and get you."

Yang scoffed. There was no way the threat could ever be exercised, so he decided to have some fun. "Be patient, Hunter. When I find a way out, I'll be sure to tie up all loose ends – one being the collection of your son." He waited, but heard nothing but empty air. He could imagine the confusion from the man.

Yang threw out a hand to keep his balance as he negotiated a particularly slimy group of boulders. The stink was near overwhelming the closer he got to the water – decay, slick mosses, and something tangy that stung his eyes.

Yang enjoyed the distraction, and decided to continue goading the American. "Your son was lucky last time, but even now, we know where he is. *Joshua* ... that is his name, yes? He is on the American base, alone, while you and his mother are down here." He couldn't contain his laughter, or the jubilation he felt – the submarine was so close now. His success was assured.

He sneered. "Your American military can't protect its secrets, its technology, its people, and it certainly won't be able to protect one small boy." There came a sound like a growl over the walkie talkie and Yang gripped it harder. "Imagine how much more valuable he will be, if his father, the original Arcadian, is now dead?"

Yang concentrated on running for a moment, and wished he could see Hunter's face, even just a glimpse. His breathing was becoming ragged, and he coughed, not just from exertion, but from the stink in the air around him that hurt the lining of his nose and throat. The submarine was no more than fifty feet away, half rolled towards him, and he could make out the hatch on top. He'd be inside in another few minutes.

The gunshots were loud in the cavern, and just as the twinkling blue pinpricks of light went out, he felt the hard punch to the back of his thigh. The pain was excruciating, and he stumbled forward. He cursed, holding his leg to stem the bloodflow from the bullet wound, and climbing quickly to his feet.

The lights began to come back on, and he lifted the walkie talkie once again. That was the best they could do? He shook his head;

one more taunt before he was inside. He turned to look back over his shoulder.

"*Huh?*" He blinked in confusion; only one of his men was following him now. His last soldier, who had been lagging from his injuries, had vanished. There was the rocky shoreline, the dark water, and further back, the twisted mangrove-like plants. But there was no sign of his soldier, and nowhere else he could have gone.

Yang, still limping from his bullet wound, turned back towards the sub, hobbling in a restricted sort of jog, as he tried to lift his pace. The stink got worse as he got closer, and though his breath rasped loudly, he thought he heard the sound like someone had something stuck in their throat, and then came the soft splash of water. He turned briefly to his lone soldier, but saw he was now alone.

The mist wasn't so thick that they could be hidden; *no*, they were both gone. There were no pursuing HAWCs, no ropes dropping down from above, and no bodies lying on the shoreline, shot by his enemies. They had just vanished into thin air ... or water. Suddenly the stink became more recognizable, and for the first time, a surge of fear ran up the PLA captain's spine. Ignoring the pain and his bleeding leg, Yang began to run for his life.

Yang's vision blurred as the acrid odor was now so strong it became a stinging gas all around him. He didn't want to turn as he could sense something behind him – cold, huge, and indomitable. Water dripped onto his head and shoulders.

He heard a small whine that could have only escaped from his own throat. As if it had a will of its own, his head began to turn. He couldn't stop the scream escaping his lips, and he lost concentration and coordination as his fear began to short-circuit his muscle movement. He raised an arm over his head and fired his revolver several times.

The loud report of the revolver made the lights go out. In the pitch darkness, he felt the first touch of the thing – cold, like slimy rubber, and immensely strong. His mind conjured up an image of an elephant's trunk, and then the lights came back on.

He screamed again, sanity slipping from him. The tentacle had him, circling his waist. He followed the limb to where it snaked from the water, and could see the behemoth just beneath the surface. Yang's scream was long and loud as the thing lifted him, and then began to tighten.

CHAPTER 56

Aimee let Casey take the gun from her hands. Luck more than skill had guided the shot that had struck the PLA captain. She continued to watch, a grim smile on her lips.

Yang's body was held aloft, and then the green and black tentacle around his waist began to tighten. Yang's screams became a moan as the squeezing continued until the coil met in the middle, just stopping at his spine. His body was crushed like a tube of toothpaste, all the contents forced to either end. He flopped in half, just the skin holding the two separated portions of his body. Only then was the carcass drawn silently down below the water's surface.

"Straight back to hell," Aimee whispered.

The group stood in silence for several moments more, and Aimee could feel Alex's eyes on her. She wondered whether he was shocked by her callousness. She faced him, and raised an eyebrow. After a moment he nodded and turned back to the water.

*

Shenjung felt Soong burrow into him, pressing her face hard into his shoulder. He didn't want to watch either, and though he detested Yang, no man deserved the fate that had been inflicted upon him and his men.

"Oh god," Jennifer said. "We'll never make it past that." She looked around, almost panicked. "We'll never make it. We need to go back, find another way."

"There is no other way," Alex said.

"Then we're dead ... *dead*." Jennifer turned away, and Franks went to her, talking softly.

"It's a suicide run," Jackson said softly.

"It'd be suicide to sit here and wait for rescue," Aimee said. "We've got to check that sub; it's the only chance we've got."

"If it works," Cate said, her face pale.

"We overheard Yang and his men talking," Soong said, with a glance toward Shenjung. "The *Sea Shadow*'s power source is nuclear, and everything internally was designed to deal with a highly damp and extremely caustic and corrosive environment."

"If the hull wasn't breached, then it could still be operational," Alex said.

Rhino joined Jackson's side. "Good enough for me. And one more thing to think about. If the hull wasn't breached, then there could be survivors."

Shenjung grimaced and looked back to the pile of skulls. Though some looked ancient, there were a few still a glistening bone-white. "This is wishful thoughts," he said to Soong. Blake was nearby and nodded, his face still pale.

"Your submarine disappeared in 2008," she said. "If there was anyone inside that made it here alive, we doubt they survived for long."

"If it works, then it's got to be our way out," Aimee said.

"No, it *is* our way out," Cate added.

"What are you thinking?" Alex tilted his head.

"When you and I first dropped into the water, the sea," Cate started, "we passed through a column of freezing water – a vortex. This corresponds to algal blooms in the Antarctic's coastal zones. We think it's due to an upwelling of warm water, an unexplained phenomena in the freezing waters of the Southern Ocean. The water obviously came from here." She pointed. "That sub, we need that sub. If it can still do what it was made to do, then that vortex might be a way out for us – an open sea tunnel."

Alex exhaled and turned back to the far shoreline. "Well, I got nothing else."

"But it's beached," Jackson said. "How the hell do we get it back in the water?"

"The props are still in the water. Reverse thrust and that thing will pull itself back in," Alex said.

"Then we need to get to it," Rhino said, and smiled. "This is going to be a rush."

"We need to think about this. There must be another way." Jennifer grimaced. "Please."

"Every option now is probably a bad option," Aimee said, her eyes on the group. They lingered on Alex. "We just need to choose the one that gives us the greater return on our risk."

Jennifer put a hand over her eyes and rubbed. "By risk, you mean our lives."

Casey cradled her gun. "Well, I ain't staying here to become a member of the clan of the cave squid." She pointed a thumb at the small being that was still standing docilely behind them. "And I like my teeth as they are."

Alex turned to the small being and drew his knife. "Best if she's not here when we're about to go to war with her god."

"Wait," Shenjung said. Soong turned to him, and he tried to continue in English. "You said the ultrasonic sound they made … scared it off."

Jennifer crowded in. "Make her do it." She grasped the small being by the shoulders. "Make her do it to protect us."

"How?" Alex asked. "I don't think I can make her understand. I'm not sure she'd want to help anyway."

He went to cut her bonds and Jennifer pushed his hand up. "Then we keep her with us … as a shield."

"That might work," Shenjung said. Alex looked over at the Chinese engineer, and Shenjung immediately knew that the American leader didn't trust him. He sighed. "Perhaps not then."

Alex cut the bonds, and placed a hand on the being's shoulder. She lifted her mask, and the huge dark orbs stared into Alex's eyes for a moment, before she looked down at her cut bonds, her long deathly white fingers picking away the remnants of the cords, and dropping them to the ground. She turned to Alex again, staring for a few more seconds before lowering her mask, and then in an instant, she scampered away, dancing over the rocks like a goat. As soon as she was within a few feet of one of the openings, dozens of the small pale folk appeared, to grab at her and take her in. They all held spears, knives, and loops of rope. They stared down at Alex and the group for a few moments, before backing silently into their caves.

"Look's like we got an audience," Rhino said.

"I think we always had one," said Jackson.

"Mighty Aztlan, center of the world, and possibly the seed of all human wisdom, now reduced to cave dwellers," Aimee said.

"All civilizations fall. It's not a matter of *if*, but *when*," Alex said. "One thing these guys learned to do is survive, and anyone that can do that down here is pretty clever." He turned back to the group. "We can't take this thing head-on with the weapons we have. Options?"

"Diversion," Casey said. "I take one group over to the other side with the rifle, and attract its attention, draw it to us. Keep it off you guys as you make it to the sub."

"Oh please, can I be in that group?" said Jackson, grinning. "Because that sounds like a real long-term career option." He turned to the wounded HAWC. "What do you say, Blake?"

Casey grinned back. "I accept your volunteering. Especially since you'll make the bigger target."

"Forget it; Jackson is right," said Aimee. She folded her arms, turning to Casey. "You'd last about two minutes. It'd finish you off, and be all over us again – your death would be wasted. And then what do we do once we're in the sub? That thing is obviously big enough to move it around – it dragged it in here for godsake. And as for outrunning it, it probably overtook the sub when it first grabbed it all those years ago. We could just piss it off." She shrugged. "Sorry, Casey."

Jackson exhaled. "Thank god for that."

Jennifer looked pale, her eyes red-rimmed. "Then we just get to the sub and seal ourselves in. Wait it out."

"Fish in a bottle," Cate said, shaking her head sadly. "Ever heard the story of the biologist who gave an octopus a puzzle once.

He placed a small fish in a jar, and screwed the lid tight. Now, the octopus had never seen a jar before, and didn't know how it operated. But it wanted the fish real bad." She sighed. "It took the octopus ten minutes to work out how to undo the jar, and then it ate the fish."

"Oh god, we'd be the fish." Jennifer giggled. "We'd be the tuna in a can."

"I don't think it'd even need to wait. It could rip the sub in half if it wanted to," Alex said. Aimee looked back towards the vessel. "We use what we learned – this thing flees from heat, and we know it vanishes at the first hint of a cave-in. How can we use that?"

"We create a cave-in by pushing some of those boulders down on top of it." Casey pointed. "Up there, that overhang should do fine."

Hanging above the ships was a shelf of stone, hundreds of tons of dark rock, jutting out over the lake.

"No, too risky; we could crush the *Sea Shadow*," Alex said. "But I like the idea of creating a cave-in and panicking it. We can simulate a collapse with an explosion." He held up the grenades he took from the PLA soldiers. "At least we can give it an upset stomach."

Cate raised her head to peer over the rock barrier at the lake. The mist was rising again. "All quiet, maybe it's sated for now and gone back to its midden. That's where it ..."

As if in response, the water broke as a tentacle lifted from the water just in front of them. They hunkered down, but it wasn't seeking the group. Instead, it gently unfurled at the mound of skulls, dropping another onto the top of the pile. This one was fresh, and with streaks of flesh still clinging to it. Another tentacle snaked from the water, and a similar skull was carefully placed beside it, and then rearranged, until the creature decided it was in its right place.

Alex could see the gigantic mass spreading below the water. The monstrous bulk just beneath the surface looked like a mottled green and black stain. Two car-sized unblinking discs watched its own handwork as it arranged and rearranged its toys. Satisfied at last, its tentacles eased back below the surface without a ripple and then the rubbery mass dove into deeper water, to digest its last meal or wait for more to come.

"I feel sick," Jennifer said, sitting back down by Blake.

Alex held out one of the grenades. "Casey, you get one, and I'll keep the other. On my word, you launch yours. Hopefully we won't need two, but we don't know what it's going to take to scare this thing off."

"Scare it off?" Jennifer giggled dementedly. "Did you see that fucking thing? It's as big as a jumbo jet. And you think throwing a firecracker will scare it off."

Jackson put a hand on her shoulder. "It's okay, Jenn, I'm scared too. And you know if you get a firecracker in the eye, you're gonna have one hell of a bad day." He smiled and shook her shoulder. "So, good a plan as any, and if it leads to us getting out of here ..."

Jennifer hugged herself tighter, lowering her head and moaning.

With the plans rapidly forming, Shenjung suddenly felt nervous about his place in the group. "Will you take us too?" He had an arm around a shivering Soong.

Alex turned, frowning. "Huh, what?"

"Will you take us on the submarine?" Shenjung asked again. "We can help ... once onboard."

"No one gets left behind," Alex said. "But you need to keep up. This is a one-shot deal. If anyone falls behind or deviates, then no one is going back for anyone. Understand?"

Alex held his eyes, and Shenjung was sure he meant it when he said if they fell behind, he would leave them without blinking.

Alex turned away and sucked in a deep breath. "We go two-by-twos. Rhino, with me at lead, followed by Aimee and Cate, then Jackson and Jennifer, and then Soong and Shenjung – you are each responsible for your partner. Blake and Casey, you're my bookend at the rear. You've got to have eyes in the back of your head; you ready?"

Casey grinned, holding the grenade in her fist. Muscles and veins bulged in her neck. "Let's fucking do this."

Jackson drew forth the jawbone axe he had tucked into his belt, hefting it. "Ready."

"Not much of an arsenal," Cate observed. "It'll have to do."

"We don't need much," said Aimee. "This thing sees humans as little more than food or something to play with. It hasn't regarded us as a threat for perhaps centuries, and I'm betting it underestimates us. We will have the element of surprise."

"We teach it a lesson ... or at least give it damned good bellyache," Rhino said, hitting Jackson on the shoulder.

"Ready?" Alex asked.

There were nods, and Shenjung felt his pulse start to race. He squeezed Soong's hand, who looked up at him with an ashen face and round eyes. She nodded.

"Three, two ..." Alex looked at each of them as he counted down. *"Go!"* He turned and leapt over the boulder and began to pick up speed.

*

They were about halfway to their destination, and to where the cliffs intruded close to the lake, forcing them all nearer to the oil-dark water. Tactically, Alex realized, if he was planning a sea-based ambush on his group, this is where it would come from.

Sure enough, he began to sense the creature, and looked to the lake's misted surface. He knew down below, it was gliding closer, its excellent vision seeing the small bodies running along the water's edge.

"Heads up," he yelled, watching the water as he ran. He saw the mottled stain spreading beneath the surface. Luminous circles began to flare, and the creature's body changed from green-black to a brick red, and then to a muddy brown, as he guessed the massive cephalopod's chromataphores were firing, matching its excitement level. *Why not?* It was enjoying the game, Alex knew, especially as it got to eat its toys at the end.

The monstrous creature surged forward and Alex pulled the pin on the fragmentation grenade and threw it. "Fire in the hole!"

The group crouched, as the explosion thumped below the water, sending a geyser into the air. The lake erupted for hundreds of feet as the creature shot away from the bank so fast it left a huge whirlpool eddy on the surface.

"It's working," Aimee said, and the group began to increase their pace.

A bow wave raced around the farthest side of the lake, five feet high. It was like the wave given off by the bow of an ocean liner, except the huge moving object wasn't above the water, but below. The wave turned when it was about half a mile away, coming back towards them for a few hundred feet, before slowing over the deeper water.

"Gone deep," Cate yelled. "I think we did it."

"Nope; it's coming back. Faster," Alex shouted. "Franks, you're up."

Casey fingered the pin on her grenade, but held it. "I got nothing back here."

"Shit." Jackson started to run harder, dragging Jennifer with him.

When they were only two hundred feet from the sub, the wave rose again in the middle of the lake, and then between them and the first of the ships, the thing exploded from the water, beaching itself, and dwarfing the ships behind it. The creature continued to boil from the water, coiling and tangling like a handful of monstrous worms knotting and crawling over each other. The acrid smell was overpowering. Suddenly, the idea that a single remaining grenade would send it packing seemed a hideous joke.

"Franks!" Alex yelled.

The female HAWC sprinted forward, her arm raised.

A tentacle shot towards the group, and Alex lifted his pitiful Ka-bar blade. But the club moved past him, choosing a different target.

Jackson saw the coming appendage and pushed Jennifer to the ground. "Shut your eyes." He moved to the side, drawing its attention and lifting his makeshift axe, swinging with all his might, striking the rubbery mass, and opening a foot long gash in its flesh. Purple blood splashed the rocks.

"Fuck you!" he yelled. He readied himself for the next swing while the thing lifted higher, as though wary now.

"Get moving!" Blake yelled.

Jackson stood, legs planted, holding the jawbone axe ready. The tentacle hovered about fifty feet above him, and then came down with blinding speed, swatting down upon his body, flattening him as if he were an annoying bug. When the thing rolled back up, there was a large red smear across the plate-sized suckers, and only a pulpy mess where the huge man had been seconds before. Jennifer's scream was like a siren that stretched across the water.

Casey was finally close enough, and pulled the pin on her grenade, throwing it like a pitcher. It flew fast and straight, tucking in under the creature's bulk. She kept running to dive across Jennifer, who was getting up from her knees and looking like she was preparing to run, somewhere, anywhere.

The fragmentation grenade detonated in an ear shattering blast. Gobbets of meat showered the group, and there came a hideous, alien screaming like something from the very depths of hell. Rocks were pushed aside as the thing coiled in on itself, wrapping tentacles around the train-tunnel sized wound in its side and drawing back into the water. It fled, moving impossibly fast for a creature that big, and soon sank without a trace.

"*Now, now, now,*" Alex yelled, running hard.

CHAPTER 57

"Sink the USS *Texas*." Minister Chung Wanlin stood immobile at the head of the group in the large meeting room, his expression implacable. Around the polished table, General Banguuo sat in the center and fanned out to his left and right were eight other generals of the Chinese armed forces. This was a war council, and Banguuo knew that cautious words mattered now.

Banguuo felt his comrade peers waiting on him, as he was the ranking officer in the room. Though Minister Chung Wanlin was the senior party official, when it came to military matters, it was not up to him to drive armed forces strategy.

"Then what?" Banguuo asked.

Wanlin narrowed his eyes. "Then, General, we will have educated them. We will have shown them what happens when they disable our ships, blow up our bases, take our soldiers captive, and *kill* our personnel." He smiled coldly. "Should I go on?"

Banguuo observed that the man looked agitated, energized, and there was a fire of zeal behind his eyes. He needed to be careful with him.

"Honorable Minister ..." Banguuo remained ice calm as he leaned forward. "The moment I order that strike, China and America ... the entire world as we know it, will change forever. And perhaps not for the better for us."

Wanlin's lips compressed.

Kraken Rising

"Dear Minister, do you know how many nuclear warheads China has?" Banguuo asked. Wanlin stayed motionless, and Banguuo responded for him. "About 280." He tilted his head. "Do you know how many nuclear warheads, including tactical, strategic, and nondeployed weapons, the Americans have?"

Banguuo waited for a moment, and then smiled with little humor. "Approximately 4,800." The general held out his hands. "I am not afraid to die for my country. But I will not consign millions of my citizens to the same fate, over some minor friction, which history might contend we initiated. We should be careful about poking a bear, Minister."

"A bear?" Wanlin harrumphed. "A dragon eats bears." He stared unblinking at Banguuo. "I did not know that courage was something in such short supply." Wanlin craned his neck towards the general, his face going red. "I have already discussed first strike option with the president." He smiled. "We can contain them, and minimize our own losses, if we strike first – hard and at multiple targets." He scoffed and leaned back. "Do not fear bears in the age of the dragon, General Banguuo." He lowered his brow. "You will initiate a strike against the American submarine. That is the order, General. Launch the strike or resign your post."

Banguuo didn't move, didn't even blink. He feigned indifference, even though he had a burning urge to leap from his seat and pound this upstart into the ground. Neither of the minister's options were acceptable to him. But he needed more time; Wanlin was a politician, not a soldier, and that meant he dealt in persuasion, subterfuge, and outright deception. Wanlin was moving too fast. Banguuo needed to slow him down.

"Show me the order."

Wanlin bristled. "I just gave it to you."

Banguuo smiled, his eyes calm. "Not from you. An order of this magnitude needs to be sighted by all the generals ... and myself. Please show me the directive from the General Secretary of the Chinese Communist Party."

At the use of the president's full title, Wanlin's face looked about to explode. But after a moment, the angry color leaked away, and he seemed to ease. Then he smiled. This worried Banguuo more than anything else.

"Then you shall have your presidential order." Wanlin's phone beeped and he took it from his pocket. He looked at it briefly before putting it to his ear. He grunted, and turned away for a moment.

"Put it up on screen," he said quickly, and immediately, the wall behind him came to life. He stood to the side, with his back to it, facing Banguuo and the other generals at the table. "You think the threat is over? While you hesitate, they murder us, and then insult us by picking over our corpses."

The satellite screen image drilled down from the heavens to focus on the blackened stain on the snow and ice. The wreckage of the Chinese base could barely be made out among the still smoldering debris. A figure in a white snow suit, with an American military snow ski parked to the side, walked in among the debris, stopping now and then, lifting items and dropping them.

Wanlin's eyes slid to Banguuo. "A further insult. Deal with it, forcefully. *Show them your metal!*" He turned and left the room, the door banging shut behind him.

Banguuo sat staring at the screen. He sighed. "*Dragons eat bears,*" he whispered, shaking his head. He turned to the man next to him. "I have no choice; get me the *Kunming*, priority one."

*

"*Launch – launch – launch.*" Klaxon horns blared within the USS *Texas*, bulkhead doors were sealed and the interior lights switched to red. Men moved to their posts, fast but calm.

Commander Carmack ran to the bridge, yelling orders as he went. "Who fired, what and where?"

In the bridge room, Hensen was beside him in an instant, and the pair quickly took to their stations. Here too, the lighting was now a hellish red, with multiple screens making the attending officer's faces glow an alien green.

"The *Kunming*, sir, fired one ship-to-shore missile. Possibly a silk worm or dragon claw." The officer stared hard at his screen, reading lists of data as it rapidly scrolled. "Reaching Mach 1 now; determining course and target."

Hensen went and stood behind the man, reading the data along with him. His face green with the light and his eyes fixed.

"Goddammit." Carmack gritted his teeth and prayed it wasn't on its way to McMurdo. If it was, he would have no choice but to retaliate.

"Prepare to dive." He licked suddenly dry lips.

Hensen looked up, frowning. "Target is the Xuě Lóng Base, *their* base."

"What?" Carmack rubbed a hand up through his hair.

"Maybe they're sanitizing the site?" Hensen said. He turned back to the screen. "Forty seconds to impact."

"*Sanitization* ... I hope that's all it is." Carmack folded his arms.

*

Sergeant Monroe's guts ached. His people were out of range, missing or even dead, for all he knew. He cursed Jack Hammerson for involving his team – they were regular soldiers, not Special Forces. He kicked a smoldering beam from his path, and cursed some more.

Monroe bent to pull up another smoking piece of debris – there was nothing that remained of the Chinese base – no survivors, no clues, and he had no idea what he was looking for or actually doing on the foreign nation's site. *Rendering assistance,* he might have said if someone asked him.

He lifted something that might have been the sole of a boot. In reality, he just wanted some sign, anything, any clue, that might tell him his team had all gotten into the tunnels, *and even better*, that there was a way he could get them out.

Sergeant "Wild' Bill Monroe paused and tilted his head, listening. He could swear he heard a bird whistling. He turned.

*

The missile impact and detonation carved a crater fifty feet deep and a hundred wide. It melted snow and blasted ice and rock far out over the landscape. Nothing remained of the already decimated base, or the last human being to ever set foot there.

*

Sam leaned over Sulley, watching the wonders and monstrosities that passed in and out of *Orca*'s tunnel of light, which was thrown forward into the black water. A while back, a fish, if that's what it could be called, had glided into the light. It was big, its head armor plated, and its eye was like something set in a mechanical swivel. Sulley had halted the submersible, lest the living battering ram decided to turn and make a run at them. It circled for a minute or two, and then glided off into the darkness.

Earlier they had been traveling on the surface, using the blue twilight to navigate, instead of the energy hungry lights ... but that too had proved a mistake. They had been forced to dive again, as something the size of a glider swooped down from the huge cavern's ceiling. It was all leathery wings and needle toothed snout, and it had snatched at *Orca*, but probably been surprised to find there wasn't flesh to sink its talons into, but hard shell. *Orca* had dropped back into the water and they had immediately dived again.

Sam straightened, wondering what it would have been like to be in that warm water, free floating, exposed to all that. Or maybe worse, in that land with just your wits and a truck load of courage. This was the job they did, he knew. But this was one helluva tough gig. He grimaced, remembering that Aimee Weir was also down there somewhere.

Sam's comm. unit pinged, and he walked a few paces away from the scientists. It was Hammerson on the line.

"Boss."

"Sam, please tell me Jack Monroe is with you."

Sam frowned. "No, sir, haven't seen him for several hours."

"Ah, goddammit. He must have gone over to the Chinese base." Hammerson exhaled. "The Chinese just put a ship-to-shore missile on their base. There's nothing left."

"*Fuck it.*" Sam had liked the McMurdo sergeant. "Did they know he was there?"

Hammerson snorted softly. "What do you think?"

"Yeah, no accident. They wanted to send us a message," Sam said.

"Time's just about up. Tell me what you've got."

"Nothing more than what we know – we think Alex survived, and we're following the shoreline. The Brits here have calibrated their submersible to pick up the *Sea Shadow*'s distress beacon. We're following it along a type of coast where we believe Alex has entered. All we can do is watch and wait."

"Time is the enemy now, Sam. The Chinese fleet has assembled in the Southern Ocean, and we'll be there within the hour. The president has moved us up to DEFCON-2, so a lot of fingers are on buttons across the globe. Pray Hunter gets to that submarine first."

"Pray for sanity," Sam said.

"And if that doesn't prevail, then pray for a quick and overwhelming war," Hammerson responded evenly. "Keep me updated." He clicked off, and Sam turned back to the screen, feeling a knot of impatience coil inside him as he watched and waited.

CHAPTER 58

Time: 00 hours 30 minutes 18 seconds until fleet convergence

In another few minutes they were at the hull of the submarine. Up close, Alex could see the damage. The entire vessel looked compressed, as if by a huge hand. It was lying half in the water, with one side tilted towards them. Alex clambered up first, seeing the hatch swung wide, as if the submarine crew had climbed out and left it open in the event they needed to scramble back in fast. He doubted any who left ever made it.

He looked around at the cave of the Kraken one last time. If the *Sea Shadow* crew did survive, he imagined they must have thought they'd arrived in hell. He looked back at Aimee and then nodded before jumping into the hatch.

He was first to drop down into the vessel, and crouched, staying motionless and trying to sense anything or anyone moving inside the metal tunnels of the submarine's interior.

He inhaled – dampness. At his feet, there was some water. But not enough to indicate a tear in the sub's skin. Further in, he saw there were a few small lights on. He knew that without a breach, the nuclear powered electric generator would have kept on humming for fifty years.

One after the other his team dropped down behind him. Alex stood slowly and sniffed again. There was something missing – the odor of decay and corruption – there were no bodies here. Even ancient corruption could paint the walls with fats and oil that lingered for decades.

Rhino was last in, thumping down heavily and then turning to pull the hatch shut behind him and screwing it tight. He stood leaning forward, breathing heavily and with his forehead pressed against the metal ladder bars. After another few seconds he pushed back hard.

"*Goddamn Jackson!*"

He rammed one huge fist into the sub's wall, making a dull thud run through the hull. He lowered his head again, crushing his eyes shut.

Casey held onto Jennifer; the McMurdo woman looked to be in shock. She lifted her head to look at Alex. Her mouth worked but no words came. Rhino punched the sub hull again.

"*Rinofsky!*" Alex's voice brought Rhino's head up. "Brave men die young." Alex then turned to Jennifer. "He was a good man, but the time for mourning is later."

"Let's go home," Soong whispered.

"Works for me," Casey said.

Rhino stood straighter and nodded once, and then Alex spun away from him. "You heard the lady; let's go home. Blake get to the bridge, Franks, see what's working. Rhino, down to the torpedo room. I want to know what we're still packing. Everyone else, a quick reconnoiter of stores – what have we still got? Five minutes, double time, and then we meet on the bridge."

Alex went quickly along the steel corridor to the bridge room. It was small, and there was a central column with a periscope. Casey immediately pushed at it but nothing happened.

"Dead," she said, looking around in the confined space. She whistled. "No wonder we want it back."

Even though the submarine was nearly a decade old, it looked more like the inside of spaceship than that of an undersea vessel. Gleaming panels with banks of now darkened lights and small screens set into bench tops and walls. A single steering column with a U-shaped wheel had a swivel seat that Blake immediately slipped into, and began fiddling with buttons.

Alex saw that blood ran from Blake's multiple wounds, down his arms and onto his fingers. "Fix that bleeding, mister."

"On it." Blake wiped his hands on his pants, turning about, searching for something he could use as Alex went to the main console, the only one that still glowed softly. There was a single square light blinking at its center, and one word printed there – REBOOT.

He placed his fingertips over it, and exhaled slowly. *Come on, baby, you can do it.* He pressed down, and waited. Images of Joshua flashed through his mind, and his hand pressed even harder onto the glowing button. *You damn well better do it,* he urged.

There was nothing. Alex imagined the electric drives reaching out to ask the question of the high-energy reactor plants, and receiving empty silence in response. He waited and felt a chill creep up his spine. There was no Plan B. The blinking REBOOT sign had vanished, and the screen remained dark.

Alex could feel eyes on him. If the engines wouldn't start, they would expect him to come up with something else. He knew there was *nothing* else. *Please, baby, please.* He placed his fingertips against the screen, praying now to everything and everyone he could think of.

There was a tingle at his fingertips – *static.* And then a tiny hum and a sensation of a draft as if the sub was drawing its first breath in years. The nuclear onboard computers and reactors would have been sent into hibernation mode, awaiting a call to arms. But, receiving the call, they fired up, and then bank after bank of light panels came on. Overhead, lights began to cast a soft glow down on them as the machine came to life.

"We got juice," Casey yelled, as she was able to launch the periscope. It slid up silently and smoothly, and she leaned in to the eyecups. She began to pan. When she finished her rotation, she pulled her head back a fraction. "*Yo;* clear on all quadrants."

The speaker pinged, and Rhino's voice came over the comms. "Good morning, ladies and gentlemen, welcome aboard the USS *Sea Shadow*. For your pleasure and protection, we have four torpedoes, conventional fish, and all looking like they just came out of their wrappers."

Alex smiled. "Good work, and that'll do ... *it has to.*"

*

Aimee was one of the first back, trailed by Cate, and then the rest of the team crowded into the small bridge room. They shared information; there were no rations, and the quarters were in disarray. It suggested that the men and women who had survived lived for some time onboard. Perhaps finally venturing out, to their deaths.

Aimee shuddered at the thought of these brave men and women who were destined to have their heads end up as mere playthings, stacked neatly at the water's edge. She watched as Alex moved fast to the side of the room, and she stepped out of the way, knocking something from a panel top to the floor. It looked like a folder.

Alex turned to Blake. Jennifer was now fussing over his wounds, tying strips of her shirt over the deepest of them. "Here we go, people, pumping ... now." He engaged the pumps and a steady vibration could be felt through the vessel. He straightened, looking relieved. "Good, let's give it a few minutes to do its job. At least then we won't tear the *Shadow*'s belly out on the bottom."

Aimee bent to pick up the folder, surrounded by a hard plastic cover. She opened and began to read.

"What have you got?" Cate looked over her shoulder.

"It's a log ... of the *Sea Shadow*." She frowned as she skimmed the pages. "Log of Commander Clint O'Kane, USS *Sea Shadow*. Dated 13-Oct-2008." She looked up. "That's a day after it went missing, isn't it?"

"Yes; read it; *read that day*," Alex yelled as he and his team rushed from console to console. "Might give us an idea of what the hell happened."

Aimee started to flip more pages through to the last few entries.

"Here we are," she said, and started reading aloud.

Log Entry 112. Date 13-Oct-2008. 1300 hours.

Most of the crew rendered partially deaf from rapid depth-compression. Hull has held, and the reason why we are still alive. Somehow, we've run aground, and it is impossible to reconcile what we are seeing with the instrument readings – it says we are at a depth of over 6,000 feet, well below crush range. But we are on dry land, or partial dry land. Whatever attacked us seems to have vanished. Did it bring us here? Why? Periscope and view screens show semi dark atmosphere, like twilight. But chronologically it's all wrong. Sending a crew out to investigate. We will attempt a refloat when they return.

End Log Entry 112.

Aimee's hands gripped the log tighter. "It proves they made it, and were alive when they got here." She licked dry lips and turned the page, reading aloud again.

Log Entry 113. Date 14-Oct-2008. 0200 hours.

Last night the thing returned, shaking the submarine, rolling it, and lifting it up. Like a child with a rattle. It's gone now, but our sanity is being tested. Worse is, there is still no sign of crew. Party gone for over 12 hours. This exceeds orders for exploratory time frame. Sergeant Anderson was leading party – not a man to deviate from orders. Will not attempt a refloat until all crew accounted for. Communications are not working – no signals picked up. We are transmitting and hope to god someone can hear us. We know now, we are in some sort of cave ... below the ground. There are other ships, all sizes, some from ages long past. What is happening here? Insane. Some sort of Bermuda Triangle, or perhaps we all died and are really all in hell. I must look for my crewmembers, and will personally lead a second team to find missing men.

End Log Entry 113.

She looked up, feeling a wave of nausea run through her. She could feel the man's fear and confusion in every word. The other ships might have given the creature nothing but drowned bodies to pick over. But the *Sea Shadow* and its doomed crew was the first vessel the massive cephalopod had brought to its lair that contained something alive, and something to torment.

Aimee wanted to help. She wanted to save them, or at least yell out to O'Kane and his crew to stay inside the submarine. But it was all too late; *years too late.* She pushed the images of the piled skulls from her mind once again.

She swallowed a lump in her throat and felt the eyes of the group on her now. Even Alex had slowed in his workings to listen. She looked up at him.

"Go on," he said softy.

She turned the page.
Log Entry 114. Date 14-Oct-2008. 0600 hours.
It was in the water, waiting for us. It took the men, snatched them up like they were nothing. It must be the thing that dragged us here, and has been stalking us ever since ...

Aimee paused her reading. In her mind, she saw the huge Ben Jackson swatted like a fly, and the Chinese soldiers snatched up like they weighed nothing. It would have been a nightmare to tear at these poor submariners' sanity. She continued, wishing for the log entries to just end now.

It's been waiting for us to come out the whole time. Sidearms distributed, and we have sealed the hatch, but we know it is out there, we can feel it pressing against the hull. I think it could come in if it wants to. Down to three men – Morrison, Drake, and myself – just enough to run the submarine, but not even sure what we'd do then – go where? We are trapped.

End Log Entry 114.

"Oh god." Aimee could feel the men's fear – she had felt it herself. When she had escaped from the caves before, she had then spent time researching the giant creatures. Something that had caught her eye was an ancient Hawaiian tale. The tropical waters of the islands sometimes played host to the giant creatures. Though nothing like the monster down here, the threat to their fisherman was well understood. The Hawaiian ancestors had thought that these many-legged creatures were actually aliens who came to Earth long before humans existed.

Perhaps this is what O'Kane and the fragmenting minds of his crew would have imagined. That their submarine had somehow been transported to a distant world, and the horrifying unearthly being attacking them was a denizen of that world.

She drew in a deep breath. "This next is the last entry."
Log Entry 115. Date 25-Oct-2008. 1800 hours.
Ten days sealed in now. Morale low, but first sign of hope has presented itself. There are people out there. Can see them moving in the shadows. The creature is gone, for now. Maybe they have scared it off. We're going out to try and talk to them – we'll leave the hatch open in case we need to run for it. Maybe the people can help us.

Our distress beacon is still active. Can anyone hear us? God help us all. Commander Clint O'Kane, USS Sea Shadow.
 End Log Entry 115.

Aimee flipped a few more pages, shaking her head. Her eyes were blurred, wet. "That's it. They went outside, and then that's it."

The room fell silent. O'Kane had been given a devil's choice – stay inside and starve slowly, or leave the metal coffin they were in, and die quickly. Aimee knew it was the same coffin they were all in now. She shut the log.

"So, going out to meet the people probably wasn't a great idea," Casey said at last.

"And if we stay, that'll eventually happen to us," Cate said.

"Then we get out," Aimee said. "This lake, in here, must join up with the outside sea, somewhere, somehow."

"That's what I was thinking." Alex looked up from the instruments. "Maybe during king tides, or during quakes it opens and shuts, makes another vortex like the one we encountered in the sea. This thing slips out, grabs some more toys, and then comes home where it's nice and warm, so it can play and eat in peace."

"This is its home, we are the intruders," Soong added. "It has all the time on its side, and we have limited food, water, and breathable air." She licked dry lips. "We cannot wait for an earthquake, or for the monster to return and pry us out of here."

The group was silent, but most nodded, agreeing with the Chinese scientist's bleak assessment.

Alex rubbed his stubbled chin. "Soong's right." He stopped in front of Aimee. "Aimee, anything we can use? Cate, c'mon, what can we use?"

Aimee frowned, her eyes on the floor, remembering her experiences and research. "Cephalopods are learning creatures," she said. "Every encounter with mankind it has had, it has learned more about us, what we are more or less likely to do, how we will react." She looked up into Alex's eyes. "Those boats out there, some are hundreds of years old. That means it, or its ancestors, has been doing this for centuries. It knows us, but all we know is that it's voracious, aggressive, and smart. In the wild, this thing's smaller cousins have all those characteristics, and are very territorial. This is its turf. Maybe if we can move it off its turf ..." She shrugged, knowing it wasn't much.

"That's right," Cate said. "Orthocones were the alpha predator for millions of years. When most life in the oceans was tiny, these things were already thirty feet long. It can outrun us, outwait us, and certainly outlive us. We're only alive because it doesn't want us just yet."

"That fucker has got us right where it wants us," Casey said, fists balled.

"Then let's get the hell out of here, or die trying." Alex turned, opening the comm. to the torpedo room. "Rhino, load tubes one and two. Blake, it's crash or crash through time. This lake is separated from the main sea by some sort of sea wall, and the creature has got to be using an opening in it. We need to find it."

"Excuse me." Shenjung's voice was almost apologetic. "But we could bring this entire place down on top of us. We have already seen that this type of rock is subject to fracturing."

Alex gave the Chinese scientist a flat smile. "And if we stay, we get eaten alive. Which is better?"

"No, no, I agree, we must leave. But we may be able to use the fracturing to our advantage."

"Selective collapse of the geologic substructure," Aimee said.

Alex nodded. "Okay, good. Franks, anything outside?"

"All clear on the scope." Casey pulled her face back an inch. "What's the plan, boss?"

"Once we're out, we find that sea vortex, and ride it out. If it's within the depth capability of this submarine, we may just pop up outside. If not, we're a crushed can on the bottom of a cold ocean."

"Maybe not," Soong said. "If there is a vortex causing the water column to be in agitation, then the pressure might be bearable." She turned to Shenjung. "I think this might work."

Shenjung nodded. "Yes, I see. We have observed that the properties of water molecules remain disparate the more the water is moving. Also warm water will be much less dense than the outside deeper, cold water."

"As long as we stay within the vortex column," Cate said, "then pressure could be more benign ... at least until it dissipates as the water slows."

"We stay in the vortex, we can make it. Best news I heard all day." Casey grinned. "Nobody, but nobody back home is going to be able to top this." She put her face back to the periscope visor once again, and her eyes went wide. "Oh fuck – *incoming!*"

Alex pushed her aside and looked through the periscope. His expression became grim. "It's on us."

*

The submarine groaned, and then rocked. The slight angle the vessel was resting at suddenly was righted. The group stared straight ahead, arms out for balance, faces pale, waiting and listening. Alex grabbed a railing, looking up, sensing the monstrous weight bearing down on them.

There came a horrendous scraping sound as the hull was drawn along rock – they were being moved, sideways.

"*Hang on!*" Alex shouted. Someone screamed as metal popped and groaned around them. The submarine was designed to withstand enormous pressure, but pressure evenly distributed along its hull, and not pressing down in any one spot. It could buckle, or worse, split open.

The torpedo room comm. came to life. "Standing by, boss. Just say the word," Rhino yelled.

"Water's too shallow. We'll just blow ourselves up," Alex yelled back.

The submarine scraped again, a painful, metallic, nails-on-chalkboard sound magnified a thousand times.

"Fuck it." Franks stepped back from the scope, the thing only half up. "It's jammed."

Alex bared his teeth as more scraping sounded along the hull. "Can't let it damage the props." He held out his hand to Casey Franks. "Rifle."

"What?" Aimee looked momentarily horrified, but then she slumped, seeming to understand what he had to do. She nodded to him. "Save us."

Franks shook her head. "Boss, let me, sir. I'm dispensable."

"*That's an order!*" Alex's voice boomed in the small room.

Franks looked like she was about to say more, but Aimee pulled on her brawny arm. "Let him go. Only he can do it; you know that."

Casey looked torn, but after another second ripped the rifle from her shoulder, her face furious. "Three rounds left."

Alex took it. "Seal the hatch after I'm gone, and be ready." He half smiled. "If I get ... separated, then do your best to get the hell out."

"Yeah," Franks said. "Count on it. I'll help you up."

Alex quickly headed down the steel corridor towards the hatch, and put one hand on the ladder railing. Franks waited silently beside him. He stared up the ladder, his sensitive hearing picking up the soft sliding weight moving above him. He felt the light touch of a hand on his shoulder, and Aimee turned him around.

"Programmed for destruction." She smiled softly.

"I have to," Alex said, not sure what else he could tell her.

"I know. Jack Hammerson's monster, Hammerson's weapon of mass destruction, take your pick, but it's what you were created for. You can't escape it." She dropped her hand.

"You have to get out, for Joshua, and if I can give you even a small chance ..." He sighed, feeling the pang in his chest, at all the wasted years without her.

"Make it back. I'll be here." She went to turn, but stopped, and then just stared hard at him. "Was it real? Did we ever truly make it out of here before, or have we been trapped down here for the last five years, like O'Kane, in our own version of hell?"

He smiled. "If you were here with me, how could that be hell?" He leaned forward to kiss her on the lips, but Aimee threw an arm around his neck, and pulled him close, kissing him back, hard.

Alex smelled her, tasted her, and felt a moment of dizziness as if he was intoxicated – and perhaps he was. At that second, there was nowhere else he wanted to be, and no one else in the world he wanted with him. He had found her again, and that was all that mattered.

Aimee then pushed him away, her eyes shining, the pupils heavily dilated. "Goddamn you, why do you have to be ... *you?*" She turned and walked away.

He watched her disappear down the dark corridor. Alex didn't want to go up that ladder; instead he wanted just one more moment, even just a few more seconds with her. But the submarine rocked again, and he knew what pursued them now would kill her in the most horrible way. She was worth living for, worth killing for, and if it came to it, worth dying for.

Alex knew she was right; it *was* what he was made for. He turned, seeing Casey smile awkwardly. She shrugged.

He pointed a finger at her. "Not a word."

"Didn't see a thing." She saluted. "Good luck ... *fool.*"

Alex sucked in a deep breath, and then went up the ladder. He spun the hatch wheel.

CHAPTER 59

The first thing that assailed his senses when Alex made it to the deck was the acrid smell. The biological ammonia was so thick in the air it was like a poisonous gas. He had to move quickly, and hope for a lucky shot. If he could target one of the huge eyes, he may be able to get a bullet into its brain. He had no idea whether that would kill it or even slow it down, but his goal was simple: make it back off just long enough for them to get the hell off the shoreline.

Franks slammed the hatch shut, and immediately the huge creature surged over the submarine. Alex fought back the urge to move quickly, as the massed tentacles rose around him. He saw they were whip-thin at the tip, but at their base they were as thick around as a freight train. There, they coiled and wrestled with each other like grotesque pythons fighting to be first to consume him. The submarine was now in among the Kraken's nest of flesh, with most of its monstrous bulk still in the water. The huge sack of its head lifted, pulsating, and eyes the size of cars rose up to fix upon him.

He thought he saw it shiver, not from fear, but perhaps with eager anticipation of a new game. Alex could sense its intelligence – not quite that of a human, but certainly a cold intellect that was almost alien. Colors flared in bands as excitement rippled through its body.

Alex carefully raised the rifle. One of the eyes was turned towards him, rising ever higher. At this range, it was impossible to miss. He fired twice, dead center. The huge lidless eye quivered and pulled back, but there was no explosion of optic jelly, or even blood seepage. It was impossible to tell if there had been any damage at all.

Not a thing, he thought. *One left.*

He raised the rifle again, once more sighting on the huge disc of an eye. What Alex couldn't have known was that behind the massive eye, the brain was protected by flexible cartilage – and on the monster before him, that shield was a dozen feet thick.

Alex's neck prickled, and then came a soft, wet noise behind him, followed by a sensation of growing coldness. Alex turned to see the watery figure drifting up and over the railing, to then alight on the deck. Captain Wu Yang, looking expressionless, wet, and staring, his arms by his sides. Alex froze, knowing the figure wasn't a figure at all, but another tentacle, stalking him.

So real, Alex thought. Yang's face carried a tortured expression, like the man's very soul had been trapped inside the animal that had consumed him. Alex felt hopelessness settling over him. As real as Yang looked, he, *it*, was just a huge pad, dotted with softball-sized suckers, each with a cruel hooked talon at its center. It seemed the creature had decided to play with its food before it struck.

Alex carefully eased the gun around, but knew that as much as he wanted to fire point-blank between Yang's eyes, it would be like trying to stop an elephant by jabbing its toe with a toothpick. Beside him, he saw the periscope lens swivel towards Yang. He imagined Casey cursing her usual curses, and he hoped his orders held, or she'd be beside him, fighting to a sure death, in another few seconds.

Indecision wracked him. He could think of only one insane option, to dive over the side. But that would be into about six or more feet of water, where the huge cephalopod was king – he'd last about six seconds. He waited, as Yang glided a little closer, the thing's face slack, urging him to make a move. It was so lifelike that Alex almost felt compelled to talk to him.

He turned his head at a glacial speed, to do so any faster would invite attack. He could see the massive bulk of the Kraken still in the water. Now both its white, goat-slit eyes watched him intently. He bet it'd be smiling if it could. Its colossal size and strength meant they never really stood a chance. It dwarfed the submarine, and he didn't doubt for a second that if it wanted to, it could rip the steel hull apart to get at the tender morsels inside.

Yang glided so close, Alex could see the cold aura of death surrounding the thing, and the stink made his eyes stream.

Alex stood absolutely still, waiting. Another tentacle tip edged over the railing towards him, and the tip alighted on one of his arms. The cold sliminess was immediately replaced by fire, as he felt the suckers engage, penetrating even his toughened suit. The tooth-rimmed discs felt like they were searing down into his flesh. He remembered Aimee telling him years ago that the cephalopods could taste their food this way.

I don't want to end up like Yang, he thought, his mind whirling, but with zero options. He worked to ignore the fire on his arm that now snaked up to his shoulder, and tried to separate his mind from his body, preparing for the bloody annihilation he knew would surely come. From the corner of his eye he saw movement, and easing his head around, saw that there were hundreds of tiny pale figures standing on the jutting ledges and broken balconies of the fallen city. Like stadium crowds at a football game, the barrackers were all there, and he bet his side was not the local team.

Alex felt his armored suit being slowly stripped away and knew his flesh would soon follow. He calmed himself, and then saw her: she was out at front, smaller than the rest and she lifted her mask free, the glossy oil-black eyes watching him.

Help us, he mouthed.

The tiny woman's head titled, and he had no idea whether she heard, understood, or even cared about his fate.

There was a metallic squeal from behind him as the hatch wheel started to spin.

Goddamn you, Franks, Alex thought, his teeth grinding. He half turned. "Keep that hatch closed."

Yang shot forward, passing right by Alex, and hitting the hatch door. The door, now unlocked, was pulled upward, dragging the huge form of Rhino with it. The expression of surprise on his face would have been humorous, if his appearance probably didn't spell a horrible death.

Alex spun, fired at the eye again, and then dropped the gun. In one swift movement, he drew his pitiful blade and stabbed and slashed at the huge muscular limb. His razor sharp knife cut into the flesh, but it was like trying to sever something that was a combination of leather and rubber. More tentacles inched upward over the hull as the exposed Rhino was trying to keep the impossible figure of Yang from its sticky embrace with the hatch lid.

Alex felt the limb freeze beneath his hands, and he thought his mind was playing tricks as a haunting whistle sounded from ahead of him, behind him, all around him. A fist gripped tight inside his head, and he grimaced from the agony, as the sound stabbed deep into his brain. The tentacles stopped their movement, and hung in the air around the submarine like a huge flower with mottled green and black tentacles, blooming all around them. Alex looked over the side, only just able to stop his eyes crushing shut from the unbearable pain. He knew a hungry mouth the size of a truck was there, beneath the mantle of the creature, and just below the waterline.

Gradually the Kraken pulled back, and then silently slipped beneath the surface. The whistling stopped, and with it went the pain. Alex turned to the small figure on the far shoreline. She pointed at herself, then at Alex, and made a breaking motion. Alex could feel the thought slide easily into his tortured mind. *You once freed me, and now I freed you – we are even.*

The ghostly pale figure with the mask of tentacles turned and danced back over the huge tumbled boulders, skipping away and disappearing into one of the broken holes of the last refuge of the mighty city of Aztlan.

Rhino was lying on the deck panting, his hands covered in slime. "I came up to lend a hand, boss."

Alex growled, and lifted the big man with one hand and shoved him towards the hatch. "If we live, remind me to kick your ass all the way back home."

They slid down the ladder, and Rhino sealed them in. Alex sped straight for the bridge. "This is the only chance we might get. Fire up those engines and give me maximum reverse thrust."

The sound of running boots on steel grating echoed in the steel corridors. Blake and Casey followed Alex to the bridge room, and headed to different consoles, while Rhino sprinted back down to the torpedo room.

Aimee tilted her head as Alex appeared in the bridge room. Their eyes locked – he could guess what she was thinking: *another life used up*. And he also knew then that they would need to have a long conversation about what the future may hold, for them, and for Joshua. *If* they survived.

She smiled and nodded to him, looking away and releasing him. *When* they survived, he thought.

"Hey, check this out." Casey turned away from one of the screens that showed a camera view of the outside.

"Got it working. This would be an underwater view ... if we were underwater."

"Engines at full power, boss," Blake said, his fingers dancing over the consoles.

"Okay, here goes." Alex sucked in a breath, saying a silent prayer. "Full reverse, and let's hope the prop still turns."

"And we don't just spin it to shit on the rocks," Casey said.

"Think positive thoughts," Cate replied.

Casey snorted. "You do the chanting, lady, we'll do the driving."

Alex turned to the group trying to see over the HAWCs. "Everyone else, sit down, strap in, or just wrap something around yourselves. This is going to be real rough."

A throb went through the *Sea Shadow*, then a vibration they could all feel right down to the bones. Alex gripped the console edge, willing the vessel to move.

"Sixty percent turbine," Blake said, pushing the small handle a little further forward. Bands of light on a panel illuminated another few bars up a scale. He pushed a little more, and the bars lit up towards the top. His voice was calm. "Seventy percent ... seventy-five ... eighty ..."

The submarine lurched violently. Soong got down low, and wrapped both arms around a steel pole. Shenjung crouched beside her, hugging his arms around her and the pole together. Cate slipped and screamed, and Aimee reached out to grab her, while keeping one arm looped around a strut.

"Move, you sonofabitch," Casey screamed as the entire submarine juddered again, but stayed in place.

"Ninety percent ... red lining, boss," Blake yelled. He spun. "She canna take anymore, Captain," he said in his best Scottish accent, then grinned.

Alex laughed grimly, and held up a fist. "Then punch it, Scotty, we got nothing to stay here for."

Blake pushed the lever all the way up, and the bars of light, once green, now changed to full red. There was a steady thrum, and then a smell of burning. Finally, there came another sound, and it was the sweetest they had heard in days – the sound of the metal hull grating on rock.

The submarine slid a few feet, juddered and bucked, and then slid a few more feet. As soon as the curved propeller hit the deeper water it could create more drag. Waves flowed up the bank as the props grabbed, and then threw water in great geysers over the submarine and onto the shoreline.

Suddenly, there was a grinding rush, as they slid backwards.

*

Aimee gripped the railing, bracing her legs as the *Sea Shadow* slid into deeper water.

"Ease down, Blake. Bring her about," Alex said, moving from console to console.

Aimee continued to watch him – pride, love, desire, and joy near overwhelming her. But there was also something else underlying it all ... a darker emotion. Fear ... fear of the unknown. She knew he still harbored personal demons like no other man. Could she ever trust him? Inside him lurked a stranger, *the Other,* Alex called him, and she'd witnessed this being's callous brutality in the past. He was a force that answered every question with violence, and his volatility was a threat to her safety, and perhaps even to Joshua's.

Aimee sighed; thinking of Joshua was a shot in the arm to her spirits. Joshua too was different – stronger, faster, and smarter than normal – but she knew now he was constantly in danger. She vividly remembered the attack on her house, and Peter shot and unable to protect them. She realized that to defend against violence, maybe someone of strength and violence was what they needed. And who better to guide her son, and be a father to him, than someone exactly like him? She was torn.

"Okay?" Cate's voice made her start.

"Huh?" Aimee smiled. "Yeah, or I will be, when I see the sun again."

"I heard that. Let's just hope it happens soon." Cate turned to watch Alex as well.

"Okay, people," Alex said. "This is what we've got. We're currently in a small pond with a very large marine predator. It got the vessel in here, so we need to get it out. We will find a way out, or we will make one."

"It had to have used the vortex," Cate said. "My guess is it's the far wall of this cavern that separates its lake from the greater underground ocean. We need to be out there."

Alex nodded. "Makes sense to me." He moved behind Blake. "Ping the wall; find me that hole. If not, find me a weak spot. And Franks, keep your eyes and ears open. That thing was enough trouble *above* the water."

"Got it," said Casey, hunched over a sonar monitor.

Aimee crossed to where Shenjung and Soong stood quietly. "Do you think we can navigate the vortex … if we can find it?"

Shenjung shook his head. "This is unknown. The opening in the cave could be smaller than we anticipate. This creature can compress itself down very small. Maybe it can fit into tight spaces, but we cannot."

Soong wrung her hands, and Shenjung took one of them in his. She smiled up at him, but then turned to Aimee. "If there is a constricting of the geology, there could be a funnel effect that will make the water extremely turbulent. Very difficult."

"Great," Aimee said. "Then we need something else – luck."

CHAPTER 60

The submarine turned fast, the steel fish incredibly maneuverable. Alex felt a glimmer of hope as they moved along the eastern shoreline, on the edge of an underwater shelf and about twenty feet down.

Casey Franks frowned and leaned in towards her screen. "*Gross*, what the hell is this?" She turned. "Hey, Doc ... uh, *Docs*."

Cate and Aimee joined her, both leaning over the female HAWC. Cate's brows shot up as she straightened. "Unbelievable, but I think that's *eggs*."

The group crowded around Casey's screen. The underwater shelf created an overhang, and suspended from the rock roof there looked to be gigantic bunches of grapes, each egg pod about six feet in length. They swayed slightly in an invisible current.

"So, this is where momma raises the kids?" Casey said.

Cate leaned back. "Also answers the question on whether there is only one of them. Got to be at least two, huh?"

"And going to be a hell of a lot more soon." Casey looked like she had just smelled something bad. She panned the external camera around. "Looks like a pretty strong current coming from somewhere."

"Oh god, yes and no," Cate said, spinning back. "We need to get away from here." She leaned over Casey, staring hard at the screen. "A current, yes, but not a natural one. The female stays close to the eggs, protecting them and blowing water over them to keep them oxygenated." She pointed. "There."

At the end of her finger on the screen, they could just make out the tips of tentacles flattened on the bottom. The rest of the creature was so perfectly camouflaged, it could have been part of the rock shelf itself.

Casey pulled back on the camera's magnification, taking more of the gigantic cephalopod in, but like a submerged mountain, much of the animal extended beyond their scope.

Alex leaned forward, studying the image. He felt a surge of adrenalin at seeing the size of the thing, and so close to them in the water. Down here they were vulnerable. Inside the submarine, they had nowhere else to go. He straightened.

"Okay, if this is where the thing is, then we want to be somewhere else. Blake, get us out of here."

Blake swung the submarine away towards the far wall, and the lake bottom suddenly fell away beneath them.

"Getting deeper here, we've not got fifty fathoms beneath us." He checked his instruments. "No sign of any breaks in the wall."

"Take her down another twenty," said Alex.

"You got it." Blake eased the U-shaped wheel forward and the sub gently inclined as it dropped. "Hold the phone, ladies and gentlemen, we might have an opening. Sonar just missed a few pings along the western wall ... means the sonar pulses passed right through and didn't bounce back off anything solid."

"There, a blue glow up ahead." Casey clapped her hands once as she watched the screen. "A big beautiful hole in the wall." She grinned. "And plenty of room – got to be eighty feet up and across – easy."

"Take us through," said Alex.

"*Incoming*'" Blake yelled, making Jennifer cringe as though she had been struck.

"What?" Alex spun to the man, crossing the bridge in two strides.

"Big bogey, coming right at us ..." Blake's neck jutted forward, his round eyes fixed on the sonar. "Hold it, hold it ..." He half turned, a relieved smile on his face. "Going to miss us ... it's going right past, and it's in a helluva hurry." Blake's smile evaporated. "*Ah* goddammit, it's headed for the hole in the wall."

"No, you don't." Casey pounded a fist on the bench top. "It's gonna shut the door."

"All stop," Alex yelled, crossing to Casey and leaning closer to her screen as the engines powered down. At this depth the water was darker, but the blue glow of the hole they had just glimpsed was now obscured.

"Try this." Casey flicked a few switches, and external lights came on.

"Oh my god," Aimee said, grimacing.

The huge cephalopod hung in the water, with many of its tentacles extended. This was no random action; it had moved to fully block the hole. It hung suspended, mid water, looking like a large mottled web, waiting to ensnare them. Its mantle fully spread, blotting out the weak light from outside.

Alex stared at the monstrous creature and cleared his mind. He pushed his senses out and felt the thing in the water, its bulk, and its cold consciousness. It knew they were inside the submarine, and it even knew how many of them there were.

Alex felt a stab of pain in his skull. It wanted all of them. It wanted them for food, and it wanted to use them to break the boredom it felt, in its eternal twilight.

"A monster, a real monster," Cate said.

"It's just sitting there, staring at us." Casey's fingers flexed on the console.

"Look at its eyes." Blake seemed mesmerized. "Who was it that said that when you look into an abyss, the abyss also looks into you?"

"Nietzsche," Aimee said quietly.

Alex folded his arms. "Looks like it doesn't want its new playthings getting away."

"Let's put a torpedo up its ass," Casey said, with her jaw set.

Alex slowly shook his head. "Don't know if just one will work, and don't want to exhaust them just yet."

"And if we miss and hit the wall, we might collapse our only way out," said Aimee, coming and standing by Alex.

He turned to Cate. "You said it was protecting its eggs."

"Yes, they have a strong maternal instinct. If we can outrun it, it might turn back," she said, nodding.

"Can't outrun it in here," Alex said. "It leaves us no choice. Blake, bring her around."

Blake engaged the engines, and turned the *Sea Shadow* away from the monster in the deep.

Alex waited for a few moments. "Is it following?"

Blake shook his head. "No, staying right where it can act like the biggest cork in history."

"Time to take it up a level." Alex reached towards the comm. "Rhino, stand by." He looked back to Blake. "Hold course, but on my word, swing away hard, and make a looping course back for the hole." Alex watched Casey's screen.

"Coming up on the shoreline, boss," Blake said. He gritted his teeth, occasionally looking across at the depth readings. "Getting real close." He half turned.

"Stand by." Alex had the comm. line open. He kept watching Casey's screen, until he could see them, the huge dangling bunches of eggs.

"Fire one." There was a small kick, and on the view screen there appeared a trail of bubbles racing away from the nose of the *Sea Shadow*. Alex spun.

"Blake, bank hard, *now!*"

Blake turned the U-shaped wheel like a racing car driver, and the steel fish yawed in the water. They all held on as the submarine tilted.

Alex urged more speed, and in another second came the detonation, and then a judder ran through the skin of the vessel.

"That got its attention. Creature is on the move," Blake said. "Coming fast – *real fast* – brace."

They waited, but there was nothing. As Alex had hoped, the creature had raced right by them to save its eggs.

"Now, give it all you've got. Let's get through that hole." Alex paced as Blake pushed the lever forward to maximum, pushing every ounce of energy into the rear propulsion, and willing his own strength into the turbines for good measure. The submarine kicked forward, speeding away under the dark water.

Alex saw the blue glow of the hole approaching, and counted down the seconds. *Come on, give us some luck*, he prayed, urging the machine on. From deep within his head, he could feel a sense of anguish and pain emanating from the cold mind of the creature. He tried to shut it out, but the distress came at him in waves.

Alex put his head down, concentrating on the blue glow ahead. As the echoes of the creature's misery dimmed, he finally felt it morphing into something much more hard-edged; *hate*.

No one spoke. Everyone was focused on Blake and Casey's screens and panels. Soong and Shenjung just stayed seated, waiting and listening for the sound of something huge settling on the skin of the vessel.

"Gonna be tight." Casey's teeth were clamped together.

"Exit coming up," Blake said. "500 feet, 450, 400, 350 … say a prayer ladies and gentlemen, we're going to thread the needle. 200 feet, 150, 100 …" Nothing else existed but Blake's voice.

Time slowed, and then stretched. Alex looked to Aimee, and her eyes locked with his. In the ice-blue gaze and the tiny uptilt of her lips, he saw resignation, perhaps to fate, but also trust. He hoped it was not misplaced.

"Hold onto your asses-*ssss* …" Blake yelled through gritted teeth as scraping and grinding sounded against the hull. They bounced hard to the left, something popped, and metal squealed from somewhere back in the bowels of the vessel. The makeshift crew held on as they passed through the hole in the wall.

"Yeah." Casey leapt from her chair, high-fiving herself in an overhead clap.

There were sighs of relief and cheers as the submarine sailed out into more open waters. Alex leaned forward onto his knuckles and exhaled, realizing he had been holding his breath.

Aimee grabbed his arm, holding on. "You know it will follow us," she said softly.

He half turned, feeling a sense of resignation. "I wish I could say it won't." He straightened. "But I can't." He pressed the comm. button connecting to Rinofsky. "Rhino, stand by on all tubes."

*

Project Ellsworth – English Antarctic Research Base

"Whoa."

Sam Reid turned at the sound of the scientist's voice.

"That's weird," Sulley said.

"What's up, sunshine?" Schmidt pushed his chair back.

"Got something?" Sam wandered over and stood behind Sulley's chair.

"Yeah, but something that shouldn't be there. A big object, but really weird. It's giving back a metallic signature." Sulley's fingers flew over the console.

Metallic signature – Sam's hopes skyrocketed.

"You been putting too much sugar in your tea again?" Schmidt leaned over the young scientist. "Could be some sort of high concentration of ore in one of the cliff walls – anything from platinum, nickel, copper to gold down here. Let me see that." He straightened, frowning. "That *is* weird."

Sam put one large hand on Sulley's shoulder. "Please tell me yours is the only probe down there?"

From behind, Bentley scoffed. "Of course we damn well are, Reid. We must be picking up some sort of manganese node amalgamation or the like."

"That's what I thought, but it's moving, and damned fast … and that background signal is getting stronger," Sulley responded.

Sam folded his arms, grinning. "Follow it."

CHAPTER 61

Cate paced in the small bridge room, having to maneuver around the huge Rinofsky who had just joined them. She strained to draw the most minute details from her memory.

"I don't know where it was exactly. I was kinda focused on staying alive." She stopped and turned. "The best I can guess is that it was close to where we came up on the beach. There was a column of cool among the tropical water mass – a cold water vortex; it might not even show up above the water."

"No idea if we can pick up temperature variations. Might be able to, but haven't really read the manual." Blake shrugged. "Doing the best we can."

Alex nodded. "We'll find it, we have to." He looked at Aimee and Cate, and also motioned Soong and Shenjung closer. "We haven't got a lot of time. You guys are the brains trust. If we can't detect the temperature variation, and can't really see it, then how else can we detect it?" Alex looked along their faces. "Water movement; like a current? Color; would it be full of debris, or less debris?" Alex paced. "What about density, could it …"

"Wait … *density,*" Soong said. "This might be a way. Ocean water has different densities. The colder the water, the heavier it is; the hotter the water, the lighter it is." She turned to Cate. "When you passed through the column, did you rise or fall?"

Cate nodded. "We dropped … dropped down about fifty feet in a few seconds. And it got real cold."

"Good." Soong nodded. "Cold water is heavy water; it sinks."

Shenjung put his arm around her and beamed.

"*Density*, we might be able to pick up," Blake said. "We can ping it, maybe listen for some sort of soft echo or at least a distortion."

"Do it," Alex said.

"Where?" Blake half turned.

Cate cast her mind back to the dark water. "I think we were around half a mile offshore."

"Then let's take a trip along the coast," Aimee said.

Blake nodded and just slightly turned the U-shaped wheel.

"Franks, give me external acoustics. Let's see if we can hear anything out there." Alex paced.

Casey flicked some switches and suddenly the room was filled with the sound of surging water, and the pips and squeaks of a large ocean … a large *living* ocean.

Cate listened intently, frowning as she concentrated. The sounds danced at the edge of her memory – things that could have been whale song, but weren't. That could have been triggerfish, dolphin squeak, or even the click of crustaceans, but were all slightly different from what she had heard in the past. These creatures she was hearing were things that no one in her lifetime, or a perhaps a million lifetimes, had ever heard. Or maybe *nothing* had heard them *ever*, if evolution had taken them in a myriad different directions.

"Boss, got something up ahead. Just registering a change in density. Not solid, but just on the scope." Blake raised his eyebrows. "It feels right." He switched the sound to the console and small pings, just audible, came from his panel.

"Let's take a look," Alex said, continuing to pace.

There came a louder ping from the console that brought everyone's heads around.

"Ah, shit." Blake leaned in closer. "Got another bogey, big signature this time. Coming at us fast." He turned, grimacing. "And from where we just came from."

"Put the pedal down," Alex said.

They felt the surge as the vessel picked up speed. Jennifer looked like she was praying.

"Still gaining on us, doing fifty knots now. Impossible speed."

"Not for this thing," Aimee said softly.

"We can't outrun that." Casey's teeth were gritted as she turned. "Boss, we need to surface. Fight it up there."

Rhino scoffed. "With what, our bare hands?"

Casey rounded on the big HAWC. She was carrying multiple facial wounds and was still streaked with dried blood from her battle with Mungoi, giving her a fearsome painted warrior look. Jennifer had wrapped a cloth bandage around her battered forehead, that was now also bloody, and it dragged down one of her brows into a permanent scowl. Soong and Shenjung shrank from her when she passed in front of them. Casey's eyes blazed as she glared at Rhino. "We fight it with tooth and claw if need be."

Rhino held up a huge pair of hands. "Okay, take it easy, *huh*?"

Alex half turned from the screen. "Everyone just cool it. We're trapped in this tin can together for now, so we might as well conserve our energy. If we need to surface, we will, but that's not yet. If things go to plan, we'll find a way out. If not, well, we might all find ourselves swimming back to shore."

Soong blanched, and Aimee put a hand on her shoulder. "We'll be fine. Captain Hunter was only joking."

"Rhino, get down to the torpedo room." Alex turned back to Blake at the consoles. "Keep heading to the vortex. If need be, we'll bring her around for a torpedo launch, but as a last resort. Not convinced we'll even hit something that fast and smart underwater." He looked up. "And we know it learns, so now it knows what those torpedoes can do."

"Yeah, and I'm betting it remembers exactly where those torpedoes came from, and wants to tear us a new asshole." Casey growled. "Floor it, soldier."

From the acoustic speakers there was an increasing sound like the clacking of a giant castanet.

"What in hell's name is that?" Casey asked.

Aimee hugged herself. "That, I think, is the sound of a Kraken's mouth, the beak, opening and closing."

"Oh fuck. It sounds to me, like someone really pissed off, grinding their teeth." Casey flexed her hands on the panel top, and Cate and Aimee looked over her shoulder. Her view monitors showed nothing but a soft blue above and a pitiless black below them.

"Vortex coming up in 500 feet, boss." Blake read more numbers. "Plenty of water. Deep, but within our crush tolerance."

"Come on, come on." Casey urged more speed from the submarine, her neck straining.

"Bogey about to overtake is. Vortex in now in 200 feet." Perspiration ran down Blake's face and his forearms bulged from the strain as he squeezed the wheel. "It's running us down, boss. We ain't gonna make it."

"Vertical dive, straight into the vortex," Alex yelled. "If that column of cold water has some drag we can ride its wake."

"Into what?" Cate asked. "We don't know what's down there."

"Well, we know what's up here, lady." Casey's jaws bulged as she bared her teeth. "Hold your ass, say your prayers, and enjoy the ride."

"No choice," Alex said as the deck tilted.

"Bogey coming at us, going to hit ..." Blake yelled the words. "*Hold on!*"

*

The laboratory was silent as the four English Ellsworth base scientists stared hard at the camera feed. Their mouths hung open.

Orca hung motionless in the dark water, its sensitive lenses trained on the submarine as it came out of the dark, and then shot past. It was immediately pursued by what looked like a huge mottled shroud. An enormous eye with a slitted pupil, momentarily swiveled towards them, but immediately went back to focus on the fleeing vessel – the thing obviously wanted that craft, and nothing else.

Sam Reid's huge hands curled into fists. He felt a wave of frustration and rage wash over him, and had to swallow it down hard, knowing he could do nothing but watch.

The screen image wobbled as the small probe was buffeted by the pressure swell, as the creature surged past, and then was gone.

"Oh my good Queen Lizzie." Sulley leaned back into his chair, his hands to his head. "That was a *fucking* submarine, being chased by … I don't even know what it was, but it was as big as an office block."

"*Follow, follow,*" Schmidt screamed.

"Huh? But …" Sulley looked confused, and simply pointed at the screen.

Sam leaned in. "Get after them … *now!*" He paced like a huge lion behind the men, his weight making the floor creak beneath him.

Sulley swiveled the submersible and accelerated, and then bounced in his seat, looking like he couldn't decide whether he wanted to sit or stand, or something in-between. He pointed at the screen again, grinning. "*That was a submarine.*" His brows were so high on his forehead they nearly touched his hairline. "*That, was, a fucking, submarine.*" He put his hands to his head. "Getting chased by what looks like a giant squid-octopus thingy."

Sam felt lightheaded. He'd read the reports from the Antarctic mission, and of the creature that had once pursued Alex and Aimee through the ancient tunnels. But nothing, *nothing*, could have prepared him for the reality of the thing. He straightened, trying to calm himself, and remembered a few lines from a favorite thriller writer he read:

"*When I look down into the abyss, Down into the merciless blackness, Colder and deeper than Hades itself, There I see the Kraken rising.*"

And so it was, he thought, and now Alex was right in its path. Sam suddenly jolted, and then turned to stare hard at the mini-submersible's screen. *What if it wasn't Alex?* What if the Chinese had won the race? Shit! He turned back to Sulley.

"We need to contact them."

Sulley shook his head. "How? *Orca* has no conventional communication hardware. I'm afraid no can do, Bill Bunyan."

Sam was pushed aside as the other scientists jostled for a closer look at the spectacle.

"How … who?" Bentley asked.

"Who?" Schmidt grinned. "Does anyone else think Cate might *not* be onboard?"

There was silence for a few seconds, until Bentley finally spoke. "Of course, if anyone could find a submarine in a warm, primordial sea, start it up, and then get into a fight with a Krakenesque sea monster, it'd be her – could *only* be her."

Not just her, Sam felt a knot tightening in his stomach.

"That thing was twice the size of the submarine." Timms was now on his feet. "They're going to be crushed."

*

Sam stood out in the cold corridor and tried to shut out the whooping of the British scientists in the control room as he made the call.

"Confirmation, *Sea Shadow* is on the move. But still below the ice."

Colonel Jack Hammerson grunted. "That's only half the answer I want. Who exactly is in control of that vessel?"

Sam exhaled. "I don't know, sir. Until there is contact, it could be Alex, and it could be someone else entirely."

"Goddammit, that's not going to stop a war, Reid." There was a sound like grating teeth, and then Hammerson came back on the line. "Seconds count now. Make contact, somehow, some way. If it's Alex, move heaven and earth to assist. If not, I don't want that submarine ever seeing the light of day. Tell me the second you know for sure. Out."

Sam turned back to the crowded control room. In front of the excited scientists, the screen showed nothing but endless blackness as *Orca* was on the trail of two leviathans of the subterranean depths.

CHAPTER 62

Time: 00 hours 08 minutes 02 seconds until fleet convergence

Aimee felt the beat of her heart in her throat, racing faster and faster. She willed every ounce of her strength to the engines, so they could stay in front of the pursuing monster. They were so close now, almost free. She just wanted to see Joshua, the sunlight, the surface, just one more time.

"Oh, for chrissake." Blake's brow furrowed and he looked about to leap out of his chair. He spun. "Now we got another signature – coming right at us."

"What, you sure that isn't some sort of sonar echo?" Alex yelled.

Blake shook his head. "Nope, big mama is still right on our tail, but something else coming in at twelve degrees starboard – fast."

Aimee cursed and hung on to a railing, her legs braced as the deck tilted downwards. She grabbed Cate, who began to slide past.

Cate nodded her thanks. "Might be another cephalopod? After all, the creature didn't fertilize those eggs by itself."

"Jesus Christ, we can't even fight one of them down here." Alex rubbed a hand up through sweat-slicked hair. "Blake, how long till bottom?"

Blake read numbers from the screen. "Four hundred feet until we hit the deck, and whatever is down there better be big enough for us to pass through, or we're a paint smudge on the rocks." He looked at another screen and grimaced. "We're not gonna win the race."

Over the external speakers there rose a noise above the background clicks and squeaks of the underground sea. This one a deep rumbling that sounded more like a low moaning.

"What the hell ...?" Casey sat back, staring into space. "That doesn't sound like it did before."

The sound came again, louder, as whatever it was drew nearer.

"No." Cate's face had drained of color. "I've heard that before. When Alex and I were first in the water." She looked across to Alex. "Just before the pliosaur attacked."

"Well, Doc, if that's what it is, there's two of them this time." Blake stared at the screen, eyes wide. "The new bogey coming in from starboard has now broken into two distinct signatures, one about seventy feet long, and the other about fifty."

Cate nodded. "Makes sense, probably male and female. I'm betting they're territorial ... and we just wandered into the front yard."

"Two more of them? *Ha!*" Casey rocked in her seat. "Well, if they want to eat us, they're going to have to wait their turn."

The *Sea Shadow* momentarily shuddered, and then totally stopped. Everyone was either thrown forward or swung on the struts and handholds they had gripped.

Aimee flew forward. Alex shot out a single arm to catch her as she went to fly past. "Oh no," was all she could think to say. Frustration welled up inside her – so close. Perhaps they were never meant to escape.

The next noise made even Alex's face pale. It was the sound of the submarine's metal skin groaning around them.

"It's got us," Blake said.

*

The *Sea Shadow* was twisted one way, then the next. Blake was whipped forward, smashing the bridge of his nose on the wheel, and Casey's forearms bulged from the effort of keeping herself in her chair.

Alex felt the cold hatred enveloping them just as surely as the train-tunnel thick tentacles of the giant cephalopod. He looked up, hearing the steel complain at the tightening of the rubbery, striated muscle.

"Blake, get us the hell out of here." Alex knew they couldn't just wait for it to rip them open, but also knew there was little they could realistically do. The Kraken was far larger, and far stronger than they were, and at home in this environment. They were just sardines in a can, waiting to be peeled open.

The strengthened steel hull groaned once again as monstrous pressure was applied to its surface. The control panels popped, lights began to go out, and one of their screens went dark.

"We're fucked; not going anywhere," Casey yelled.

Behind them, one of the walls started to compress, and then one of the reinforcing elliptical-frames began to lower from above them. Alex was underneath it faster than anyone could follow, and he reached up to hold the curved beam. He felt it then – *so close*. He and the creature were separated by a thin skin of strengthened steel.

He glimpsed its alien mind. It wanted them, not just as food, or as playthings, but it wanted them for revenge. It wanted to torture them, rip them to pieces slowly, and then devour the bits. It knew human beings, and knew what made them scream the loudest.

Alex gritted his teeth, as the steel started to come down hard. He focused all of his strength, and locked his arms. The steel bending stopped momentarily, but he knew he wouldn't be able to hold it for long. He turned slowly, and could only let the words hiss from between his teeth.

"*Blake – get us – out – of here – NOW!*"

"Trying." Blake wiped blood from his nose as his hands flew over the console. "Already at full power. Trying something ..." His hands flew again. "... reversing." After a few seconds, he swore, smacking his fist down hard on the console. "Nothing; we're stuck."

There came an abrupt boom of steel from somewhere back in the metal corridors. Soong screamed, and Shenjung covered her head with his arms and then together they sank down in a corner. Alex turned to where Aimee stood. She was silent and ghost like, clutching a wall strut. She just stared at him. There was resignation in her expression.

He heard her: Joshua, her mind repeated, over and over.

Alex turned back to the hull, screaming his defiance, releasing every demon from his id, and throwing them into war with the thing on the ship. He felt his bones start to bend, and tendons popped. But with all his great strength, inexorably, the steel beam still came down.

He turned back to Aimee. "*Sorry,*" he whispered.

"Fuck it." Casey was on her feet, and punched one hand down on the torpedo room comm. link. "Rhino, fire all ..."

"*Belay that order,*" Alex screamed through his pain. "You'll blow us wide open."

"We're opening up now," Casey yelled back. Her fists were balled. "We're dead if we don't."

Alex was torn; the roof continued its slow drop. He was a flea holding back an elephant. "Not here, not now." He prayed.

Blake hunched forward, one hand to his ear phone. "Something out there – mechanical." He switched it to external. Over the speakers there was a tiny rotational whine. "What is that?"

Suddenly there was an impact explosion. He spun. "Was that us?"

"No." Alex immediately felt the weight on the *Sea Shadow*'s surface vanish. They lurched free.

Blake clapped once, grabbing the controls. "Hey, we're free, *we're free* ... it let us go."

"Something just happened out there," Cate said.

"Don't care. We've been given a chance. Blake, take her down, soldier." Alex dropped his arms, and immediately felt the pain of torn muscles and cracked bones. He nodded to Casey. "Now you can get Rhino."

Casey grinned and pressed the comm. "Hey, big fella, still there?"

"Yo, shaken, but not stirred," came the reply.

Alex smiled. "Ready on all tubes."

The deep voice came back immediately. "Standing by, just say the word."

*

The orthocone squid was an old female, the largest in its territory, and it had known more centuries than it could remember. It knew joy, boredom, curiosity, excitement, it knew love for its offspring, and it knew rage and hate. When it battled its own kind for territory or for food, or when the rocks fell from above to try and crush its limbs or its home, it had raged.

But these times were nothing compared to the hate it felt now for the destroyers of its brood. The small playthings that were warm and sweet to eat had managed to attack it from within the hard-shelled sea swimmer.

Excitement surged through it as it planned to drag them to the surface, tear the hard shell open, and take its time, stripping the tiny things of their limbs, watching their small faces twist in agony, before it finally consumed them.

As it pressed down on the shell of the hard thing, it sensed the humans inside. It could feel them scurrying about, and also feel their fear. Bands of color pulsed along its limbs and it flexed its muscles.

But frustration surged as it sensed the two massive leviathan creatures closing in on it. It immediately knew them, had fought them before. It would attack them if it ever found a small one alone, or weak, or old, but always avoided the strong ones, especially when they hunted in groups. The huge marine reptiles were fearsome predators, not as smart as it was, but they were fast and had a fearsome arsenal of teeth that could severely damage it ... perhaps even kill it.

It held onto its hard prize, and hung in the water, indecision now tearing at it – should it flee, or stay and fight? The two huge creatures circled it, wary of its size and danger.

The decision was made – the giant swimmers attacked. The first impact was hard, and one of its limbs was grabbed and shredded. Then another, as the second reptilian predator came in from another angle, grasping and tearing at a second limb. Again, it lost flesh. It grasped one then, coiling around its flanks and holding it tight. It squeezed, applying colossal pressure until it began to feel the reptile's mighty bones break beneath its skin. After another few seconds, it released the body, and briefly watched it sink into the dark void.

The other leviathan's huge mouth closed on it, the tusk-like teeth each more than a foot long were sharp blades that sunk in deep and then ripped away a car-sized mound of flesh. It wrapped massive limbs around this one too – it had it now, and the sea reptile's teeth were of no use if it couldn't bring them to bear. It squeezed harder, feeling the satisfying sensation of crushing flesh and bones.

Just then, there came a tiny metallic whine.

*

"Do it." Sam's voice boomed.

"Hey, but ..." Bentley went to object, but then blanched as the huge form of Sam leaned over him. The bearded scientist waved a hand and just shook his head. "Okay, okay, do it."

Sam knew he was taking a chance – if it was Alex in the submarine, he might, just *might*, give them a fighting chance. If it was the Chinese in control, then ... he knew he probably should be ramming *Orca* into the sub, or leaving it to its fate.

"Rigging to detonate its fuel core on impact," Sulley said mechanically. "So long, fella. Thanks for everything."

The mottled hide of the cephalopod filled the screen, and then a large slitted eye became *Orca*'s entire world.

Schmidt's arms dropped to his sides. "Good luck and god speed, Cate."

Sam turned away. There was no way he could determine who was piloting the submarine, so there was no more he could do here. He walked heavily to the door, and opened it onto a freezing landscape.

If things went bad, he needed to prepare for war. He pressed his collar stud and the full head shield telescoped up over his face as he walked out into the snow.

*

The Kraken swiveled one giant eye and saw something tiny coming at it. The small, whining creature had a single luminous eye at one end, and it increased speed to fly fast at the cephalopod's bulbous head. The tiny thing struck and then suddenly erupted in an explosion of red hot pain.

The cephalopod freed the fleeing hard shell and the last reptile, and squirted its camouflage ink into the water, rolled, knotted, and coiled on itself, and then jetted away.

The Kraken propelled itself towards the dark sea bottom, to spread out flat, changing color and blending in perfectly with the rocky depths. It was hurt, in agony, but it was alive, and it still had one thing left ... its boiling hate.

CHAPTER 63

"We got a vent, dead ahead." Blake hit keys and pulled back on a small joystick as he read numbers scrolling up multiple screens. "Another big cavern in there, but we have strong water movement. That's the good news." He eased back on the stick. "The bad news is, that opening isn't wide enough for us. We're going to tear ourselves apart on its edges." He turned. "Or get wedged."

The proximity alarm sounded.

Alex leaned forward. "Full speed ahead. This is going to be close." He hit the comm. button. "Rhino, fire tubes two and three."

They all felt a slight judder, as the torpedoes sped away from the submarine.

"Two and three away." Rhino replied.

On the view screen they saw the trails of bubbles zooming away from them, heading down into an impenetrable blackness.

"Okay everyone, *hang on!*" Alex yelled as the submarine careened towards the sea bottom, caught now in the whirlpool that accelerated its descent. He looked quickly to Aimee. Her eyes were round, watching him. A nervous smile just flickered across her lips.

The two torpedoes struck the cavern edges, detonating and sending shock waves ballooning outwards into the water. The submarine bucked and shuddered as it passed through the blast compression wave, but still surged on.

Viewing screen visibility was obliterated, and they relied on the *Sea Shadow*'s electronic eyes and ears.

"We're alive," Casey said. "Blake I could kiss you, if you weren't so ugly."

Blake grinned. "We passed through, and we're in the pipe." He navigated the tunnel that led them many miles from the warm underground sea towards the freezing world waiting for them. The temperature began to drop against the hull so quickly that the sound of the metal contracting drowned out conversation.

"It's a natural barrier," Cate said. "No sea creature can pass between tropical water, and crushing icy water. It'd kill them."

"Except one," said Aimee. "One that has been doing it for perhaps too many centuries to count."

"I hope it's fucking dead," Casey said. "We should blow the hole closed when we get out. Seal that motherfucker in forever."

"Not a bad idea," said Alex.

"We're moving fast, real fast, riding a strong current," Blake said. "Still on a slight incline, but getting heavy down here now, 450 psi water pressure. Much more and we're gonna be in a world of pain."

Jennifer snorted. "And where we just came from wasn't?"

"Boss, got a wall coming up," Blake yelled.

Alex leaned over him. "Is the current still moving? If it is, then we got another vent, hopefully going up. Follow it."

Blake started to pull up on the U-shaped wheel. Shenjung and Soong stepped closer to look at his screen and then braced themselves on his chair.

"Slow it down. Don't want to end up a skid mark against the wall," said Alex, hanging on now.

"You got it," Blake said. The deck started to tilt as they lifted and headed up the huge natural tunnel. The *Sea Shadow* bucked and then slowed down to just a few knots.

"Not that much," Alex said.

Blake shook his head. "It's not me. The current just changed direction. It's rushing back at us now. We have got one mother of a headwind. Going to punch it." He pushed the lever forward again; the submarine only slightly increased its speed.

"Sonar says we've got another small opening coming up, gonna need to blow it to fit through."

"Rhino, fire tube four." Alex gripped the table edge. "Lucky last, people. Let's hope it also shuts the door behind us."

"Last fish away," Rhino said over the speaker. "Cupboards now empty."

This time the explosion was felt and heard through the skin of the vessel, followed by rocks bouncing against the hull. The screens whited out.

*

Time: 00 hours 00 minutes 00 seconds – Convergence

Eric Carmack, commander of the Seawolf class submarine, USS *Texas*, and leading the American fleet in the Southern Ocean, was in the conning tower, watching his rivals jockey into place. He paused and turned as his officer handed him the microphone.

"Carmack, go ahead."

"Commander, we have a sea shelf detonation. Medium-sized torpex impact at 210 fathoms. The blast signature was consistent with a heavy sea-borne torpedo strike." The seaman paused, and Carmack knew he was reading new data as it came in. "Got something coming up, sir. Depth now 810 feet, and speed at 25 knots – metallic signature." His voice took on a sense of urgency. "Computer can't identify it from our libraries, but it's got to be a medium sized submarine."

"What the hell are they playing at now?" Carmack swung to his chief of boat, Alan Hensen. "Signal the fleet and sound battle stations." He was handed a life jacket which he waved away. "Not yet. But I want batteries ready to engage, and all torpedo tubes locked and loaded."

Hensen relayed orders, and then held the microphone away from his mouth. "We dive, sir?"

"No, but full astern. Let's give 'em some room." He lifted his glasses and scanned the semi-circle of Chinese ships. Combined with his own vessels, the ring of steel over the clear patch of ocean water was like an iron coliseum, the ships were the seating stands and the half mile wide patch of water, the battle arena.

"Too many ... on both sides." He lowered his glasses. *They're too close, and so are we*, he thought. At this proximity, there would be no winners.

"Okay, let's see what we've got." He turned. "Soundings." He waited.

Hensen relayed the information as it came in. "200 fathoms, and still coming fast. 150, 100, 80, 45 – breach imminent – relative bearing 310 degrees port bow." He pointed.

The entire crew watched and waited. Then, like a salmon jumping from a pond, two thirds of the submarine's steel body lifted from the water. It fell back, creating a massive wave, and was carried back beneath the surface for a moment, before then powering up to sit silently at all stop.

"*Jesus Christ, the* Sea Shadow." Carmack grinned through his whispered words. "Put it on hailing frequency." He lifted his field glasses again, training them on the hatch. "Come on." He knew what the stakes were now. If the first voice that came from the speakers was Chinese, then they would know they had lost control of the submarine.

"Alan, get the admiralty on the line, ASAP." Carmack blew air through puffed cheeks. The stakes had just gone up. In seconds they would know which way the chips had fallen. And as his missiles, heavy guns, torpedoes, and circling planes all had their targeting systems locked in on Chinese strategic targets, everything would hinge on the call from HQ, and the one from inside that damned vessel. He looked at his floating opponents; he had no doubt the Chinese had their weapons primed and pointed right down his throat as well.

Carmack could feel the heart beating in his chest. He was once again handed a life jacket, which this time, he donned over his uniform, and then put on a helmet. He knew that the waters in this part of the world were down around zero degrees. Five minutes in the drink, and you didn't need to worry about going home anymore.

He lifted the glasses again, watching, waiting, and praying.

*

Jack Hammerson sat in the darkened office of James Carter, the secretary of defense. Spread around Carter's desk were five-star General Marcus Chilton, Jim Harker, his staff sergeant, and various assembled generals and other senior military brass. They all stared hard at a huge screen and watched the events unfold real-time from one of their Southern Hemisphere satellites.

On Carter's desk there were two speakers arranged; one was a direct line through to the Commander in Chief, President Paul Banning. On the other was Fleet Commander Eric Carmack.

Chilton's eyes went from Carter back to the screen, where circling planes, multiple boats, and submarines formed a one mile halo of clear water. At its center was a single vessel – the *Sea Shadow*.

"Damned crowded down there, Eric." Chilton looked relaxed, but Hammerson bet inside the big man was as on edge as the rest of them.

"That it is, Marcus. Like a goldfish bowl. Problem is, we're all in the same bowl." Carmack still sounded good humored.

Chilton half smiled, but then sat forward. "Eric, could you share with us your assessment of first round, send and receive?"

Hammerson knew what Chilton was asking. If the firing started in the first few seconds, how many would he sink and how many would he lose.

"Marcus, we're all too close. At this proximity, it will not be a tactical fight; more a metal storm. We estimate a one hundred percent sinkage on their side, and perhaps seventy-five percent on ours. Of the twenty-five percent still afloat, there will be significant structural damage to all. Remaining aerial assets would have to land at McMurdo ... if that base somehow avoided being caught up in the firefight. Personnel losses and injuries in the high hundreds – lot of sick people in the water."

Chilton's lips momentarily compressed, but then he slowly nodded. "Expected." He glanced at Carter. "Acceptable."

Carter swiveled in his chair, turning side-on to the room. He steepled his fingers. "Other option progress, gentlemen?"

Chilton's eyes slid to Hammerson. His brows went up, but Hammerson knew he had nothing concrete to give his superior.

He shook his head. Chilton tilted his head back slightly, and then faced the secretary of defense.

"No known progress, sir." He turned back to the screen and the lonely looking submarine ringed by the wall of aggressive steel. He then leaned in towards the president's comm. link. "Mr. President, if that hatch opens, and our people *do not* emerge, then we need to be ready for what that means."

John Carter turned back to face the room and the president's speaker. "Further instructions, sir?"

The president's voice sounded tired. "Nothing has changed. Bottom line is, that vessel cannot fall into foreign power hands. Are we in agreement?"

Chilton nodded. "I agree, sir." The room all voiced their agreement.

The president softly grunted his acknowledgment. "Then do what you have to, General Chilton."

Chilton drew in a deep breath, his jaw set. "Commander Carmack, that vessel is the sovereign property of the United States of America. We take it home, or we blow it to atoms. Anyone or anything that interferes with your order, or fires upon an American vessel or individual, will be taken to be committing a hostile act against our country. Full use of force is therefore authorized." He sat back, but his gaze was now hawk-like.

"Yes sir, understood, sir. God bless America." Carmack's voice was clipped.

"Good luck. And God's strength to you and your forces, Eric."

Hammerson gritted his teeth. This was what was called the sharp edge. Everyone in the room knew just what they had committed their country to; in fact, what they had just committed the entire world to. For some reason, the only thing Hammerson could think of was how he was going to tell Joshua his mother wasn't coming home.

He straightened his jacket. Maybe that wouldn't matter, maybe nothing would matter, in the next few minutes.

CHAPTER 64

Whoops and high-fives filled the bridge room. Alex grinned and turned in time to be grabbed by Cate who hugged him hard. A pair of hands levered them apart and Aimee pulled Cate out of the way to hug Alex and then kiss him even harder.

He smiled down at her. "Mission accomplished. Sunlight, and guess what? The world still seems to be here." He kept one arm around her and leaned into the console, hitting the comm. button. "Rinofsky, get up here before the champagne gets warm."

"I heard that," came the response.

Alex turned to Blake. "Open a line. See if we can raise Commander Carmack on the USS *Texas*. He's an old buddy."

Behind him, Casey and Rhino were doing a waltz in the small space. Casey put a hand up into the big HAWC's face and pushed when he tried to kiss her.

"When you two lovebirds are finished, perhaps someone could pop the lid."

"Aye aye, skipper." Casey saluted and ran down the steel corridor.

"Let's go up, I'm dying to breathe in cold, clean air." Aimee grabbed Alex's hand. "And see some sunshine." She led him away.

Casey climbed the railing ladder and spun the wheel, pushing the lid up. Fresh, freezing air burst inside, and nothing felt or smelled sweeter. Alex helped Aimee up behind Casey.

Alex and the small crew were now all jammed on the conning tower. They turned their faces to the sun, luxuriating in the fresh air.

"Smells like heaven." Rhino opened his huge arms wide, turning his face to the sky.

"Smells like someone needs a bath," Casey said.

Rhino looked mock-hurt, but Casey waved him away. "Forget it, you smelled like that when we went down." She squinted in the glare after so many days in near twilight. "Holy shit, we got half the world's navy down here."

"And I'm betting they're not all here on holiday. Looks like things escalated after all. We need to fix that. Get the USS *Texas* on the …" Alex paused and turned. "Belay that last order. Shenjung, you need to speak to your people first, pronto."

Shenjung took the comm. device. "5727 kilohertz, please."

Blake adjusted the signal frequency, and then nodded to the Chinese engineer. Shenjung spoke rapidly in Chinese, listened for a moment, grunted an acknowledgment and then waited. He lifted the receiver from his ear. "They are routing me through to the commander of the fleet, Admiral Zang Do."

Alex watched and waited. He saw the man suddenly snap to attention as a deeper voice came on the line. Once again Shenjung spoke fast, but this time deferentially. There was a smile on his face, but the more the Chinese scientist listened, it rapidly changed to one of concern, and then of frustration.

Shenjung looked to Soong, and slowly shook his head. He licked his lips and his focus turned inwards as he spoke softly once again. Alex could see now that he wasn't being allowed to finish his sentences. In the end he lowered his head and handed the earphone back to Blake. He turned to Alex.

"The admiral refused to countenance that an entire squad of PLA soldiers were wiped out by anything other than … *you*. He thinks that the concept of there being a world beneath the dark ice is fanciful and the product of dehydration or my delusion." He smiled sadly. "Also, my suggestion of a creature being responsible for Yang's death was seen as more brainwashing." His smile fell away. "He called me an American spy."

Soong sighed. "We cannot go home."

"I'm sorry." Alex took the comm. from Shenjung. "My turn, after all." Alex changed frequencies, and called the USS *Texas*.

"Code name, Arcadian, urgent communication for Commander Eric Carmack aboard the USS *Texas*."

Alex didn't have to wait long before a booming voice blared out from his earphone.

"Thank the lord, and are we ever glad to hear you." Alan Hensen sounded like he had a grin from ear to ear. "Here's the commander, the line is secure. Go ahead, Arcadian."

"*Hallelujah*, son," Carmack almost shouted. "You just saved me having to deploy a lot of expensive armaments, and I and the US Navy thank you for that." He laughed heartily, and then breathed a sigh of relief. "Please tell me you have control of the *Sea Shadow*."

"That we do, sir. We're all looking forward to a hot meal and then going home." Alex turned and nodded to Aimee.

"You can tell us all about your adventure when you bring that submarine alongside. As you can see, things are still a little tense here." Carmack lowered his voice. "Best we take our toys and head home, before someone does something they regret."

"Works for me, sir." Alex could feel warm sun on his neck, and for the first time in days, felt at ease. He turned to grin at Rhino and Casey, just as a blaring alarm screamed out from Carmack's line that jolted him upright.

Aimee grabbed at his arm. "What the hell is going on?"

"Commander ..." Alex began.

"Sonar warning. Were you the only guys down there?" Carmack asked quickly.

"Yes." Alex overheard Alan Hensen talking rapidly to his sonar and communication officers before relaying information. "Another reading, sir. This one coming up from the deep, fast, and big, *really big*."

"Attack sub?" Carmack asked.

Hensen listened some more. "Too big for that. Non-metallic signature ... and silent as a ghost; it's weird. Going to come up at the *Sea Shadow* in a few minutes – collision course."

"*Jesus Christ*, Hunter, what in God's name did you just drag with you? We got something coming up underneath us and traveling at about eighty knots. Signature is all wrong. Non-metallic and silent as death. Looks like it's coming from where you just came from. What the hell is it?"

Alex shook his head, confused, but then tilted his head back and closed his eyes. "That sir, is the Kraken rising, and our worst nightmare. It'll sink us, if it gets to us."

Alex heard shouted orders before Carmack came back.

"Not on my watch, son. Get below decks, we'll take it from here."

*

General Banguuo rose to his feet, listening carefully as Admiral Zang Do gave his urgent report.

"General, deep sonar contact. Single heavy-mass signature rising from over 300 fathoms. Breach zone is estimated to be directly below the fleet, sir. Unknown object has accelerated to 80 knots."

Banguuo's eyebrows rose. Eighty knots? "Seems the game of bluff has ended. A new stealth submarine perhaps, Admiral?"

"Or the Americans have initiated their first strike protocol," Admiral Zang responded quickly.

Banguuo heard the frantic orders being yelled aboard the admiral's ship – *battle stations, tracking target, ready all batteries* – it was the familiar language of war. His free hand curled into a fist.

"The Americans are foolish to think the Chinese navy would be caught off guard so easily." Banguuo decided: first, they would destroy the submarine coming up at them, and then they would engage.

"Authorization to launch, Admiral. Fire at will."

"*Jue-zhan-jing-wai.*" The admiral roared.

Banguuo grunted. It was an armed forces battle cry, and meant *decisive battle*. He gripped the phone so tight his knuckles went white. He closed his eyes, and in his mind he saw the bubble trails as the heavy Yu-4 homing torpedoes were launched and would already be speeding down to meet their doomed target.

Perhaps Minister Wanlin was right, he thought. It was inevitable – the age of the dragon was here whether he liked it or not.

*

Commander Carmack stared hard through the dielectric reflective coated binoculars. Before him, the iron-gray ocean was being whipped by a freezing wind, sending horsetails of stinging spray along its surface. There was one oasis of calm, and that lay at the center of the flotilla. The few square miles of ocean were ringed by two of the most powerful naval fleets in the world, and nothing else mattered but that large circle of freezing water, with the small, sleek submarine at its center.

Carmack, and every other captain and commander on the water, and back at their home bases, watched the *Sea Shadow*. Everyone else watched consoles, stood by weaponry, or waited impatiently for orders to either fight or stand down. Until then it was up to someone else to make a first move. Fingers were on hundreds of multi-ballistic triggers.

The closest vessel was a Chinese Jiangkai I Type 054 Ma'anshan class destroyer. It was a big warship, at 450 feet, and displacing 4,300 tons. The floating death dealer was armed with an octuple rocket launcher, anti-ship missiles, AK630 CIWS turrets, ASW torpedoes, and a variety of mines. Carmack's communication officers had detected the launch of several of these moments before, undoubtedly convinced there was an attack coming from below – they were only partially right.

The explosions that occurred deep below the Ma'anshan class destroyer were too deep to register on the surface, and Carmack and Hensen were just lowering their glasses when there came a flurry of activity onboard the ship. Whooping alarms rolled across the water, and more mines were flung over the sides, these rigged for shallow detonation, and their plumes of spray showered the deck.

Men started running wildly about, and there came the pop of automatic rifle fire as the sailors leaned over the rails to shoot down into the water. There was something there only *they* could see, but as yet, Carmack and his fleet could not.

"What the hell is going on?" Hensen said, frowning and moving between using his field glasses, and trusting his own eyes.

"I think we now have a new player," Carmack said slowly.

A mottled green and black tree grew from the water beside the destroyer, higher and higher, lifting above the ship's bridge, to then topple across the metal superstructure, bending the steel like it was made of matchsticks and paper. More of the giant things rose up, and then the cold mountain began to follow its limbs.

"Oh my god." Hensen backed up a step.

The Kraken was revealed in all its monstrous glory, clinging to the side of the battleship, tilting it as its bulk came out of the water. It bloomed open, a gigantic flower whose petals coiled and thrashed.

"What the fuck is that thing?" Hensen whispered.

Carmack lowered his glasses, his face drained of color. "The thing that all sailors dread – the sinker of ships, the monster from the abyss – *the Kraken*."

The thing rose once more, and then seemed to swell, flowing like liquid up and over the Ma'anshan's superstructure. Tentacles wrapped the ship from stern to bow, their tips thin as a wrist, but where they joined the bulbous body they were as thick as redwood trees.

From across the water, Carmack heard the sound of metal complaining, and the 450-foot ship tilted even more, its nearest deck now close to the icy ocean's water line. The muscular strength of the tentacles radiated inevitability, and the coils started to compress.

"Orders, sir." Hensen waited.

Carmack exhaled. "Hold fire. We can't do anything. We might hit the destroyer."

Shenyang J-15 fighter craft swarmed and fired GSh-30–1 cannons and armor piercing rockets. Mottled flesh was blasted away, but they were pinpricks to the monster. An acrid smell wafted across the expanse of iron-gray water, and Carmack watched as men were encircled in tentacles, and then crushed like flies. The Kraken seemed to be acting in a furious desire to do nothing but kill the ship and everything on it.

Admiral Zang Do, aboard the aircraft carrier *Liaoning*, maneuvered the huge ship closer. It was the only thing larger than the monster, but with hundreds of tons of slimy flesh almost fully engulfing his destroyer, he obviously hesitated to fire, knowing a missile passing through the rubbery hide would strike the vessel.

"Fire at it, goddamn you, *just, fucking, fire*," Carmack hissed.

The hesitation lasted another few seconds, and then there came the sound of an enormous cracking, as the huge destroyer bent in the center. Both the bow and stern rose up sharply, as the combined weight of the creature and its crushing tentacles had weakened the hull structure to a point of collapse.

Only then, was Zang Do shocked into action.

Hundreds of missiles, cannon rounds, and heavy machine gun fire lanced out at the huge creature. They were fiery harpoons, striking the flesh and embedding deep. Some blew car-sized chunks of flesh into the air, and dark blood stained the sea around the stricken destroyer.

"Send it back to hell," Carmack whispered. He half turned to Hensen. "Back the fleet up."

The creature slid back to the sea. But it didn't relinquish its grip, as it dragged the broken ship down with it, ensuring its kill was complete. On the surface, there was a spinning whirlpool of debris and dead bodies where the monster had once been.

"Dead," Hensen said.

"Dead? They hit it, sure. Did they kill it? I have no idea." Carmack stepped back. He nodded towards the Chinese boats trying to pull surviving sailors from the water. "See if they want any help." He sighed. "But I doubt they'd take it even if they needed it."

"Well," Hensen said. "I'm betting that episode might go a long way to adding some credibility to our story."

"But a terrible price for finding out the truth." Carmack turned away. "Bring the *Sea Shadow* in close, and get Hunter and his crew onboard. Time to go home."

CHAPTER 65

"Show him in, Margie." Colonel Jack Hammerson got to his feet, and came around from behind his desk.

Alex Hunter pushed open the door, grinned, and held his arms wide. "The world still stands."

Hammerson smiled and held out his hand. "Only just ... and no small thanks to you."

They shook hands and Hammerson led Alex to a couple of leather arm chairs, with coffee waiting. He'd read the flash report Alex had put together – he and his team had been through hell. That they managed to succeed in their mission, let alone survive for more than an hour down under the ice, was a miracle and a testament to their skill and fortitude.

He patted his soldier on the shoulder. "Great work ... great work. General Chilton read your report, and wants to meet you personally."

Alex raised his eyebrows. "And the president?"

"I'm sure he would as well, if he knew about you." Hammerson poured Alex a coffee. "Plausible deniability; you know how it works."

Alex shrugged. "I wouldn't know what to say, anyway." He eased down into the chair, and Hammerson saw that he let his body relax. "We got the *Sea Shadow* back, so now what happens?"

Hammerson bobbed his head as he poured himself a coffee. "We scrap it. The design was superseded years back. It's just that the vessel is decades more advanced than anything anyone else has, so if they want top tech, they can damn well work for it themselves."

Alex snorted softly. "Of course." He turned to Hammerson. "The Chinese were really going to go to the mat on this one. The PLA Special Forces went there to fight for it ... and kill for it. There was never going to be a negotiated outcome."

"Had to try." Hammerson put his mug down. "At least now they know why that area of the Antarctic is off limits." He smiled and raised his eyebrows. "Sometimes trust has to be proven."

Alex didn't return the smile. "That PLA captain, Wu Yang. It was him that tried to abduct Joshua. Did you know?"

Hammerson steeled himself. "We suspected it was Chinese operatives. Didn't know Yang was involved; you have my word on that."

"But Jack, they knew about Joshua. Knew that he was ... different. That's why they wanted him." He turned his laser like eyes on Hammerson. The mirth of just moments ago was gone. Alex sat forward. "They have their own advanced soldier program. Their soldier, Mungoi, was a giant. But he was flawed. That's why they wanted Joshua, to perfect their program." He sprang to his feet and crossed to the large windows overlooking the grounds. "The Arcadian program's secret is out, and so is his." He laughed softly. "The Israelis, the Chinese, the Russians ... it's not a matter of who knows now, but who *doesn't* know?" He continued to stare down at the grounds.

Hammerson rose to his feet and joined him at the window. He could see what had Alex's attention. Below Aimee Weir and Joshua chased each other on grass so green, it looked like stadium turf.

"Without me, he is vulnerable." Alex sighed and watched his son run faster and faster, leaving Aimee long behind. He turned to Hammerson. "Only I can protect him."

Jack Hammerson watched Alex for a moment. "Have you spoken to him yet?"

"No. I wanted to give Aimee some time alone with him first. But soon." He smiled as he watched the pair. "For the first time in years, I feel ... nervous."

Hammerson sipped his coffee. "I can't order you to do anything here. I can advise, but that's all. And I want you to know that any advice I give is from a friend, not as your superior officer."

Alex turned to scrutinize him for a moment and Hammerson felt the gaze reach deeply inside him, and knew Alex was reading him. He nodded and turned away.

Hammerson sipped and then lowered his mug. "And for what it's worth, my initial advice would be to keep his abilities secret. Not everyone knows about him. Sure, they may know *of* him, but not *who* he really is." He placed an arm on Alex's shoulder. "This is a big decision. You need to take some time out, spend it with them ... see what happens."

Hammerson crossed back to his desk. "I won't lie to you, I hope you decide to stay with us. I'm selfish like that." He watched as Alex stared down onto the field, a smile still on his brutally handsome features.

"See if family life suits you for a while." Hammerson continued to watch him. "Just one thing ... you said they're vulnerable without you. Remember, they will be getting more than just Alex Hunter."

Alex turned, his face stony. "The Other one."

Hammerson nodded.

Alex continued to stare at Hammerson, his eyes unblinking. "I can control him ... *it*."

"Can you really?" Hammerson returned the gaze for a moment longer. "Only you can really know the answer to that. But my view, I think these ... missions, let some pressure out. A good thing ... for everyone."

Alex turned back to the window. "I can control it," he repeated.

*

Alex came around the corner of the building and paused, watching Aimee and Joshua. They played for a moment longer, but then his son stopped running, and turned to face him.

Alex could feel the force of the boy's gaze. Joshua studied him, his face relaxed, but the familiar eyes penetrated him to the core.

The boy held up a hand and waved. Aimee turned then, and seeing Alex, stiffened.

Alex felt a sudden jolt of disillusionment, as she stepped forward to pull Joshua in close to herself. There came a soft voice into Alex's head: *this is your reward; she doesn't trust you.*

Not me ... *you*, Alex thought.

A soft laugh. *You are me, and I am you.*

Joshua lifted Aimee's hand from him, and continued his scrutiny. Alex tried to relax, and waved. He smiled and first went to Aimee. "*Ah*, I saw you two playing, and I wanted to say hello."

"It's good to see you," Aimee said. "It's ..."

"It's about time," Joshua cut in, reaching up to take his hand. "You were always there, but not there ... and now you're finally, here." He cocked his head. "I know who you are. You're my father. Not Peter."

Alex went down on one knee, and Aimee stood behind Joshua, resting her hands lightly on his shoulders. "Yes, Joshua. I'm your father. I've been away, but I've been wanting to see you for many years." He held out his hand. "I'm back now."

Joshua took it and smiled. "Good."

You'll hurt him – maybe not today, maybe not tomorrow, but you will. The voice didn't carry its usual sneering tone, but instead was simply matter of fact.

Joshua gripped Alex's hand a little harder, a frown creasing his small brow. "I don't believe that," he said.

"Huh?" Alex froze. "Don't believe what, Joshua?"

"I don't believe you'll hurt me." Joshua lifted his head, confident.

"What?" Aimee leaned forward.

"No, I would never ..." Alex began.

"But *the Other* one might." The boy tilted his head, eyes narrowed slightly.

Aimee frowned, and knelt beside her son. "You okay, honey?" Joshua looked briefly at her, and nodded.

Alex felt a stab of pain deep in his head. *And you'll hurt her too. You have before, and next time, you'll kill her.* Alex's jaws worked as his teeth ground into his cheeks. He tried to push the disturbing thoughts away.

Suddenly he felt another pain, this one from his hand. He looked down to see Joshua's hand on his, the fingers now closing hard, harder than was possible for a normal five year old.

"Don't worry, you won't hurt me, or Mommy." He smiled. "I'll make sure." He leaned in close to Alex's ear. "I can help."

Alex felt the pain in the center of his head relax. And after another moment, it felt like a door was slamming shut in his mind, the tormenting presence locked behind it, and silenced.

Alex exhaled. "Yes, I think we'll be fine, Joshua. Let's see how things go."

"As a family." Joshua held Alex's eyes.

"Yes, as a family." Alex smiled. "Hey, can I call you Josh?

The boy's face lit up. "Yes, I like that. You can call me Josh ... Josh Hunter." He let go of Alex's hand. "And one more thing; I want a dog ... a big one."

EPILOGUE

The massive creature sunk to the sea shelf, tried to hang on, but the damage to its body was too great. It gave up and let itself slide off the edge of the underwater cliff and sink into the cold, dark pressure of the abyss. It took an hour for it hit bottom and spread over the rocky surface of the abyssal plain like a gigantic mottled carpet. Beside it, the broken ship floated down to lay like the broken skeleton of some long dead beast.

Many miles away from the Kraken's graveyard, in a cavern hidden away beneath the dark ice and rocky shell of an underground world, several bulbous six-foot eggs bounced along warm shallows of the shoreline. Their coiled contents wriggled, shook, and the rubbery shells burst open in an explosion of writhing tentacled horror.

The creatures immediately changed color, and blended to their environment. Their large disc eyes with slitted pupils examined their new world, and they tasted the warm water, which was thick with the signals of life, movement, and food. They propelled themselves into deeper water, already hungry.

AUTHOR'S NOTES

Many readers ask me about the underlying details in my novels – is the science real or fiction? Where do the situations, equipment, characters, or their expertise come from, and just how much of any legend has a basis in fact?

As in my previous novels, there is always the germ of a story, or legend, or ... something. And in the case of the Kraken there are numerous seafaring tales dating back many centuries.

The Kraken is a legendary sea creature that was first said to dwell off the coasts of Norway and Greenland. The legend dates back as far as the late 13th century. An old Icelandic saga, Örvar-Oddr, tells of a journey to Helluland (Baffin Island), where a sailor sees the massive sea beast called Hafgufa. This is believed to be the first ever reference to the Kraken.

It wasn't until 1735, that the Swedish botanist, Carolus Linnaeus, first classified the Kraken as a cephalopod in the first edition of his *Systema Naturae*, a taxonomic classification of all living things. From then on, its sightings continue to this day.

Was it – *is it* – real? Perhaps. After all, the deepest trenches in the ocean are thousands of miles long and seven crushing miles deep – sunless, pitiless voids where impossible pressures make it an unexplored and alien place. Who knows what treasures, and horrors, they really contain!

Was The Kraken Real?

> *Below the thunders of the upper deep;*
> *Far, far beneath in the abysmal sea;*
> *His ancient, dreamless, uninvaded sleep*
> *The Kraken sleepeth*
>
> *Alfred Lord Tennyson, "The Kraken"*

Wherever there is deep or dark, the unknown and unexplored, then also come the legends. Tales of a monstrous, many armed sea creature exists from ancient times. Like the Greek legend of the Scylla, a monster with six long necks, each with its own frightening head and a body with twelve tentacle-like legs. And later, in 1555, Olaus Magnus wrote of a giant sea creature that was like a mighty tree up by the roots.

The term Kraken appeared in 1735 in the *Systema Naturae*, where stories about this monster dated back to twelfth century Norway. These tales often refer to a creature so big that it is mistaken for an island. Even as late as 1752, when the Bishop of Bergen, Erik Ludvigsen Pontoppidan, wrote his *The Natural History of Norway* he described the Kraken as "incontestably the largest Sea monster in the world" with a width of one and a half miles.

Disappearing islands – fanciful? Well, as recently as 2012, scientists found that an island (Sandy Island) that had been on ocean charts and even shown on Google Earth since the year 2000 ... wasn't there anymore. In fact, navigation charts showed a water depth of over 4,000 feet – nothing there but deep, black ocean depths. Was it something from the fathomless void simply basking on the surface temporarily?

The myth of the Kraken has been colored by reality over the years, like in 1896, when the rotting carcass of great sized creature beached itself on the coast of St. Augustine, Florida. It was first seen by Mr. Herbert Coles and Dunham Coretter on a bicycle trip. When the young men saw the carcass, it had sunk into the sand because of its immense weight. The next day, Dr. DeWitt Webb, founder of the St. Augustine Historical Society and Institute of Science, arrived on the scene. The creature's skin was of an extremely light pink color with a silvery tint to it. They concluded it weighed roughly five tons and the visible portions were twenty-three feet in length, four feet high, and eighteen feet across the widest part of the back. Webb decided that it was not a whale but instead some kind of cephalopod.

Myth and reality collide again and again. For example, in Japan, there is a legend of an enormous sea creature called the Akkorokamui. Its home is Volcano Bay, which is located in the southwestern island of Hokkaido. The Akkorokamui is said to be a giant squid-like creature, 300 hundred feet long, a brilliant red color, with giant staring eyes and a noxious odor. It was greatly feared by the local fishermen, as it was said to swamp boats, taking any fallen fishermen down to the depths, never to be seen again.

Just recently, for the first time, a giant squid was photographed live in the Sea of Japan. Brought to the surface, the smallish creature (around twenty feet) gave off a smell of ammonia (a substance in great quantity in their flesh that allows them to manage the huge pressure of the depths and also attain negative buoyancy required to float and hunt in mid water).

An ancient Japanese legend tells of a creature with massive trunk-like tentacles, noxious smell, giant eyes, and striking red color. And then one brought to the surface exactly like that described all those centuries ago – how could the legend have been so accurate, when this describes the giant squid, *Architeuthis*, so clearly? We know that these giants live down there … perhaps they aren't miles long, and can't be mistaken for islands that can be mapped, but did they once exist? Well, the Kraken is said to be the monstrous cousin to this giant Architeuthis squid. And though scientists have come across many strange things in the world's seas, they have yet to find trace of the legendary Kraken … or maybe, until now …

In a presentation made at a meeting of the Geological Society of America in Minneapolis, Mark McMenamin, a study researcher and paleontologist at Mount Holyoke College, presented evidence for the Kraken. His theory derived from some deep scoring found on the bones and remains of nine forty-five-foot ichthyosaurs from the Triassic period (248 million to 206 million years ago). Perhaps the fingerprints of the legendary Kraken?

How these particular huge ichthyosaurs died has long been a mystery. In the 1950s Charles Lewis Camp hypothesized that the ichthyosaurs had fallen victim to a toxic plankton bloom or became stranded in shallow water. But recent work on the rocks surrounding the fossils seem to suggest that many of the creatures died in deep water ... very deep water.

Obsessed with solving the puzzle of how these beasts were killed, McMenamin looked hard at the fossil evidence. By arranging the vertebrae of some ichthyosaur remains, he noticed something odd in the patterning. Something that resembled the gigantic sucker marks like those from a giant cephalopod's tentacle. According to McMenamin, this "Kraken" would have been nearly a hundred feet long and most likely caught the ichthyosaurs and dragged their massive corpses back to its underwater lair.

Comparing this hypothesized behavior to that of the modern octopus, McMenamin said, "It is known that the modern octopus will pile the remains of its prey in a midden and play with and manipulate those pieces." So, the Kraken may have been monstrously large prehistoric cephalopods that fed on some of the Triassic ocean's largest predators, and stored their bodies in a larder for later consumption.

We know more every day. We already know that the giant squid can grow to enormous sizes, making it one of the largest animals on the planet, that they are intelligent, and fantastically strong. But what we don't really know is just how big they can get, or how long they can live, or how often (and why) they come to the surface.

(Taken from my blog post in ThrillerCentral – "Fingerprints of the Kraken".)

The Southern Seas Devil's Triangle

Bass Strait is a channel connecting the Tasman Sea on the east with the Indian Ocean on the west, and separating Tasmania on the south from the Australian mainland on the north. The first recorded disappearances in the area go back to 1797 when the ship, *Sydney Cove*, was wrecked. One of the vessels engaged in the salvage operations, *Eliza*, mysteriously vanished on her way back to Sydney. From 1838–1840, seven vessels were lost in the area but only wreckage from three has ever been found. The remaining four remain a mystery to this day. Over the following century dozens of other ships have mysteriously vanished after entering the Southern Sea's triangle, never to be seen again.

In 1858 a British warship, *Sappho*, vanished into thin air, along with over a hundred crew. The *Sappho* had been seen by the crew of the schooner *Yarrow*, off Cape Bridgewater, Victoria, at the western entrance to Bass Strait on 18 February. But she never reached her destination of Sydney. Numerous ships took part in a search, but all failed to find any trace of the missing ship.

With the introduction of aircraft in the beginning of the 20th century, the Southern Sea's "triangle" continued to make headlines with mysterious vanishings. The first aircraft to vanish was a military Airco DH 9A. It was being used to search for a missing ship, the *Amelia J*, in 1920. No trace of the plane has ever been found.

Ocean Submarine Mysteries

USS *Scorpion* (SSN-589) was a Skipjack class nuclear submarine of the United States Navy and the sixth vessel of the U.S. Navy to carry that name. *Scorpion* was lost on 22 May 1968, with ninety-nine crewmen dying in the incident. The USS *Scorpion* is one of two nuclear submarines the U.S. Navy has lost, along with the USS *Thresher*. It was one of four mysterious submarine disappearances in 1968; the others being the Israeli submarine *INS Dakar*, the French submarine *Minerve* (S647), and the Soviet submarine *K-129*.

Massive Antarctic Algae Bloom Seen From Space

The bloom, estimated to be around 500 miles wide and 200 miles long, was captured by Australian scientists monitoring a satellite 1,850 miles above the Earth. Scientists from the Australian Antarctic Division say they are still not sure exactly what caused the bloom but they predict it may affect the local wildlife. *ABC News, March 05, 2012*